Cascade

Cascade

a ✦ novel

Barbara Lalla

University of the West Indies Press

Barbados • Jamaica • Trinidad and Tobago

University of the West Indies Press
7A Gibraltar Hall Road   Mona
Kingston 7 Jamaica
www.uwipress.com

ISBN 978-976-640-233-4

A catalogue record of this book is available
from the National Library of Jamaica.

Cover photograph of Mount Plenty, St Ann, Jamaica,
© Cookie Kinkead, 2009.

Book and cover design by Robert Harris.
Set in Dante 10.5 / 15 x 24
Printed in the United States of America.

FOR BILL AND ELSIE, AND FOR MISS AVIS

Prologue

THEIR TALK RUSTLES PAST. Quivering behind the back wall of the house, a frail aerial root missed by the blade of the machete reaches down, tentatively.

"A guest house, missis, now you young and strong. That way, you hold onto the property make it work for you, especially now the war done and things picking up so nicely. Ivy, what you mean – who would pay to stay here? Then you never hear bout tourist? Haw!"

It is as it is by chance, pollen strewn accidentally by a wasp blown in from nowhere, and now a young plant, lodged on its receptive host, huddles thankfully in its niche and extends a fragile root towards the earth. Unaware of it, the twelve-year-old trying his hand at a weekend wo'k in the garden straightens his back and flicks the sweat away, but no one minds Basil and the talk continues without pause.

"Turn it into a guest house, so you keep your home and stand on you own feet."

In the end, little is as it seemed. Rooted at last, and indistinguishable from the bush around it, the free-standing plant thickens, thrusts up and outward in knotting muscle and in bright then darkening leaves scattering and reflecting light from a thousand polished surfaces, swirling dense and glossy. Postponing its claim to a discrete existence, it leans on the cassia, embracing, clenching, fusing – up here, in full view. As a mongoose sprints over, an odd child sitting alone on the roadside bows to it respectfully, pausing in his task of sifting the gravel along the curb for shards of glass, and above, a parrot guffaws briefly. A speckled guinea hen darts, head extended in alarm, back to the discordant huddle of hens, ducks and the occasional turkey. Far beneath, the young plant reaches into the earth, probing crevices, shrugging aside rubble, cleaving the irrational stubbornness of brick, fracturing the coldest and most sullen stone. And through myriad surfaces it extends an invitation to moisture.

Destructive? Possibly. And unstoppable. Intertwining noiselessly with their affairs, it absorbs all that passes from their lips. Year in, year out.

". . . an old higue, I tell you, Ivy. Well. Dead and gone."

"She was well miserable, and must be that why it happen. Butchered, the *Gleaner* said."

"Well, we won't talk about that sort of thing in my condition – my condition at long last."

Life teems in the crowding foliage that soaks up and transpires again the droplets of their lives. Two women sit close together on the back porch, and one rests a listening hand tenderly on the belly of her friend, her tears washing away her own regrets in delight over the brief surge beneath her fingers. Then they hug each other wordlessly. Scattered thoughts, randomly sprinkled, pool under knotting branches, diffuse through root-hairs and flow on in secret through the pores of the earth. With time, some minds reveal themselves; others grow indecipherable to each other.

"Then, Ellie, you sure she wasn't just old and miserable?"

"Stupidness, Ivy. Her own sister called her an old harpy. She was twisted inside her head."

Unnoticed, the ficus sends out its roots like the years and who can see, over four decades beneath the green and burgundy and bronze of ground cover and scattered stone, what they shatter, what they bind.

ONE

Rosemarie

. . . FROM NOWHERE. Ten o'clock in truth the back door open, but not a sound in the yard. Now, when we think back, we say it was too quiet. Not a bird, not a cricket, not a frog. And as for the dog – the less said about Venables the better, especially since car lick him down only weeks later anyway, poor fellow. So, as Miss Ellie like to say, *the rest is silence*. We certainly hear nothing from no dawg that night. Only the pulley squealed when Dan hauled the line from the landing beyond the door, and I walked out to pull the clothes off as he held the line within reach. All the time Ellie was folding and stacking the clothes as fast as I tossed them in to her, for we done become sisters long-time – she could all read my mind.

I tell you our eyes well fasten on that door and even from inside we could see right through it and past the laundry room door. The zinc roof sloped towards that dark corner under the mango tree where the Bombays weighed down the branch. One or two must have dropped since I came in from watering because the smell reached way into the house, so Ellie started to mutter about churning ice cream – but we were never going out after them into the black shadow of the tree even if we could have found them. Apart from those corners and the top of the laundry roof, the light under the eave flooded the rest of the yard.

Then, missis, that blow stun me. Like a vice close on my head same time the two heavy boot crunch down behind me. And the grip wrench back my head and yank my face up so I see the steel flash before I feel that cold metal flat under my chin. I suck in my breath to just hold my throat from the blade and the fingers clench on my skull was iron, tug my neck back so although my eye darting darting all I see bend over me was this hood with slits. Dark, frayed slits.

Only then from my eye corner I glimpse the other one, like a shadow. Now he break away from the dark under the palm and spring up on the parapet. Light, weightless. Is almost like he float in between Dan and the door. He hooded too but his hands odd – transparent white like duppy fingers on the black gun. Then Lord, Master – he level the muzzle in Dan face and circle him jabbing, jabbing with the gun.

Nothing we could do but inch backwards inside the house.

When the muzzle nudge at his head Dan freeze, but since I come back and I get to know him again I come to realize his mind racing even when his voice soft. Only this cool . . . murmur, over and over. Polite.

"Nothing valuable but our books. See for yourselves." Calm.

But is like I went crazy. I said this is not happening and they will be gone or Dan will behave normal – scream, curse, shake.

But he turned up his palms and spread his hands and said, "Look around if you like."

When I tell you – was one madness. Or must be was me crazy. I flatten against the wall watching this gun at my brother's head and it was like I catch fire inside. I begin to blaze. Years apart and now this . . . this loss again hanging over me – a rage roar in my head, whatever happen I feel I must kill at least one of them.

The dundus man with the gun fixed his eye on me (eye colourless, like ice). I glared back at him but I could feel Dan's eyes boring into my brain: *Don't antagonize them.* And he was right bout me for I was never one to consider anything for long, and then the gun slide around from the back of his head and settle at his temple.

The dundus push his head in Dan face and . . . and growl, "Don' make no trouble!"

I see it now – books, notepads scattered on the table, the mahogany like a mirror how it reflect teacup, bookmark from the Holy Land, one New Orleans paperweight, the photo album open on coconut tree criss-cross at Manzanilla. Ellie began to scream and the gunman swung towards her. Dan tried to call them off, to distract them from her.

"Take anything you want."

"Shut her up," one of them said. The grip on my hair relaxed, and the blade swept out and flashed at Ellie. "Nobody have fe dead here tonight. Just learn fe cooperate."

"Quiet! Hard-ears old bitch you!" The gunman grabbed at Ellie as she slid over to the window screaming, screaming. He bawled at her, "Don't make we kill you."

When he bring down the gun butt at the back of her head was like a warning, not vicious, and she pay him no mind. She slide from his hand and scream one scream after the other without pause and is so they leave the two of us to try stop her.

Dan wail out, "Nooo!" For he saw her drawing them away and the gun butt raise, miss, connect, miss while she duck out of their way, screaming all the time. Then they pitched her down on the tiles and turned back to Dan, and he whispered, "Do what you like with *me*."

Outside over the whistling frog and cricket, an owl shrieked and I cursed it. I could see the swelling, three lumps on her head back but no blood really, nothing you would expect of a head wound. It was a dream, how they shouted at me when I opened the fridge door and tumbled out ice cubes in my skirt and wrapped them in the kitchen towel and pressed against her head.

They flash the knife at me and I just tell them say, "Beg you get 'way from in front me."

Ellie whisper, "O Jesu, *careful*," but I never give thrupence for them.

"Likklemost I box him down," I told her, and I swear I was ready. Only then a siren wailed in the road – maybe is the screaming draw attention fe true – and they chase back out into nowhere.

So we survived – except for this feeling they could walk in again. Anytime. It was over. Except in our heads.

"Everything's riddled with uncertainty now," Ellie explained over the phone to Ivy when I passed on the receiver. "They've left a sort of void lingering on in . . . little pockets of bewilderment."

The house looked like nothing happened, but how to *live* after a thing like that?

Ellie said if General Patton were still alive, he would have barked and raised hell. The General was the dog I met when I came to them first and that was over thirty years ago. Their daughter, Rachel, was just a little thing then – younger than her own Andy was when this thing happened.

"The General would've ripped out a few pieces too, good fellow, not like this little docile mutt we have now. But, Rummy," Ellie said to me when we went over it again, "they *must* have fed Venables something, for you remember how he staggered when he woke up. All the same, I don't doubt that the dope was all that prevented him from taking to his heels. Heels? Dawg have heels?"

Oh Saviour. I mean I loved Ellie for being able to smile even in pain, but sometimes she drove me mad, always finding something to laugh about even at the weirdest times. True.

All Dan could find to say was, Just suppose Andy had been here. "First time I've felt relieved the little fellow is far away."

He closed his eyes and the strain in my brother's face tugged at my heart. They were writing the children of course, Rachel and her husband, Rabin, and Ellie muttered aloud as she finished it off.

Going now. Carbon paper nearly in rags. Just slipping this in with your father's epistle. Rummy sends love. DV, Mom – P.S. Hug my little Andy.

Of course they had phoned Trinidad that same night to talk to Rachel, but there were details to add so they wrote too. Dan and Ellie were like that. They would write letters.

The whole awful thing replayed in our minds, as Ellie put it, and some parts we had forgotten came back later. And then, for that matter, how much was blotted out? The attack was reason enough for any of us to wake the next morning shattered, but the relief of having us all safe buoyed us up over the shock, and Ellie insisted the gunmen were not so beastly as they might have been when we think what we see sometimes in the *Gleaner*. Headlines screeched at us from the newspaper spread open on the table between Dan and Ellie, and he slapped the paper closed and rolled it tight.

"But at least they never tormented us," Ellie protested, "and perhaps at heart they were not so . . ."

I swung away refusing to hear it and slammed my fist on the wrought iron bars between me and the white anthurium beside the porch step. The colours outside glowed rich, deep, and this was the hour ferns were supposed to get the little water. But instead I dropped down into the wicker chair, sucked my knuckles, and did my best to take in what I could. That was September 1985, I remember, that first evening I was locked away from the garden, and its perfume was all around me.

"Why they didn't shoot us then, if they were so evil?" Ellie insisted. "How we know they weren't just hungry and desperate?"

"Don't ever make the mistake of underrating the situation we were in," Dan snapped. He was quiet but so furious I stared at him, for he never had a bitter word or rough tone for Ellie, but she just laid her cheek against his and they let the matter go, though he refused to speak of it ever again.

"So here we are on the porch with a tale to tell, like in the old days." Ellie stretched for my hand. "But those times were nothing like these. We called Ivy about it, didn't we?"

Right away, and Ivy spoke with each of us. It was always Ivy we turned to and, in fact, it could have been her house – the guest house – that cemented us together. Of course the guest house itself had been Ellie's idea, as Ivy told me herself.

"But downstairs has so much space, Ivy," Ellie had said. "Listen. Your papa's big bedroom and den could cut up make guest rooms. You have this porch down here, not only on the southern side, but on the east – when there is all that glorious space upstairs. You could enclose just one side down here make into rooms. Then, Ivy, you don't see you can get at least six guest rooms downstairs? Cho! What you waiting on?"

Over the years we would drive north through the hills for a weekend, just as Dan and Ellie had always done before I came to them, and we would arrive at Miss Ivy's, shouting for her above the uproar, for Dan held down the car horn to drown out the dogs.

"Hysterical as always," he would grumble.

Basil would saunter out with that mournful smile ("lugubrious as usual," Ellie would say, and grin) and he would calm the dogs. Basil's title was Butler but really he functioned as general handyman and gardener, so right away someone would hound him to produce a breadfruit and get it on the coals.

"Just pick it fram one of dem tree right here so, Basil. Nuh go hill and gully a look fe it."

While she ordered Basil around, Petrona would tumble ackees out of the bankra and rummage for Scotch bonnet peppers. Eventually, it was Ivy's place that inspired it all.

"I sometimes dream of escaping the gathering confusion in Kingston for good," Dan had been saying of late.

So, now that the madness had actually touched us, it was Ivy's we longed for, for sanity.

And what if I had lost one of them – the brother Ma deprived me of all the time I was growing up, leaving me parked there in New York with her crotchety old Aunt Miriam, from the earliest I can remember, so she could ensure the education of her precious son? And what if now I was actually back with him, what if I had lost him or his wife, who brought us back together? Dan and Ellie. Long-time, Ivy would say they grew together like two pimento trees. It was the sort of thing she would say. Yet since that fall and the broken hip we saw less of Ivy.

"On the phone we debated it," Ellie lamented, "and I could only agree with her. What she could do but let the guest house go? At least she made enough to keep the place, before her hip gave out, not to mention the tourists going more and more for the hotels springing up on the beach. Only now, in between our visits the house just gapes around her, empty and silent."

She never married, poor Ivy, so she had no children – save Evan, the boy she seemed to see as some sort of protégé, and of course her nephew, Scotty. Because I thought of him as mine – my stepson, after all – I forgot sometimes that Scotty was her sister Maisie's boy. Otherwise, Ivy was left with only the facety puss that was too full of itself to be company for anyone – though of course Miss Ivy insisted Marie Antoinette was devoted to her. It got to be just at the end and in the middle of the year that the guest house was full, and sometimes Ivy was alone. It was then we would go, mostly, but there was always always room for us.

The times we had there. I lived in the garden and worked on it each visit. Now where I had nestled tiny plants, lush shrubs marked the edges of the lawn and their perfume drifted up to the porch. I remember Dan complaining one dusk as I sprayed Ivy's geraniums for her, "All this green bush we can't even eat, Basil. Why they don't clear it plant likkle corn?"

"Me fada 'ave a bull cow," Basil said, coming to a halt in a tangle of boney limbs. "Me fada milk him naat', sout', heas' an' wes'. Where im don' milk im?"

"Eh?"

"Bull cow cyan't milk, sah! Is nat dat im for."

"Haw!" Ellie turned on Dan triumphantly. "So not everything God plant make for you to eat. You better start grow gerberas now."

But Dan just grinned after her and muttered his stock phrase, "I'll take the matter under advisement."

And Basil raised his hat a last time before clapping it on his head to make his way downhill.

Later that evening, though, Dan stopped and reflected. "This morning," he recalled, "no, earlier, first thing this morning, Basil was decidedly sullen. It bewildered Ellie for she always insists he is good-natured in his own wooden sort of way. Ellie asked Basil if he was sick, for he really isn't sour usually, and after some disgruntled writhing, he grumbled it out."

But I knew the story already. Scotty had refused to let Basil chop down a scrawny cassia tree that some type of ficus was overpowering. More important, Scotty refused to let Basil "chap" the ficus itself. The idea was to give more privacy to the upstairs bathroom windows.

"But the roots, Basil," Ellie had protested, "is right against the wall."

"I tell Mas' Scotty, m'am." He waved the machete murderously.

"Is a beautiful tree," I lamented.

But Ellie planted her hands on her hips furiously. "Frost the panes, or put up curtains. Ficus *root*? He will mash up the house! And after all Ivy has gone through?"

"A so me tell him, Miss El. Me tell Mas' Scotty say strangler fig wicked, but him say fe mind me business and fertilize it."

That was when Ellie held her head in frustration and called in Dan.

"Then Scotty not listening to Basil about *plants*? Ignorance top o' ignorance."

And was no point going to Ivy to complain on Scotty, especially as I very well did as *I* pleased.

Under the lignum vitae tree my own plants thrived and jostled one another. Even the grass was thicker, silkier, and the orchids I had set showered almost to the ground. Basil and I had spread coconut husks behind the tree and now the anthuriums flourished up to the wall bordering the yard. You could see the garden from every room of the house, and beyond it westward at the front, but also on the northern side there was the sea.

So as often as possible we drove over to Ivy's, and in the long run I suppose it *had* to come up: Why leave at all?

"Why we don't just remake the guest house into our own old-people home?" I had demanded.

"Rousseau's Rest Cure?" Ellie intoned, turning it over on her tongue.

"Rest? What we want is to ensure some intelligent conversation," objected Dan's friend Cecil, who generally drove over when we were to spend more than one night. Cecil was lonely, Dan confided. Not much interest from his children since the wife died. "I'm ready to join up." Cecil raised his right hand.

"Call it Ivy's League!" Dan ripped away the tough red-streaked green outer layer from a column of sugar cane and split each section into four.

"Get Scotty to put up the money to start with," I added, leaning back to clasp my hands behind my head so I could think better. Scotty was not only my stepson but Ivy's nephew. He could very well do that for her, and here I was – prepared to run it.

After all, Ivy and I were sisters-in-law-in-law – and it happen this way.

Before I came back to Jamaica, Ivy's sister, Maisie, married Jesse Cunningham, and after that first miscarriage eight years pass before the child born. Same way Ellie wait years to have Rachel, but in Maisie case is when the time come that the baby just wouldn' born. Well then all Jesse did dream about turn to nightmare. Ivy told me everything – the screaming, and Maisie like some pale shadow not like Maisie at all, she toss, bawl till she tired. When the baby came at last she just let go in a final unforgettable sigh, Ivy said, and the frail scrap of a infant hardly able to cry. Poor Jesse.

After Maisie's death, Ivy devoted herself to this baby – Scott, they christened him – and somehow she kept her brother-in-law alive too. But then, when Ellie told her I was home and living with them, Ivy begged me to help her. To help her *again* (for there had been that other time I mustn't talk about). What Ivy needed now was for me to help her with Jesse's baby while he was at work, for it was the season and the guest house was busy. So I took leave and spent a month with Ivy – and is that started it, for Jesse was ready to idolize anybody who cared about his child.

But it was years, while I hemmed and hawed about Jesse. A second wife, I couldn't help thinking, and a child involved. I talked it over with Ellie as I never talked with anyone before.

I had been hurt, you see. In New York. I was lonely over there, unaccustomed to compliments, dazzled by the uniform. My mother gave no advice, gave nothing as usual, as usual wrapped up in herself and her son – though I don't hold that gainst Dan no more. Ma had come to spend time with her Aunt Miriam and to help get me ready for the wedding. But two weeks before my wedding Ma picked up and returned to Jamaica. No notice, no explanation. She just cut short the visit to get back to her precious son and left me to marry or not marry a wo'tless man. My fiancé made a joke of it like he made joke of anything that cut me, my . . . gallant soldier. Crude, cutting little jibes, was what Ellie called them when I told her. When I cried, he laughed.

"You cain't take a little *hazing*?" he would jeer.

So I learned not to cry. I don't believe I even remember how, and I suppose I have him to thank for that.

He didn't mind the old witch flying out, he said; what worried him was that she might come back.

"Jealous you got a man, that's what!" he would taunt me. Then he break out in a song about some Dirty Gertie and that bust up the whole thing. And is *that* my mother abandon me to.

"Is God make the man show up himself so," I told Miss Ellie. "Because I feel say, if I didn't end it, he would try beat me one day, and then I woulda kill him stone dead."

"God of course," Ellie agreed. "But not all men stay so. Look at Dan. And then think, darling – a child." Her glance turned to the baby picture of Rachel, on the piano, and I almost thought their eyes met.

So eventually I married Jesse – '56, that was – and Scott he came to be my own child, the son I could never have otherwise. Jesse did well working with the Tourist Board and what with bauxite taking off the place was flourishing. At any rate, we did live good, and after a while this child that was so puny began to shoot up like bamboo. Always Scotty hand was in my own while Rachel danced circles round us till I was dizzy. Rachel resembled both her parents, first more like Dan then more and more favour Ellie as the years pass. "Rummy," she insisted on calling me, for she couldn't say Rosemarie. "Rummy to put Scott *down*." All the years the two of them were like my own. And is so I grew as close to Ivy as the rest of them.

Eventually, of course, I was back with Ellie and Dan and it was just the three of us in their house, which was my home as much as theirs by then. Rachel was married and moved to Trinidad, and Scotty was out of touch, but we filled the emptiness with each other. As often as we could we drove to Ivy's, grumbling about the hotels that were taking over the beaches so it was harder to get a swim.

". . . which bodes ill for Ivy's business," Ellie fretted.

With Rachel gone, the three of us drew closer and closer – I must have been even closer to Dan's wife than to my brother self – and, as for me, as one desertion after the next swallow up in the past I suppose I heal up somehow and the bitterness disappear. I just never have it in my craw no more. I did cry when my mother died – not over no loss, for is not to say she was ever mine, but *because* she was never mine. So is not glad I was glad she gone. I just feel lighter (in a sort of guilty-ish way) that nobody couldn't part the three of us again. *Dis aliter visum*, Ellie muttered when I said that, but I never retain a word of Latin – and God knows how she could keep it in her head or why the way she say it echo on in my own. But that was Miss Ellie for you. I see how Dan woulda just look pon her and blind to whatever else move. Is dazzle he dazzle. He have an amazing mind too. From small. People would say, "That boy brain don't stop here." But his was the quiet sort of bright. Ellie . . . sparkled.

Dan, Ellie and me. Funny – *he* never called me anything but Rosemarie, but she picked up Rachel's name for me. Rummy.

Great-hearted. So I sum up Ellie. Dan and I came back together through Ellie, after not a word to each other for eighteen years. Our mother self at the root of it of course but, anyway, Dan and I had no use for each other till Ellie set to work on him. When he wrote me, it was a stranger inviting me to spend holiday with them. Stranger meet me at airport take me to his house, then Ellie hurtled down the front step and flung her arms round me. Dan and I, awkward as we started out, we never stood a chance against Ellie's warmth.

A year later, with not a soul of my own in Manhattan, I came back for a rest after my hysterectomy and I never went back.

"We have hospitals right here for you to work in," Dan pointed out.

By the time I was matron, I had married Jesse and mothered Scott. Then Jesse died and Scotty set out to college in the States, calling home so little that in a way I lost them both, but still I had Dan and Ellie on one side of the island and Ivy on the other. Whensoever Scotty come home he would fly into Mo Bay instead of Kingston and just find his way along to Ivy's, for he liked the heap of loud music which Dan wouldn't have put up with, while his aunt just let him do anything, even to fix up her storeroom with some cork or foam business so he could make himself happy without annoying the guests. So what with one thing and another, I would be back and forth to Ivy's.

Me same one was the first to set it in a plan.

"We just retire together right here with Ivy. Watch me. I retiring next year and then is a free matron you have."

"Needs management, though." Just like Ivy to throw herself into it one time. "It would be one thing for Ellie to do the accounts but we can't make her carry the whole thing, and you know my hip rules me out. We have to bring in some-one younger."

"Well, don't Scotty self qualify in Management?" I demanded.

"But if your stepson is indeed an executive in New York, green card and all," Cecil teased slyly, "why would he leave all that and return to run our old-people home?"

"He says he doesn't feel challenged again." I held onto my patience. If we were all going live together it was time to practise. "He might move back if his Aunt Ivy ask him. What you think?" I tried to sound careless, watching Dan and Ellie, but was on tenterhooks, for I wanted this but I certainly wouldn't be walking out on them. From the time I sold Jesse's house and moved back to theirs I know we three were staying together for good.

"Why uproot ourselves if we're comfortable as we are?" Dan sounded reluc-tant to bother, rather than against the notion itself. "And what about Rachel, Miss

Ellie?" With a flourish, he added, "Our children Mr and Mrs Seenath and Master Andy Seenath! Well? What about them?"

"We're on the move now." You could see her leaning towards it. "But what about when we slow down? We can't just land on the children, and when they visit they can come to us here. Otherwise, we'll get isolated. Then, Dan, what you expect? We just dodder in our separate corners?"

"I was rather hoping," he said in his ponderous way, "to be permitted to dodder in the same corner as yourself. I'm to be cast forth?"

"Dope!"

"Communal doddering!" Cecil ruled, and slammed his palm on the card table.

"*So let it be written*," Ellie crowed, and as Dan relented and pronounced the response we all chorused with him, "*So let it be done.*"

Is that why our first thought after the gunmen come down on us was to drive go visit Ivy. Only now our house was harder to leave.

"Suppose the gunmen come back?" Ellie said.

Apart from organizing for plants to water, Venables to feed, we had to call in carpenter to check locks and put in bolts. Then, as he done land up there already, Ellie say he might as well work on a facing or two that hollow with termites. He re-shingle piece of the roof. Welder come bout broken twist in wrought iron gate. Painter to touch up. Christmas pass.

"Just as well," Ellie argued. "We have fruitcake to take with us, and the rest of the ham."

In the chill of the morning, the mist curling through the Bog Walk Gorge made me glad of the delay, and when at last we turned in at Ivy's gate the poinsettias were still heavy in bloom. We sliced up the fruitcake on the porch and she called Petrona to bring out sorrel.

"I can't carry a tray with glasses again," Ivy grumbled. "I have to hold on to walk. When next you come I mightn't be able to get down the steps."

"And who knows when next it's going to be," Ellie said, "with this move coming up."

"Then is soon?" Ivy wailed. "And I here licking my chops that the whole of you coming to settle here. When you told me on the phone I thought you meant years and years away."

"Rachel will be here to help us pack up in a couple months," Dan said, as I watched him reach for another slice of cake. "She's organizing our room over there."

"We'll be back to visit." Ellie picked up my lifeless hand and squeezed it against her cheek. "And Rummy will come to see us as often as she can."

"Then what about your house?" Ivy wanted to know.

"Sale complete. Repairs done."

Ivy's voice lowered and began to tremble. "But how I will manage without you? All the way in Trinidad?"

Ellie sounded cheerful and comforting as usual, but like her voice float to me over a far distance. "You still have Rummy."

Is the first time I hear one thing about it.

TWO

Ellie

SOMETIMES WHAT SEEMS transparent grows opaque and mysteries drift up, like fog over clear river water. Dan always said I could see straight into the heart of things, but I am not too sure. I do know though that Rosemarie sees her stepson as the man she hoped he would become. He was quick enough to come back to Ivy and take up free lodging, like tadpole in wildpine. But what Scotty ever care about his Aunt Ivy – one of my oldest friends – let alone his father's second wife, Rosemarie, even if she did sacrifice everything to raise him? Rummy, you have sugar cake? Rummy, watch me knee! Rummy, after I don't have no bus fare. But – a tough woman, Rosemarie. Never seems . . . bruised.

Except that coldness a while there just before we left – what to make of it? A sort of frozen incredulous silence as if there were a pain beyond words. Why couldn't we have talked, as always? I never found out what it was. Then one day the ice just melted.

"Rummy," I had said, "you don't think we could get a flat in Trinidad, the three of us, near to Rachel?" She stood considering me for a while and I gave in. "I know you say you have your heart set on Ivy's place and Scotty's family. It's just . . . I no longer know how to live without you. Promise you will come soon."

"How would you know what my heart is set on?" she asked as if she were choking.

"Well, you said so. When we discussed the whole move."

And then she seemed bewildered, for a moment frantic.

"What is it, darling?" I touched her cheek and she shook her head.

"Ellie." She seemed dazed. "Ellie, something has gone wrong." She went grey. Terrified, she seemed. But before I could enquire the phone rang and from that time on it hardly stopped.

Like a convulsion in time, the days warped and whirled around us. One small case each, Rachel insisted. Dan and I would go ahead and Rabin would meet us, but soon she would follow with everything else. Everything. It comes back to me, the storm of conflicting sensation. Elation over the prospect of this future with Rachel – and with Rabin who is just so warm and . . . and jolly. And then Andy, my own only little grand. I had never expected it, this unlooked for . . . this grace. And Rachel was taking care of the move itself. Everything. Except that this *everything* churned around me, inside me and beyond me, in a haze.

Boxes. They slide one out of the other, fill and stack.

Amid the constant murmur and query and admonition of visitors, the phone ringing, and the snarl of tape around boxes, trays of sandwiches, patties, plantain tarts float silently by on upturned fingers. Tissue and china, the crackle of newspaper and clatter of clothes hangers distract me yet I insist on wads of old blanket around Mama's mirror. Then, outside the doors and waiting to be discarded, lurks the terror of garbage bags bulging with unknown contents I have no time to enquire into, what with the continuous wrench of parting hugs. So many friends so close now for so few minutes and so much left unsaid, and when shall we all talk like this again?

Sybil, my friend from Wolmer's Girls', reflects with her eyes sliding away from mine that what with her respiratory problems she won't be able to travel by air to see me, and I feel like a snake.

"We'll be back to visit," I protest.

Evening melts into morning and water gurgles out of my face basin with a finality that melts my legs, but two small cases thump down in the trunk, and I refuse to lock up – not that house, not to slam the door once and for all – so I kiss Rachel loudly, hanging onto the knowledge that this is what it takes to be with her again and that Rosemarie, who has driven off already, will visit soon, then I am down the step and up the drive with its unruly border of blue plumbago and out of the gate as fast as I can walk, but of course the heels make it difficult, you know, for the road is not paved as it used to be, and when the car stops and the door opens I am thankful to jump in.

"If we may be permitted to offer you a drive?" Dan extends a hand and envelops mine. "Or were you planning to sprint all the way to the Norman Manley International Airport?" So we end up screeching with laughter after all, as Long Mountain flashes by and the harbour ripples back far out to the right while the wilder sea on the other side of the Palisadoes hurls spumes of foam up above the humps of sand and macca bush.

As the plane lifted us from the runway, the harbour in its embracing mangroves, Kingston – at once laid back and traumatized – and the whole land with its unflinching backbone of mountains dwindled, and I lost balance and felt (even when I landed once and for all) as if the orbit of the earth had shifted. It was never like that before '86, when we just visited the children. And here now, after only a couple years, I find my mind clinging to those old days, times I thought were left behind but that now crowd solicitously near me. Yet the present too is warm and insistent, and I bend over my letter to Rosemarie again.

Those two went fishing again last night and Andy caught a "monsrous fish" and had it for supper. He is fascinated by all Dan's tackle, but of course Dan keeps it safely locked away.

Ivy, Sybil, Cecil. Rummy. And in between us, the sea. Between my new home with Rachel and Ivy's house in the mountains the shared years mutate into intervening miles, and now the people we meet know only what they see of us. At the bank yesterday a young chap expounded on investment and, poor fellow, he addressed himself to Dan of all people. I was polite, I think, though I have been investing in land since this lad's head was at his knees, for we are determined not to become miserable old people. I mean, we could have been headed for some home, and certainly not a fancy one like Ivy's.

In a way all these separations began years ago when I dismantled the firm. The file before me has carbon copies of my old correspondence.

This is a short one, Rachel, for I'm no writer like your father. Just a note that the final papers are signed: business sold.

Not that I regret the years I gave to my brother Bonny's firm, though I was never at heart a businesswoman, nor ever wanted to do anything but teach English.

I just read, then, more than ever. Not only the classics (which indeed I began to reread) but the novels that had been coming out in our very midst, by Reid and Mais and Hearne.

"Why?" Cecil demanded. "I want to be lifted out of our problems, not have my nose rubbed in them."

"Miss Ellie is a rebel," Ivy had chuckled years before. "She better join Claudius Henry." For that had been all the talk then, that pocket of revolutionary ferment.

But it was the world of business that I wanted to be lifted out of, only Bonny had needed the help and he was my brother. Years later – late in the sixties, it was – when Ivy persuaded me to ask Bonny whether he had room for Scotty or Evan in the business, Bonny said, over his dead body (though I suspect he might have considered Evan). Ivy never took offence though: no one could hold anything against Bonny. Of course, he was a handsome chap and girls threw themselves in his way, but my brother never cared for anyone after Agnes, poor fellow. One of the others threw herself a little too hard. The copy of that old letter to Rachel comes to hand again.

Now I can properly enjoy the book you sent with Jocelyn's daughter. Jocelyn never remained friends with us, for reasons I can't discuss. I tried because she was one of our old set, but she nursed her hurt and kept her distance. *The daughter dropped the book in the mailbox and drove off. Sourpuss. But don't be afraid to send more, for Dan is hammering away at another bookcase. (I know: "What else is new?")*

I'll save the rest of the news till I see you. Kiss my beloved Grand. DV, Mom. – P.S. With the business off my hands I'll see if Dad will think more clearly about the move you propose. Bless you for wanting us. Your father has pasted your letter inside the cover of his Bible (with the Easter bun recipe!).

Before the move we had begun to read about the other islands, stranger to us than Europe which at least we had learned about in school, and Rachel had sent a book written by a man named Naipaul. It was like glimpsing a new world, seeing the Caribbean in print. We were going to another world.

"And the business is one thing I won't miss," I remember confiding to Dan.

Of course, there were aspects of it that I had dispensed with years ago when Rutherford threw us over. *Business* – his assistant savoured the word, rolling it off profoundly in explanation of why Rutherford was withdrawing as the colony became independent. They had given no notice. Our firm had been the local distributor for his brushware for years. Decades. But, tersely, Rutherford's letter referred Bonny to a representative who would come down to close the matter up.

"We thought, after twenty-six years, Mr Rutherford would have shown consideration . . ."

Bonny struggled for words, aghast at the unexpectedness of it, and the young man handling the matter locally for Rutherford fidgeted with the papers impatiently. "We thought . . ." Bonny resumed painfully, one eyelid drooping and the papers sliding sliding from his hand.

"More fool you!" the lad dealt him smartly, gathering up his files.

After Bonny's first stroke we persisted over the next six years and the business survived. He would take long walks to unwind and to keep down his blood pressure, but one evening in '68 he did not come home.

"He will not come home again," I whispered to Dan when the call from the emergency room ended, and I placed the receiver carefully back in its cradle.

I salvaged what I could – handkerchiefs and guest towels embroidered with hibiscus, lignum vitae and prancing natives in shiny black thread; mahoe boxes, and plaques carved with laden donkeys and burdened women. I discontinued some lines – mutinous about stereotypes however well they sold, and on my own terms I built back the rest of the business. At that stage it was all I could do for Bonny, or at least for his estate. So eventually I sold it in good shape, and it was time, for the children and even Dan seemed anxious about my working late, especially in the Christmas season, as crime crept into the area. I thought of hiring protection, but Dr Maxwell said I was developing an ulcer, and I was just about the age to retire anyway so I sold it off. Faint flurries of scratching remind me to poke out a bit of carrot for Hazel – though how a rabbit can possibly be out on her own is beyond me however capable she may be. Before going to put her up I slap a rubber band around *Notes of a Chat with Rosemarie* and re-examine a cluster of brochures.

Ivy's was a fine old house left over from bygone days. Downstairs was almost surrounded by porches, cool and breezy, but, oh, upstairs was like floating.

There were three ways up. The kitchen steps we rarely used because of the dogs, who were boisterous and had appropriated the landing. Then there was the inside staircase at the other end of the corridor in from the porch. This was how it was both upstairs and downstairs – a corridor from the front porch to the back of the house, with the bedrooms opening onto it from the western side. A separate door (closer to the driveway on the eastern side) led into drawing and dining rooms. The main structural difference was that, upstairs, Ivy's room opened onto the porch itself. And of course there was the kitchen. Unless rain was blowing in at the front, the inner staircase was used mainly by the maids up and down with laundry and food, or by Basil bearing the heaviest trays down for dinner, because whatever the little kitchenette downstairs might produce in terms of snacks, the main meals emanated from Petrona's big kitchen upstairs.

The paying guests Ivy used to have were mainly downstairs, their rooms opening into the corridor or the central sitting space. The downstairs front porch was wide enough to accommodate scattered round tables for dining. They were welcome to it as far as we were concerned. As soon as we arrived at the front entrance downstairs we charged straight up the stairs ahead of us to the porch, with its stunning view of sea and hills, and across it to Ivy's door or, turning sharply left, through the living and dining room towards the kitchen. We knew the three bedrooms on the western side behind Ivy's were never assigned to strangers, so we could arrive and take up residence whenever we liked.

Now, upstairs of the home would be Sybil, perhaps even Jocelyn, and by evening the whole of them would be up there gathered around Ivy. The fiery sky, the melting coconut tarts, the liqueur and laughter – all that would be upstairs. Downstairs, the tourists would produce the real profit – a motley crew, it seems, for (whatever his Aunt Ivy or stepmother, Rosemarie, might have had in mind) Scotty wanted the guests merely so he could collect and deposit, while his wife, Pansy, dreamed of some sort of high-society watering hole.

"We could paint those black lines across the walls for the traditional look – *Illisabethan*," she enthused when we had visited Ivy before moving here to Rachel's. "The elites would like that, don't it?"

To avoid Dan's eye, I had focused on Marie Antoinette, who groomed herself with Bourbon unconcern despite my efforts to attract her attention. My outheld fingers dishonestly pinched together made no difference to the rhythm of pink tongue and silver silk fur. Now she may well be holding court downstairs, amid the tourists, but all the richness of twilight camaraderie would be upstairs. Going on without us. Always. I am haunted by that other life, that other future Dan and I did not select.

For Rosemarie will run Ivy's home as it should be run, whatever line Scotty draws between the locals' retirement home upstairs and the tourists' vacation house downstairs (and Scotty is good at drawing lines). Rosemarie has the stamina and compassion. A little too much of the health food perhaps – cerasee tea, ugh! I don't mind mint, but cerasee! Fish tea, now. (Or Dolores's good conch soup, mmm – from when I was a child. Mama always said she could close her eyes and leave the kitchen to Dolores.)

But Rummy will do it well. (*Rummy! Rummy!* The children, Rachel and Scotty, bounce and clamour in my mind. *Coconut drops, Rummy!*) Not that it's Rosemarie's home. Mainly she seems to be caring for Scotty's daughter – as sullen a child as I've ever encountered, but I suppose anyone must soften to Rummy eventually. A handsome boy Scotty was in his own feckless way and perhaps he too will come to appreciate her.

"Rosemarie likes to fool herself," Dan disagreed.

True word.

Of itself, though, it was not a bad idea, this group retirement we had all worked out. But one must reflect: Scotty part with a shilling? And Pansy, the lacklustre wife he produced shortly after Rachel's wedding, Pansy is not much better. Dan is astute about people and he insists that Rosemarie never thinks things through, especially when they involve her stepson.

"I for one am not impressed by the old Scotty," he muttered. "Scotty achieve this and Scotty buy that. Scotty making so much money in New York. But what has he got to show or actually contributed anywhere?"

What he ever bring for his Aunt Ivy when he come back on holiday to cock up his bare foot on her porch – much less invest in a phone call to Rosemarie just to call his stepmother say, "Dawg, you alive?" Apart from the other lad, Evan, whom did Ivy have to call on, and what hold had she on Evan anyway? What living thing was there to call her own, unless you were prepared to count the puss

– which had an attitude of its own, by the way. Haughty silver-grey puss, spectacular enough to command attention but routinely shrugging off Ivy's affection with elaborate indifference. Ivy lived for our visits.

It is a close circle – some of us friends from the old Wolmer's School days and on through the civil service. Dan alone seems unchanged, tall, broad and full-faced with rich dark brown skin, his eyes keen under bushy brows, eyes full of calm humorous regard, and lighting, when he turns to me, with a sort of wonder. From the first we had friends in common, like Ivy. As for Ivy and me, our mothers rocked us on each other's porches, and I was the one she reached for when we were young, when her life turned inside out. Ivy Rousseau.

After a while she had Rosemarie as a friend as well, especially when Rosemarie married Jesse, Ivy's brother-in-law, years after his wife's death. But close as Ivy and Rosemarie became they never quite clung to each other as they each did to me. Rosemarie said I was the one who turned her life around. And it had been a mess.

But then, who was to advise her? Dan once held that Rosemarie deserted their mother in favour of some lout from the army and, even now, Dan swears the separation was not all their mother's fault. Rummy insists she was eighteen when her mother turned her back on her just before the wedding and flew from New York back to Kingston "so as not to leave her son alone any longer". And this son was a grown man with a job, not to mention a wife. Thank God Rosemarie's engagement to that oaf fell apart before they exchanged vows. But all Dan knew was his mother's side of it and the silence between brother and sister deepened with the years.

"Invite her for a holiday," I urged. That was a Sunday, for we were negotiating the approach to St Andrew's between services with me clutching Rachel on my lap, Dan wrenching the steering wheel about in the eddy between incoming and outgoing worshippers. I tapped Mama's old Bible pointedly to emphasize that the situation between Dan and his sister was not the sort I thought the Founder would approve of. So at last he agreed, and after a year or so Miss Rosemarie arrived.

Straightforward, sturdy, tireless Rosemarie. A lot less vain than I, sensible shoes, tougher than I have ever been, but in a kind, sheltering way. Like a tree. Rosemarie's solid figure was well-proportioned, so her clothes set well and her square frame mirrored somehow a firm – well, yes then – a stubborn jaw. Yet there was that vulnerable mouth and the searching eyes that lit at recognition and affection. She seemed restless, almost hunted, until she was outdoors. Space – I saw it at once: she needs space. How did she ever survive in an apartment? As soon as she arrived she embraced the freedom of an open house, was outside by daybreak, and everything she touched sprouted, flourished, bloomed. Immediately she took over the garden.

She was never a reader, but she did love a performance. She was in her element when we packed her into the car to see Miss Lou. Then we were swallowed up in the crowd, in the mass response to the solid, bold gestures on the stage of the woman who spoke in all our voices, communicated through every movement of her body, seeming to embrace the whole crowd, lifting, scolding and reassuring at one time, palms up and open in excitement, eyes shining and open in discovery, mouth a great O of amazement, and we in the thick of it all, rocked with delight.

"She has changed it all," I began eagerly afterwards, in the hangover of chuckling as we made our way home. But that was of no immediate interest to Rosemarie.

"She's a scream," she gasped, going off into another peal of laughter.

But Rummy, Rosemarie, can be serious too – well (let us come clean with it), even domineering when she chooses, but not to me. I never allowed her to rule me. As old-time people say, *Duppy know who to frighten*. But when you think of what she became after her return, marshalling the wards in what amounted to a war zone of Kingston, with dwindling money and fewer trained nurses and more gruesome emergencies, once at least to the staccato of bullets raining on the outside walls and the screams of traumatized staff – how could she just stop being Matron Cunningham, suddenly, on retirement? You don't just stop being who you are.

For Rosemarie, Ivy's old-people home offered the ideal retirement job.

I can see the place now. One of those old houses with only latticework half-sheltering the porch and louvred windows that were never closed and just all open to the breeze.

Open, open all the time – for between the vacation seasons, apart from a fitful flow of businessmen during the week and a scattering of tourists on vacation, it bustled with a turnover and overlap of friends unpacking a leg of pork here, a box of biscuits there, munching Petrona's gizzadas and swapping anecdotes. Basil, gangling over some palm to be repotted or fence to mend, was normally taciturn around strangers. Yet he was amiable to us, and he sorely taxed the cook with his riddles.

"Basil, you don' chop de coconut fe Doctor yet?"

"Miss Petrona, which dacta don' go a callege?"

"Basil, don' try me!"

"Dacta bird!"

Orchids cascaded from that three-legged table in the corner, and a bird might just skim through trailing its satin ribbon of a tail.

Outside – let me see. Stone pillars towered on either side of the gate, flanked by silver-green fountains of aloe vera. The garden itself was defined by the old brick walk that was chalky in some places, ochre in others, then interrupted by that gate creaking on hinges coated with verdigris. Even inside came this clean smell of earth bordering the atmosphere of fresh linen, of wood polished with oil and vinegar, of green gungo peas simmering in coconut milk with a Scotch bonnet pepper, and a yellow yam roasting somewhere. You could paint it – like the battered-looking Irish woman who visited every January – set up your easel, your colours, but there would be no capturing the smell. A whole dimension shifted on the wind.

Sometimes, though, as I recall, just before catastrophe there comes the scent of flowers. Lulling . . . That is when one must be most on one's guard because after all from nowhere, on just such an evening, heady with clusters of brief cereus blooms and timeless damp moss and fern between the tree roots, it fell on us in our own home, that random, casual assault.

Just dusk. There they were, and always will be in my head, brutal and eerie at once. Some images I would gladly wipe from my brain but the silent pictures reel on relentlessly: death rammed against Dan's temple so his pulse pounds in my own skull, black metal pressed into his flesh chilling my own. Dan's big hands, powerful but elegantly tapered, strong skilful fingers, spread palms up. The men paused – I can only think they were for a moment arrested by his unshakeable dignity, and by his courtesy . . . almost disarmed. I close my eyes and his face is indescribable. Kind, fearless, serene. With the gun pressed to his temple. Life, deprived of him, flashes before me. Of course I screamed.

Afterwards we retraced it, agonized, pondered, and questioned whether we could ever feel safe again. Still. Did we do right? I wonder. For we could all have been together – Rummy, Dan and I. And perhaps the others. Not like being with one's children, but, if anything, at least we would have been in the same boat. Shadows prowl the edges of my mind, but I dismiss them sternly. Nothing can compare with being with one's children. In any case, traces of our old lives are scattered now – a beer mug from Belgium, Bonny's ancient typewriter, a stone from the edge of Loch Ness, a pillowcase full of Mama's gloves for all occasions, salt from the Dead Sea. The table Papa carved with his own hands. Still, I can feel Rachel's palm on mine and Andy's tousled head thrown back on my lap, and the fragmenting past is nothing to that. And not to say that I deserted anyone.

Yet at night regret reaches deep into my skull, sifting the years with bony fingers, probing pain I had methodically suppressed.

"I'll make it up to her," Bonny whispers in my mind. He clutches his temples. "If I do nothing else."

Nothing comforts him. However I try, however hard I work, I cannot heal him. My brother adores me, but to no avail. I support him at the office but against this bottled-up agony I am useless.

"My fault, mine," he insisted. "I'll make it up to her if it's the last thing I do." I remember the veins standing out on his neck.

Over and over I urged him, "For God's sake just turn aside and *live*."

But when life throws up a wall he tightens his shoulders and rams his head against it.

"Stop!" I scream. "For God's sake!"

He raises a face awash with blood, and says through his teeth, "If it's the last . . ."

Dan holds me struggling and still gasping, "Stop! Oh Jesu. Stop!" And I find myself in bed in a different room and it is too late for Bonny.

Yet he was tough in many ways. Never think he wasn't. He built the business from nothing, he dismissed advice against taking me into it and he flatly refused to employ Scotty, no matter how bright Ivy said he was (and they say now he actually has a degree in Management, whatever that is, from some unidentified college).

"Wo'tless," Bonny insisted. "Scotty change, what? You can wash speckle off guinea fowl?"

Highly qualified in Management, Rummy argued, when we came to discuss the retirement home. Yet Scotty, if my memory serves me right, could hardly manage his zipper, and I wonder now how he will run a home. And if he disappoints them – well. As I told them, you can't fire family.

Some homes are nightmares, so I hear. But then, there was old Miss Minnie. Probably no one else alive remembers her besides me, for there is more and more of the past that survives in my head only, but the further back I look the clearer these things shine. Miss Minnie lived in a home for years and seemed happier than I had ever known her to be; but she had been dreadfully alone in that house and, before that, with her old dragon of a sister. Then there had been the ordeal of finding the sister – butchered, they said – and in the end here was old Miss Minnie with her own little flat, so to speak, but not isolated. As for me – I'm accustomed to a full house.

Twilight draws all memories rushing back. From we were children – that was when we pieced it together, a kaleidoscope, the day's events, things recollected, read, made up – stories brief as dusk. Perched there half in, half out the house on the wooden railing that rimmed it beneath lacy fretwork, I lost track of what was real or not real as the sun plunged behind the tamarind tree which printed its own black tracery of branches on the glowing sky. As a child I searched that sky for wings of every possible sort, but in no time the flame-edged cobalt deepened and swallowed imagined terrors at one gulp.

Everything double-stacked on the shelves I read and read again. Eventually Verne, Austen, Donne, Wordsworth, Gibbon, Wells opened door after door into other spaces I could inhabit or escape quicker than thought. But even before, as early as I can remember, at unusual speed outlandish stories deposited characters and events in my head. They loomed so starkly against my uneventful life sometimes it seemed adventure was for everyone but me. It was all well and good for Bonny, my brother, who was three years older, proud, and tensely resolved to prove himself. Bonny shone at the centre of his own tales, but I suspected we were too dark, Kingston too far from everywhere, and the times (even in that young twentieth century) too well advanced for monsters – and I a girl on top of everything.

"You coulda never be the hero, Ellie," Bonny goaded me. "You woulda have to be the sacrifice."

So I set my back against the tamarind and smouldered.

"You like poetry, don't it?" he jeered. "Watch me!

Eleanor, what a bore,
When she hear de monster roar
Faint and drap down pon de floor!"

He grabbed a branch of the Julie mango tree and hoisted himself out of reach without pausing.

"Hear de chorus now:

Ellie, Ellie, shake like jelly,
Wake up inna manster belly."

"I going show you," I cried, for I knew I could face anything. In fact, I could hardly wait. There are two tragedies in life, they say. One is not to get your heart's desire; the other is to get it.

I can hear the chatter still, big people talking. Arguments about Garvey and whether England really was the mother country. Papa was more anxious about what would happen to bananas with the US changing the market and what with Panama disease and something called leaf spot.

"And where will they all go when they can't get work? Kingston? No, of course I don't mind. It's just – what will they do here? What will happen to the country if everyone comes to Kingston? And what will happen to Kingston?"

It frightened me, the thought of some unnamed thing happening to Kingston, and Mama saw it and said, "The real problem is – what will happen to the people?" But I didn't feel better, for I thought *we* were the people.

Now, in my mind's eye, I see the house at Lincoln Road as clearly as I did in those days. I hear the whistling frog who found himself in the bathroom and had to be conducted outside firmly but kindly on the upside-down chamber pot to which he had laid claim. I can feel under my fingers the grooves of the carved bedposts in Mama's room, and hear the bicycle bell clamouring that the boy who lived next door was home at last. I wanted to stay back and play with him but Mama said we must get ready to catch the tram.

"Not today, Mama. Not Miss Minnie today. Her stories are all sad."

Even years later they haunted me, these tales of incredible cruelty that revolved around Minnie's sister – Tita, they called her still. I was grown up, of course, for Miss Minnie to have said in front of me, "Imagine, the mother abandoning that poor little baby boy in the pit latrine," and I was shocked although it had happened five years before. Certainly I never connected Tita's bitter repudiation of the Cockburns with her own daughter's *predicament* until later, when I was a grown woman and Mama enlightened me in her roundabout way. I was still little, though, when Miss Minnie described how Tita, her sister, had punished her own daughter for stealing sugar. "She took the flat iron from the coal pot and burnt the little girl on her . . . well, she raised the back of her skirt and burnt her there." I was not surprised the child had run away and lost herself in the streets of Kingston or that she had thrown away her own child. For what had she learned of love? Only she threw him back on the mother from whom she had fled.

Later, he ran too.

As I find myself distracted the song blurts from me. *"Run, mongoose!"*

But did we run too, Dan and I?

Before the gunmen came in on us, I had never wanted to run away from anywhere. I rooted, poured my life into places and could not withdraw it easily. First it was Lincoln Road that was my world, and when Papa died and Mama talked of moving I cried all over again, day in, day out. I was just a little thing, not even ten.

When she relented I called next door, "Dan, we're staying here forever."

Then I wondered if *he* might go away, my best friend, for he was a big boy writing exams. When I asked him he said no, he had thought about things and when I grew up we would be married if I liked. I asked him for a ring and he laughed and said I was too little for a ring, but he picked a silverback fern and pressed it against my finger and said not to be afraid if it washed off, for the mountains were full of silver ferns. And so I knew it would be all right and we never spoke of it again until it was time.

When Mama made Easter bun she sent one over for Dan, because he was my best friend, and like me he had no papa any more. Dan's papa had died in the Great War. He had volunteered but was never allowed to fight white people, even enemy white people, and so he had to dig trenches and move ammunition and died there in one of the trenches in the rain. They said he drowned.

Dan said one day he would study at a university, so he was full of talk about

Marcus Garvey, and how Garvey said there must be a university and a technical institute in Jamaica. But Dan was ahead of them all, and it only came true after Garvey's death, so Dan studied . . . by post, I thought, till I understood about the external degree. When the University College opened, Dan had his degree already. He said I should go, but at last here was Rachel and I could not tear myself away . . . I was always reading anyway. Even when I was little I had begun to read Dan's books.

Dan and my brother, Bonny, got along well enough, but they were not best friends. Dan and I were best friends. And now here we are.

There were some from those old days that I kept a bit at a distance though, like Cockburn. Sherwin Cockburn was *Bonny's* friend, and (to my way of thinking) entirely out of order, but impossible to avoid and not bad-hearted. He turned out to be a faithful friend to my brother and for Bonny's sake I suppose I accepted him with resignation, as an act of God. In any case, Bonny fell in love with Cockburn's twin sister, Agnes.

Now so many of them would be there at Ivy's. It was how the house was, always either overflowing or empty. Then Rummy (my Rachel named her when she was too little to say Rosemarie, and it stuck) – wasn't it Rummy who said, "Why we don't just stay?"

It was idle chatter at first but there was no denying Ivy's guest house would make a delightful old-people home. Town was not what it had been, but there was no grillework at Ivy's, no clatter of helicopters, or distant claps of what might be gunshot. Outside there was only the sound of running water over stone on the hillside, eternally, infinitesimally honing, and ever winding, splattering, pitting, gurgling down.

"Miss Petrona, what lie down inna bed an him bed always wet?"

"Oh Saviour! Basil, don' torment me!"

"Ribba!" He belted it out and ducked away awkwardly in his huge shoes, trying to compress the tall gaunt frame out of Petrona's notice.

Outside the gate the local madman, hardly more than a lad really, searched the gravel for fragments of broken bottle that he collected meticulously in an empty condensed milk can and packed into the garbage when the bags were put out. He was harmless, Ivy agreed, and Dan pointed out that he did the establishment a service by removing broken glass from the path of car tyres.

CASCADE

In the day brief scraps of advice emanated from Glass Bottle regarding the balance of power among the servants of the house: "Mankind nat to be hold in subjection to womankind!" Glass Bottle would pronounce.

"Is to drive 'way de likkle old wo'tless," Petrona objected when Basil smuggled him a fragrant wedge of breadfruit hot from the coal pot.

But Basil would cut his eye off her and mutter, "Mout' long like alligator."

Cecil would have collected Sybil, my friend from schooldays at Wolmer's, and they would sputter in later than ever in his old Austin.

"About time," Dan would exclaim, as I made the general announcement. *"All men come to the hills. Finally!"*

"If you're going to quote that troublemaker – I'm going straight back," Cecil threatened, but he bowed over my hand nevertheless and kissed the air above my fingers.

At night, when it rained and thundered we were inside, singing, playing. A parry of words on the Scrabble board, a swoop of cards, a clash of dominoes. Someone would trundle down to the storeroom and pull out a bottle from the common stash we kept replenishing, and soon the aroma of pimento dram wove through our laughter. Our fellowship was . . . impregnable. Lightning perforated the darkness, as it must, but each rent mended instantly. So it does when the shafts come from the outside. And even in broad daylight, among us, *forever* hovered momentarily – an emerald shimmer, then darted on.

"Scotty has a degree in Management," Rosemarie said one day.

In a twirl of silver fur, Marie Antoinette uncurled herself from what was certainly the most comfortable chair in the room and stalked away scornfully, tail aloft, so I sank unobtrusively into her warm dent in the cushion.

I kept very quiet. For one thing, I could hardly help wondering whether, if we moved in together, we might not be permanently afflicted with that man Cockburn. For another, the last thing I was retiring for was to take on a whole new enterprise. So there had to be some independent means of running it.

But Scotty's success – I remember once asking Dan what exams the boy had passed and I can hear Dan now, suck his teeth and say, "Pass *exam*? Scotty? Boy couldn' pass worms!"

"Haw!"

THREE

Evan

IF YOU WANT know the truth, some woman good till they stupid. No, me not making no joke. Is true.

Miss Ivy me know from me born, and is she give me a start in life for no good reason. She say my mother who was her maid in the States get fool up by a wo'tless white man and die in labour. So when she Ivy come back home to Jamaica she bring me with her and get a woman on the property to take care of me. Miss Millicent do her best with me but I wasn't easy. You know? I like to play in the river and dig hole to make cave in the hillside, and I like to drag bush into the house and bring in ground lizard and mongoose, say I making a jungle. And one day when I swing out of the Nelson mango tree (I think I was Tarzan that day) I come down through the roof and break down the dining table.

Of course I land without a scratch because I come down foot first in a cowboy boots one of Miss Ivy guest give me say his son outgrow, and is the big heel punch the hell of a hole in the old shingle.

But Miss Ivy say, "Give the boy a chance, Millicent. Is a good boy. He just want something to do." So she buy me a little goat kid and that is how I begin the farm. Of course I was still Tarzan but the young goat was my elephant and I name him Tantor, only Tantor turn out to be a girl and later on she start the herd.

Is Miss Ivy why I go to school in the first place, but is Miss Ellie why I finish. I get fed up with school early and was looking to leave and Miss Ivy say she wouldn't force me, but Miss Ellie get to hear and she call me and ask me if I want to run a farm for myself or if I want to work on somebody else farm. So I stay and finish school and after I sow a set of very wild oats I start thinking to go and train as a vet, but I meet Pinkie and she was a vet already so I just build up the farm till it begin to run itself. Once the men fraid you and love you at the same time everything go smooth like cocoa butter.

Now is not to say Pinkie take to me at first, as how I loud and out of order and she full of broughtupsy. I first buck up Pinkie in a friend wedding and I believe she hear my mouth long before we introduce but them seat us at the same table and after she watch me a while with her mouth wide open and her eyebrow in her hairline I suppose I grow on her, and even though when she take me home her mother nearly faint (I say afterwards I shoulda never wear the yellow silk tie) the parents come round eventually.

And we do well. Don't mind Miss Ivy say she giving me the piece of land, I invest my part of the profit from the farm in a small property adjoining her own, so I get a place for myself but still oversee her own. Pinkie set up her clinic just outside of Ochie, and when Evadne come – well, she is my little eyeball. I never expect to feel so and is when they put the baby in me hand I feel the eye-water running down. Hold on a minute, because I never really come back to myself.

Right.

Anyway, from Evadne could talk she turn me round her finger and is Evadne bring me through when we lose Pinkie to the breast cancer. I just . . . I lie down wanted to dead and Evadne make me get up and shave every day and paint the gate and fix up an office, and she say we have an extra Land Rover, why we don't rent it to tourist. And the bigger she get the more head she get for business and next thing I know I running One Love Tours from the office near the farm gate and Evadne is the consultant in her frilly skirt and pigtail. Tourist calling Evadne from all over the world and arranging Land Rover discovery trip. They plan they route with her and we supply information on accommodation and sightseeing and rent them a Land Rover from the fleet. When they arrive and sign up we hand them the vehicle and the key, a map, a hot patty and a beastly cold Red Stripe beer (or a june-plum juice if they prefer). The fool-fool tourist dem doing all the work and paying through they . . . well, through the nose to drive into the back of beyond just because it have a name like Gimme Me Bit, or Nonsuch, or You No Send Me Nuh Come. And they come back mash up from the rough road and blister from hot sun and salt water, grinning from ear to ear and thanking us like we give them a free holiday.

Well, if truth be told some of them not bad. In fact some of them nice to raatid – or, as Miss Ellie would have corrected me primly, very nice indeed. One pair take to us so much we stop charge them and they just collect the vehicle from us when they land. And it turn out they look after Evadne when she gone over there – like they own pickney.

Because after a while Evadne gone abroad to study since she done set everything up here and the workmen terrified of this mawga little pickney and adore her would dead for her, so One Love Tours running itself, and she not even seventeen but she say she must gone to study Business and Design. But I feel the college in for a shock for she must going take over and teach the professor dem a whole new approach to running a business.

But you know is a little thing can make or break a pickney. When Evadne was small small with the hair ribbon bright on her head top, a woman I never like did try to drag her into domestic work. This woman, Pansy, marry to Miss Ivy nephew, and Pansy and her husband, Scott, was plastering themselves onto Miss Ivy because they see she have no children and them angling for her to leave them the property. It might sound coarse, put so, but is so I see it and me no 'custom to mince words. Well, the Pansy say to Evadne how she is a nice bright little child and if she want come learn how to help out in the kitchen so she could make a money.

Is good I only get to know about it afterwards or I mighta box down the woman, but thank God is Miss Ellie overhear and she say no, leave the little child let her do her schoolwork and play and read in her spare time. She will learn what housework she have to learn in her own house, and one day she will manage her own business. Well, after that Evadne begin to manufacture necklace from john-crow bead, and construct violin from shoebox cover and rubber band, and all the time Pansy only throwing words behind Evadne to make her feel small. But Miss Ivy buy a necklace from Evadne and wear it all evening and after that from time to time, and one day when Miss Ellie and Mas' Dan come up from Kingston they bring Evadne a book about handicraft. When night come Evadne sleep with that book.

Anyhow, is so Evadne turn out to be a businesswoman instead of somebody servant, and she say when she graduate and come back we opening up a branch of One Love Tours in Kingston. But I don't know, because me mind tell me not fe leave up Miss Ivy for Pansy and Scotty to take advantage (set of old johncrow dem), and, besides, apart from Evadne, everything I want right here a country.

FOUR

Dan

IT STAYED ETCHED into my mind – that brochure Scott left on the table when he first brought Pansy to holiday at Ivy's. The man in the picture wore formal academic dress and flashed a hungry grin that prompted Ellie to dismiss him as some politician. Then she looked closer, brought it to me and we studied it together.

"Dan," she whispered. "This can't be . . ."

But it *was*. An advertisement for an instant college degree. Taking only Ivy into account, Scotty had made no effort to conceal it.

"The ungodly know no shame."

Ellie was still quoting Zephaniah that evening when she slapped down the brochure in front of me once more – as if for the first time – and when we had finished spluttering all over again she folded it small and tucked it in a corner of her escritoire. Shame, I reflected. In large doses it can destroy you, but controlled amounts are healthful.

I knew I could not live with any significant level of shame and I determined from the outset that I would do nothing illegal in the effort to leave Jamaica. Certainly, when Wally, my lawyer, enumerated ways of dealing with the man who was trying to take over my land, I refused. I had never broken the law in my life and was not prepared to at this stage. Similarly, there was no question of my smuggling money out of the country, particularly as it was not my money but Ellie's.

As a civil servant of the old colonial days I had a pension payable through Britain. It was cumbersome and when given the choice of more direct payment many of my colleagues had opted for a change in pension arrangements, but I never had – which turned out to be just as well when our dollar (which had begun as half of a British pound) collapsed to a dwindling fraction of the US dollar. As burdening the children was out of the question, the move to Trinidad was possible only because I had access to more than the fifty US dollars per person that the government was allowing us to take out of the country at that time. My pension could go straight to Trinidad.

For Ellie it was quite a different matter. Every cent she had was in Jamaican and devaluing rapidly. Moreover, the house and her other property had all been converted to cash which she could not move. Fortunately, her lawyers agreed that if she gave me her cheque and I gave them mine, they would write me an equivalent sum from their US bank and send it to Trinidad, where I could pass it on to her. That way, she need not even come down to the office – which was just as well since Ellie lived by the rule that anything circuitous was likely to be shifty. It was their account in the States to do with as they liked, however, so it was entirely legal, and they were happy to assist a family with whom they had done business for generations. Their US cheque would be posted to arrive even before we did, and there it was waiting on us when we moved in.

The only problem was that it bounced. Every thousand dollars of it.

I called Wally and he sprinted over to Hammond and Sons to sort it out. It was, as he confirmed, a complete accident, though he questioned why I had gone to them instead of doing the whole transaction through him. I had begun to wonder myself, but Ellie would never have agreed to let her money pass through Wally and I could hardly tell him so. I was in bed for a few days but they got my pressure down without ever knowing what sent it up.

Most important, Ellie was none the wiser.

So whenever Ellie encountered the advertisement again among her papers, I could laugh with her over Scotty's shamelessness without any sense of irony.

"I always felt he was just full of prunes, Dan," she conceded, "but you – how could you know from the first that the degree was a hoax? Especially after Pansy preen herself about certificate in gold frame?"

The mention of Pansy impels us to fall on the sofa together, and we howl in chorus, *"Alimentary, my dear Watson!"*

Scotty and Pansy were hardly at Ivy's until recently though, and, all in all, we were tempted to retire there. But it was Ellie who had built our house and I could not predict whether it would be that easy for her to give it up.

Kingston, now – both hard and easy to leave. Once, Ellie, who was licensed but reluctant to drive, would jump on a bus and head downtown. But *now*, wrenched by voracious cycles of poverty and violence, Kingston had been riven into uptown and downtown existences alienated from each other. The government grandiosely described the local situation as war – shifting attention away from its persistent inability to solve crime.

"Evan says them should just do 'way with de police," Ellie chuckled, but she had a stubborn respect for Evan. Ivy's protégé has done quite well for himself and seen his own daughter through college. It was true though that the police were generally distrusted. "Nobady cyan't trust Babylon, according to Evan," she continued. "Better we just arganise justice we own way. Farm a new *arder*."

Outrageous. He always was.

"Evan has the weirdest ideas," she agreed, "but – good hearted, and *fond* of Ivy." If only we could say as much for her nephew, Scotty Cunningham – although he is around more now and quite attentive – and his wife. Or, at least they are in the foreground, Scotty very much the lord of the manor. Pansy especially postures as the daughter of the house and subjects everyone to her concept of elegance.

"We must get something from a *good year*, for that cellar," Pansy proclaimed one evening.

But it was all hot air, as I told Ellie. Pansy knew no more about wine or cuisine than I did.

"Not the remotest," Ellie concurred. "Then, after the poor old pantry get confused into Scotty's music room, and now it turn *cellar*? Pansy is *so* full of prunes."

The truth is Pansy was there that day of the mutton, and we have always sworn she cooked it. Certainly Petrona said *she* knew the beast had eaten guinea hen weed and the meat was worthless, but still Pansy served it.

"After all the soak them soak it in vinegar, nothing couldn' tek it out, Miss El." Petrona kissed her teeth, a prolonged expression of scorn.

And Ellie was particular about food. There was that pompous Englishman who was Bonny's business connection. Old Rutherford was in shock when he saw "how the people here lived", as he put it. When he had gone back to Sussex, still bemused, Ellie, Bonny and I laughed till we were weak. Rosemarie missed it because she was staying with Ivy for one of Scotty's visits. Ellie tried to spare me but I overheard Rutherford telling her he was considering doing something nice for our lovely lady*like* daughter. Had we thought of sending Rachel to England, he asked, to a proper school? Well, he dumped Bonny and never looked back.

Then before we knew it there we were, packing up to join Rachel and family in Trinidad.

The road here, home to Rachel, runs alongside the house, the lawn edged by ixoras that Ellie set when we arrived. The driveway, flanked by unruly bougainvillea (but the children seem to like it), bends around the back of the house to a wide paved area on the far side. There is space for Andy to get up to all kinds of shenanigans and a fine old shade tree with a garden seat for keeping an eye on him. Rabin and I have long chats there. The front has a good porch – not like Miss Ivy's but pleasant, shaded with potted plants like Ferncot, our old house in Kingston. We love it here.

Still, Ellie was not only elated but frankly amazed that I agreed so quickly when Rachel and Rabin proposed the move. There was the alternative of Ivy's at least for a time, but I could not risk it. Rightly or wrongly I decided to conceal the threats I had received about the land. It was a piece I had bought from Ivy and was refusing to sell in case Ivy should find it possible someday to buy it back, as she had originally hoped. The hold-up, and the question of whether it really was only a hold-up, set their pincers in my brain and squeezed tighter and tighter. Yet when the phone call came two days afterwards, I was not prepared for the fear that clenched my throat and sent my stomach plummeting. I could think of nothing but getting Ellie out of our house and into Rachel's. I was satisfied Rosemarie was in no danger and could follow later. Never did I see it as a permanent separation from Rosemarie. The competing forces that impelled me then flutter now at the back of my mind, fragile and faded as the carbon copy of Ellie's letter:

My Darlings,

What a delight over the prospect. Of course we can't move overnight after nearly forty years in this house (and then, to another country too) but the sale is settled and I'm to chat with the lawyer (Hammond of course).

Can't wait to see you for the packing up and trying to do what we can in advance, but the issue is: what not to pack! When Dan and I were getting married, Bonny carved this dining table with his own hands. He made it from the old mahogany boards Mama had under her house for thirty years, for her coffin she had said, but then she decided this was more practical. I would like to bring the escritoire Papa made for me if at all possible, and I can't see your father being parted from his desk, but I'm not sure he needs all the fishing tackle (although he keeps muttering threateningly about tilapia and wabine). And, my dears! I must warn you! He's talking about pulling all the bookcases apart and reassembling them in your house. Call *him. This is no time to be delicate. Nowhere in the world has that much extra wall space.*

Though, she was the first to admit we couldn't leave our books.

All around. *Sir Winston Churchill: His Life and Times* and *Popular Mechanics* lay at the periphery in case there was space, but Wodehouse and Shakespeare clustered near to the planter for the silver fern we bought at that country fair when we got engaged, and her mama's lace centrepiece, folded in tissue, rested on *A Tale of Two Cities*. Beside was Emily Post's *Etiquette*, not so much for its content but because it was from Jocelyn – sad, driven, determined Jocelyn whom none of us took as seriously as she deserved until it was too late.

Longing to see you all. Will you bring our boy?

"What to keep; what to let go." Ellie threw up her two palms for divine guidance. "*The Life of Enos Nuttall*, from Miss Ivy. They must decide how much more they can take in their house."

"Ballast," I had insisted.

P.S. Dan says, Do you have a hedge trimmer?

This was the letter Ellie was writing when the news came about the Hammond boy, a junior partner in the firm that handled her affairs and, I believe, Ivy's. Gunned down in broad daylight, no one knows why. He was on a street he had no business to be on. Whom could he have gone to see there, and why? Someone walked up and shot him in the face. Later, Wally told me that the mix-up with the cheque occurred because of transactions left dangling on the death of the young partner. But why did he die? Rumours flew about him being "in the wrong crowd" but that seemed unlikely – Hammond's son, after all. Nevertheless it was unsettling that those who had the care of our affairs should be so vulnerable themselves. And what if they too or even just one among them were tainted. Well. She would have none of Wally.

"Our papers must be in order," she insisted, so we sifted through our correspondence before the move. Every day, this paperwork: some to the lawyer, some to burn. "Ha! Our school reports – Wolmer's Girls' and Wolmer's Boys'." She unfolded them eagerly.

"You remember your headmistress trying to grow that bougainvillea hedge between the boys' and girls' schools?" All at once I was alight with recollection. "For years, Cecil and I had been watering it with sulphuric acid from the lab."

"Brutes. Just as well though, for *we* had no lab."

"By the time you got there I was almost ready to leave."

"And head boy. Poisoning the school hedge. Good Lord!"

"Well, I wasn't head boy till the following year. Anyway, I look back on it with a clear conscience – solidarity with one's peers. The other side of the hedge was of little importance to me before you arrived."

"Liar. Anyway you got me an order-mark."

"How?"

"Waved at me through the half-dead piece of hedge in February of '33 and when I waved back all hell broke loose. If Bonny hadn't told them you were our neighbour and *his* friend, I think I'd have been expelled for loose behaviour at twelve years old. And see – look at my marks. But there was no university here in those days."

"You should have had the chance."

She packaged up the school reports reverently.

What was strange was how Rosemarie held herself aloof. She cleared cupboards far into the night but with a cold hard silence that baffled me.

"Rummy's vexed with me I tell you," Ellie said. "It has to be about the move."

But that was out of the question for nothing had been finalized before she and Ellie had talked, and from what I understood she was determined to join Ivy. Particularly unsettling was Pansy's inviting "their Rummy" to come and live with them – not Scotty, Pansy nor for that matter Cindy, the daughter, having ever shown much interest in Rosemarie. We all accepted that the three of us could not move together. Even one elderly person can become a handful, Ellie agreed. But Rosemarie's determination that her stepson wanted her jarred on me. Where would this sudden devotion of Scotty's spring from?

"To be a drudge," I fumed.

"She believes in them." Ellie shook her head sceptically.

What could I say to Rosemarie even when she did calm down?

"No one can have all of us," my sister reassured us staunchly. "Rachel is your child and at least Scott is Jesse's."

But it was when Pansy and Cindy came for her and were driving away and when Rosemarie waved through the back glass of the car that this new parting became real. Rosemarie had put her arm around Cindy, who raised her face coolly, weighing the latest development.

"I wish you had brought our Andy," Rummy had said, just before stepping into the car, and squeezed Rachel's fingers.

For Rachel had come in the night before. We had planned it that way for Rosemarie to see her. The morning was like any other till Rachel called, "Rummy's ready to go. Aren't you going to kiss her?" Then Ellie was in a daze. Perhaps we all were.

Rosemarie waved from the back seat, looking perplexed.

Still it was not our last glimpse, for Rachel stayed in town to finish packing up for us and she insisted we go ahead to Ivy's. So we rolled over the mountains in the old Rover, polished inside and out for its last long run with us and the first major outing in months. How could we not drop in on Ivy, Ellie insisted (as if anyone were arguing), especially with Rummy going to be there?

"And Ivy herself. How can Ivy travel again – heavy as she is with the thick legs crumpling uselessly under her? They must be so disappointed in us."

The composite retirement had seemed a good idea for a while. But when I attempted to disencumber the land I owned adjoining Ivy's – for I wanted, one day, to sell it back to her as I had bought it – when I refused to be badgered into selling it to anyone else, then the threats began. I stood firm when the first, subtly menacing note arrived. The next message, in smudged capital letters, suggested they would send gunmen for me, and I halted the action against the squatter. But then, nevertheless, came a muffled voice on the phone promising to throw acid on Ellie, and the blood surged to my head leaving my feet like ice, my mind numb. Even if I agreed to sell, what was it I would be dealing with? I dropped the land matter altogether, instantly. I'm getting out and the land can rot, I told Wally. I said nothing to Ellie about this, for she was gifted at investment, at turning over real estate, and it would have been hard for her to accept throwing away land. If I died before her (as I should hope to) I feared she might reopen it, once we had stayed in Jamaica. So I determined that that time must find her in Rachel's house. The nearest I came to telling any of them about it was to inform Rachel I had put the land in Wally's hands.

"Never enquire about it," I directed her when I found her alone among the packing cases. She slid down the handkerchief she had tied over her nose and stared, chin tipped rebelliously.

"Why not?"

"That constitutes an enquiry."

The retort hovered at her lips then diffused into a good-natured suck-teeth, which I overlooked, and she never brought it up again.

So I walked away from the problem without a backward glance, but on the way out to the plane whom should we see but Scotty, way out where they meet the VIPs, and he stopped us to ask whether we would consider selling him the land. Then he promised to call, and hurried over to the man he was obviously there to meet, some bejewelled businessman before whom he began practically genuflecting.

"Funding for the home?" Ellie groped for some explanation to account for Scotty's grovelling. "But what a spectacle! Scotty really *would* sell his soul for a deal." Certainly he had reinvented the home for a market we could never imagine. The brochure Pansy distributed boasted Seafood Night on our airy veranda with live band, and (if you please) fortnightly barbecue surrounded by lush tropical gardens against the sound of gentle falls.

"After most of them won't have teeth to tear meat," Rosemarie had snickered. "All this fe serve mineral water. Anyway, the boy just young and enthusiastic."

We waved as we walked away, and Scotty acknowledged us with a perfunctory nod, too engrossed to waste attention on two old fogies wandering in the other direction from that of his home.

We didn't give tuppence about him because we were going to our children.

Rachel and Rabin have a comfortable three-bedroom house, so whenever we visited we had always stayed upstairs near them with Andy's little bedroom in between. Now of course he was growing up so they had very rightly moved him to the larger room and kept the smaller one as a spare. But that presented no problem because what had been maid's quarters and laundry room downstairs were now painted and re-tiled to become a bedroom, bath and study for Ellie and me. So as soon as we entered the kitchen from the side of the house parallel to the road, there was our little apartment on the right, the bedroom and study side by side with a door between, and each with a door to the kitchen. But we had our own entrance too on the other side of the house, for Rabin (and it was *just like him*) had had the carport transformed into a small porch for us and extended the roof at the back for the cars.

Among the carbon copies, another line caught my eye and I reached for the paper while Ellie peered over my shoulder.

. . . *head is not what it was. Things fall in and out.*

"You didn't feel right?" Ellie probed cautiously. "You want a cup of tea?"

"Tea is nauseous," I responded automatically.

"Nauseating."

"That too," I grumbled. I peered at the paper, preoccupied, then pushed it deep into my pocket, averting my eyes. In glancing around I realized how, in little more than three years, the books had spilled over from the study into the bedroom.

Rabin inspects the bookshelves from time to time, leaning his tall frame in the doorway and stroking his short neat beard. We had always liked him, from the day Rachel brought him home from campus. Somehow he forced her to pause in mid-hurtle from one overstuffed day to the next, interrupting her intensity with comedy, a single wild strand running through him of wacky unpredictable humour.

"If it were not for Rabin, she might be like Bonny," Ellie reflected. "He has saved her."

"You notice any change," I overheard Ellie whisper to Rachel, "any change in Dan's face, his expression?" Then she turned away, as if appalled at her own question, to a volume on the bedside awaiting repair. The title on the thick-ribbed spine, gold bordered, glowed proudly on the peeling chocolate surface but the binding was worn away from the spine altogether and the cream ends of strings dangled. And what if it were all becoming undone? I could see her reaching back into her head – she does that visibly. *"No more shall grief of mine . . ."*

Rachel whisked past and, *sometimes*, I thought, glancing at her, *if you moved more slowly you would last longer and even get more done.*

"Are *you* going to sit still for five minutes?" I asked Ellie with interest. "Just so I can eat without getting the galloping indigestion?"

"I only got up to find a grapefruit knife."

"Rachel doesn't have."

"I do."

"Did. Disappeared in the moving," I announced triumphantly.

"That's what you say," she pondered. "But what would a thief want with a grapefruit knife?" To which there was really no answer.

Andy thundered down the stairs and collapsed at the bottom to put on socks, howling for someone to tell him where he had left his shoes, scandalized at the notion of combing hair.

"No one *does* that!" he protested.

"And how would I have known if I stayed in my room like a fool?" Ellie stared at him with her mouth hanging open. "So they go out with it sticking out so?"

"Hair's supposed to stick out," he confirmed.

"You see? If you want to learn, travel!"

"Just hold still!" Rachel grinned, tugging a hairbrush through the mop of curls with one hand and with the other producing mail that Rabin had forgotten to hand over yesterday.

"Ha!" I swooped on it, but there was no good news. "Dollar plummeted further. Almost everything we have there is half the value it would have been if we had been able to shift it."

"It would have devalued just as much if you had stayed," Rabin reminded us, rifling through a tray in the fridge in search of mangoes.

Yes, we were better here in the surge of lives under construction around us. I wanted the chatter, the clutter, the bickering that collapsed into laughter, and most of all I wanted it for Ellie. Andy – every day a new crisis of outgrown shoes and vanished music book, a puppy to name and some baby squirrel to be fed with an eye-dropper, or a false gold tooth flashing unannounced in his grin. When they were away, the house grew unbearably still, and during their trip to visit Rabin's family in Toronto we entertained ourselves more systematically.

"The agenda?" I prompted.

Ellie hovered in front of the wardrobe, considering the location of her handbag. "Always ready for a jaunt. Comestibles?"

"Naturally."

She had always been serious about fun, but the meticulousness with which she planned outings and equipped picnics became instantly invisible at the actual events, which came off with all the spontaneity of an accidental occurrence. Besides, barefoot on the beach or precariously perched on horseback at the outposts of Ivy's land, she radiated exhilaration and wonder. Her head thrown back, plaits sweeping her back then, later, lapped across the crown and eventually clipped to a neat bob, hands upraised, shoulders scrunched up with hilarity, even her feet rubbing each other, hers was a complete physical surrender to the moment. She was quick bursts of movement, smart collars and dramatic borders on sleeves and hems, crisp pleats, exquisite lace, skirts that hobbled or swirled, deep glowing colours and rakish hats. But at the same time she was pragmatic, direct, fearlessly outspoken, infuriatingly stubborn and uncompromising, ready if not eager to die for a principle. But most of all faithfully, selflessly loving.

"When did the soursop drink come to pass?" I rejoiced.

"*They, while their companions slept,*" she returned briskly. "All aboard, big fellow?"

Every so often when it was dry enough we wandered along the perimeter of the lake. It was a brief drive, but slow because of this stiffness in my limbs. I kept the sandwiches, leaving Ellie's hands free to steady me on the loose stones, and we strolled, now and then dipping in and out of each other's thoughts. Once when it began to drizzle we ducked into a shelter along the path.

"Shh! Look!" she said. "That little frail bird, dapper in black satin, negotiating the surface. See? Stepping delicately on . . . cobweb legs across those lily pads."

Without her I would never have *seen*. Huge concave leaves swayed their green velvet, glossy veins muted by beads of water, and raindrops pearled their edges. But the rain beat more and more heavily, filling them like shallow bowls of champagne with a splash and bubble raised to us on slender stems.

"Cheers," Ellie pronounced, and I inclined my head graciously.

Filling, tipping gently, pouring their drink and then, empty again, righting themselves to fill once more. We could have watched forever while the hours slipped by. Yes. Why *should* we ever move again?

Still we pounced on every scrap of news from home.

"Wheelchairs arrive at last," Rosemarie reported over a crackling line, "and the pillows, which *supposed* to be non-allergenic but is me unload the crate and I can tell you I was in *one* state. Talk bout sneeze? Let alone poor Sybil and the asthma. Sybil say is not what we agree on and pay for and I have to say is true. I mean you can't take people money then short them. I sorry to see Sybil so, and I tell Scotty myself."

"Sybil had this asthma from we were children," Ellie protested later. "People don't outgrow it?"

"If so, she's taking her time," I chuckled. But on reflection, I sobered. "The problem is the combination of asthma with heart."

"She have heart too?"

"Cho! Long-time." Reaching for a slip of paper I folded it three times to clean my nails with the edge, but it was an awkward business now, what with the tremor, and Ellie searched out her nail file to finish up with the pointed end.

Ellie always chose the chair she said Rosemarie would like, straight-backed, affording a perch from which to peer over my shoulder at the crossword puzzle on the clipboard over which I manoeuvred with the battered pencil, leaving her own rocker empty for the time being, till Rosemarie's visit to Trinidad. The smell of cocoa curled shawl-like around. Time trailed behind us, forking into countless paths taken, avoided, taken, missed, refound. We browsed through each other's memories, teasing out the clues.

"*With hey, ho, the wind and the rain,*" sang Ellie, spinning the hint through her mind. Between the damp, crowding darkness and ourselves, the reading lamp threw a field of light and warmth. Our murmurs melted and reformed in its glow.

"What's on the last line, Miss Ellie?" I held up the confounded newspaper to the ceiling to see the bottom of the page, which shook rapidly till she took it away and slipped her arm under my elbow.

In the struggle to find my feet, seemingly out of contact, Ellie steadied me with her glance as much as with her hands, and the certainty in her voice restored me from momentary panic to balance. Outside was dark and wet, but Gawain's panting sounded clear and close. Yet even he settled quietly when Ellie began to read. He had become part of the routine.

A stunning mind, St Paul's. Tonight's passage transported us back to the pale sand-coloured stone we saw at Jaffa, the bumpy palm trunks and a radical ministry to the gentiles. A new beginning, as outrageous as any.

"Young people," Ellie reflected admiringly, drawing the sheet around us and pressing her back against mine to fold us into a sheath of warmth. "But what trips we had. At least we can stretch out properly though. Remember the little beds we saw in those old palaces?" She chuckled. "They slept sitting up? Or they were shorter than us? Both?"

"Mm."

"They weren't uncomfortable? But you don't have mouth to answer?"

"Probably spent limited time in their own beds."

"Out of order!"

"You sought my view on the subject."

She sniggered comfortably. It could rain outside as much as it liked. This was the bed we had slept in for nearly half a century, my increasingly angular lines framing the contours of hers. Inside, the night enfolded us. We were safe.

Next morning, as we dressed for our appointment, the phone rang.

"Front right button," I bellowed when Ellie reached the receiver.

"Miss Ellie, if I didn't phone you me mouth would weld shut." The speaker brought Rosemarie right into the room. "When I tell you – *days* pass without them utter one word to me, and even if people chat and is only bout money, what I must tell them? Then, Missis, next thing: the Mas' Scotty him bring young girl in the house when Pansy out."

"No!"

"And young, you know. Little tight skirt like bandage, and gold ring in navel. Hear, nuh? I in me room hemming Cindy school uniform and I hear this . . . Sorry, Missis, but I hear this *thumping,* and I frighten because I did think is me one in the house. So I take time lock me door and then I bawl out, 'Who there? I calling police!' Everything go quiet. Then I hear a voice say, 'No, is okay, Rums. Is me, Scotty.'

"So I open my door and there they are coming out of him room rumpfle up. Well, me jaw must be drop because him stare at me bold bold and say, 'What happen, Miss Rosemarie?' "

Rosemarie's voice paused, and I broke in, "What you said to him?"

"Wait, Dan. You there? Sorry, Massa, I thought it was just us girls."

"But what you told him?"

"I just say, 'I feel like I coulda lick you down dead right here.' "

"So what the thumping was?" Ellie demanded.

"Lord God, Ellie!"

According to Rosemarie, all Pansy talk is money, money: funds for a security gate, cost of bad dawg with pedigree and papers, salary for security man called Jarvis who facety you see? Then they want put in electronic alarm system – and who going to break into an old-people home? And in the hills too. Then the strangest thing: imagine, they going reduce nursing staff to hire dog handler.

"So much security?" Ellie pondered afterwards. "Then the place really get that bad? I mean this is not West Kingston."

"And you noticed that with the reduction in nursing staff they need Rosemarie's help there even more, so she's not coming here yet." I glowered through the window.

"Something is rotten." Ellie turned back to me. "Did you pick up that Scotty wants to buy adjoining land for some investment? But what do they have adjoining – besides his and Rummy's pieces, and of course yours? Well, there's Evan's own as well, eh? But stop! Don't Scotty said he was going to call you?"

"He needn't. He's welcome to talk with my lawyer." I swung away, back to my book.

The volumes clustered around from every flat surface. When I manage to open one my parting glance feels more like recognition than enquiry, but their words swarm on in my head.

"You need new glasses," Ellie insisted.

"I can't change them every month." A chill passed across her face. "It's not two months," I hastened to say.

"It *must* be your tablets," she agonized. "Some side effect. How else could you forget how long . . ."

Her repressed anxiety set my fingers quivering on the volume in my lap, an old favourite. The dark green fabric covers with burgundy binding at spines and corners are eaten by time. Inside each cover is lined with a pastel marbling of green, pink and pearly cream but the unevenly sized pages are crisp brown at the edges, crumbling to dust, and a corner is worm tunnelled.

"We must shop early, before the rush." I interrupted our anxieties sliding out of control by bringing the tumult of the season back to us. In the fifties Bonny's office had hummed and bustled with Christmas sales on the gift items, and Ellie reminded me how the higglers had demanded cards powdered with snow.

"Is dat de people want," one had insisted. "Dat is Christmas fe true!"

"Cho, man! Me prefer pansettia."

One thought ignited another in flare after flare of recollection. It came back to me, the assurance with which she had stepped in years later when Bonny collapsed – towards the end of the sixties that was – how she had shouldered the business.

"You have such a mind," I whispered again, just as I had that time twenty years before. "Why you don't sign up for that degree at last?" I had demanded then. "Literature?"

But then Bonny fell ill and she took over.

It was that extraordinary competence I had in mind when Rachel asked, almost twenty years later when we were packing for Trinidad, whether I had talked to Mom about my property in Jamaica, whatever the problem was, and I said I could not afford to begin a conversation with Ellie that I must not finish. How would Mom know, Rachel protested, whether the conversation was finished? Just stop short of whatever distressed me, Rachel suggested. "What you forget" – I remember staring away into the past and the future at the same time – "is that your mother's mind moves at the speed of light."

Yet beside me this Ellie waited out the boredom of cars chasing each other meaninglessly across the screen and men leaning through windows to fire at each other, and I realized that the knobs under the television screen presented a mystery, different as they were to those on our old set. My feet simply refused to take me in the direction necessary for me to turn the TV off, so the car in front of us drove off with the body of the man it had hit draped over the bonnet like a banner.

Fortunately Rosemarie's call intervened.

"Left button, TV. Right front button, phone," I intoned.

"Petrona and all get vex and leave the work," Rosemarie reported, "and the food have no taste now. But I don't blame her after Pansy speak to her like a hog, only that is how Pansy talk to everybody. Wait! Either of you remember old Lazarus?"

"The one who was raised?" Ellie asked, playing for time.

"Behave yourself! Irvin Lazarus, who was organist at Valley View. Him head funny now, you see? And Jocelyn self not doing well."

"Oh, that Lazarus. Not raised fully," Ellie agreed. "Made every hymn a dirge. But he was always odd. You know he used to buy two *Gleaner* every day?" she added.

"To give 'way one?"

"Nah. To have a spare."

"Rockstone!" Rosemarie exclaimed, then resumed. "But nine of us upstairs and most in good enough shape to poke fun at Pansy and laugh after the tourist them. All the same, downstairs they have one local gentleman come sometimes for the quiet because him pressure high, but what he must be paying to stay downstairs have to be enough to drive it up more." She dropped her voice to a whisper. "But here this, nah? Poor Scotty. When I tell you – he *cannot* let a woman pass. Petrona did tell me he even carry one mattress put down in the pantry, and is true – I see it for myself. And then some of these women so fool. One of the new nurse in love ready to dead fe him. Mitzy she name. So she hate Pansy like poison. Poor Pansy don' know why this woman only watching her like snake."

"You mean Scotty running a racket with the nurses now?" Ellie asked.

"If? I wish I could see you two to talk. You know, I believe Cindy know bout it, and I can't excuse Scotty for that."

"Cindy?"

"Scotty's daughter," I recall.

Both of us are anxious for details of Rosemarie's visit but she has nothing encouraging to report.

"Listen, I understand you lose the seat because you don't pay by the deadline."

Ellie tried to keep the disappointment from her voice, though I could hear it flooding up bitter and choking. "But when you say your money wasn't released . . ."

"Why don't you go to the bank yourself?" I demanded.

"Massa, if me did know say I couldn't walk as I like I woulda think twice before I come live with them. Scotty really let me down. True. I thought he had more in him. But even so I woulda manage myself, and you know me no like lock-up. Of course, what could be more lock-up than town?"

Then the connection went dead.

"Sometimes I wonder whether we did right," Ellie said after breakfast as we cleared up, and I knew she was thinking of the move three years ago.

"We were perfectly right!" I insisted. "What would happen when I couldn't drive? We would have ended up as prisoners in our own house." The thought that driving was already becoming onerous startled me and the box of eggs slid from my hand before I could get them in the fridge door. I recoiled from the mess, staring at my hands in the horror of their unpredictable tremor.

"If Basil were here, he would say, 'Go up white come down yellow!'" Ellie grabbed my hands and kissed them, before diving down with a wad of kitchen roll. "We should call Rummy and tell her to make sure and keep her money in the bank. I wouldn't put Scotty to watch a farthing of mine. And don't Rosemarie said he was into some sort of banking or investment business too? Mercy!"

"He may well have his doctorate in financial management by now," I said, dialling. "He's always flying back and forth, and you can buy anything in these big cities."

"And Basil leave too, you know," Rosemarie lamented. "I don' know why I miss the old wo'tless so."

"Entertainment value?" I suggested.

"And he so facety too. When I used to ask him why him don't believe they can run a good home, him say, 'Why fowl cyan't pray, Ms Rose?' And I say I don't know. And he say, 'Because him knee turn backway. Him nah make so. Same way the Cunningham dem cyan't make no home.'"

"What's become of him?"

"Massa, gone Basil gone a town fe look im fortune. I hear he build squatter house in West Kingston."

"I hope they don't shoot poor Basil," Ellie said unhappily.

"Nothing hangs together," I said later, then resolved it. "She must come next month. I'll fix it from this end."

"What tied up her money?"

"Some legal transaction."

"Then is not hers?"

"As usual you go to the heart of the matter." Suddenly exhausted, I reached for her fingers. "What's to be done, Miss Ellie? Tell me your mind."

She struggled to piece bits together but there seemed too few to assemble and instead she reached for the *National Geographic* that Rabin had left for us.

"I'm worried about Rosemarie," I brooded. "I told her to speak to a lawyer, and then she said she met some legal . . . specialist."

"How would she know someone like that? Who put her onto him?"

"Exactly. Then Scotty has invested in another pharmacy but is worried about security. He talks about needing protection, more expenditure again. All this capital he's reaping from the home and what are our people getting back? That's what I want to know."

"You know what I think?" Ellie nudged me.

"Mm?"

"I always knew Scotty was no philanthropist, but I don't consider him any great entrepreneur either. I feel he's just a dutty tief and probably not a good one at that."

I agreed but the mirror reflected my face blank of all I felt, and I realized why at times she thought I was not listening: I offered no answering expression. Part of the condition, the neurologist had said, was the effect on the muscles of the face. I squeezed my eyes closed, and when I opened them I turned resolutely from the glass to focus on my feet, marshalling control to get them up on the hassock.

"So?" she insisted. "Where does that leave Rosemarie?"

When I shook my head and closed my eyes again she pursued it no further – at least, not aloud. But I sensed the questions skewering her mind even as I sagged against her and let my thoughts drift to the children, who would soon be back.

I was too tired to speak for much longer, but, unlike Rosemarie, Ellie still has others to talk to. Only a week before the young people left on their three-week holiday to see Rabin's family in Canada, she had chatted with Rachel over a collection of leaves, flowers, sprigs, and the oddest pod, dark and shrunken on one side like a mummified brain, dissected, riddled with holes, rimmed by a dry horny ridge.

"Now for God's sake," Ellie protested. "What a gruesome sight!"

"How?" Rachel asked.

Too thin, our Rachel. Well, she never stops.

Ellie could not explain. It seemed mutilated, I suppose, sterile and contracting. "Ghastly!"

"Same flower you were admiring the other day," Rachel retorted good-naturedly. "It's the lotus pod. Stunning in a dried arrangement."

"Story!"

"See." Oasis and a twist of floral wire. "Sometimes we spray it, but there's no need really."

In fact, it was extraordinary – unrecognizable in relation to a flower, of course, but dramatic in its own stark symmetry. The bloom swayed on in Ellie's memory, for she spoke of it often, tracing its shape with her fingers on the pillow. Soft cream veined by pink, she recalled, swelling and parting, an enchanting glow, hovering above the mud. Yet she drew back her fingers nervously, frowning as if, below the flower, something churned in her mind, ill-defined, threatening to surface. I remember her stepping away from the edge of the lake, which was spongy with wet leaves.

"I don't want to leave the place dull and boring for you," Rachel had continued. "What else can we do to liven things up?"

Later we went with her to borrow some movies, but it was hard to find something decent we had never seen. After a while we slipped out for a walk, and would have bought June plums (under some other, alien, name) but they were all green.

"For chow." The vender leaned forward when we seemed confused, and repeated it, raising her voice and slowing her speech patiently.

Rachel was surprised to find us outside.

"I thought you'd have liked to pick out a few films."

Once they had left for the airport the house was so still I wished we had chosen *Gone with the Wind* again. Still there were the books and the garden.

"*Much abides*," Ellie confirmed.

On the corner table swept the curve of a long leaf, coiled, a tendril spiralling from beneath a softness of white petals, set off against a dry pod bared to the tough honest lines of its original form but contracted to exaggerate each ridge and depression.

"I'd have dumped *you*," Ellie admitted, examining it once again. "But look at you there."

"We got Mom's message, and of course we're fine." Through the speaker we could hear Rachel bawl faintly from the other end of the line.

"Dan saw it on the news. The earthquake. I understood the damage was terrible," said Ellie.

"But that was Japan. Far away. See you soon."

"When are you coming?" Ellie shouted, relieved after all our anxiety about Rosemarie.

Instead of going out to feed Gawain right away, Ellie hurried over, unable to wait, and leaned down to put her cheek against mine, and she whispered, "They're coming!"

"Aah!" I put aside my own turmoil and rushed on. "I'm looking forward to my trim. I must be glamorous for their return." The wedding picture signed *Rabin and Rachel* caught my eye and I waved inexactly towards the smaller photographs on the dressing table. "We must get the one of your mama enlarged." My voice was more urgent than I had intended, and the inconsequentiality seemed to unsettle her. "Put a note on the fridge," I urged all the same. "Write 'Mama's picture'."

"Here."

She held out a pen but I responded only with a delicate wavering stroke on the back of her hand, and there in her eyes I glimpsed recognition that fraction after fraction was slipping through her fingers, as my physical problems proliferated. But suppose, behind this spectre, there lurked another. I watched obsession and avoidance play out their hide-and-seek over her face. I could see in expression and gesture how, endlessly evading only to collide again with it bruisingly, she would duck behind some other thought, but that gradually as change after change flayed the edges of consciousness, an unaccustomed inclination to tears had begun to build.

When she had washed her face secretly and come out of the bathroom, a new miniseries was being announced on the screen. Some disaster movie.

"It would be nice to have some flowers in the house for their arrival," I suggested, startling her with an idea that I suppose seemed out-of-character for me.

"Here?" However she tried to avoid exciting me unduly, she could not veil the delight.

"But where else? And if we call the florist, we could get something delivered in time. You know Rachel's as crazy about flowers as you are," I grumbled. "Didn't get it from me."

"But don't be foolish. What could be more beautiful than flowers? I don't mind spending the little money. What do you think?"

"Good idea."

It rang so close behind me that I could reach the button and immediately Rosemarie was crowing through the speaker.

"I have the ticket," she sang, and suddenly I discovered in Ellie's face that she had been sitting on the recollection of their parting as a jagged blade pierced into her vitals. Rosemarie, the sister she never had, torn from her. And by me? Rosemarie must come, I thought, for that wound to close, before the next opened.

A faint wheeze at the window commanded me to stretch my hand through the louvres. From the bed, I just reached through to rub Gawain's head briefly. Every night this ceremony of pressing forward on hind legs to strain in over the sill.

"There should be some way of avoiding the cold nose," I pretended to complain, but there were the dog's eyes closed and the quivering tip of pink tongue celebrating the deliciousness of being touched.

Ellie would get up to bring a soapy washrag, in a while. It was all right, she insisted, no trouble at all. What was one to do – not pat the dog?

The moment she opened her eyes she was ready for the start of a busy day.

"Brush your teeth as early as possible," she reminded me briskly.

"I always do." I stared at her, scandalized.

"Earlier."

"In bed?"

"You can make joke. You remember that camel by the Dead Sea? What his breath was like?"

"Merciful Lord!"

"A word to the wise is enough!"

Soon we were clearing the breakfast table and Ellie had the melon skin ready. Then through the windows I followed her progress around the house, tugging a dry frond away here and there, but gripping the skin tightly to keep track. Behind the wire, a whisk of brown and – where? Ha, sitting up and quivering with expectation.

"What ho, Hazel!" Rattle of the door as she checked the latch, for Gawain would have made short work of Hazel, given a chance.

The first major item on the agenda would be our boy's vital supplies: Coke, mango, chicken wings, and we must have eaten out the frosted flakes. We could drive *there*, just down the road.

Cars whizzed by and a truck blared, swerving around us.

"Mercy!" I pulled into the supermarket lot thankfully, for every week the traffic seemed more frenetic than the week before. The parking lot was wide and empty and Ellie's eyes searched for . . . perhaps some landmark. But at least the cars here queued and manoeuvred sedately.

"We have to go back out into that?" she gasped.

"Well," I said, "we could just bed down on the back seat. The stupormarket is right there, and the bank. Bathroom facilities are limited, but I could accommodate you with a turn at my bottle."

I reached under the seat and produced it triumphantly in its little plastic bag.

"Beast! You walk with it?"

"Not on the street, but once I drive out. It seems safest. You're not getting out?"

While she pondered the logistics of it all, I got around to holding open the door and leaning on the window to hand her out of the car.

"I wonder if I shouldn't carry the stick too," I muttered. "But you wouldn't want to be seen with an old fogey like that?"

"Perhaps I shall get one too. Or a few, matching the accessories – don't you know? Cut a bit of dash!"

So we arrived at the supermarket door giggling like two fools.

"Soon it will be time to shop for Rummy's visit," I gloated as we got the last bag onto the kitchen counter.

But now lunch was late, and she insisted on the big iron pot with the arms akimbo, to make rice and peas.

"We didn't bring that," I objected. "Rachel's is steel."

"I used it last week," she whispered. "You washed it yourself. Remember?"

"Let's make potato salad instead. They're coming in late. Besides, rice is a terrible thing."

"Just because you don't like it doesn't mean other people don't have sense. Anyway, remember?" she insisted.

"I remember lots of things. Ivy's. The two of us on my bike. Our trips abroad."

"Aren't you ever tired?" Ellie had laughed as I stood outside the back door, home at Ferncot, covered in grass chips after mowing, gulping from one of the pewter beer mugs.

Remember? Remember when we walked tirelessly, hypnotized by a dream fulfilled, on a mount in Jerusalem. A column soared in my mind, inscribed ZKOR – *lest catastrophe repeat itself*. Now she made a note of where she put everything, so I could manage if she was out, but she rarely left me, and whatever of yesterday slipped away we recalled the old days as sharply as ever.

"Dan, don't there's a legal way of changing your name?"

"Why should I?"

"Not you, dope. Cockburn."

"Aah. What brought him to mind?"

"That woman on the TV. The one with the heck of a bosom."

"Oh my, yes. Flourishing." Then I returned to the matter at hand. "He probably didn't care though – Cockburn, I mean. About his name, especially since it's inoffensive when pronounced."

"But for God's sake, he had to see it in black and white sometimes. I would have gotten rid of it early."

Then the basket of flowers arrived and she felt almost guilty about enjoying it before the children came. I care less about flowers, and it was only a yellowish blur to me anyway.

"Nice shade of blur, admittedly," I conceded.

"True word." She closed her eyes, rubbing her cheek on my hand and extending one finger. She took in the textures of petals and sprays and the cold droplets at the ends of leaves, and inhaled the scent, opening her eyes narrowly to see how they looked as my blur. But it was not the sort of thing you could keep up for long.

"The basket is just filled with . . ."

The name escaped her, but she said it was some more recent variety of orchid. It replaced Rachel's old arrangement which had, to one side, a sort of pod against which the blooms unfolded in stunning contrast. They would not have been the same without it, she commented, and now that they were all scattered, it alone endured. She saved it on the counter for Rachel to use again, and turned quickly away from it back to this new basket Rosemarie would love if only we could work out her visit. Altogether, she concluded, it was a shower of gold.

"Who are they for again?"

She turned to me, her eyes sparkling and the question echoing in the tug of her hand on my shoulder, and her strength and brilliance seized my breath, and I pressed her head between my palms to hold it together as long as I could, to hide it from Rachel and most of all from Ellie herself for as long as I could, even as the shards of the future pierced my brain, and I leaned my cheek on her hair.

And all I could whisper was, "Enjoy every second."

FIVE

Icy

I KNEW ELLIE'S opinion of my nephew and perhaps Scotty did take me for granted, but the truth was that my troubles began with her own brother, Bonny. It was Bonny who introduced me to Stanley Croft.

They had all arrived to spend the weekend with me early in the forties (I think Ellie and Dan could only have been married a couple years) when Bonny said he had told this chap, a businessman doing his rounds to the country stores, to drop in at the Rousseau house for a hand of cards. My father was the most hospitable man in the world and loved Bonny like a son, but in any case Stanley was handsome and good humoured and everyone took to him at once – except for Ellie. At first I found him confusing, sweet-talking me but staring at Agnes (Bonny's Agnes) all the time. Of course, I wasn't that fond of Agnes. I suppose I may have been a trifle jealous to begin with.

Agnes Cockburn was clear-skinned with fiery hair and grey-green eyes. She was tall, slim, elegant, and I was thick and clumsy beside her. In fact, she was always way ahead of the rest of us girls, with her manicured toenails and the little chain around her ankle, from New York. I know she wore pyjamas, and people said she smoked cigarettes though that might not have been true. But however much truth there was in what they said, it was all all done when she away from home because her mother was stricter than anyone else's.

Her mother had become a cold, pious, ascetic woman, however she may have started out. Having the twins had almost killed her – and so destroyed "certain aspects of her married life", to use the phrase Ellie eventually gleaned from her own mama. This took me years to figure out, but I eventually pieced together that Mrs Cockburn had determined never to go through another childbirth and so old Pastor Cockburn, Agnes's father, proud as he was of his beautiful and saintly wife, lived in utter deprivation except when he could comfort himself with one of the servants. So he was a terror to the poor young girls of his parish whom he brought home one by one, ostensibly to do odd jobs for his wife. Agnes's mother confided to Ellie's that she could never contemplate anything that could lead to so much suffering again, so she had told Pastor to do whatever he must, but leave her out of it. She would understand.

Their son, Sherwin, was spoilt and delighted in saying anything that might shock or embarrass, but it was essentially just talk for Sherwin was not a bad boy. It was different for Agnes though because, between them, Agnes's parents cocooned their daughter in a life of utter monotony from which she would have done anything to escape.

But they trusted me.

"Ivy is a good quiet child," her mother pronounced, "not like these town girls."

So, sometimes Agnes was allowed to spend a weekend with me. She was with me when Marcus Garvey arrived in the island, deported from the States after serving the prison term, and the crowds cheered him on the docks. Our parents exchanged outraged reactions to this welcome but all that made no impression on Agnes. What mattered was that she had escaped from her house and that her parents had faith in me.

Mine was not the strict home her mother believed it to be, though. In fact, I was thoroughly indulged by my own father – a comfortably-off country landowner, widowed, preoccupied, doting on me and my younger sister, Maisie. Well, Maisie married her Jesse just barely in time. After her wedding I was convinced once and for all that I would be an old maid. Oh, everyone believed in me and I in everyone, animals adored me and I surrounded myself with cats, dogs, parrots, even a transient peacock. But I was convinced, locked in my unending battle with my weight, that no one would ever marry me. So I was quickly befuddled by Stanley Croft and utterly amazed when he proposed.

The first meeting continued to trouble Ellie, though. She said it had made her uncomfortable trying to work out whether he was eyeing Agnes or trying to see into Bonny's hand of cards. I shrugged it away thinking he had offended Ellie by remarking that Dan was darker than she was, and men generally were darker than their wives in those days, so why should she care if Stanley observed that? As far as I was concerned Stanley was gorgeous, witty, fun-loving. I could not even pretend to take my eyes off him.

As always, Ellie and Dan were full of talk about books and politics, and Ellie especially prattled on about artists who were just names to me, Huie, Dunkley, Abrahams. Of course I knew about Edna Manley, but as to the rest –

"I went to the Institute too," I protested, "but some of it was so gloomy. How could pictures like that decorate anywhere?"

"Well, dark dreams and indeterminate landscapes, yes," Ellie admitted. "I don't think Huie's interested in decorating your house though. The work is . . . troubling. Like all the unrest. All part of the same turmoil."

There she was gazing at me expectantly, but I never pretended to be any intellectual.

"I like art to calm me and match my cushions," I laughed, and Stanley smiled back and applauded.

Then he clapped Bonny on the back and urged him to get together a few business associates and bring them boating, but as he waved to us before backing out of the gate, Ellie leaned closer to Bonny.

"He's a sharper," she said.

Oh, but Stanley was devastatingly charming and his smile made my head swirl. So when, after a hectic courtship, he proposed to me I accepted ecstatically. Nineteen forty-two and it's like yesterday.

The wedding was to be at home, under the lignum vitae tree with its canopy of blue flowers and hung with orchids. "Anything," Papa said, beaming. "Anything you like."

I was still dazed with joy when Ellie arrived two days before the wedding to help us prepare. Then I saw she was in torment.

"How can I tell you? How can I not tell you?" She clutched me tightly. "Don't hate me, Ivy. Oh Jesu, Ivy, don't hate me."

"What is it?" My teeth chattered.

"Bonny and Agnes will be coming over from tonight. Look at Agnes carefully. Watch her interactions." Then she continued brightly, "You know, Bonny is utterly under her spell. I want your advice about that."

Bonny's addiction to Agnes was old news and I sensed Ellie had more in mind, only I was too enthralled to work it out.

But that night there was no mistaking it. Stanley was mesmerized and once when he leaned to whisper something to Agnes he touched her ear with his tongue.

Pots of flowering plants were gathered around the lignum vitae, ready to be set out for the wedding, and I was watering them that last morning before the day of the ceremony when Stanley came up the driveway.

"How's my sweetheart?" he demanded, spreading his arms, and I turned the hose in his face full force.

When he yelled, Papa rushed out just in time to catch me as my legs gave way.

"What? What?" the old man shouted, pulling the hose from my hand.

But all I could whisper was, "It should have been a gun."

I left for New York shortly afterwards on the edge of a breakdown and was away for a year.

Ellie had Bonny to deal with during that year, but in the end she was never forced to tell him anything, for Agnes took it out of her hands. Agnes gave Bonny an ultimatum, Ellie said, and the end was inevitable.

"But where would we live?" he gasped. "I have to save *something*."

He was terrified of losing her and so his mama helped him build up the business, but it was too late – the madhouse of her parents' marriage was tightening around Agnes, and Stanley seemed to be making a fortune and was showering her with gifts. Bonny was desperately scraping together the money to start a decent life, but it was taking him too long. So Agnes left Bonny for Stanley Croft – my Stanley (as I thought of him, even then) – who turned out to be vulgar, dissolute and violent until his death.

I returned from New York for Papa's funeral in the midst of the labour unrest. My disappointment and absence had been too much for his heart. I could keep no one, not even Papa. They gathered around me, Ellie and Dan, and Bonny, and I healed on the surface as it came home to me. I began to recognize that Stanley had fallen for my father's property, rather than for me. Then, as I heard rumours of the pair and realized what I had been spared I recovered at a deeper level – except I began to think, if only Bonny had loved me instead of Agnes, we could both have been happy. Ellie would have been my sister. But it was never so. I know Ellie thought of it. She had me visit with her for a while and we picnicked by the river in Castleton Gardens and went to the Edna Manley exhibition – but Bonny never really saw me.

By August the pimento berries clustered on the trees east of the house, ripening and filling the air with their scent. When they were picked in, a little lad from some poor family nearby spread them on the barbecue to dry. The same boy, Basil (I've never known his surname), covered them against the September rain and turned them faithfully until they were ready. Ellie and I made the liqueur together before she went home, and I told her that Dan's sister, Rosemarie, had nursed me in New York, though Ellie hadn't met Rosemarie yet. I am certain Rosemarie told her nothing of what passed between us, even later, close as she knew we were. I had been Rosemarie's patient and she never broke a confidence.

But how close they grew after all. When Ellie and Dan married, a little before the war, the question of Rosemarie coming for the wedding had never arisen and, even afterwards, it took years for Ellie to heal that breach.

Over the years my house came to be Ellie's haven when the burden of the office crunched down. Her mama had helped Bonny start the business in the old days, but as she grew frail Ellie took over from her and worked along with her brother. Until the stroke. What had blazed through like a fuse, driving him, now burnt him out. The worst of it was Bonny's eyes, emptying of alertness. A stillness overtook him, then a sort of wistful vagueness as if, Ellie reflected, as if he sensed a loss he could not quite define. He recovered enough to know . . . to know he had not recovered. And I now, I could see it all the clearer, the old days of tall tales and cricket. Bonny dangling from a branch by one hand singing nonsense. Bonny leaning forward to clinch some plan then springing up to shake on it. But now, the lithe, tireless action stilled.

He had always trusted Ellie unquestioningly.

"I told Agnes we should wait till I saved a bit more," he had agonized twenty-five years before, according to what Ellie relayed to me. "But was that right, you think?"

"Yes. What she said though?"

Twenty-five years later he repeated to Ellie, "She looked through me like I wasn't there."

To distract him, Ellie would pass the ledger for him to see the figures, but he brushed it aside. He was impatient to be off.

"Don't is *you* add it?"

He had this fiery competence, and then it sputtered and went cold.

Yet they had already expanded the business. When Bonny's most important associate, old Rutherford (the big brushware man), had came down from Sussex I heard all about it. Of course they had him to tea, with her mama's Bavarian china set, and there was Rutherford pleasantly surprised to find them civilized. Dolores outdid herself with the plantain tarts and Bonny practically purred with satisfaction. The business flourished and over the next fifteen years he overdid it, poor Bonny, and when Rutherford threw him over it broke him, so Ellie took it up. It was the sort of thing Scotty should have been able to do, but Bonny had always been reluctant to have Scotty.

Yet in no time news came of Scotty's degree, then of the Big Job. The wedding had been in New York and Rosemarie and I heard about it when it was all over.

"I would have gone. If the little sinner did only pick up the phone!" Rosemarie grumbled. "We could have flown over together, Miss Ivy."

The degree, though, was another matter. Scotty's wife, Pansy, invested in the overseas call to tell Rosemarie, and reminded her to "pawss it on to all the folks",

I felt a captivating boy like Scotty could have done better than Pansy.

When I visited Kingston in the old days I stayed with Ellie. Then she and Bonny would accompany me back for the weekend. The plain after Twickenham Park stretched dry and dismal, but then the land greened and rolled by lush again. A poinciana leaned precariously over the river beyond Flat Bridge and Ellie pointed to the petals flaming beneath on the surface of the water till they swirled slowly apart.

When we were children the three of us would sing, *"Carry me ackee go a Lin-stead Market . . ."* Then the old people would say "Shh!" because it was a bungo song. But Ellie's mama shrugged, and said, "Make the children have a chance, once they not *boisterous.*"

Ellie was always well behaved, although they were never able to cure her of The Laugh. It was never a vulgar bray like that of Agnes's brother, Sherwin, though. Just an explosion of mirth. She was irrepressible.

The last time we came back together as youngsters we crawled along the wind-ing road behind a huge yellow truck crammed with passengers and gaudily cap-tioned *Wild Hog,* and . . . Look! Stone slab steps wound up the hillside. But where did they lead?

Ah! Here it was. A side road branched, sudden and steep. We lurched up the wet uneven surface with the tangled hillside on one hand, still drenched from the rain, and, on the other, rougher bush broken by glimpses of the sea near the hori-zon, distant and leaden. It opened up as the road rose. I don't recall which was my own last trip back up here to the house and now I don't go out, but I can see it all from here.

On the last visit from Ellie and Dan I watched from the kitchen window upstairs as they arrived. Leaning over the sill I could see Rosemarie run out laugh-ing and she hugged Ellie and Dan at once.

"What you fern baskets doing on the ground?" Ellie gasped.

"Missis, if I tell you, you won' believe it." Rosemarie tugged away Ellie's purse, pulled the usual bag of Bombay mangoes to her face and inhaled blissfully, then planted everything on the back step, to march them around the house. But, before turning the corner she paused and almost crushed Ellie's hand in warning. "They chop down the tree."

I made my way painfully to the front and looked out from the porch.

The ancient lignum vitae was cut down, chopped up, rooted out. Around its remains the land lay mangled. A crushed red hummingbird feeder showed up in its fallen foliage, as the dying leaves curled and shrank. Dismembered chunks of wood, pale mottled bark contrasting with the severed trunk of raw yellow and brown, lay where they had fallen. Basil sat dejectedly on a piece of the trunk, his long, angular body looking even more disjointed than usual. He raised his eyes mournfully to me and shook his head.

"The birds don't know what to do." Rosemarie pointed at the garden bench that had been moved to a picturesque place in the full blast of the sun where no one would sit. "Jesse and I courted under that tree."

Who wouldn't? I forced from my mind the recollection of Stanley and instead recalled the patina of moss that had greened the thick base of the trunk, deep toned and velvety, thinning upwards to a film. Into the deep gash in my life had come my sister's child and Scotty had practically lived with me before his father remarried, so Jesse was almost continuously at my house and grew closer and closer to Rosemarie. It had come to be their bench then, shaded by bright fountains of fern fronds and jaggedly sharp spears of wildpines, pink blush muted with beige, that sprang in clefts of the lowest branches which had bent down and twisted up again with a grey-green tangle of old man's beard and gold-green tendrils of creepers accommodating the pale jointed stalks of green-white orchids and the iridescent hummingbird shimmering among them. When the lignum vitae bloomed, its dome was random clusters of small blue flowers.

It was a whole world in itself and had been there before us all, and who would rip open the land and tear out a tree like that?

"Scotty," Rosemarie confessed, then turned away to give Basil some direction, so I caught Ellie's whisper to Dan just below me.

"But what a jackass this boy is." She stared incredulously at the ficus towering over the house from the back wall where it had been going from strength to strength. "Then why Ivy allows it?"

"Ivy? Cho! They don' ask her nothing."

"What you mean?"

But Rosemarie's explanation was lost in the general bustle, for repairs were underway already, and in the clang of iron being delivered for the grillework. Scotty issued forth in his lilac-coloured shirt, snapping directions till he glimpsed them, and then, aah, pleasant greeting, wreathed in smiles, and concern regarding their journey and whether they had eaten. Even at a distance I was warmed by his aura of charm and hospitality – such a beautiful beautiful boy, tall, lean, smooth-shaven, soft-spoken, with a flash of that mysterious school ring.

Scotty brought them upstairs and for a few moments it was like the old days.

"Cindy! Say 'Hello'!" he commanded the child peering around the door, but she pouted and withdrew quickly.

Rosemarie had shifted a pot of orchids from the fallen tree to the porch in an effort to save it, but along the edges of the cattleya leaves open wounds wept away the vital substance of the shoots. Still, Scotty gestured proudly towards the ones Rosemarie had positioned opposite my door, showers of lavender and cream.

The home was materializing around me. There had always been arrangements for live-in staff behind the house, and the vast kitchen had been wasted for years, apart from routine triumphs like Petrona's rice and peas.

"Petrona!" Ellie hailed her as she came out to greet them. "I smell fresh lime juice."

Dan dropped his voice conspiratorially. "Don' tell me is for turtle. Turtle soup?"

"Turtle, sah? No, sah! After dem no buy dem ting again, sah!"

Oh well. But turtle soup, with the precise hint of mace! Anyway.

"Whatever Petrona has," they affirmed, wandering to the front steps, though Dan added, "Once it's not rice."

Remarking that he must secure that porch or the old people might drop off and mash up, Scotty bustled away for a skirmish with the welders. Dan lowered himself a little stiffly into a chair and closed his eyes decisively, while Ellie settled in between Rosemarie and me. Outside the fence the madman, Glass Bottle, wailed, "God tree not fe chap down fe serve mankind iniquity."

"All this . . ." Ellie gestured at the iron, the lignum vitae crater and some boxes of computer equipment. "Don't it will drive up the charge? You think you will get guests who can pay for it?"

"Scotty advertising in foreign too," Rosemarie explained, "and he talking about approaching interested parties for funding, some wealthy philand . . . *philanthropist* they call it? One Ashmead."

"Related to old Miss Minnie?"

"He must be from away. He rich. Perhaps he's one of Scotty business associates."

"Which leaves one no wiser," Dan muttered, and Ellie glared at him.

But – let that go. For, sitting up here looking over the grass and out to sea takes me back to a time where the children would be playing just before twilight, when the scent of jasmine rose and everything slowed down and we sat contented after warm cornmeal pudding. Marie Antoinette landed suddenly, without a sound, on the cushion of the chair nearby and flicked her elegant tail. She rubbed her shoulder on the chair back as though she might condescend to let me pet her – in case I was desperate. Then she curled up with her back to us. In a corner, the others were playing rummy, and the impossible woman currently trailing after Sherwin Cockburn leaned a bit too far forward for that neckline and admonished him to "pick a kyawd". And look, one of the little ones came strumming on a shoebox cover laced with rubber bands.

"What stupidness it is you have there now?" Pansy demanded.

"Must be a violin!" I shook all over, no longer caring how my arms quivered like Jell-O. "This is Evan's daughter, you know," I told Dan.

"I guess is not so good." A little girl's face falling, preparing to accept defeat.

"But it is," Dan interrupted swiftly. "It's excellent . . . just not a violin. Certainly a related instrument."

"Could it be a crwth?" Ellie wondered, and Evadne, seeming relieved, skipped off again.

Pansy's voice snaps me back to the present and that child is grown now and has studied something or other far away and come home, but I haven't seen her. When I ask for Evan, Pansy changes the subject quickly.

They have never liked him around me.

'Fraid you leave him the house – Dan's theory comes back to me.

The ban on Evan is easily organized now I can no longer manage the stairs to get outside, for he is not allowed up here any more.

Rachel's house bursts with activity, over there where they have gone. From the beginning Ellie's phone calls were full of Andy and his wagon and noise and mess. Her mama was jolly too, and Bonny – a little raucous at times. Ellie's earliest memory, as she tells it, is of climbing the latticework and being so afraid to look down she froze there. She thought: Bonny will laugh at me. Instead, he hollered admiringly, "After I never know you coulda climb!"

From then on not even the guinep tree was safe from Ellie.

"All that is vivid, like yesterday," Ellie told me on the phone. More vivid than yesterday, for now, she said, it was hard to believe how the ixoras she had planted when she first arrived a couple years ago had overgrown in a hedge, a riot of colour. "Aha! My boy is here," she reported on a rare occasion recently when Pansy took the time to hand me the phone. "Andy is stretching up quickly," she rejoiced, "all limbs, knees, elbows and tangle of unruly hair." Now and then all I have missed pierces me like an ice pick and the thought that no one knows this wound drives the point of regret deeper. For Ellie is out of reach. Well, Rosemarie brings me all of Ellie's letters to her. Sometimes they mention me, refer to writing me, but I never receive any mail.

Dear Rosemarie,

In the evenings we stroll by the lake, because the poui is in bloom. You and Ivy will love it when you visit. When we get to the end of the path the birds are coming home and the sky is full of their cries and the water streaked with the shadows of their passing over. Sometimes the little old man with the dachshund (they look so alike) passes us, and he does give a little grunt nowadays, but still no actual words. Dashy wags, nice little thing, should teach the old sourpuss some manners. Dan is practising the grunt every evening and says he's going to start returning it when he gets it just right. But we don't care, because the path is so peaceful that when they've gone it's as if they were never there.

Then the water is like glass for a while till a line zips it open slowly with just the two knobs of the caiman's eyes skimming the top . . .

So I lost Ellie, and even Rosemarie is mainly at Scotty's house, although she jumps in his car whenever he is coming here directly from home, and she comes to see me. She told me they have repaired my card table at last.

"It was in the storeroom all the time," Rosemarie reported. "Everything clear out of there now and they replace the old door with one big brute iron someting. Lord, they can waste money. The table looks just like it did in the old days though. What a pity it's downstairs where you can't see it."

Closing my eyes I can see the smooth green felt with the jokers dumped in the corner and I inhale deeply as a draught from the windows Rosemarie opened draws in the smell of baked bananas with a squeeze of lemon. I know the old coconut man comes twice a week because I hear them haggling at the gate. Rosemarie will see I get a glass. Behind the narrowing life in this little room lies another life I carry in my head. Left undone. Beneath . . . well. I back away, dodging the shadows not only of the past but the present and future. It may be everything they dreamed of, but not for me. I am alone in the crowded house walled off from me.

Ellie reminded Rosemarie to let me know she received a Christmas card from Evan. Fancy he remembered! She slipped it into her file with the brochures about the home, she said.

Miss Ivy's, they used to call it when I lived alone and they were visiting me, before the house was full around the bare little room that is left to me since my dream of what it would be faded to an old woman's querulous stutter, though Rosemarie brings fresh flowers as often as she can and combs my hair and opens windows that are no longer mine, not really, not at all. Still that's the least of my troubles now I can no longer see Evan and his child, and Scotty shrugs and his daughter, Cindy, curls her lip in disgust and Pansy hasn't time (even to pretend). And now they tell me Rosemarie is needed elsewhere and it makes no sense to drive her here just to listen to my foolishness, and Petrona has work to do in the kitchen, I must not keep her back. So I squeeze the teddy bear Petrona brought before she left (someone said she left) and keep my eye fixed on the gate. In case someone comes through. Someone to me.

Outside is beautiful unchanged not like me. Beautiful outside. Now as I catch in the distance that sound of water, rolling down and slapping the stone of the hillside, and as my mind turns back to the foam parting and swirling together again like a veil, I think they are right about the name for the home.

Cascade.

SIX

Ellie

"A FINE, healthy girl," crows the midwife on the screen, searching with her fingers.

A shaft of sunlight plays directly over their faces and the baby blinks. Only the baby. Aha. But science fiction is something I can't watch late at night, so I urge Dan to his feet.

"I can't sit here all night. You mean I *one* must go on the bed?"

"No. That wouldn't be fair." At once he struggles out of the chair. "Show's over?"

He may well ask. How does he sleep through everything?

"Practice!" His ready grin. Triumphant. But he just stands there.

"You have to move your feet to get here."

"Wasn't I? Oh, very well." He is so bent he kisses the top of my head without stooping farther. "How was your show?"

But the theme of the show, some unspeakable condition, has unsettled me.

"I don't hold with these harrowing films."

He sinks down on the side of the bed and stares at me from a room in his head that I cannot enter because his face is expressionless, throwing my mind which is already frayed by worry into tatters.

At the back of my thoughts a certainty gathers, so grim that I block it with other things – good things where possible but, more successfully, with other, lesser terrors. I have thrown up so many screens that I cannot always distinguish the central issue, but I know it is there. I cannot block out the tremor in his hand, the blankness of his gaze. The part of me that searches ruthlessly for the truth intercepts that part that knows the truth to be unbearable. For there is a place in the dark for those who have little-understood diseases and need to become slowly and inevitably invisible. Once a gully or some remote corner of a canepiece, but now, here in the twentieth century there is still always to be found some mysterious place for throwing people away when their disorders grow inescapable and embarrassing. It is a mindset that renders them invisible. But submerge even that thought. Hide a shadow with other shadows.

I wake and the bed is bare on Dan's side, paralysing me with its silence and emptiness. Summoning a prayer, I inhale raggedly and prop myself up to search out his profile against the window. Then the tension explodes in irritation instead of relief, searing my throat.

"What you doing in that chair at this hour?" I hear my voice rasp as if independent of me.

"Well, I came back from the bathroom and thought I'd rest a minute before having to lie down. Getting off the slippers, the whole ordeal."

"You could have called me. What have I missed?"

"Just an old man sitting in a chair."

Suddenly as it flared my annoyance cools.

"Well, I can't afford to miss that," I say brusquely, making my way to him. "So next time call."

That sounded sharp, I know, but it lights his face and his eyes snap with mischief as in the old days.

"Bring the crossword, then – or you think a hand of Patience, considering the hour?"

"Raisins?"

"Obviously."

Outside is blackest night, seared with lightning startling then fading in the mind to a nagging anxiety, like recollections of dragon fire in a dream after an old tale. The General – no, *Gawain* barks once under our window, a deepening, cautionary note.

✦

We must have fallen asleep in a muddle of playing cards and raisins, for when the phone tinkles the sun is glaring in with the inside light still on. Night and day flow into each other now we need not get up for the office. Then, thank heavens, I find the phone before it stops ringing.

Rosemarie is frantic. Scotty and money. He is squeezing them, these people he has known from childhood, but it seems he wants funds to pay for protection of some sort. Money, money.

"Missis, is like a cancer. And don't talk bout chase woman," Rosemarie continues. "Anyway, Cindy catch on and she tell him she getting a trip to Miami or she having a long talk with Mummy."

"No!"

"I didn't get the whole story," I complain to Dan later. "I would have called you, but you were sleeping." I rest the plate well away from his hand and curl his fingers around the cup.

"Nauseous fluid," he grumbles automatically. Then he reflects, "But you say Scotty came and took the phone from her? He actually said Rosemarie isn't well?"

At a table beside Dan's desk in the study that opens into our room, Andy looks up from his screen and a bowl of . . . green plums. Good Lord. And a little mess of salt and pepper. Mercy.

"*Rummy* sick?" he croaks. The voice is breaking already.

"Hard to picture," agrees Rabin. He has washed Dan's glasses and slips them back onto his face.

"Odd," Dan agrees. He glances at Rabin. "Thank you, my boy," he says, then continues. "Seems no way of getting to the bottom of it. How do these places work normally?" Frustration intensifies the rolling motion of his head and jerks his hand, sloshing tea across the mat. Andy comes and dumps paper towels on the spill and steadies the hand by diverting Dan with a quick gesture at his screen. He shares Dan's study now, and what could be better?

"Who you want to find, Gran Dan? You know about the Net? It have this thing called the Net. Nothing you can't find out on the Net. If we could get on it we could find out all the stuff you want. Then we could store it up." Our boy clicks and shuffles the little hand business, and in a while I have drawn our chairs through the study door close to his. "Like this. See?"

"You mean you can contact people?" Dan probes. "And find out about standard operations in retirement homes and that sort of thing?"

"I can't. We don't have it. But if I could get on I could track it down and store it up for you." Andy waggles a little gadget on a cord. "Look, I'm going to open a file for you."

"You can do *what*?" Dan gasps, unfolding his stick again and using it as a prop to lean forward and peer at the screen.

"You can see it, Gran Dan?"

"Just about."

"You shouldn't put your face so close," I fret.

"Leave him," Andy advises. "See? I'm going to type up the addresses you have here."

"Paper."

The boy stares at him from under a mop of uncombed hair. "*Paper*? Why?"

The page my boy prints for us tucked away into a wide carved drawer with mementos of Rosemarie and I push the drawer in gently with a touch of the tiny brass knobs. Suppose Bonny had had this gadget of Andy's at the office, I reflect. But no, he had to do it all for himself. Meanwhile, Agnes was vivacious, fun-loving, elegant, quick with a sharp answer but not malicious. She had no patience to wait on Bonny, to wait for him to be satisfied with himself.

"Hey! Got to go," Andy exclaims, glancing at the new watch we gave him for Christmas. His rapid movements mirror Rachel's and Bonny's. But his face is Dan's. Dan on Lincoln Road.

"I'm glad he likes it there, near to us," I muse happily after Andy has switched off the machine and headed out. I finish some chips left in his wake and reach under the table for his shoes incredulously. "Then the foot is really this size?"

"He's in big school now."

Dan stares unseeingly at the screen, but behind the vacancy I sense his mind bounding on; only I can no longer glimpse that mind in his face so I lean back into our intertwined pasts. That mind, balancing, soaring. How mine has challenged and romped and danced with it.

"What a gadget." His voice is almost tearful, though his face is unmoved. And why shouldn't he enjoy a computer too? Especially as he no longer has the steadiness for fishing.

"You don't want to get one?" I ask.

"We shall see."

The wistfulness in his tone deepens to something else, and he strokes my arm with one finger as if consoling me. I could work out what it is but sense that would not improve matters so I cast my thoughts instead to the lake with the lotus leaves. And, among them, enormous heady blooms of cream blushing to rose surprised us, some virginally folded still, but others with just parted lips or open ecstasy. The woman who was leaving as we made our way down the path managed to pick one – for a *puja,* someone said, and I had the feeling it might be rude to ask what that was.

The incredible flowers drew me too, but they are out in murky water, who knows how deep – or what swims there, down among the roots. Instead I let my mind alone roam through this forest of tall shifting stems with stately blooms and leaves like champagne glasses.

By evening a familiar motif ripples from the television.

"Look," he says. "Your show. That series."

After a few minutes at sea I catch up just as the parents find out. Their baby has this obscene ability of which almost everyone had been purified since The Error. The child can *see.*

I drop my voice to explain to Dan. "Which puts them in danger of a Cleansing."

"What's that?"

"Shh! Some sort of summons, I think. Yet people seem . . . festive, almost." The thud of drums under our window seems to confirm it. "And I don't know why they have to play the dub music so loud."

"Ask him to turn it down. Andy's a good child, just deaf like all young people."

I open the window and call, for he has hung a lamp outside and is washing the car with his music blaring. "It can be a little softer, sweetie?" But as he turns, I call after him. "They won't be vexed?"

He must not have heard the second question above the music, because to my alarm he just thrusts a dripping arm into the car and turns it down.

"Aah!" Dan sighs in relief, then chuckles. "Bernard Shaw, or one of them? *Youth is a wonderful thing.*" And we chorus his version: *"Too good to be wasted on youth."*

But, seriously, I grip his hand, and he raises mine shakily to his lips.

"What's troubling you?" His eyes see everything, sorting the anxieties churning in me.

"Well. I'm wondering if it isn't dangerous to interfere with them."

"Whom?"

"Who." And since he looks at me in amazement, I expand, "*Who's* interfering with them, you mean?"

The theme rises again, fastening me to the screen, though there is no hiding from the fact that Dan does not keep up as he used to. Not just physically – and who could ever have kept pace with Rachel? She would just fly along tirelessly – at least she would have when she was in training, which she has no time for now. ("I'm off track," she quips.) No. Dan has slowed down. It is hard for me too – this uncomfortable trek along a stony path that bruises the feet of the man directly in front of me on the approach to the quarry. I would stop it but the knob eludes me and, in any case, the quarry lies inescapably ahead, because we zoom in now and then to its honeycomb of echoing caves. I squeeze the arm of the chair, for I was never able to go into a cave. The apprehension tightens to terror of being trapped in a deep place, and I shrink down into the cushion, pressing my back against the cane.

Dan snores, although something momentous is about to happen, but . . . he . . . Yes. I have to say it, though it tears me . . . that he can be so . . . callous.

The donkey lurches to a halt. My heart races as the company join hands and spread out while the prisoner struggles and shrieks.

"No idea what we're doing for it," grumbles a dishevelled woman just opposite.

But what are we doing? The shrieking tears my nerves and I bite my lips to keep silent.

"They should gag it," snaps a woman in the crowd as they draw him to the cave spitting and cursing.

And now I am frantic to escape, for I don't belong here, in this drunkenness and frenzy. One staggers in the lineup, feeling for the heaps piled near the entrance. They surge forward shouldering and bruising each other as the rocks grate into position in the growing wall and the voice behind the pile hoarsens, muffled by the increasing barrier of stone.

My heart grows leaden with realization but the protest dies on my lips as the alert faces of the guards, deadly with threat, flash before me.

"Kinder in the end," a more subdued man mutters, a little gruffly. "After a while the aggression passes. They quiet down. Wait for us to pass the food in. When the time comes . . . prepared."

I shake Dan and he jolts upright.

"How could you sleep through *that*?" I cry. He has always sat up with me, for the outcome of each election or on bad nights during Mama's illness – always.

"What's upset you, love?"

"You crazy?" Don't tell me he hasn't made the connection. "They seal away anyone who is different! Next thing they kill the child!"

Parents whisper frantically. Some conditions are almost impossible to conceal. Sometimes I pray to wake up. *Pretend*, I urge the child silently from my side of the glass. *Pretend you are like everyone else for as long as you can.* It unfolds around me. Excuses enable us to avoid crowds. I summon all my strength and compose my face with my teeth clenched.

"Are you sure you want to watch this?" Dan interrupts thoughtfully.

"Well, you can cut yourself off from what's going on," I retort, "but I think it's better to be aware."

The child is growing up and no one knows her secret.

"The best thing is to ask no questions," I say when there is a pause, "to draw no attention to yourself at all lest they notice you are different."

"When I was a child," Dan says suddenly, at my side, making me jump, "life was a bit like that over there – the States, you know. Difference was a guilty secret. What do they know about it here? All this racial tension they like to talk about."

"Mm!"

"Ma left the States and came back to the Caribbean so my hair 'condition' would be better accepted."

"I always wondered why she went in the first place."

"To get work. Then she sent for me. She was much fairer, remember, and perhaps she hadn't noticed . . . little things. But when she saw them happening to *me* – then. A man at a candy counter told me I should eat only licorice. For my complexion. There was the whole issue of bathrooms. Then the school she wanted wouldn't accept me whatever grades I showed. I was back in Kingston in no time so I would be in line for Wolmer's Boys'." He manages to get to his feet.

"You never told me all that before. We only talked about your mother's visit later, to Rosemarie."

"I suppose so," he admitted. "It was so long ago it hardly matters." He turns off the TV.

But the things of long ago are clearest. "Your mama came back with you? How she knew she would get work here then?"

"Ma didn't."

"Didn't which?"

He laughs. He still laughs. Always. Despite the effort it has become.

"I missed that one," he gasps.

"Didn't which?"

"Neither."

"Neither what?" I ask.

The thread has broken and he is laughing at something that would normally have tickled us both, but here I am, alone, on the outside of the joke, and he grows serious and runs his fingers over my brow, smoothing it. He holds my head between his unsteady hands and presses it gently as if trying to put something back together.

"Mother didn't know whether she would find work at home, *and* she didn't find any – at least for some time."

"But she did, eventually. And you were okay. So why are you crying?"

But he just sits clutching my head in both his hands, with his eyes streaming. And I remember against my will that mood swings can be a symptom. I hold him, locking my arms behind his back and straining him to me.

"You will be fine!" I almost shout it. But, sometimes I *am* afraid. There must be a way to find out once and for all if there is something wrong with him that he is hiding from me.

Medical records, it occurs to me.

Later, while he sleeps I search for a file that might give some clue.

. . . *unfounded in my own view but, in any case, your dear wife is now safely out of the country.* I read on and the lawyer's letter is illuminating but does not clarify whether money has actually been paid for the land. Apart from correspondence on some legal matter and a tirade from Cecil about his children there is little new to be found and nothing whatever about Dan's medical status.

✦

Tonight, in any case, he's back to normal. Quiet, lying propped up to watch me ordering the cards for Patience in crisp rows. Now we know the old pack so well we can place every ace, king and two, by its bruises and nicks.

"It's that fellow we want, you know," he says. "Look at the blighter skulking in the middle of the row."

We regard the offensive card sourly for a few seconds before I scoop them all up and shuffle again.

Before bed I comb my hair as usual and slide the needle from beneath the embroidered linen runner to neaten a fraying edge on the lace of my nightie. He peers at me with interest.

"Remember you have a whole box of new nightgowns. You keeping them to sell?"

"Too forward!"

But I pick up my Bible and clamber up onto our bed which is not like these new beds they make now so close to the floor (which can't be wholesome).

"In the morning," he says, beginning his usual mental preparation for tomorrow, but orally instead of in the small maroon diary, "we need to talk to Rachel about Rosemarie. I wonder if there isn't someplace here where she can be happy. I would be comfortable knowing you have each other."

Close to Rummy as well as Rachel? Too much to ask, even of God, but I let my mind play with it.

To assuage the pain of waiting to see Rummy, I shuffle the homes of my past idly in my head. At Ferncot, the driveway swung in through ordinary square gateposts to a riot of colour. When the petrea bloomed, cars slowed at the gate and passersby pointed. Some returned with cameras. The sash windows of our bedroom opened on the most fragrant corner of the garden, partly obscured by this blue, so vivid it throbs on in my mind.

Well. We were comfortable together. It reassembles obediently as I close my eyes, and concrete, foliage, stone and wood materialize more delicate than in the original incarnation, to a fragile lacework I drape across my thoughts before sleep. Ribbons of tattered banana leaves flutter along the back fence and perforated philodendrons to the side. Moonlight illuminates a latticed arbour. Rachel is reading on the porch, one of my favourite books, and I can't wait for her to finish so we can talk it over. The lights from inside shine behind the wicker porch chairs and out through wrought iron grillework, and Rosemarie weaves in and out of light and shadow in her routine watering of baby's breath and ruthless hunting for slugs. Filaments of longing and thankfulness weave delicately about my thoughts stirred faintly by Dan's breath on my cheek, and my mind steadies, for if every other light went out in my head he would glow on, pure and intense.

The picture of my mother has arrived and his delight is touching. He was good to her, who wouldn't be, but I had never sensed quite that force of feeling. A little photo, I think it was originally. He watches me lean the frame on the dressing table, beside Rachel and Rabin, and he nods with satisfaction.

"Now you will always have her close at hand."

A teenage girl in jeans hovers at the kitchen door as Rabin heads out and Rachel gets ready for work.

"To keep an ear out in case you need anything when Viv is upstairs," Rachel explains.

"But to do what, just sit here?"

"Well, she could help you with Dad."

"How?" A thought pops into my head and being a straightforward person I say it right out. "You don't mean she'd be in our bedroom?"

"Only if you need help. As he's not so well."

"She's a nurse?"

"Well, no. I'm paying her just to be within call. I'll feel more relaxed."

Which is all she has to say for I can see her strung taut, tugged in every direction.

"Because however fast I move I can't pull it together. I'm running just to keep in place," I heard her say the other night when Rabin asked her why she couldn't be still for even a moment. "No," she sighed when he asked if it was the office and the house that divided her. "Not at all. It's between how I thought it would be and all I could never have foreseen. The time I wanted to spend with . . . I don't get to spend it that way. Before I can get a grip on one crisis the next is underway."

So I don't argue with Rachel, poor child. But later, when she has gone to work and left me with the problem, I find the new girl crying by the door.

"I missing my baby," she sniffs. "I never leave she before."

"You have a baby? You?" But see here. *She's* a baby! "Then go home, darling. There's nothing for you to do here."

"The lady might vex."

"No, no. I'll talk to her."

She jumps up gratefully and gathers her things.

"Now run along and kiss that baby for me." In a minute I've dipped in my purse and slipped a crisp bill in her hand.

"Thank you, Tantie." She hugs me. Sweet child, really.

Jocelyn comes to mind and I wonder what ever became of her. She loved Bonny, no doubt about it. Jocelyn was plain though – no use tiptoeing around it – she was plain, with that sharp beak of a nose and her complexion so speckled. Like a fowl. She was no match for Agnes, but she had her pride. Desperate as she must have been, when Bonny offered she turned him down because it was out of . . . well. And she would have been compared to Agnes all her life. Pity. She was, after all, the better woman, and it is so painful to lose a friend.

Anyway, this little girl who was just here has gone her way so that's that. But Dan doesn't care about any of it. Rachel knows best, he says with a shrug, and if we were all together at Ivy's, the staff would help us in all sorts of ways. But I think they're helping *themselves* at Ivy's. Poor Rosemarie told me she hasn't one good nightgown left.

"It's time to get up, Dan," I insist. "You need a bath." But not liking to rush him I sit close by on the bed and complain that the TV is full of rubbish.

"Well, it was good to have it during the coup," he says.

"Coup?"

"The thing last year. Abu Bakr. We stayed quietly glued to the TV."

I stare at the TV but it is just vulgar people wriggling up themselves and it is all so wearisome. If they won't go away, at least we could.

"What about a sea bath?" I urge. "In the old days we didn't just sit home. We went on jaunts – if it were even across to Hellshire!"

Between my scattered reflections on the recent past are interspersed the ruins near Rodney's Arms. Maypoles and candelabrum cactus jut above the macca bush. Limestone, parched countryside, ruins, a wall at which to mourn over inconceivable losses. If there were a sycamore tree of such dimensions I could climb and see more clearly, for I would like to see it all, once and for all, once again. I wish Bonny were still there, but at least there are the places we enjoyed together.

Bonny adored me, but I don't know why for I never did enough for him. I tried to but still he flayed himself.

Within my head the continents sheer again, fracturing foundations of stone, and the remains of countless lives precipitate, fuse, and centuries of rain pit the rocks. Out at Hellshire we could see shells in the limestone, an egret stumbled past, a johncrow wheeled, there was some warning about crocodiles, eventually a rumour about iguanas, but far more going on in the crevices we could not see, life teeming on invisibly in every perforation of the rock.

In my album elsewhere a limestone setting in the Holy Land is broken by columns of enormous strength and grace, firmly grounded, no longer supporting an edifice but strongly rooted at massive bases, the flagstones between them eaten by time and they are still a structure with the gaunt beauty of parallelism and consistent intricate tracery.

"A sea bath," I urge. Floating in the Dead Sea was easy, getting to one's feet . . . a different matter. But one did not drown.

"Hellshire? I don't feel to drive all that way today," he says apologetically.

But more and more he stays later and later in bed. If I remember rightly he did not get up at all yesterday, and one can't have that. And I must get this dog *out* or Dan may trip over him when he does get up (though, now I think of it, the General always reverses out of his path, wagging the whole way. They do that sometimes, when they sense something wrong. May's dog used to.)

"General, out! No, good fellow. But *out!*"

I remember – just like yesterday – when we dropped in on May after her heart attack. All that anxiety, with her mother. And I remember having said to Dan, why don't they put the old lady in a home? He was shocked, so it was just as well I found out how he felt and I never suggested it when his own mother got difficult. Still, I wouldn't have; she was just difficult, and had never been easy – a ten-minute egg from I knew her. But May's mother was different, the sweetest woman and the soul of propriety. And then now in her old age when she should have one foot in heaven she was . . . she was a hellhound. Mean, suspicious, foul-mouthed. Whole personality utterly destroyed. I mean your body falling apart is natural. Even your mind – though that's harder to accept. But your personality shattered? It shook me, I can tell you.

Now they have a name for it, but no treatment. Fat lot of good having a fancy foreign name, except of course I suppose it needs a name if they are to get funding for research. One day they will find out what to do – too late for May's mother. Too late for May. You know she had another heart attack? Died before the mother.

That's what made me sit Rachel down years ago and talk to her. When I get old, I told her, if I get like that put me in a home.

Dan was scandalized. "Do you know what some are like," he demanded, "even if you can pay for them?"

Ready cash is one problem Rosemarie does not have apparently. She said Scotty cashes her cheques all the time – in fact sometimes they give her more cash than the value of the cheque. "As is me," she says, though she feels they want the cheque rather than the cash. But how can that make sense?

"Then Ivy is happy with the whole set-up?"

"Poor Ivy, she don't talk again. She hold a teddy and hug and kiss it all day."

"*Ivy?*"

"When it comes to homes," Dan had warned, "if you are lucky to find a decent place you may die on the waiting list."

But how unfair, for there are terrible places abroad too, while right here in Jamaica Miss Minnie was happy at the Verley. There *are* good homes here.

Anyway, I told them, if I get out of hand at least sedate me. I *knew* old Miss Rita. May did her no favour leaving her in such a pickle. She needed something to quiet her. Dan said sometimes medication is unpredictable, so I told Rachel in that case work with a doctor. If some medication puts me to sleep and I never wake I still am better off. You didn't plan it; don't let it devastate you. Remember, I said, I am telling you now, in my sound mind, for how could I be happy destroying your life?

Stupidness, having to word something so obvious. May tiptoed around the whole thing. Don' want give Mama this, don' want do Mama that. 'Fraid all the chemicals. Rubbish! Where was the Mama when May dropped dead?

Well. Thank God my mother never went through that. Sometimes, though, as I watch Dan I am so afraid, but of course I'd be going in with him if we ever had to locate a home for him. Anyway, right now he is engrossed in a letter from Scott, who has written to say Rosemarie is senile. Just like that he *says* it right out, says she talks stupidness she makes up in her head and upsets Cindy who is so devoted to her, so they are shifting her to the home which is equipped to deal with "people like that". Senile my foot. Living in his house she sees too much of his dirty life, that's what. Tell me stubborn as a mule. Tell me miserable even. Domineering – we all know. Senile?

And who in hell is Scotty to diagnose? Don' mind he have degree from some-where we never hear of. Just the other day Rabin brought home an advertisement his secretary in the principal's office had printed to show him:

UNIVERSITY DEGREE PROGRAMMES
Increase your personal prestige and money-earning power
through an advanced university degree.
Eminent, non-accredited universities will award you a degree for only $200.
Degree granted based on your present knowledge and experience.
No further effort necessary on your part.
Just a short phone call is all that is required for a BA, MA, MBA or
PhD diploma in the field of your choice.

The notice gave a number to call for details.

"I could swear it was something like that I saw years ago. Was it some paper on Scotty's table?" I searched the past.

"And now he knows everything," Dan mutters.

"He says the occupational therapist is to have sessions with Rosemarie."

Dan rallies. "Good. She will find the blighter some occupation and straighten him out."

A *real* doctor came to see her, an old colleague from her days at the hospital, but Pansy turned him away because it was not visiting hours. "But I'm a doctor," he had protested.

FAMILY DOCTOR VISITS MUST BE ARRANGED TEN DAYS IN ADVANCE.

He was so furious he invested in the overseas call to tell us – this man we do not even know. "I drove for two hours on that road, at my age," he fumed. "They never offered me a seat, let alone a drink of ice water. Your sister's in an uncivilized institution, and I thought you should be aware of it."

What is behind it? We often have difficulty now getting Rosemarie herself on the phone, but we continue to try.

"Matron says Rosemarie is resting," a nurse reports crisply. Resting at ten forty-five in the morning my foot. Well, Rosemarie never wanted to hear anything against Scotty.

"So fortunate to get *in*," Pansy cooed when we caught her on the phone last night and tried to prize actual information out of her. "We normally don't accept convales*cents*, out of *con*sideration for the normal guests. We want to avoid the ospital hatmosphere, to encourage members to make it their permanent *home*."

"But stop, Dan, Pansy never used to have such a problem with her aitches?"

"Nerves, I suppose. She's terrified of you, you know."

"*Me*? Then something really wrong with Pansy."

"I have it! Senility."

"Can't Rosemarie just move out?" I mean, she has property of her own, up the hill, almost opposite Dan's. "She can't build her own little place? Or sell her piece to finance the building and put it up on yours. Or you selling yours?"

But his face closes and he falls silent at the mention of his land.

Dan's land was originally Ivy's. Ivy's own was side by side with that of Maisie, her sister, who was Jesse's first wife, for their father left them each a half of what he had. They were so alike, Ivy and Maisie Rousseau – same peak at the hairline, same laughing eyes. They loved to dance and were light on their feet despite the extra weight. They didn't care whether Mussolini attacked Ethiopia or Buzz Butler's people in Trinidad burnt down the oil wells. Ivy and Maisie cared about what was unfolding in or around their own lives. When more and more people left the countryside for Kingston, they wondered what would become of them, country people as they were. "And who will work the property?" they protested.

They lived here and now. Batista or Machado could have furthered America's interests at whatever cost because Cuba was remote, a rumour, and the sugar workers in Guiana could run raving mad – wherever Guiana was, in whatever jungle – for the Rousseau girls knew themselves to have been born and bred in a civilized society. Yes, they were riveted on Jamaica, on the grand sweep of Busta's arm as he rallied the workers and the subtle nuances of Manley's debating. And, most closely of all, though, they followed news of Edward and Mrs Simpson and admired the dutiful stand of the new king as war loomed in Europe.

And then, suddenly, Ivy was alone. After Maisie's death, Maisie's land passed to Jesse and later when he remarried he put it jointly in his name and Rosemarie's. When the hotels went up on the beaches and Ivy's guest house drew fewer and fewer visitors and fell into disrepair, the debts mounted and Ivy offered to sell Dan part of her property. So he bought it, promising to sell some back when she recovered financially, but she never did. For years what had been Rousseau land was mostly Rosemarie's and Dan's, and Evan could reap what he liked, poor fellow, until Ivy actually transferred a piece of what she had left, to Evan (for safety sake, she said).

"But the paperwork, Dan," I had insisted. "*Is* the land transfer from Ivy to you foolproof?"

"So my lawyer assures me," Dan replied, a trifle wearily – which hurt me, though he did not intend it, for I understand these things he cares so little about.

"And *his* lawyer is a bloody shark, or so they say," I remember snapping at poor Rosemarie.

"They who? Who say so? Then Dan mus' know what he doing. And don't the lawyer is his friend?"

"Worse yet! In a legal transaction? *Friend*? Dangerous!"

I nailed my affairs in place with the help of Hammond and Sons, who had handled Mama's matters and transactions for Bonny's business. My own two lots were downtown and rapidly increasing in value but small and easy to keep track of. Dan's and Rosemarie's sprawled over almost forty-five acres, with what remained to Ivy separated from Dan's only by barbwire and the smaller lot beyond, which she had transferred to Evan, similarly fenced. To further confuse matters, Rosemarie insisted that Jesse had meant to divide their parcel because, after all, it had belonged to his first wife, Maisie, Scott's mother. So we brought in a surveyor and eventually Rosemarie turned half of hers over to Scott, and facety enough he was to her regarding the rest.

"I'll have Wally arrange to survey mine again and write it all up," Dan sighed when I insisted – which is something.

I close my eyes and the old place rises around me – huge gnarled trees and the ground damp and scattered now with mangoes, now with naseberries or guavas.

The grass is trodden down along the paths and the vegetation thick and fragrant, though the stake and barbwire borders sag in places and wood rot is setting in at the inner gates.

"But we sold off the cattle years ago, so the inner gates don't matter," Dan said.

"Nevertheless . . ."

"I'll take it under advisement."

Well, that's that! I fold my own correspondence from Hammond and Sons with a sense of relief, and a lurking anxiety about Dan's lawyer. ("You mean wily Wally?" Sherwin Cockburn had sniped once, his eyes disappearing into crinkles of laughter which would have been infectious but for the awful braying, and it was all I could do to keep a straight face for Dan's sake.)

But who knows how Rosemarie has things disposed? I have my business filed away (*Deeds/Will/Titles*) and I never ask other people their business – even my dearest people. But Pansy does, interestingly enough. Rosemarie says Miss Pansy grilled her about the land Jesse left, and was shocked to learn that Ivy had sold most of *her* own to Dan.

"How did he manage to persuade Aunty I?"

The recollection enrages me. When Ivy was floundering in debt Scotty never returned one of her calls. The money Dan paid for the land enabled Ivy to repair the roof before it fell on her head and to pay off loans that had been accumulating for decades. Persuade Aunty I, *my foot*! Ivy's property would have joined up nicely with that piece Rosemarie turned over to Scotty from Jesse's estate, and Pansy and Scotty were just licking their chops, that's what. I sip a glass of ice water to cool down.

With Rosemarie in this fix Dan has been wondering whether we should contact the philanthropist who we hear has befriended the home. Or has he just been seduced into parting with his money to Scotty? Anyway, we might contact the man, whoever he is, Dan says, for it can only be the finances tying Rosemarie down.

"Ashmead," I pronounce.

Dan stares at me in amazement, but it came back to me easily for although I have never met Scotty's benefactor his name is one I have known from childhood.

"Ashmead," I repeat.

Our boy insists one can find almost anyone, and I stare, an anachronism, from the sidelines. A website, he says, skimming light and fast along invisible threads. But there is no trace of anything that can help.

"Supposed to be well known for work in a range of charities," I reflect. "One man doing so much, eh? I must be wo'tless."

"Well, I'm the one who just sits about now," Dan objects.

Rachel strokes his face. "Are you settled? See? I told you we would have you back home without the old gall bladder." She turns to me, relief shining out. "So we have our boy back."

"Back." Yes, it has been has been . . . a tumult. Too fraught with . . . urgency, anguish, to . . . to think even. "Oh Jesu." I lay my cold forehead on his warm arm. "You haven't been too good, big fellow!"

"Well, I like that!" His lips waver to a grin. "After what I go through they tell me I'm no good."

Rachel bustles in again, hugs, hugs all round, and shows in a big pleasant-looking woman in crisp white. "Laid-back" is how Rabin would describe this woman. And seeing her beside Rachel brings home to me again the tension in this child, a woman now, tension that never eases. Work she must, and her posi-tion in Human Resources (as they call it now) comes with this house – but other people have been busy too from the beginning of time and she was always on the move but now something more, something . . . importunate has seized her: she is nervy, taut, never stops, hands and feet never still together. Always doing three things at a time – see, on the counter a letter beside the egg scrambling in the pan and the Spanish vocab Andy would prefer her to overlook and keeping an eye on the newcomer she has just introduced and her head cocked in my direc-tion as if . . . in case. Lithe (and she has lost more weight, I realize), thin like a marathon runner, poised for take-off.

"Remember I promised to bring a little help for the time being?" she chirps. "While he gets back to normal?" What? "All set up! A team will be here round the clock to take pressure, help with the bath, keep track of medicines. The works."

Rachel kisses me and whisks herself out, her purse strap hitching on the door handle, as usual. Car keys dropping and being snatched up with a mutter, as usual. Gone.

And the morning splinters into brisk movements about my bed, in and out of my cupboard, back and forth from my bathroom. The washbasin is rearranged and all Dan's things are put in their own little cup with mine in another. And the soap is in a new place. My bed linen is changed all wrong – not matching, and one of the pillowcases is from the set I keep for guests. And I must just watch?

"Wait!" I have to intervene. "Wait one minute!" Though perhaps I am louder than necessary.

"Yes, Mom?"

But who is this fat woman I have never met in my life calling me Mom?

"Excuse us a minute please." I am polite if a trifle crisp.

"What's the matter?"

I have to spell out everything?

"I need a little time alone with my husband – to get him ready. He will talk to you in a moment."

"Okay, Mom. Okay. You want to settle down over on this side?"

I suppose I just stare at her, for next she looks me full in the face in the most extraordinary manner.

"Sit down," she says, in the firm voice one saves for a recalcitrant child. Then she says it again, louder, and she uses my first name. "Eleanor, sit."

The strange thing is that Rachel does not respond with . . . well, outrage. She is concerned and, yes, assures me she will speak to the woman and tell her what to call me. But the inappropriateness – Rachel seems not to grasp it.

"He needs the help, my love." She smiles at me wonderingly. "Don't you see?"

"But how can you ask? I never move from his side. I see him, as he is now, and I feel . . . I feel . . ." I pause, waiting for the storm in my head to die down. I reach in for even half a line to retrieve my balance (*and not to yield*). Then I get back to her. "What is there that *I* wouldn't do?"

"Nothing." She strains to see into the raw pain of my watching him labour through simple movements, putting on his glasses, his watch. "There is nothing you wouldn't do. But they are trained. You must have help."

"*Now*, Mom!" My own dear boy aims a wave in my direction as he pulls Rachel through the door.

"Where are you off to again?" I call.

"Lessons," Rabin replies, edging past them into the kitchen. "Need anything?"

"*Dominus vobiscum,*" I call, but they are already in the car. I pat Rabin's face and turn back to the room, searching for closure. "*Dominus vobiscum.*"

"*Et cum spiritu,*" Dan whispers.

And so it has been all the years. Driving in the Lake District, curling up in the car, and as we dropped off to sleep, *et cum spiritu.*

At night, all is quiet again as I set out the cards, but the TV is angled towards the bed.

"Someone is in your study?" I say. "Can't be." But the shadow goes and comes against the thin curtain.

"Same lady." He shrugs. "Seems efficient."

Sir Gawain puts both paws up on the windowsill and Dan puts out his hand, but the bed has shifted so that Gawain's head is inches out of reach. Dan's hand wavers for a bit towards the louvres then withdraws regretfully, and the dog whimpers.

"Sorry, old man," Dan says.

Disappointed, both of them. But I can't shift back that big bed all by myself.

"Raisins?" I offer.

And then, from the next room, a voice interrupts firmly. "I've brushed his teeth already."

Startled, I jolt upright, upsetting the cards.

"What's that?"

He squeezes my hand. "Look," he whispers. "Who's in the movie tonight?"

And I am quiet, so as not to disturb him.

But the truth is I cannot watch. There is so much to think through even though nowadays we talk mainly to each other. For Dan, in any group now, the conversation rushes on as he frames the words, and the moment flits past. The issues remain unresolved and he turns them over and over in his mind, so later we go through it exposing facet after facet, but meanwhile the talk, the chatter, sweeps giddily this way and that, and we stumble and fall silent. Yesterday, though, at the little gathering of Rachel's friends, as I made ready to offer my point of view in the general discussion of chaos in the society, someone popped a grape into my mouth, aborting thought. Just as I opened my mouth – a luscious grape, but such an intimate gesture, from a stranger.

I would like to keep up. I wish Dan could get to say something in time. The children pause, but the pace of their lives makes prolonged contact impossible. By night, when I try to piece it all together, there are gaps.

Then, like anyone else, I have nightmares from time to time. But now, occasionally, one prowls over the edge of its own territory. Last night something actually crawled out of my head and smiled at the children, licking its lips. It looked at them out of my eyes and grinned with my lips showing jagged yellow razors. I opened my mouth to scream and found myself looking into my own maw, a bottomless, suctioning void, and my regular voice withered to a thin hiss. The distorted face stared at me through glass, slobbering eagerly.

"What do you want of me?" I gasped. But the eyes that impaled me were my own. It flicked a talon through my temples and gouged out a chunk of raw tissue.

When Dan called me I was already awake, yet it seemed to squat half in, half out of me. Anathema.

Thank God for bright daylight. Though, standing here, it is not easy to tell whether I am walking to the house or away from it. I pause to cradle in my hand a heavy burst of pink bougainvillea at the entrance to one of the driveways, postponing the decision. But why move a landmark? If everything were in place there would be no chaos. (Or is chaos, as Dan proposed yesterday, just some divine construct we cannot read?) Home? Fountains of deep pink blooms dip and sway, creation of which I am a part. A part? Apart? A rough carpet of toast-brown grass stretches before me, cut, through drought, by deep cracks riddling the lawn.

Not to know the way home is to stand on the edge of chaos. Or is it some new design after all, unreadable at first, but in harmony with an alternative scheme? Enigma. I study the road for the new design to become apparent and Rachel drives past waving at me through the car window and swinging into the driveway with a scrunch of dry gravel. Which more or less puts things in place, and I turn in behind the car. And, for the time being, there the matter rests.

I get in just in time for Rosemarie's voice on the speaker.

"And talk bout lock-up? I mean is long-time now Scotty enclose the downstairs porch on the eastern side and make two more rooms, but, Missis, now he gone with the upstairs sitting room and make four narrow likkle box out of it. He say he moving all the local like Archdeacon and Cecil upstairs because they old and depressing, and he want downstairs to have a holiday atmosphere – to be just for tourist because that is where the money is."

After a while we get to the main topic, that of the visit, but she says the plane ticket for next year will be more than she can manage, in view of the monthly cost of her room at the home.

"They charging you rent?" I scream into the phone. "After they beg you stay with them and help with they child?"

"Well, Cindy big now – sweet sixteen party and all, and she hardly want anything to do with me. She say I always prefer Andy, and even Evan daughter. And when I say what about all the nice dress I sew for her, she say she didn' hax to be born. Anyway, Scotty say he going take over the cost for my room soon as he clear the debt for their new house."

"But your pension . . ."

". . . no access to my account any more . . ."

"He's addicted to money," Dan moans. "Frantic for it. This . . . this frenzied pursuit of every last cent."

"Will she never come then?" I cry as Rachel and Rabin come through the door. "Won't we ever see Rummy?" I hold my tears back, because I owe them that, but the disappointment twists in me like a knife. "How long have we been here? Over six years, you say? Impossible. But, so years . . . years since we saw her . . ."

"Not two months," Dan protests. "She was here just six weeks ago."

I glance at Rachel in horror, for now she will see his situation and what will it do to her, but she nods gently, yet firmly.

"Of course, Mom. Rummy spent Christmas with us as we got the inflammation down so Dad could have the surgery. We were able to do without the nurses all that time. You and Dad sent the ticket for Rummy. She stayed over a month."

They are serious. Rabin too, nodding. How am I to doubt them?

"Rosemarie? Here?" I whisper it. "Come and gone?"

"Yes, love." She lays her cheek on mine and her warm hand rubs the life back into my fingers before she leaves.

And I search my mind, but it is all all missing – no trace of Rosemarie's visit. Anywhere.

I turn over what I can of it in my head, all I can, as I wander back outside the hedge to the bushes that are a riot of flowers, and I bend and interlace some thin branches, pulling others free. So I missed Christmas too. Then I could not have bought presents. Could Andy have got no present – my own little grand, tall as he's got so suddenly? Then Rosemarie came and went. And not a word from me. Did we speak, cry, laugh, hold each other? Months (years?) of agonizing over the visit. Where did it go if not into my mind – in absentia, some alternative abyss?

What else is in the abyss? The thought brings to mind nightmares I had safely put away.

In the old days, you know, marauders occasionally came in at night from the outside and did various kinds of skullduggery. Now it's all changed and just when you feel safest, tucked into the sweetest sleep, things come out of the dark bleak inside, places you never knew you had, and they come with talons spread and jaws agape, breathing contagion. They come for no other reason but that you have managed to be content and they are wretched, no other reason but that they are locked out of consciousness. Against all odds you piece your life together and exile them from your thoughts, and when they have lurked long enough in the depths for you to be sure they don't exist, that is when they swim up from the murk and prowl the perimeter and you feel the chill but deny it, and that is your mistake. Suddenly they are out from the inthere to rip your heart and shred your life and you wake in your bed, mangled.

No one can do anything for you for no one is aware. No one can see them. No one knows they exist. And after a while you forget. You settle your soul in peace.

And then they come again. Bloodier than ever before. Out of the inthere.

"I can see how disturbing it must be." Dan clutches the frame of the stroller to make his way to the porch, and he shows me a pot of orchids Rosemarie bought for me while she was here. The label he shows me says, *Ionopsis*. The same, he reports, as the little piece she smuggled in her suitcase from Ivy's garden and fastened to a tree outside. She brought a card from Evan too, he continues, but he says I kept walking around with it and no one can find it now. "You had a wonderful time," he assures me, lowering himself thankfully onto a chair and placing the stroller aside, "especially in the garden. I was happy for you both."

"And you?"

"Well, I *had* rather wondered whether I would ever see her again. And here she was." He fastens my thoughts which have been unravelling into panic. "You did not miss it."

"Which would be some relief if I had something to show for it in my head. You know, there is so much I meant to ask her and if I did her answers are all lost now."

"Like what? Perhaps I can help you to remember."

"Well, like this sad business about your land, for one, as you won't talk about it." He doesn't comment so I charge on. "The little fool-fool man squatting on it can't have been the trouble. There has to be someone more substantial involved. Particularly since the lawyer seems stumped."

"Where have you got all that?"

"Are you sure it's not Scotty at the bottom of it, or one of his cronies? Mind you, I doubt that even Scotty is stupid enough to threaten you all the same. And do you think they would really have hurt me? Dan . . ." I lean down to his ear to confide in him. "Dan, do you think that hold-up had anything to do with your piece of land?"

"Good Lord."

And as I get nothing more out of him I promise to think it over more when I take my walk. Instead, though, old Miss Minnie rises in my mind. One day Mama went without me and came home ice cold.

"The house will have to be locked up," she said faintly. "Miss Minnie can't live there any more. She will see it always before her. Blood everywhere."

Tita, her sister, was dead of multiple stab wounds. That case was never solved.

As I pause on my stroll along the road, a lady whose name escapes me stops to kiss me, to enquire and soothe, to turn me back to the house. This happens around here. Other places, if I seem busy, people stop me, take things gently from my hand, push a chair towards me. At home of course the children and their circle are quite normal, but in a store clerks rarely meet my eye. They respond to my questions by addressing Rachel, show Rachel what I should want to see. Strangers whom I meet look . . . through me, as if I am becoming transparent.

The borders of my world shift, melt and reform, and some of the fun has seeped away leaving areas of darkness.

Here I am with no recollection of Rosemarie's visit. Worse, the topic of a discussion I had with Dan only an hour ago has slipped away and only a sense of its importance remains. It is one thing to move house as we did a year or so ago, but to embark on life in a new place without memory is to set out into completely uncharted territory, and the thought that I may lose my way in the void takes hold icily on the edge of my mind.

But then I call myself sharply to order, for eyes do adjust in the darkest power-cut, and somewhere there is always a candle to be found. And a match.

SEVEN

Rachel

AND YET SOMETIMES when all hell has broken loose at work, my secretary says, "You look so cool, as if you just stepped out the shower. How do you keep this calm?"

Ha!

But, for now at least the house is quiet, and at last that TV series that seemed to disturb Mom so has come to an end. It was a rerun of something Dad said she had liked years ago. She was frantic about some girl in the story who had to seem like everyone else.

"They seal them off," she whispered.

Something about it reminded her of *Tomb of the Pharaohs*, she said – apparently a horror movie from the old days which must have been, as Andy bluntly pointed out, quite lame. But after all what else, other than the show, could have disturbed her so profoundly?

Always a night person, reading, baking, balancing the ledger, now more than ever Mom roamed the cool stillness of the house, sometimes urgently, as if the bed had become a rack on which she was stretched out and which she must escape at all costs. I too sensed a trap closing. She and I had always shared sensations imperceptible to others and perhaps, sometimes, shared our nightmares.

Usually, like her, I could fix my face not to show fear. But I felt a tightening of the skin, as if against the dread of something cold-blooded and poisonous.

All around us things looked the same but her instability sent a tremor through me and a sense of some catastrophe underway set off aftershocks in me so intense my head swam and my world shuddered on its axis. When the room settled I pulled myself together, for I had learned from her that I could handle anything.

But the jolt in consciousness dislodged something – everything, disturbed the rhythm of nature as if, at some inner shore, the tide had changed, rushed out, reared, towered and slammed forward over her. So now her expression alternated between crisis and stillness, as if at times a fury thundered along her veins, roared through her brain and then receded, leaving her dazed in its wake of silence. And the shock awakened something none of us could have foreseen. In some cave, it groaned and turned. Stretched. Eyes opened in the darkness and regarded the world from an angle hitherto unknown. Sourly. In her head.

Yet there was Mom as she had always been, as we knew her. She held your heart in place. You know? There she was. And then, there was this. She could not help it she had nothing to do with it it would just wake up and take over. There was my mind and hers all interlocked with all the books we read and the holidays at Aunt Ivy's and the walks with Rummy (only we didn't snigger over Pansy when Rummy was there) and our analyses of Rabin when he first came to visit. And there was Mom with Dad which was this incredible . . . this . . . I mean that is how you knew there is eternity. And when you were little and you heard hurricane was going to hit the island you went to sleep because they were there. And when you woke up and everything was bright and orderly you asked whether it came because after all there they were and they accounted for whatever order persisted irrationally despite hurricanes.

Then as I grew up I began to become her, not through coercion or brainwashing but by effort – she was what I wanted to be though I never told my friends for they would have laughed at me – and now, so now this thing that was overtaking her was happening to me and all her terror and frustration and denial was mine as well. So I began to awaken conscious that Mom was awake and that along some fault line a fissure widened, eroding certainties as if (in little trickles of sand and shale) the foundations of the world were giving way, and something baleful yawned in the ruin, waiting to be uncovered. Perhaps I slept fitfully again another twenty minutes, then sprang up, sleep shattered into unrelenting daylight.

When I opened their door her soaked clothes clung, bound, tripped her as she slid off the mattress.

"Damn one foot shoe," she snapped, stumbling to her bathroom for the tap. Aah, soap. "I don't know this towel. Where is mine? *Mischievous.*" She hurled it aside and reached for her dress, scrunching it together and rubbing herself off. "At least I know this is mine." She accepted a dry dress with the usual "Bless you" and healing smile.

But the bedsheet was soaked.

"Wake up!"

Dad smiled and yawned, reaching for her fingers waveringly and she snatched them away.

"Come on. Get up and get in the bath."

He felt the bed in bewilderment and she turned back swiftly to hug him, soaked as he was. Her voice softened.

"It's not your fault though. Get up, darling, come in the bath. But you need a check-up. Don't Maxwell will be in today?"

"Nope. Died twelve years ago."

As I turned back to the kettle, she lowered herself onto the chair by the bed.

"Dr Maxwell died?"

"Long-time."

"Our Maxwell? Then you couldn't tell me?"

"You knew."

"Nonsense!" she exploded. "After the man has been so good to us? A man like that? I would have gone to the funeral. Jesu. What his wife must think of me."

"Not a problem."

"Chat nonsense! How could it not be a problem?"

"Esther's dead too. In the glory these eight years. Doesn't care if you . . . went to funeral . . . or not. Which, by the way, you did. Any dry shorts?"

I believe she was on the point of telling him to get his shorts himself, but her eyes locked on his hands and widened as his anxiety intensified the tremor.

"Stay quiet today. I'll sponge you, and perhaps Maxwell can drop in and have a look at you. Only you say he's gone. Who has his practice? Try to remember while I get the basin. Lie still, darling."

The nurse bustled in with basin and towels. "Good morning!" Louder than either Mom or Dad could be expected to handle.

So I called, briskly stirring a cup of tea, "Mom, swallow this while it's hot. You don't look yourself. Are you coming down with something?"

"That wouldn't be sweet enough by the look of it. Nor necessarily recent. Then stale tea they heat up an give me? But never mind. Poor child, you work so hard, and tea is exactly what I need. This *headache*."

She sat at the kitchen table for a moment with her eyes closed, then sprang up and made a new cup, sipping it in relief, while I threw food into the fridge and out of the freezer.

"Now this is tea," she murmured.

I left her searching for Dan's new pyjamas in the study cupboard. Instead, there were all types of gear, but no longer stored with his old fastidiousness. I already knew the fishing tackle was now a tangle of line and hooks and his fine old knife with the carved bone handle was not in its sheath. The loop for the flashlight hung empty too, and lures were dumped about and their case had vanished. Quickly, before they wheeled him through, she closed the looted cupboard and hurried back to the wardrobe for clean pyjamas as I went back upstairs to dress.

I suppose it was there Viv found her. From the landing, I could hear Mom accost her about searching their belongings.

"What happen, Miss Ellenie?" It was quite true that Viv managed to make Mom's name sound like Miscellany.

I dashed downstairs again but before I could intervene, Mom had accused her of rifling through their things, and shock and pain alternated in Viv's face. Mom's tone was cold. Never a hypocrite, she cut to the core of the matter like a knife. Then, strangely, the expression of outrage passed and Viv touched her hair, gently, almost sorrowfully, her eyes swimming. Instantly Mom grabbed her hand and squeezed it.

"I don't mean to be unkind."

"You not unkind, darling. I know you long-time. Forget?"

"You must be so busy you forget to ask for whatever it is and now I rough you up and you don't deserve it. Let me help you," Mom suggested. "I'll set the hose while you're down here where you can hear him."

I ran upstairs again to finish dressing and get out. Their voices rose up behind me.

"The nurse here too, Miss El."

"Don't remind me!"

The rope hummed and slapped, hummed and slapped. Through the window I could see the children bouncing in the road, bright skirts ballooning and flopping as they jumped. As they turned the rope their friend tripped and dropped out.

"Too bad," Mom called.

I saw no harm in her wandering over to them and the ready laughing faces tilted to her, and the rope kept turning as she nipped in and jumped a few times. But she withdrew quickly – *young people need to be on their own,* she always said – and she called, "Thank you for the turn," throwing a kiss over her shoulder, then heading back, pausing to examine the hedge. One ran after her asking how come she jumped rope better than the rest of them, and she laughed out, "Been practising longer."

She shrugged it off but couldn't help a little cocky toss of the head, for (as she liked to say) she was not bad, not bad at all.

To her left the bougainvillea swayed and bobbed in vibrant pink, thick clusters of blooms with hardly room for a leaf anywhere, and she gestured towards them as a young woman walked vigorously by, then slowed and regarded her uncertainly. I could hear the neighbour I had had no time to meet (Indira, I believe) call out to her: "Shall I walk you home?"

"Certainly. A cool drink?" Then on closer observation Mom exclaimed, "You're sweating." ("Horses sweat" – she used to describe her form mistress flicking her eye across the class like a whip – "gentlemen perspire, ladies glow.") "But you are *sweating!*" she protested. "And it can be a sign of some condition. Have you seen a doctor?"

By the time I reached the kitchen door Indira had warned Viv to keep a closer eye, and jogged away with a reproving glance in my direction.

"What is it?" Mom whispered to Viv. "Somebody hurt?"

"No, thank God." Viv turned the key and pocketed it.

"But I'm going back out."

"Not now," I said, supporting Viv.

Mom snapped, "Who appointed any of you?"

"I think you was asking me to come too," Viv explained hastily. "Not so? But why we don't wait till after tea and put out the tea leaves?"

"Aah." That is what she had always believed in, fern fronds uncurling from earth dark with tea leaves.

By afternoon she was writing a letter when her bedroom door slapped open and the new addition to the nursing shift strolled through without knocking. I threw Mom a kiss and signalled the large old soul who had just rolled in.

"Can I speak to you?" I summoned her back to the kitchen.

"But I jus' come to find out if he want tea."

"But what I'm saying is, rap the door. It's their bedroom."

"But they ole. They doesn't be doing nothing. I take care of plenty so. An they can't tell me nothing trough de close door."

"Just *rap*. For respect."

Reassured that the world had one sane person left, Mom returned to her letter – at peace, because Dad had had a good day. He had eaten in the dining room, wheeled up to the table. He slipped the brake against the wheel himself. A friend called from Canada and they chatted like old times.

"He says he heard from one of the boys staying at Cascade," Dad reported. "You know Cecil's there."

"Cascade?"

"Ivy's old place," he reminded her. "He says our set there all seem quite strapped for money. Perhaps it's the devaluation."

"They can't be that short," she objected. "Cockburn was one man who had plenty, wasn't he? Unless he drank it out?"

"If not, Scotty would have decanted what was left," Dad reflected, trying to suppress a chuckle.

"Monster! Maybe" – she doubled over laughing – "Cockburn would have been too marinated to notice."

By afternoon, though, a shadow fell as I settled Dad in for his nap.

"I managed to get a brief word with Rosemarie before they cut us off," he whispered to us. "Seems Scott has taken charge of all she has. He *may* have power of attorney but . . . not sure. While she was living . . . working in his house . . .

his children . . . working . . ." He closed his eyes. After a minute he continued, "Whether she authorized it . . . he offered to invest her savings . . . or whether he had her declared . . ." He tired quickly and the explanation degenerated. "She has . . . no control now."

"Where are her papers?" Mom demanded.

"Seems everything is filed away in the storeroom. They . . . put on a . . . special door."

"Dan." It must have simmered for a while. "You don't think we're being self-ish?"

His eyes turned to her, troubled.

"How can we just gallivant about indefinitely and leave Rosemarie in that position?" she demanded.

"What you suggest?"

She stared at us both. "Well, we should be getting home. She might not be able to stay in the house alone, but once we're back she wouldn' need to be in their damn clutches."

"Aah!" He seemed to drift off to sleep, and I made for the door rattling the car keys distractingly.

It seems that later Mom told Viv they would be moving on.

"And then you know, the house. Just left up. Next thing, when we go back, squatter capture it."

Viv gave me a full account afterwards.

"Which house?" she asked Mom.

"My house. Our home."

Viv did what she could to reassure her. "But you living here now."

"Oh, sweet. Thank you. But you know the children have their own life here, and then my sister-in-law shouldn't be left to take the brunt of it. Is our house after all. We can't be irresponsible."

"But, Miss El, ent de house sell?" Viv called right outside the bedroom door. "Mr 'Vall! The house you did live in, ent it sell?" There was no answer. "You forget it sell?"

That was when Mom telephoned me at work, her voice ominously quiet.

"They're telling me the house has been sold."

"Yes." I must have sounded puzzled.

"Sold. My house."

"Of course."

The phone clicked gently before the implications reached me, and I grabbed my purse and headed for the car.

Building that house. She had told me. I knew Dad lived in his books. The house had been her concern. The land, her investment. Sketches, plans. Interviewing a builder. Materials.

"Good wood," she had insisted. "Nothing ornate on those columns now. Just a curve . . . here." Oh, shingles definitely. A pipe right here, so the hose will reach the anthuriums. Anthuriums were the latest. Aunt Ivy had them first and supplied Mom promptly.

Later Viv told me that Mom had begun to whisper to her, so as not to worry Dad.

"What is this about selling the house? What are they saying? Then where is Rosemarie?" she had asked.

"Your sister-in-law living with – I don't know – is a nephew? De house sell."

That Scotty had been involved was the last straw. By the time I drove in, her voice had thinned to a scream.

"Who in hell could presume to sell my *house*? What travesty of law could permit it? Then where are the papers?" She clutched her temples. "And they just sat by? People sold my house and . . . you all sat by?"

"Rachel will help us talk it through," Dad promised.

"Jesu," Mom muttered to Viv and me. "Look what it's done to him. I mean, this would make anybody ill."

"If you lie down too, near him, it will comfort him," Viv suggested.

Mom smiled tolerantly as if she had seen through her. "Well, you're trying to be kind." But her legs were giving way in any case, from the shock, so she let me help her up, and a little after I arrived she had fallen asleep patting my hand.

It was then, when I slipped away from the bed, that I first encountered the letters, fragments unaddressed, unsigned.

Writing this because I don't know how else to keep in touch or to keep track of all that is going on. I told you already that I have no privacy. They ransack my things and now my very papers are in disorder. Worse still, my movements are constrained. I call a cab and someone goes behind my back and cancels it. I have my feet and my handbag with my cheque book, but at the door I must ask someone to let me out (because of course my keys have been moved) and then they say, wait, I'll take you. Shortly. And – you've guessed it – shortly never comes. I hate shortly. I want shortly blasted off the face of the earth. No one is doing anything about it, not even Dan. What can it mean?

The porch plants withered. The works of assorted poets drooped, turned down over the arms of chairs. Volumes bookmarked in early chapters gathered dust on side tables. Silver tarnished. Mom's attention narrowed to Dad's bedside. The world receded.

When he slept she would bend again over her letters.

Once as I passed their door on the way in, the large, sagging woman who was then on duty peeped around the door, watched Mom fixedly while smiling at her in the most foolish way.

"Poor soul," Mom sighed. "Yes?" She prompted her after a while.

Poor Soul smiled and swayed from side to side. "Bath time," she crooned, swaying again.

"Pardon me?" Under the set grin Mom's hold on courtesy became tenuous. "Can I help you?"

"Ready for bath? Have to bathe every day!"

"Poor Soul my foot."

I rescued that nurse barely in time and, even so, by evening she was history.

The fragmentary letters lay here and there, weighted by books or teacups.

Dan will drive me over when he's up to it. While he's asleep I find myself rereading verse I used to read to Mama when she was ill. "Our birth is but a sleep and a forgetting . . ."

Perhaps, I thought, letting the paper fall back onto Mom's escritoire. Some things take an entire lifetime to wake up to even as others drop from memory.

I thought I knew old age. My intimacy with my own grandparents and with parents of my friends misled me. Only now I glimpsed what could never have been visible to me before. All this, our life now, as it really is, is nothing I could have *seen*. When I was younger I had no thought in my head of being anything else. I looked at people like old man Gould tottering on his way to the synagogue, people I thought I knew, thought I saw. But the truth is, *it was all made up* – what I hoped or feared the old might be. Deduced with impeccable logic on the evidence of my eyes but as if looking along time in one direction could possibly provide the same view as looking along time in the other. As if the slope had nothing to do with the view.

Now with each new day the angle shifted, and one night my clatter in the kitchen brought Mom to the door, to stare in surprise at me floundering at the edge of collapse.

"And now the dog is hungry," I moaned, for it was apparent the day would never end. I uncovered the pot of cooked dog food and braced myself to take care of yet another living thing.

"The dog is not hungry. I fed him." Her voice was crisp with its some-things-I-do-*not*-forget tone.

But I puzzled over the full pot. "Nothing's gone from it."

"That's as it may be. But do as you see fit. You know what? Keep it – your dog, your pot, your whole blooming house."

"Mom." I tried to hug her but she shrugged me away.

"At this stage. After bringing her up. Working on her Maths, her English, her . . . After, after . . . To feed a *dog?*"

"Sweetheart." Stunned, I repeated like a fool, "The pot is full."

A flood burst its dam, swirling away the usual euphemisms. "To hell with the dawg!" she shouted.

And in the midst of the shock I registered my answering fury – not at her but at the invisible . . . something lurking in its crevice to strike out unpredictably.

I put away the pot and, later, smuggled the food outside. Gawain devoured it like a wolf, his haunches quivering, his back, yes, boney, though I had not noticed it before. My hand groped apologetically down the dull coat, dry dead fur coming away and floating around my feet.

I've fed him already, love. Night after night. I could hear the certainty in her voice.

The dog paused, glanced up, and even as I caught the slightly mad glitter of starvation, he reached forward and licked the tear before I could draw back my face.

"I'm so sorry, boy," I murmured over and over. "I just didn't know."

CASCADE

It was somewhere at this point that Dad proposed I arrange power of attorney.

"Only look at poor Rummy," I pondered. "Was it best for her?"

"Well, this is not Rosemarie," he responded. "Turning myself over to you, not Scott. And, Miss Ellie, I strongly suggest you . . . do the same."

"Listen to Rachel," she urged. "We should take care of our own business and not burden the children."

But then came a thumping of books and shoes and the thud of music. "I *hate* Chemistry. What it have to eat? *Tell* me is not rice and stew something. Yo! Peanut brittle, Nan." Andy held up a warning finger. "But no kiss, eh?"

"Good thing you told me in time," Mom said.

As he settled behind his books, Mom broke the bar of peanut brittle and, finding Dad sleeping, rested his half in a saucer.

"Homework," she reflected, munching. "Remember the Rosetta Stone? Simple interest. Latin irregulars." She sighed. "In these other languages the verb *to be* is always such a mess."

In a while she retrieved from Dad's night table the saucer of melted candy and its crust of ants. "Dan should know by now not to leave things like this lying about."

Just then a chime of crystal attracted her to Viv washing glassware after their wedding anniversary.

"What you mean, yesterday? Our fiftieth? What, fifty-*four*? And celebrate our anniversary with us living in the very house and don't tell us a word?" Only Dad's insistence that they had both been there could calm her down. "Against the evidence of my senses," she said, "and only because we have been celebrating all our lives." She chuckled a little wickedly. "Imagine, over fifty years. And like yesterday."

When the nurse wheeled Dan towards the bed that night and helped him in, Mom sizzled again. "He can hardly walk," she said. "You tired him out to the point of collapse!"

"Just a little bath, Mrs D."

"Bath? You bathed him?"

Dad lay still and did not deny it.

"You let her bathe you?" she demanded.

But he closed his eyes.

107

"Oops," the nurse said unctuously. "We're having a little episode, eh? Okay, you cool it."

Mom lunged forward, her lips forming words that seethed indistinctly into a hiss of fury, and the nurse threw the towel to the floor and snatched at her purse – except that Mom grabbed at it, wrenched it from her hand and hurled it through the back door.

When I ran to them I ignored the nurse, held Mom, darling darling no, gripping her hard and waiting for the shudder of anger the shock that convulsed her face to pass yet even then inside somewhere another strut was crumbling some wall collapsing so that it might all all come caving in and smother thought or, worse, yawn in widening emptiness, and then what might rush in to fill that vacuum with flutterings, squirmings, rendings. The weight of all that was to come crushed down suffocating me, but then, incredibly, she braced herself and squared her shoulders steeling her soul as an arch that bore us up.

"Cooling." She inhaled deeply. "I need cooling. An ice pack on my temple, shave ice with condensed milk . . ."

She closed her eyes her arms tightening about me as I groaned for elsewhere some distant place some time gone by and she whispered me out into another place we had seen when I was a child, high in the hills, a fine, cold rain to which the ferns lifted shining fronds, a wind coiling mist around my feet. An incredible slope of blooms, unreally blue.

"Dan," she went on without opening her eyes. "Dan, you remember those hydrangeas?"

"Oh, the bank of them, that day . . . what about them?"

"Nothing. Just once you remember."

"Your shawl too. Blue blurring into pink just at the fringe. Like the flowers."

"You are right."

And so it was resolved.

In the morning the new nurse minced in flouncing glossy pressed curls above the baby-doll makeup. Stiletto heels clicked between the bedpan and the bathroom.

"Barbie," Mom sniggered. The girl was far too scared to look at her directly let alone address her. "But harmless to all appearances. Still, if she's here, all can't be well." She ran her fingers along a bookshelf, glancing at a powdery old volume.

"Kill the messengers," she reflected wryly. "Still, perhaps this one's only crime is redundancy."

"Have you heard?"

Mom met me at the door the following evening, her face taut. "They have swindled me out of everything. The house I lived in for forty years, the land, Mama's place, the business – sold. I tried to talk to your father and he closed his eyes. I insisted he get up and go with me to the lawyer, but he announced he was too ill. I shook him to bring him to his senses and they parted us. He is lying there now pretending to be asleep. None of them fool me."

How to see this new place she inhabited after the sheering, the slippage, the alignment to new dimensions, the re-peopling, how to perceive it so as to maintain contact even when . . . how to see it without the cracks riddling my own mind. She stared from her state of emergency at me, eyes piercing with urgency and I had barely time to think before grabbing her hand and sliding into it.

The landscapes of our past had been open and airy, but those of our present included forbidden places. Sinkholes rugged and inaccessible. We wound between them along hairpin bends and their recesses were fertile and tangled. But sometimes up against a wall of rock one could go no farther. Assault after assault. Atrocity after atrocity.

"Stand and fight." She braced herself, for eventually even the land itself played tricks and nothing was left but what one had inside. "I tell you it is not merely as it seems. Look at all these young women who come and go. Where they trawl them from, I don't know."

I could see the nurse too through her. Short skirts, tights. In and out of the room, one leaning over him with the big sloppy blouse gaping. He lay there without objecting, making only brief responses and never any regarding house or land.

"You know, baby, he seems genuinely ill," Mom agonized.

Once she paused and glanced at her hands and they were steady though a bit plain. A scrap of song moved in and took over briefly.

"You hand full a ring an you cyan' do a thing,
Who de go married you?"

Then where *was* her wedding ring? She rubbed the finger frantically and I began the search till a movement on the bed caught our attention. Dad held out his hand unsteadily with it on the smallest finger above the joint where she always put it before washing dishes.

"I would be able to keep track of everything, even now he is ill, if only I had Rosemarie." Her eyes filled.

"Call," he prompted, but she shook her head.

"I made a note of the number, but I can't find it."

"We need . . . a file."

Rabin offered to run upstairs for the number, but there was no need, for Dad remembered it, and papers Mom could handle. In the next room, from a shelf high above his desk she pulled out a folder with a ribbon that tied securely. She brought it to the writing table and knotted it to the same ribbon as the pen Dad had tied in place there.

"Even I can't lose that."

His grin of approval showed through a slight grimace in the effort to marshal his mouth for a pronouncement. "Write on it. *'Rosemarie'*."

The label was small, so she wrote only *Rummy*. I added a note that the file must never be moved, and we put it on her desk.

Later when I looked in he was sleeping, and Mom hugging the file.

"Rummy," she whispered, then crushed her lips tightly together.

"We'll call her." I dialled and pressed the speaker button.

Rummy actually answered and was overjoyed to hear us. If Dad were awake he would have remembered everything and repeated it as often as need be, so I put the call on speaker and paid what attention I could amid the dog barking at workmen, the plantain burning and the inexorable march of ants that had identified a house out of control.

"Missis. I on my feet all day. But you have no idea how the place has improved." Rummy's voice rang clear and strong. "Mr Ashmead, same millionaire who has been funding Scotty's project – he just put his foot down."

Mom noted the name hurriedly on the back of one of her letters. "Then, Rosemarie, he actually give Scotty money to run the place? Why?" Mom leaned to me, her voice full of mischief. *"Deus ex machina."*

And I sniggered like in the old days.

"Pharmacy not solvent?" Dad muttered without opening his eyes.

"Mr Man fix up his own flat downstairs, for his pressure high and he come ever so often for the quiet. And now he have meetings here occasionally, so the place must run good because him don't give no notice when he coming. He keep a supply of everything here – clothes, camera, medicine, and they have new medicine for pressure now, different to what Bonny used to take. He quiet though, not a word to anybody."

"How's Rummy?" Mom asked a few minutes after I'd hung up and while Dad and I were discussing the call.

"Well." He patted her hand, drifting off to sleep again, but she hid her face so no one would suspect her of being childish enough to cry about never getting to talk to Rosemarie.

"Long distance calls are too expensive for everyone to have a chance," she said, gulping down the disappointment.

In replacing the file she encountered a letter.

"Now who is this from? Why would they date it years ahead of time? Why don't they sign their name?" She sighed, holding out a paper filled with pain that seared and bewildered her:

Dan can't or will not help. In fact, I have my doubts about all the "help" he gets. I told you about the little fast girls. I caught them feeding him something and he did not want it; they were coaxing him to take it. I was so mad I boxed it away. Perhaps it accounts for his condition, even his strange behaviour. Do you think they could be slipping him something that has caused him to alter so? He hardly says a word to me now. Who could have poisoned him against me? I am constantly on guard to keep them away from him.

Mercifully, the election news on TV diverted her with its promotional drivel, but only briefly.

"They take us for fools." She snapped it off.

"Rachel!"

Pre-emptory but tormented, it ripped my sleep and I was on my feet almost before I woke. It was the tone I remembered from the emergencies of our lives. By the time I reached the foot of the stairs where the shoes and books accumulated on the last step, she was reaching for me with one hand and crumpling a paper in the other.

"Listen, I just stepped away from writing this to check on Dan and there was a young woman stripping his clothes off. Naked as the day, in my own bed. I confronted her and she said she was trying to bathe him! Of course I drove her out and I asked him what it meant. You can imagine my state, but he seemed ill. He's got ill, baby. He says the last thing he wants is to worry and upset me and I must do whatever I think best but first talk with you for your advice is always sound. What am I to think? He says, ask Rachel." She stared at me, goaded, awaiting my answer. "Whether they are ridiculing me or trying to drive me mad and have me locked up and take over I don't know. The house is sold already, someone said. But who *are* they?"

The answer must have been unthinkable for she squeezed her eyes shut against it, perhaps trying the hydrangeas again. It did not always work though. Landscapes, escapes, seascapes.

"The sea is not always as we would have it," she reflected, flinching as I guided her back to their room with my arm around her shoulders. She shaded her face as though, somewhere, a dome-like cloud system had gathered and begun to swirl, veering to high ground. Somewhere a gully thundered in spate. Old grey stone ruins mouldered on as before. "So blue a blue though."

"Yes." Dan opened his eyes and smiled at her so that even as the familiar grin skidded slightly towards tremor, the past gleamed through, the hydrangeas glowed stubbornly on.

But the newest nurse was a huge woman who glared at her ferociously every time she went near her own bed.

"What have I done to deserve Godzilla?" Mom demanded, and it was true. The woman even tried to force rice down Dad's throat.

The person they needed was Rummy, but for weeks there was no word of her, no way to reach her by phone. When I called, the line would disconnect. At least now there was a file on the escritoire, Mom could remind herself.

"So many from the old days are at Ivy's place," she sighed, "like Sybil who was in school with me, Jocelyn (poor Jocelyn, who turned out to be stronger than any of us thought), old Archdeacon Pearce and Dan's friend, Cecil. Then there are others we know of, though not well. Honourable Eric Marsh, brilliant judge once, and Irvine Lazarus who had land all over the place. Bauxite land. (Then didn't Hugh Pearce marry one of those sisters? Their father was in dry goods.) People from abroad are there too, but don't seem to mix with the locals."

She pored over and over the copy of an advertisement from the file. "Gorgeous view of Ivy's old house."

Her eyes closed as she drew on other images that seemed to rise and surround her and she turned them over with the concentration of a gourmand, her murmur summoning them up in my own memory – emerald wings whirring between the orchids, Aunt Ivy aquiver with delight, and the aroma of gizzadas. The ficus they should never have accommodated there at the back crowded its mysteries together into a hustle of glossy dark green, wrapping a dark stray bough about itself and driving its roots out to test the stability of human arrangements.

Notes from a Chat with Rosemarie. She laid them out along with the brochures. An advertisement fluttered hypnotically. Life-shares in beautiful surroundings. Exclusive clientele to retire in the sunny Caribbean on a permanent all-inclusive vacation. Superb security, swimming, physio, and ceramics classes. Special arrangements for legal advice on retirement plans, testaments and investments. A paradise.

"Yet even in those old days the yellow and black caterpillars overran the frangi-pani tree and what leaves they missed dropped and rotted underneath." The unpleasant recollection jolted her back to the evidence in hand.

The brochure boasted medical care with specialist staff in geriatric training and a speech therapist with skills in Spanish and German.

Strangely, the cost quoted was not exorbitant. Her notes of Rosemarie's call revealed that highly qualified professionals supported the home, like CEOs of large industries, with contributions on legal advice from Oliver Gray, a past church treasurer, and J.V. Hammond's surviving son. Dad, it seems, warned Rosemarie never to shift her business to any lawyer of Scotty's, so the fact that Scotty had the home associated in some way with Hammond was of relief to Mom.

"Hammonds for ever. Good thing it isn't Wally," she muttered yet again, leaning close to my ear. "I never trusted Dad's lawyer, friend or no friend. Still, I wouldn't want my house in Scotty's hands either, and there it is all left up to Rosemarie who looks at him and sees nothing but Jesse. Dan," she continued, "do you think the house is okay?"

"House sold, remember?"

"No. I mean our house."

"Little water? Throat dry."

"Just a minute. What about the house?"

"Choking."

Choking my foot, her eyes flashed. "You need to get up and help yourself sometimes," she warned coldly. "You want to turn into an invalid?" After filling the glass she slipped her hand under his head and held it to his lips with infinite gentleness, but he took only a few drops. "Then why you make me walk to the fridge if you didn't want it? You prefer Ovaltine?"

"Just stay with me. Start the crossword while I . . . catch up."

. . . best to depend on Rachel, for I cannot possibly leave now. Since he came back Dan has been quite low. The doctor has seen him and is wondering whether to put him in hospital and spoke as if he had been there before. Perhaps when I thought he was away on business he was in hospital. I know they keep things from me to spare me but I wish they wouldn't because it confuses and worries me all the more.

Relax, Rabin says. How can he possibly know the overwhelming guilt of every pause for relaxation as time vanishes around me my work lagging the garden in rags the house destabilized by nurses and my time with Andy, not to mention Rabin himself, eroded desperate as I am to give them time and time with Dad vanishing, time with Mom dissipated in confusion and even to sort out my thoughts so jagged, so edgy, and somewhere are areas in Mom still undamaged to be brought out but soon no one but I will be able to find them. And they will vanish with time, vanishing time, and I'll have left undone those things that I ought to have done, will long to have done. Torn between them all and they all love me far too much to let them see how I . . . how torn torn torn torn.

I could be more help if the nurses didn't try to pin me in front the television. The shows are alternatively asinine and gruelling.

Suddenly she would realize Dad was still in bed.

"Get up, darling. Jesu. Don't you know the longer you stay in bed the harder it is to get up? Get up *now!*" she said one day.

"Sit quietly a little and watch what coming." The nurse's tone was sharp with desperation and she shoved the rocker against the back of Mom's knees, crumpling her onto the seat.

"Lord! Hog! You have to pitch me down?"

"Are you mad?" I snapped, and the young woman cringed, whining that she couldn't do her work if the old lady wouldn't sit quiet a little. "Being gentle with her *is* your work," I said. But I knew Dad was her patient and interaction with Mom had no further reality to her than nuisance value. "Don't you want to see the show, Mom?" I hated myself for capitulating, but what other way forward was there when I was late for work?

As I went through the door I could hear Mom protesting, "Grown woman, God knows how old, and I must watch whatever foolishness is on TV? Well, this is tedious and I've had enough. Dan, get a move on – homeward bound. Where is that blasted cab?"

I clutched the wheel trying to put my mind back together. I remembered Ferncot – sitting on the front porch among the lush fountains of delicate fronds. There were big clay pots, as big as I was. In the evening the tiles were cool and I stretched my legs out straight and flat to chill the backs of my knees. They talked and laughed together while Rummy went back and forth with the goblet, pouring, remonstrating with withered leaves and exclaiming over new shoots. Their talk and laughter arched above me as the evening fell, scattering patches of light like bougainvillea petals gleaming through the leaves. The world took form around me through their words. And now, this world seemed a container from which the lid was being cranked back at uneven rates, with unearthly screeches, and ripped away, leaving me tiny, naked, raw to whatever gaped beyond.

EIGHT

Vice

"I'M A DECENT WOMAN." Miss Ellenie voice meet me from outside the house as her daughter back out the car. "Watch the screen. You think I want to be in someone else bedroom?"

Nurse flounce out and fling the old genkleman laundry on the floor before the washing machine and look back at the room and steups. Well, Miss El turn on she one time.

"Don't you suck your teeth around me. However annoyed you may be just you please remember yourself before you make that nasty noise." Then the TV took her over. "Oh no. Spare us. All my life I married to one good, clean, faithful man. I must be involved in someone else's nasty life? Watch the screen. I know her. I see her all the time. That is how she is – one after the other." Then she fling up she arm across her face. "Jesu! He hit her. No. NO." She squeeze her eyes shut but the whimpering, the pleading going on in her ears. "No!" Her voice mix up with those on the TV so now I couldn't tell whose voice was whose. "Oh God, stop it!" When the blow land and she flinch and sink down on the chair and she keep she eyes shut so long, I say, Good she fall asleep, but when she open it and look on the screen and see this face with the eyes swollen shut and the nose bloody so you can't even recognize it, she scream out.

"Jesu! Who could do this? Oh God, why?"

"Turn off!" Her husband call out so loud that like it startle her because she launch from that rocker straight to the bathroom.

She must be stumble into the shower in she clothes and turn on the water straight on she face, she hair, all in she slippers, and like the faucet come loose in she hand, but I say she going feel better when she bathe and I would mop up, for the whole bathroom must soak up as usual – but nothing in dat.

Only, like I leave it too long, for when she wrap up in a towel and crack the door open, Nurse bawl, "Whe' you clothes? Eh? What you do with you clothes?"

"God, she's a hog. I have a name, you know."

"Yes. But you don't seem to have no clothes." Nurse flag she hand at the bathroom door. "Look he shirt over the handle. Put it on, come look you clothes."

"Can you please hand me something? Look. It's my room. You should see something hanging up. I would appreciate it."

"You can't put on the big shirt and come for it youself? Since you could call people hog? Come as you are, nah? Who go want to look pon you?"

Miss Ellenie gasp out, "Jesu! You can't hand me a dress? That is so much to ask? I speak to you decently which is more than you do for me."

"What you need, darling?" I interrupt them. "Is okay, Nurse. I will see bout she."

"Viv?"

"Yes, my love. What it is you need?"

"Clothes. I beg you, for this hog has me trapped naked in here."

"I coming." I pull a dry dress over her head and she put her arms round me. "You have tea yet? You want a cup?"

"Oh, bless you. All I've had is ice water on top of my head, and . . ." It begin to come back, all she push out of her mind, and she sag against the door frame and hold me to keep from falling.

"What happen?"

She practically collapse and point at him, sleeping on the bed. "You don't know. I can't tell you." She stumble out the room. "I'm never coming here again."

"What it is?"

"What? You can ask. You can't know. You see him lying there innocently, talking softly. You don't know what a monster! How can you know. I myself . . . fooled for years. Then he turns on me. If you had seen my face. Imagine a man his size, and me. Look at me! I can't fight. That is why some women kill their husbands, after years. If you had seen my face. If you had seen the blood."

"Is what she say? He did use to beat she? Well, you see?" The nurse seem like she was only waiting to hear something and, well, she begin shrill shrill in my ears so I jump because I had put she out of my mind long-time. "Well, I see how the old wajan does get on and I ain't surprise. All like she does well look for she blows." Nurse voice get thin and sharpen she so please with the news. "Good fo' she!" This woman voice like it plunging in and out my head – much less poor Miss Ellenie. "But like she didn't get nuff. How she does get on. He shoulda straighten she out good while he did have strent."

I tell she, "Hush!" and she must be see I woulda like to lick she down. But I just hold Miss Lady and rock back and forth with her till she stop trembling and I tell she, "Shh! Shh! We goin' drink tea."

And from the time she see the condense milk pouring in she take the spoon and I have to hold her hand to stir it she shaking so much, but the minute that hot tea touch her mouth she calm down complete.

Nurse start picking picking trying find out ting I don't even know, and all I want is for she to stop talk. So I tell she, "He never touch she to hurt she in his life. It couldn' happen to she because she wouldn' take it. It couldn' happen from he because he ain' so."

"Then you mean the old woman lie on she own husband? Right so in front him?"

"Not lie, not lie."

"Well, is either he beat she or he never beat she. I mad to find out. Is either she lie or she ain' lie."

"Anyway, I here. You don' want to leave early?"

"You *know*. But I have to stay and hand over. Gyul, tell me, nah. How you does really *take* she?"

"I goin' upstairs to clean. Call me when you leaving."

As I pass Miss El and touch her hair, she speak up.

"You're a fine woman. I don't know where they find this other trash."

Then she must be gone hide in the bathroom, put down the lid with the soft cover and sitting with the notepad on her lap, for when I go downstairs again and ask, the nurse laugh, "Eh! I forget she, yes." She slap she hand hard on the bathroom door and throw it open. "What you doing so long? Is tutu you trying to tutu?" she pick up a basin of water that has gone cold and a soap and washrag. "I need to be in an out of here now because the patient have to bathe." She pause a little and stare at Miss Ellie bold bold like jamet. "I know how you does be," she say and hold out the washrag. "You want to wash his private parts?"

This poor old woman, like she mind ketch afire. Afterwards I tell the daughter I did well frighten for she. I mean this nurse – is not all stop so, only this one, but she here most of the time – this nurse don't leave her no dignity, and Miss El does get so I doesn't know what might take place. After that, she daughter well sit with the old man and talk to him about how the sedative not doing nothing for Mom and she going have to take her to doctor. An is true she need something but some of it is the situation, because look what happen the next morning.

I see Miss Ellenie studying her finger and she ask Nurse, "Have you seen it?"

"What?"

"The ring, the ring." Her voice get high one time because she ain' no boboli and she have no patience with anybody who think she so stupid she will make them take advantage of her.

"You must be take it off to wash," Nurse tell she. But I find Miss Nurse look well satisfy with sheself.

"No. Not this time. This time it isn't me." Miss El raise the sheet and check his hand, but the small finger bare. "Then where? It can't be gone. Can*not*. For there will never be another."

I help her search but I know it have no hope of seeing that ring again.

Nurse smile. "I tell you, you take it off to wash."

"Shallow and obvious." Miss Ellie nearly spit out the words in Nurse face. "My wedding ring gone? After more than fifty years? While he lies there, and our daughter pays you?"

Nurse fall back like she get a blow and next thing I hear her outside, bawling, "Is like the ole bitch possess. She dangerous, I tell you. All like she will kill somebody."

I pick up the programme for the Easter service and fan Miss El, and she say, "For Dan's sake I would cool down if I could. They don't have snow cone again, eh, Viv? Little strawberry syrup? A sea bath. Then we can't take a little holiday? Rummy would be glad to see us."

He open his eye and hold her hand to his lips.

"Dan, you don't have my ring?"

"The dresser. I . . . couldn't reach."

"My ring, Dan." She search his fingers desperate like some miracle might bring it out from nowhere.

He catch her hand and whisper, "Remember something?"

"What?"

"The hills . . . full of . . . silverback ferns."

And for a minute I say he losing it too, but she kiss him and settle down instant. "Remember something else. Important," he say.

"A secret?" She laugh out. "I *love* mysteries." She hold his two hand like they going dance. "*Allegro, allegro.*"

"So important." I couldn't tell how his mouth quiver, whether was a smile or he feel to cry or was just the same trembling for he take a while to form the words. "Stay with the children." He call it out slow like he reading a sign on the wall.

"But I wouldn' run out on my children."

"They're big. Not for them. For yourself. Stay." He was talking plenty that day. Was a good day for him.

"Of course. Who wouldn't want to?"

"This place where Rosemarie . . ." He get tired and have to stop a bit. Then he go on. "Don't like it."

But her mind take off on her sister-in-law one time. "I wish we could see Rummy." Like she was just waiting the chance. "We can't take a little holiday and go? The rest would do you good." She watch him but he eye open wide and he squeeze her fingers tight like he want to print on her skin what he can't fix in she brain.

"Never." You could feel how urgent. "Never. When I'm gone, stay here. Try bring Rosemarie." She play with his hair till his eyes open again. "Take out her file." He insist on it. "Make a note . . . *Never . . .*"

I don't know how some people so. And is not all the nurses who hand was light, just two of them, but one was this same mean one who come most of the time and the others just come to relieve her. I mean, they see Miss El situation, don't mind she difficult, but they train and suppose to understand. This woman just strip Miss Ellenie of everything she could find and the boss lady have no idea what they doing. And how I must tell her? Next thing when Miss Rachel tell them something they take it out on the old people when I gone home. And if she even send them away, all she can do is get a next set. And so it go start again.

"Then look, Viv. They clear the desk of his papers. When he get up how he going take up his work? And where the Parker pen?"

Of course I can't know whether is a pen was here recently or one gone from long-time.

"Don't what, Nurse? Don't . . . *interfere?*" Miss El like she couldn't believe she ears. "Madam, what business you have here I don't know, but my husband is a sick man. I have fixed back his desk for him and if you touch one thing on it I will call the police. Clear? Now excuse me."

Nurse plant sheself in the way and glare till Miss Ellie say, "Accommodate me. Please." And when the woman don't move she yell at her, "*Move,* blast it! And I don't care if she does think me an ole higue."

Because you have to remember the burden. She under strain, hardly move from beside him or take she eye off him. And if she look outside at the sunset, when she look back inside everything new to her. She must be find he whole condition sudden.

"And Rosemarie should be here," she keep saying. "A nurse in the family, a *real* nurse, his own sister. But she has trouble too. Trouble."

That same day the phone ring and I hear Mrs Cunningham, same Rosemarie, on the phone.

"Morning, Nurse Rose," I greet her, and hand it over to Miss El and press the button for speaker so Mr Duvall could hear.

"Boxes of cash," Nurse Rose say. "Not a normal business. They drop supplies at the home in a closed van driven by a thug with a gun and they call him Security."

"Then you don't ask the lawyer what he thinks?"

"Well, but what are their lawyers *for*? I know what Scotty think the young lady lawyer is for! He only watching her longingly like puss watch cream."

"Behave!"

"Charmaine Taitt don' business with him though. She say she have too much ambition to make Scotty tie her up. But Cindy now – I hear her say, 'Daddy, I only *hope* I getting the new luggage to travel with, because I have plenty to talk over with Mommy.'"

And don't mind I never meet this Scotty, I hear enough bout he and he wife to know how they lickrish. So I ain' surprise now that he seem to be squeezing Nurse Rose like a macajuel. But I doesn' like to seem fast so I turn away to give them a chance and I open the tap at the sink hard, but I could still hear plain plain.

"'What you think she going say about what you do yesterday?' Cindy tell him say, 'You think I went out with Mommy but I hear when you let in Julie, and I see the two of you good. What you think Mommy will say bout the two of you on her bed?'"

"Nasty set."

Mr Duvall not interested in that. All Mr Dan want hear about is a home on this side for his sister to be near he wife.

"It's what you both need." But his voice is too low for the phone to pick it up.

Afterwards Miss El on the bed with him and close her eye, but sometimes I believe her mind like it catch a cramp for when she raise up she see everything different to when she lie down.

She say, "The whole thing is one mess. And who would tamper with it?"

I ask her what, and she bawl out, "The whole blooming thing!"

She halt like something come back to her. "Then Rummy, who might help me, is in her own calamity and Dan insists I must fix it when I don't even know what to fix, and I can't go to her and leave him. And go where? Don't they say some trouble about the house?" Like a trap close round her. "Can't get out can't get in." She grab the door handle and rattle it and she throw her body 'gainst the door.

"Come." I go to take her hand but she snatch it away. When I put my hand out again though, without holding her, she give me hers.

"We going outside," I tell her.

"Can't leave Dan. He would never leave me."

"He sleeping. We can take a short walk. Five minutes."

"Gone, they tell me, sold. But, once I go abroad I leave Rosemarie in charge." Like she slide through a crack in her mind and find herself in a place she never know about, somewhere no one would want to be. "They never really loved me. I see it now. It was a sham. They wanted what they could get. Well. I'll see them in hell first."

Her face change and her lips press together thin. Like all her life have no meaning again and her heart turn stone. Talking to her don't help. Everyting drain out and the empty space pounding in her head.

I believe he must be feel how she tense beside him, why he put his hand on her face, but she dash it away and snap at him, "How you just lie and watch?"

Well, of course he completely bewilder.

"You thought I would take this quietly?" She pace and hold she head, and his eyes follow her. So Nurse march in and want to know why she making noise. "Making noise? In my own room. A dead stranger wants to know? You had better get out of my room, unless you want to be an even deader stranger."

Well, Nurse jolt to attention like she can't believe her ears, and she study Miss El from the side of she eye. "You threatening me, old woman?"

"Give us a minute," the old man interrupt, and Miss Ellenie return straight off, "What's she to you?" She steady herself on the chair back and actually begin to raise it from the floor.

"Miss Ellie." Weak as he is, his voice draw her, so she climb up on the bed. "You know me. How long . . . ?"

"Married fifty years. More?" She rest her head on his chest.

"More. From you . . . I knew. The laughter. The mind, radiating . . ." He get tired but he manage to move his hand to she face and press his finger on she temple. "How's your head?"

"Like I have ulcers on the walls of my mind." And she just whisper it but it pass clean through me so I hold me belly and bend, but then I see like she begin to heal.

"Miss Ellie," he tell she, "I . . . have loved you . . . all our lives."

And was like a stone roll from her heart. By the time the daughter reach downstairs to their room she can't know what to think. The nurse stand behind her with she hand plant on she hip.

"Anything wrong?" Miss Rachel ask.

"What could be wrong?" Miss El nudge her husband and he smile and nod like he get a joke. "Middle of the night when decent people should be sleeping this man wakes me up asking for raisins." She push one into his mouth and another in her own. "It's not an endless supply, you know." She lean over him and rest the box well out the way. "Tomorrow is another day." And she roll over and press she back against him and make ready to sleep.

"Like everything move in her head," I tell she daughter when we close they door. "Is he does really hold she steady."

And that make we look at each other then look away.

When Miss Ellenie wake up next hour or so she feel is morning but she in her day clothes, and I hear her trying to figure out why this happen.

"I don't recall having these on yesterday. Unless they from the day before. But I wouldn't wear the same dress for days. Only, speaking of yesterday, what happen to it? Wait. This not the first time." She begin to breathe ragged and she get up and hold the door frame and call out to me.

"I must catch myself . . . regain . . . this is . . . this is . . . Viv, this is what they call a panic attack. I've seen it before, though they didn't call it that then. Ivy was a girl clutching the face basin with her two hands unable to open her eyes to make a step to say the words. When I held her tight she gasped, 'My life is over. Over.' Collapsing. Is me get Ivy back on her feet enough to travel to the States." Miss El try to look at me then squeeze she eye close again. "Viv. Don't you are Viv? If I can just . . . get hold of myself. I hear them call this kind of thing a panic attack. It was on TV. But is not beginning or ending. Is a state I get up in and I can't wake. Then I have to live in this? Stupidness. I must . . . fix my thoughts."

"Open your eyes. Open them," I insist.

"Dan, Rachel, Andy. Rosemarie."

And like the pounding quiet down and she sit down to try and work it out quietly. I could hear she trying to talk it through. She lie down and figuring out what happen to yesterday. But he sleeping deep, so she pull the gown on over she clothes and slide off the bed, and when she reach the door as luck would have it Nurse march in.

Miss Ellenie shake her head and remind herself, *"Blessed are the peacemakers."*

Then she steady herself and begin nicely. "Good evening, Nurse. Have you seen my daughter, or my son?"

"They resting. They get the day off and they taking a rest."

"Jesu. I must speak to some other living soul. Comfort. I want comfort. What about my mother?"

"Eh?"

"My *mother*. Mercy. What a moron for me to be faced with in this state. Is my mother here?"

"But you mother dead long-time."

It knock her clean down. I barely reach in time to hold her before she crumple on the floor.

"Go easy," I tell Nurse.

But Miss El desperate now. "What you say? Mama? Wait. Someone will tell me. Who is here? Bonny?"

"Who now?" The nurse steups.

"Bonny. Oh Father, save me from this dolt. Bonny, my brother. He will tell me. He's home?"

"He *dead*," the woman snaps. "Is twenty or thirty years they say? Listen. Why you don't sit quiet watch TV?"

But I catch the look in Miss El eye and I suddenly see it from inside her, one loss after the next – and she husband sinking in front of her, the whole world must be crumbling round she and no one to hold responsible, no way to solve it, no one to blame, and the nurses in she face and nothing ever seem to be where she leave it and I feel so sorry for I see why she mind must mark out like a war zone even when she manage to keep her face calm and her voice polite. And I think: this old lady must be so tired.

"And now look," she sighs. "He still in bed. But he should get up. He must get up. When you grow old and lie down it gets harder and harder to get up. The secret is not to lie down for longer than is absolutely necessary. Get up, darling. This is not good for you."

He move he arms but can't turn by heself. He smile tiredlike. "Soon." It take time for him to go on. "You come."

And of course she climb up near him. "When you lose so much weight?" she wail out. "You need something to boost you. A nice custard."

His face brighten right away.

"Make it?" she ask.

"Soon. Stay." The back of his hand move as if he would stroke her if he had strength, and like he accept it all.

And she say, "No. *Do not go gentle . . .*"

"Rosemarie . . . should try to leave," he whispers. "Something rotten . . . You must help her. Keep her in your mind."

"How?" She say it soft, but like it tear open her belly.

And is then the bedroom door on the bathroom side swing open and Nurse sweep in with basin, towel, soap. She plonk down the hot wet basin right on the night table he had make for some anniversary to match the bed and dresser she mama give them.

"You don't know wood?" Miss El sit up one time.

"You have to move from the bed now," Nurse order her.

"Take that off the wooden surface." Miss El talk quiet, trying not to disturb him. "Quick, before it spoil the polish."

"You watching you furniture now? Is you husband you should think bout. Just move out from the bed, give me likkle chance."

Well, like my lady searching for words to deal with her and can't find them and I see the rage start to build.

Nurse fling back the sheet and begin to unbutton he clothes and everyting turn ole mas. He wife fling herself over him and bawl at the nurse, "What? Wait! Are you mad?"

And Nurse tugging off his clothes and the wife screaming, "Take you hands off him!"

Well, they struggle and yanking the sheet and the basin wobble and water sloshing and he begin to slide. This frail, sick old man, he head just miss the night table and he land up on the floor. Well, Nurse set up one outcry.

"Somebody help me! Look she trow the patient off the bed. Watch him tumble down on the floor. Oh God. But this ole woman will make me loss the work. Watch how she pitch him out on the ground."

Miss Ellie pull off her dressing gown before I could reach them and even while I bawling for help she covering him with it.

"You hurt anywhere, darling? Oh Jesu, I did it? I made you fall?"

"No, love." The nurse stare at him, but he eye fix on his wife. "I slid." He smile. And they both huddle up on the ground in the wet cloth when they daughter come down and reach for the bedspread.

"I don't like get people in trouble," I begin, but he interrupts.

"Somehow . . . I slid."

A look pass between he and he daughter and she stroke Miss El hair and say, "We have to see that can't happen again."

"You think I did him this?" Miss Ellenie look round in panic. "Then is me? Then who else I must be hurt? Mama? Bonny?"

"Help me," he reminds them, and we wrap him in a dry sheet and turn and twist and raise him till we can get him back to bed, but by this time her skin like ice and her legs begin to give way.

"I want Rosemarie," Miss El cry. "I buying the ticket."

And I think is about time because I wondering why they didn't do that long ago.

To my surprise, her daughter study a minute. She say, "Suppose, no suppose Pansy is right and she is . . . not herself. How we will manage *then*?"

Miss El put on a voice. "Speaking from hample experience, well, I say Miss Pansy is just full of prunes."

"Prunes." He voice quiet but firm even though he look like he asleep.

Rachel glances at him attentively. "You don't believe it either? That she's . . . losing touch?"

"Bilge."

"Hmm. Well then. I'll call and just insist on talking to Rummy myself."

"They won't let her." The effort tire him and he voice get low.

"Why?"

But nobody couldn' hear him. It sound like he say "prisoner" but that wouldn' make no sense.

Later when he rest he say, "Something must be done."

"Don't jump up and do *anything* for now," Miss Ellie warn him. "After a jolt like that, you should take it light today."

"Intend to."

She settle down beside him while they daughter sit on the bed watching, and Miss El stroke her hand and say, "What do you think bout it, baby?"

"What, love?"

"This whole development of people through and through the house." Miss Ellenie turn her two palm up flat. "What is their business? How should we proceed – as you see it?"

"They are certainly inconvenient. I know they don't belong and this is all . . . new . . . Still, there are things they can do that we can't do."

"Like what?"

"Check his blood pressure. Yes, I could learn to do that easily enough. But what would I do if the reading were high or low. They know those things."

"So they have to stay? Always?"

"For a while." She daughter look downcast for is clear it can't be long.

"Never mind." Miss El comfort her. "Mom will keep an eye on them for you."

"Thanks. You coming with me to the doctor?"

"Why?"

"Come, nuh?"

Miss El slide off the bed and move to peer into the wardrobe. "But where my clothes? Why is everything mixed up? Blast it! I can't even put my hand on my own things."

"Shh! You'll wake him. Just dress for the doctor."

"He should wake. He needs to know what is happening. He needs to know people are going through our things. Suppose something happens to our papers. What then?" Her voice raise up. "You know what hell can come of the wrong people going through one's papers? God! Don't just lie there, man!"

He turn and sigh. "Custard," he murmur like is a comfort just to think bout it.

"Oh mercy. I forgot. Yes, darling."

"As soon as we come back." The daughter link arms with she. "We going make the custard."

When Miss El kiss him say she going out, he open his eye and look at her like what he have to say must burn into her brain, and he tell she, *"Remember Rosemarie."*

NINE

Ellie

"HE'S A SPECIALIST," Rachel assures me as she snaps my seat belt, her face taut and grey.

"What's happening to you, baby?" Her cheek, silk under my fingers.

"I'm fine. Just a precaution."

"Thank God." It is heartfelt, for there must be some limit to what I can bear. "What medicine they gave you?"

"Melleril. It had better work, for nothing else has made a difference."

What tension in young people nowadays. Perhaps it is the news of town, though we are out of it and never did meddle in politics.

Politricks, Basil had grumbled. Rosemarie's report brought him back to me.

"Eehi. He come back and visit us say town not easy," she said. "Even Scotty catching hell with the drugstore downtown with so much to pay for security, but some man name Don arranging the service. It must be Ashmead help sort him out in the end – the businessman who taking an interest in the place."

But these are thoughts I'll have to come back to for here is a road I know. Aah. Home again. Praise Him.

Here, days slip quietly by towards the inconceivable but a fury is gone out of me. The strange women come and go in our room as before, but only Dan and the children matter and Dan looks content, free. In the old-time days we might have gone to Milk River Bath to recuperate but I do not think he can manage it now, and with no diversion and no anger left to distract me from the looming devastation I hang here at the centre of a great stillness.

"Sometimes," I recall a story, "things would come in from the dark, from outside. Not for light, or for company. But just to . . . to rend. Now they come from the inside too." Perhaps I have not said it aloud, for no one responds.

"It's quiet now." Rachel leans over Dan. "Our medication is right at last, eh?"

Thank you, his lips frame.

From the pillow where his hand rests he raises two fingers in my direction and I know a blessing when I see one.

"*Et cum spiritu*," I respond.

Yet in the night, while they are all asleep and only I lie awake or dream I lie awake, watching but somehow unable to intervene to stretch forth, so this stranglehold on my tongue this huge stillness crushes my throat. Something rushing swiftly silently between us, and seizes as he sleeping at my side, my life unthinkable without, I am soundless soundless make no outcry only gathering in my arms for we will close it out and both of us go to sleep both of us we drift, resist the voices around awakening only only only . . . A dream. A dream about an old tale, for it is not night at all. On my wrist the finger that was stroking it has paused and it *was* a dream for he is peaceful, gently let go, and *I* am the one it slashes.

Quickly I kiss him before they separate us.

Straighten my back, straighten, raise my head, cooperate, make it easy, poor baby, one thing less to give her pain, take the chair facing the TV to ease her up. Face it. Face. Compose face.

On the screen, a show comes to an end in rows of white letters floating slowly upwards. *Words, words, words.* Hammer them on the anvil of my brain. Forge a thought I am prepared to retain – some new alloy resistant to corrosion as if there is anything I would rather lose than this current reality. *Except my life, except my life.*

They hold me, clustering close about, their eyes wondering whether I know and how I shall go on. A new visit diverts me but from what what what what, ahh, again realization crunches its axe in my brain. Grip the chair handle, grip it and wait, await the next blow because I have known all along it was coming and, yet, because I feel our souls still entangled and my life suffused with the best part of him and faith which I grew with circulating like my bloodstream, he, I remain no conscious effort just it is that I am not cut off from . . . from any of it, from the agony or the comfort, what, what is it, tell me don't tell me looming again, hurtling at me, aagh, then so I reach into myself as Dan would have stretched for the fine brass chain that turns on our lamp. Dan.

I draw my back straight so every sinew is taut. For I know how to conduct myself. If I collapse they will crumple, if I stand firm they will restrain themselves for my sake. Viv presses my dress for the service. Long since I wore stockings, for Dan and me . . . Dan.

"Of course I'm coming," I respond. "Obviously I must kiss him *once* more."

Sitting in the church we are all together but for . . . The programme in my hand catches my eye for his name is printed across the front . . . Oh *Jesu*.

Days. Nights. I search the room again and again for clues. An old letter comes to hand, whispering of something going terribly wrong, and Dan, a strong, strong man, to slip away like that. What could I have done, fragile as he was towards the end. Or not done. Left undone those things that I ought . . . ? I try to etch each hint deeply on my brain. To jot notes to myself on cards, envelopes – the story is in snippets, disconnected, soon anonymous. But *scribo, ergo sum*. So I write them down.

Dan stepped out so quietly and I can't say what time we should expect him so I wait by the door. Outside the flowers unfold, dragonflies zigzag, leaves uncurl and a brilliant bird whirrs close, pauses in a blur of colour, and is gone, and time bears me along at a pace at once so slow and so rapid as to be imperceptible.

"We should settle the land matter and sell it as soon as possible though," Rachel murmurs to Rabin over a cup of tea in the kitchen. I can see them through my door. "What good can it be to her otherwise? It's months already."

"I thought he told you never to enquire about that land," Rabin argued.

There is only one strange face, hatchet shaped, poking about when the rest of them are out, but she takes no notice of me except when Rachel is present. I have all I need. And yet . . . *And yet I know, where'er I go . . .*

"I tell you the tablets too strong. Miss Ellenie not just calm, she sleepy. She does keep she eye close while she talking to you."

"At first I thought she was in shock, Viv," Rachel says, "but perhaps we should reduce the dosage. I want her calm but . . . but *herself.*"

They think I do not know. I know, I know all these conflicting things at the same time, intersecting and dissecting. *I know where'er I go that there hath passed away a glory from the earth.*

My eyes open to light streaming through the window and silhouetting a woman rummaging in the drawers of my escritoire.

"Excuse me!" I slide down from the bed and snatch the papers, and she squirms away and darts out of the room, so I sing out, "Run, mongoose!" But no one joins in.

The Rummy file, marked *Do Not Shift This File,* lies open on the desk and as the most recent note catches my eye I can't help feeling it would be safer not to have so much cash about in a private establishment.

"They serious." From the kitchen I catch a warning note in Viv's voice as she whispers to the weasel woman. "They have you here even though I here too, so someone can stay with her right through. If you don't mind she good, they will send you 'way."

"Anybody fire me does find bandit in they house by next night. I does know thing to read over dem when they asleep. I does know ting to say over dey food too. Dey doesn' dare fire me."

"Rubbish!" I say.

They both jump, and Viv laughs.

"Who she tink fraid *her*?" I demand.

Still, it has interrupted a trend of thought I felt important. If I could just read in peace all would be well, but I have barely started before something breaks in – the phone, the door, something, I can't tell what. Then, once the thread is broken, it's no good. *My head aches and a drowsy numbness* . . . Reading is hard.

Of course, if it's an old favourite it makes no difference how they come behind me and scramble the text. I have been that way before and it little signifies where

I begin. Then too (as the memory is not so hot, you know) if I even retrace some steps so much the better.

Half the time I hardly need the book, for most of them I have safe. Like now, my eyes smarting a little, I close them and read from inside my head. There they are. Mr Darcy. Well, she told him, eh? Sidney Carton a fine man in the end. It's guidance so many of them lack, it's those don't-care fathers – not like Dan. But where is Dan? He should call when he's going to be late. Tired of telling him. But *Remember Rosemarie*, he said.

"You see dem tablet?" Viv is displeased about something. "You need to lock them up an leave out only what for each day."

Rachel stares at her. "Viv, what you telling me?"

"I only saying. And I was thinking – you ever hear from Doreen? Doreen who did work here when I had was to stop and mind my mother?"

Viv brings me a cold drink in my own room, presses a mint into my hand and kisses me before she leaves, and, after a while, snippets of talk between Rachel and Rabin drift in.

". . . still no answers about the estate. The surveying may have been incomplete . . ."

". . . nor how much money is involved . . ."

The woman in the chair next to me shifts nearer to the door and puts her ear to the crack.

"That is out of order," I rap, "and sly!"

". . . been paying the taxes for twelve years but we have no idea who he is . . ."

". . . but not reveal the location of the title, nor do any letters from the lawyer mention any payment to Dad whatever."

"Hello?" I call to the children. "Are you under the impression that it's a private discussion you're having?"

The woman pushes out her mouth, stalks into the bathroom and slams the door.

"She's way out of line," I tell Rabin when he comes to see why I called, but I can't precisely say why.

Later I hear Rachel's voice saying, "I won't be needing you after today. I'm making other arrangements, but I'm giving you two weeks' pay." There is an altercation and Rachel's voice rises. "Don't come back to this house for any reason."

She sounds calm, but I think it is a surface calm and she is disturbed through and through. The whining that follows doesn't seem to move her though and it soon stops.

To banish it utterly from my mind I search for the tune I just enjoyed, for snatches of song, for names, the location of my cheque book, for where Mama was when last we talked. Dan? Motifs from a rich past swell and recede. The grand theme of celebration sweeps me along, but there, muted, are the occasional departures, the skipped beats or irrelevances that disturb – and, sometimes, a silence interrupts me. A chasm. And I must fill it.

"Don't grind you teeth. Come for a walk, love." Petrona is back. "It will relax you."

"Thanks, Doreen," Rachel responds, looking more at ease than I have seen her for a long time. "I can't tell you how glad I am to have you again."

Arm in arm we walk out into the garden because Petrona . . .

"Petrona?"

"Doreen, love."

. . . because Doreen has brought some clippings for us to set. The neighbour's cat squats between the tree roots and, disturbed, exits with a slatternly swagger of its hindquarters.

"Then, stop! Don't Ivy had a cat? But gorgeous silver-grey and aristocratic. Facety puss." Marie Antoinette stalks away down a shadowy corridor of my mind.

Petrona, not the old Petrona from Ivy's house but this new one, tucks her arm around me as we turn back to the house. Warm, big full-bosomed woman, shaking gently with a chuckle although her walk is stilted ever so slightly with the demeanour of one mildly in pain or recently in pain or likely to be in pain tomorrow from . . . arthritis? Ankles a little swollen, shoulder on the side of the hug a little stiff, and her walk – tilted forward to keep up, whatever the discomfort.

"No rush," I assure her, and settle firmly on a chair with a view to keeping her quiet, and I close my eyes.

I may have told you before how porous the fabric is becoming – no, no, not me (though perhaps it is true of me as well) – but of all that . . . that defined, that limited or marked-out boundaries of . . . why, of life. Look. Take time, for instance. I used to be able to explain tense, but what could I say now, now that it's all changed. The deep past and the recent past have changed places, for the old days are all about me and recent times . . . elusive, floating in and out of reach. The future, once a vast expanse, is now immediate. The present, once a point only, is sweeping away as far as the eye can see, absorbing the rest. Is all there is. The edge of eternity melts and nothing holds me in or keeps them out. We talk and laugh like in the old days.

And sometimes we cry. (*All that is in it,* is what Viv would say, touching my hair.)

"The loneliness." Miss Minnie's wrinkles assemble into a mask of anguish. "When Tita was alive she threw at me every cruel word she could muster. When I was alone with her I prayed to die. When she was gone, in the empty house where it all happened, I prayed to die – you were right, I should never have gone back there. The only relief I ever had was that boy. And vanished. I don't blame him for running away from her but he could have contacted me. I was never unkind to him."

"Forgive them," Mama says eventually, and after a long time she adds, "some-how."

I see Mama's face so clearly. It is an oval face with crinkles of laughter around no-nonsense eyes and a mouth of such gentleness but moulded to direct, decisive pronouncements and curly silver-streaked hair that resists discipline without going wild. She loves colours – soft, deep, glowing, but never garish. *The rainbow comes and goes.* Lovely.

But look at me sitting here – they will think me wo'thless. What should I be doing? Suppose they are waiting on me for the papers to sign?

"Ready?" I don't have to call often.

Petrona looks up from the clothes we have been folding.

"Mom, sweetie, where all your nighties? You used to have a whole box of them long-time when I was here first. I want to see you in pretty ting, man. I going tell Miss Rachel buy you two more. She must be don't even know they gone."

"Everything okay?" Rabin calls.

"Yes. But my head, you know. *Oh, for a draught of vintage . . .*"

He glances round the door. "What about head now?"

"Holds nothing. What do they say? Can they fix it?"

"Aah. Well. We have tablets."

"Fat lot of good." But for what? What are the tablets for?

"You're fine otherwise," Rabin reminds me. "Memory, a little trouble keeping the night for sleeping instead of walking about, more anxious than you need to be."

Did he say "anxious" or "angry"? Something nags at me. Disturbed, the night, the walking. Fury. Can't remember. The disconnected chips fall together in my head and awake . . . something. A term that eludes me.

"What is it?"

"What?"

Memory. Wandering at night. Fury. Something stirs in a recess, a deep, deep place. A cave sunken below others. A recollection not preserved, not forgotten, but hiding. So far in – that it is out of control. Beyond imagination. Once it had a . . . foreign-sounding name, but now it has hidden for so long that it is nameless. Memory. Night wandering. Anger.

An ancient, nameless terror. Disturbed.

"A picture? Or it has a name, doesn't it?"

"What?"

I don't believe him. He does not lose track of a conversation. That's my job. But already the thread is slipping away. Yet I am washed with a cold sweat I cannot account for. An unusually dense darkness yawns at the far corner of my mind.

"An eclipse?" I wonder aloud. Rosemarie clutches the prison bars of a window, signalling frantically to me from another cranny.

"Sweetheart, you don't look well. You feel sick?" Petrona lays her hand on my forehead.

"Am I?"

"You know, Doreen, I lowered the dosage like you said," muses Rachel.

"Still too groggy?" my boy asks – the big one.

"How do you feel?" Petrona's fingers on my face smooth my soul to silk.

"Mashed up." But now I can smile a little.

"I wonder if you're getting the virus," Rabin mutters. "Sit." He feels my forehead but Petrona has handed me a cup with the steam rising from it.

"Nope. It's nothing from outside. Are you staying?" I plead. Rabin rushes about so.

"If you like." He lowers himself into the chair, regarding me thoughtfully.

"I always like. But I don't want to put you out. Can I get you a cup too?"

"I hate tea."

Just what Dan would say. This is good. This is familiar.

"Tea is good for you." I get right into it and he grins sad-sweet as if recalling.

"Tea is nauseous," he whispers.

Wonderful. Now I know just where I am.

"You look better." He seems so relieved I am surprised.

"I'm fine. It's the tea."

As he takes the cup towards the kitchen his laughter floats back, wrapping me in comfort. And yet, something rumbles in the deep places. Predators, inside and out. I trip over their fragments: memory loss, walking in the night, wandering, fury. And each rumble sends a cold wave washing over me, rippling from images, reflections, a term that escapes me. Or that I escape.

Escape? Jocelyn escaped as Ivy could not. Jocelyn escaped to London. If she had been a different girl she would have kept Bonny. He wanted to be good to the child. But Jocelyn said she wouldn't take his pity. She knew he had turned to her for temporary comfort. She said if she married Bonny, Agnes would haunt her dead or alive. So then when no amount of work would fit him for Agnes because she was gone, gone for good, then everything was for Jocelyn's child. Now he lived to work only so as to make up for that, even though the little girl wanted nothing to do with him and, eventually, nothing do with her mother. They say she eventually dumped poor Jocelyn in some home. But Bonny felt he must at least safeguard her education. Now she is a doctor, I hear. I kept my promise as well as I could, left his estate in the best possible shape so she had her education.

So much flows through my mind, and most of it no one else knows. I remember what I have lived through, what I have seen played on one show after the next, what I have heard described graphically. Then there are the bits that have dropped out. The scenes weave in and out among themselves, filling one another's gaps as the gaps yawn, in and out not to be disentangled.

I check my reflection in the mirror to make sure my hair is combed. "Would you say I'm becoming a monster?" I ask. But no one answers. I consider the mirror for a while, but no. I cannot keep back the sigh of relief, for I love beautiful things and was always glad to be one. Part of the natural world.

Waters on a starry night are beautiful and . . . These things are symptoms of a condition that has a name. I am bad at names, but if one can identify a problem sometimes it can be fixed. I lean forward urgently, to ask Dan, but I can't even remember what it is that I can't remember. But wait. I do know *that* I can't remember.

"Pen and paper," I shout, "that's what I need."

And they are glad to get me the notepad. I have my name on it, and now and then I jot down things to remind myself. For I won't just give in, you know.

Not to yield. I write, *Forgetful, roaming at night, anger.*

"I think I should just book the ticket," says Rachel, in the next room but breaking into my thoughts. "I'll demand to see Rummy. I haven't laid eyes on her for five – Lord, eight or something years, and now I can't even reach her by phone. She's my aunt."

"He only needs to say it's his stepmother and his house," Rabin reminds her. "Still, I don't know what else you can do. If you do go to Jamaica you may at least be able to enquire into the tangle with Dad's land – once you're sure you should, considering what he said. For at least it's in new hands now, and this lawyer specializes in speeding processes like these."

I am settled before the TV, still holding my notes.

A war movie. Good.

"Dan!" I bawl, for a war movie is what he likes.

It begins. Some talk between the English officers. Then, a shift to the continent. The German commander barks an order angrily, and there is a name. Not one I know but one that sounds a little like a medical term, like a name I have tried to remember. Or to forget. (My memory is so bad.) Turning over the name I glance at the notepad for help. *Forgetful* . . . An impact, a splintering.

The screen disappears as I turn inward and a deep recess lights up with a gush of fire as my mind renders up the name of the disease it has hidden so securely for so long. Discovery sears every thought from my head and I look straight into the terror as it sweeps by, back into darkness.

But now I know.

The whisper of the term dries on my lips.

It eats you from inside your head, leaving a living shell. And it has started on me. It devours you slowly in the sight of those who love you best. Whom you love. Sometimes, they say, it shatters homes and blights the lives of those who share their lives with you.

A fine mind, Dan used to say admiringly. And he left me charged with something. Rosemarie, you tell me, but it is scattered now, for the thoughts are breaking up as it consumes me.

How long has it been feeding on me? At its own pace. Pausing to lick its lips, curl up and sleep for days or years and start again at will. How long has it been lapping at my brain. *How much is left?*

Outside their laughter is shaken and realigned by pain into something more. There are slivers to assemble. Something to pass on to Rachel from my last talk with Rosemarie. Something in front of something according to the message that I can't remember. Out there a fragile something with a side door, back door, trap door opens on hell. In here different passages yawn to other, elemental horrors. Terrible, but natural.

"Now I've stopped the tablets she'll be more perky," Rachel promises.

"Are we prepared?" Rabin jokes.

Beyond me their laughter is desperate.

They know. They must know. They must have seen the smoke and felt a rush of hot air. The term slashes at me again but a thought rises over it and takes hold: it's not my big fellow after all, then. Not Dan's mind, I mean. That would have been too much for me. I fix my attention on Rachel's voice.

"If Rummy really is *well,* she could be here helping – all this time. She would be happy and it would be company for Mom. If we solve the matter of Dad's property it might even help settle her nearby if she wanted, if she's well."

"You're ill?" I ask Rosemarie over the phone.

"No. But tell Rachel." Her whisper is hurried, anxious. "I want to come to you. Tell her. I never imagined, I never knew Scotty could get into such a nastiness. It look like something criminal going on and now . . . I can't talk here . . . now the other one has come. Oh Master. How to get out . . . *Leave* me!"

I jump, then realize she is talking to someone else.

"Lord! Give me a chance! I just saying hello, I not talking you business," she cries out sharply.

"Rosemarie?" I call.

A man's voice snaps, "Who's this?"

And I draw myself up and straighten my shoulders. "Mrs Eleanor Duvall. I was in a private conversation with my sister-in-law. To whom am *I* speaking?"

The other phone slams down.

At times, though, Rosemarie herself could be overbearing.

"I don't say you must hurt anybody," I remember Scotty arguing years ago, "but you forcing food and drink and medicine into old people who sick and can't cure and you just prolonging their suffering. Waste."

Before I could straighten him out, Rosemarie pressed her fingers to my mouth. "He just young. He will learn," she said. "Don't he have to grow old too? Don't bother with him, man." And she tugged me away.

"Sometimes, you can be damn officious," I muttered. "And if I can't speak my mind how will I even know I'm alive?" I shook off Rosemarie's grasp, but now I'm not sure what it was all about.

"We can't just give up on Rummy," Rachel protests in the next room. "Where else we can turn?"

"I had been thinking we might ask that lawyer to check on her for us, the one who was actually sorting out Dad's property at last. I was just thinking that when I heard what happened."

"I still can't believe it." That's Rachel, for I can't mistake her voice, changed as it is. "For a man to just walk into the lawyer's own office and . . . and slit her throat? They say no one knew till she fell in the road . . ."

"Shh!" There is quiet. "Just switch to Mom's lawyers and stay there, Rach. Hammond, is it?"

"But poor woman!"

"I know, but shh!"

That's what they say when they don't want to upset me.

✦

When I open my eyes again, ah, my boy in front of his screen.

"Aha! *What news on the Rialto?*"

"Just surfing," he responds dreamily, "sort of roaming around."

" . . . *comes riding, riding, riding,*" but I am drifting off again, a little uneasily because *they shot him down on the highway, down like a dog on the highway.* Pulling off my lace-topped bedjacket wakes me fully and I notice that, quiet as he types, a new sound begins, substituting itself for the emptiness. A rhythm, hitherto suppressed, edges through a crevice.

"What you doing, Mom?" Rabin asks.

"Eh?"

"Why you grinding you teeth?" Rachel insists.

"Who?"

She takes my face in her hands. "You. Well? Stop."

"She does always do that now." The weedling, oily voice of the new girl Rachel has taken on draws my glance but the girl averts her face. (She never looks me in the eye.) "Is a good purge she need."

"Don't give her anything, Carmen," Rachel warns.

"Is all right. I know what to do."

"No. Do not give her anything unless I tell you."

She gazes into space craftily, and when she goes outside I confide in Rachel, "She and me spirit don't walk."

Later when I am beating on the locked bedroom door, Rabin chases up the steps and lets me out.

"Carmen! Why is Mom locked up?" he enquires coldly.

"She only walking, walking all about."

"Well, your job is to walk after her. That's why you're here. You don't lock her up and sit out on the porch gazing."

"She need to res'."

When she flounces away, Andy grumbles, "This new woman you have to take care of Nan is a waste. I say is to fire she tail!"

"Easy to say," Rachel grumbles, "placing the ad, the phone jangling incessantly, interviews and continuous retrainings with no guarantee of improvement, and each time Mom must readjust to this intimate help from yet another stranger, each more . . . Anyway. Easy to say."

"Not easy," I agree. "Don't burden your mother, my own boy," I advise him. Searching for order, I impose what rhythm I can.

"Stop!" Rachel swings towards me, maddened.

"Stop what?"

"Stop grinding your teeth."

"But they are grinding *me*." I grin up at her. "You think I have anything to do with it?"

Startled she laughs back, but a little nervously to my mind. "Thank God Doreen gets back this week."

I turn back to the napkin I am folding with exquisite care, however it has come in hand. Unnecessary as it may turn out to be, how do we know what is trivial when there is no context? How can I be sure what consequences a little negligence may entail?

"It is best to be on the safe side, to avoid letting people down. For how do I know they're not expecting guests?" I slick my fingers along the last fold and lay it down. There. At least I have done my best and need not be ashamed. "I wish they *would* stop for a little though, for it is tiring on my poor old jaw."

"Don't do it!"

"But, *what*?" It is irritating to be pressed. Can I stop a heartbeat? On request? Then before anyone can answer I trot over to the phone and sit quietly, and after a while it rings and I pick it up.

"Wait, Miss El! I don't know how I even got a chance to call." Then Rosemarie's voice changes. "Hog!"

I shout for her but it is too late. The phone is dead. "After they don't give Rosemarie chance to talk!"

"That was Rummy?" Rachel crashes her fist on the table. "I badly wanted to talk to her."

"Well, they cut us off," I snap. "What was I to do?" Then I smooth my finger along her brow and try to explain. "I'm not in the . . . the main flow." I close my own eyes, reaching for the old formula. "Fish in deep water never know how fish dey a riverside feel."

As the twilight deepens about us, Rabin and Rachel talk anxiously.

"I can't bear this being out of touch with Rummy," she mumbles. "And there's the other matter too – Dad's probate. The tenant not only insists he paid taxes all these years but he swears blind he bought the land and paid through his lawyers and Dad's."

"Title?"

"He's complaining that he's been trying to get the title for years."

"I'm still not sure what you can actually accomplish by just flying over."

"Use e-mail for God's sake," Andy throws out, without a glance from the screen in front of him.

"What's going on?" I ask him.

"Browsing. Trying to find someone for Mom on the Web, someone who can help contact Rummy. You can reach people, you know, through cyberspace."

"I don't like it."

"What?"

"Rubbish. Evil or rubbish." I can't help recoiling. "The whole séance business."

"I'm not . . ." he exclaims, scandalized.

"You think you're trying to contact them. *They're* stalking *you*!"

"I not doing no madness like that. Is just a message. The Web is like a highway through space. Many highways. I can move from one to the other in seconds."

I close my eyes again, rocking, and intone, "Webs and highways. '*Will you walk into my parlour,*' *said the Spider to the Fly*. Hmm. Do not hold the handrail it is sticky. *Something spinning shining thread someone someone loves is dead.*"

"Mom! Don't be weird."

My boy just grins and his fingers skip over the keys, exactly like Dan's.

"I'll send whoever you want a message."

But Rachel says, "Suppose they don't answer?"

"You going worry bout that from now?" he grumbles.

"Plan B," she insists, and I echo stoutly, "Plan B, Plan B." I develop a little song. "*Plan B, B, B.*"

"How else you expect to find people, apart from the Net?" He shrugs.

"Phone their family, nuh?" I intervene. "Then what? Is Mars they living? Cho!"

Andy grins, scratching the little beard he seems to be nurturing for whatever reason, but Rachel regards me seriously.

"I don't know how to get the number," she responds.

Well, I am just going to leave someone else with the recurrent mystery of where to find the phone book.

I have scoured the recesses for a clue to her problem but can only grimace.

"I can't help you, what with my head, that disorder with the German-sounding name."

Rachel looks at Andy accusingly but he shakes his head, and it's true. No one told me.

The door opens with a clatter and Rabin bursts in.

"What now?"

"They just called to say one of the children bounce down."

A blow. But somehow I gasp out, "My boy? Which of the children?"

"At school, Mom. Rabin's school. Not a child you know." She watches him helplessly as he bolts out. "He is running a major boys' school alongside all my chaos."

"Too much. It's too much," I agree. But what *it* is eludes me.

"You don't think she *would* be better if Rummy came?" Andy demands in his offhand way.

"We want to bring her," Rachel assures him. "It's how to reach her though, to talk to her for any length of time. Remember it's several years since we actually saw her. We need to know *her* condition."

A drive? Thank you. My head is clear, so clear that I can concentrate on working out where we are, reading the road signs. NO PARKING.

But now the car pulls up in front of a building at the centre of a dust bowl, with rubble and scraggy bougainvillea to the right of the front steps and a glimpse of watermarked cardboard cartons to the back. A rusting bedspring leans against what, in better days, might have been a mango tree.

A key shrieks in the lock of an iron gate.

"I think the supervisor is expecting us." Rachel smiles with her mouth but her eyes are tortured.

Along the porch a row of chairs seems filled with people, though no one greets us. The walls are dark green up to shoulder level. Who would do that?

"Good morning!" My voice seems unnaturally loud, but perhaps a wake-up call is what they need.

A battered old man in a distant corner raises his head and bows with automatic courtesy. I walk across.

"How are you, brother?" I extend my hand.

He takes it, uncertainly, then looks up, smiling in surprise. "Are you new?"

What does one say to that?

"Delighted."

But I hurry back to Rachel and whisper, "You saw his nails?"

A woman waddles over to welcome us. "As you come early, we don't finish clean-up though."

Through the open door is a row of beds rumpled with antediluvian linen of various patterns faded beyond conflict, and the smell of urine is overpowering.

I lean towards Rachel and murmur, "Sweetie, I'll have to wait for you outside."

She squeezes my hand and pretends to smile at the woman. "We'll give you a call."

Back in the car and on our way I can at last talk freely. "What an operation. They have sick people in a stench like that? 'No RIGHT TURN'."

"Well, I don't know that they're sick."

"'SLOW'. 'MERGE'. Oh yes? Give them a day or two in that and they'll be dead. Most of them look like death already – death warmed over. And not warmed much. 'CHICKEN PLUCK AND GUT'. Mercy."

"Yes." She stares ahead. "When I took the dog to the clinic last week it smelt a lot better."

"General is sick?"

"Gawain. Almost fine now."

And sure enough at home he greets us effusively. "It's all right, boy. We not sending you to any dirty old hospital. *Don't* kiss my mouth!" The thing is that as I get out of the car, I can hardly contain myself. For when last have I seen Dan?

"Dan doesn't know I'm coming. Or he would be outside, waiting. What a surprise," I gloat.

Rabin, who has come out to meet us, regards me thoughtfully.

"My boy, what is it? You think it may be too much for him? The surprise? Maybe we *should* have told him." Peering out, craning my neck.

"Oh, Mom."

"Yes? What? Say what you have to say."

His lips move and the morning cracks open so that the emptiness thunders again in my head. I ward it off, reaching deep into time. Stories we loved so much flood back, trickling into the crevices of my mind. But out of the same cracks prowl all kinds of images. Grendel seized a sleeping thane. And I made no outcry. There was none big enough for the occasion.

There is no note from Dan, but Viv rests a mat in front of me and sets down nice hot crisp toast and tea. Mmm. Guavas. So I pause only to run my fingers over the satin surface of the table. Papa was making it when he took ill and I can see him now grooving the medallions on the legs. On one leg the medallion remains unfinished, but only I know that.

I close my eyes to locate Mama in my mind and, instead, Dan intercepts me with his direct gaze and whispers, *Remember Rosemarie.*

"Rosemarie." I struggle to my feet. "Lord, what about Rummy?"

"Guess what!" Rachel says. "I actually got to talk to her, though I believe someone was standing over her. She says the place is running beautifully now."

"Good. I hope they will flush the toilets. And give the linen some good sun."

She stares at me blankly; but she can't have forgotten that place we just visited. Those poor people.

"Oh. Not there!" she exclaims. Remember they refurbished Aunt Ivy's old place as a guest house for retirees? Rummy says they fired some of the staff – the wot'less ones."

"Ah. Then what they did with Scotty?"

"Still managing it. Pharmacy doing well again and he's investing in another. So Scotty's flourishing."

"He's so full of prunes," I note automatically. Still a little update is a good thing.

Remember the little song? *Oh me yerry news, me yerry.* I call out to Dan but he is out of earshot. The woman who worked here – not Petrona, she's a lady – the whining woman with shifty eyes, refused to tell me anything about Dan.

"I tired tell you the same stupidness," she would hiss.

Usually though I talk to them all. They come and go in the mist running their fingers through my hair. I am stroked by the ages of my life.

"Our souls have sight of . . . of that . . . of that . . ."

"If she can't finish *that* line it's still not right. McDougall gave me a range within which to adjust the dosage. And you see the unsteadiness. Unless we stop the Melleril altogether we'll need to fill the other prescription for the side effect."

Suddenly, everything snaps into focus. Lines, voices, thoughts sharpen without stabbing me as I have known them to. I can hold the pen steady too.

"I reduced it again, and I put her on the Artane," Rachel announces triumphantly.

At my writing table a file says *Do Not Shift This File*, and the answer is to copy Rosemarie's number from it to another slip of paper. I can't get her, so I go over an old discussion that comes to mind.

"Miss Ellie!" Rosemarie had squealed in delight. "Thank God, for I can't call out."

All the talk was about Ashmead, the man funding Scotty, only Pansy had let drop that the fortune is actually his wife's. She is older or, at any rate, an invalid in a wheelchair and supposed to be a tartar.

"Pansy say is that why he fix up his own suite downstairs here." Rosemarie's voice fell to a whisper. "The nurse dem call it de Love Nes'."

"And poor soul, she . . ."

"Oh, the wife must be think he abroad doing good works. He better watch how he play with young girl though, with that blood pressure. But I feel the wife must be have him in a vice, because I hear say he have cause to hate old women."

"Rummy sends her love!" I announce to Rachel, who seems unconvinced, especially when I explain that I placed the call, but perhaps she is only concentrating on the traffic.

The car sweeps us to an airy-looking building with verandas and huge ferns, and the lady at the top of the step apologizes about the sprinkler.

"Not at all, my dear," I reassure her. "Look at the garden. Well worth it."

"Is this your mom?" She seems surprised, shaking hands with Rachel. She takes both my hands in hers and gives the warmest smile.

"I'm so bad with names." I squeeze her fingers apologetically. "Remind me."

"Come and join us." A couple wave from the living room, as Rachel chats with Sister. Not a bad show – in fact, one of Dan's favourites, Lucille and Mr Moonie.

"A cassette," boasts the gentleman to my right. "Our daughter sent it."

His wife extends elegant fingers, tipped with clear nail polish. "Coming to stay? You'll love it. Don't go anywhere else!"

Yardley's? Hard to tell between the general aroma of smoked herring and fresh-baked bread.

Rachel and Sister come out, and Rachel says, "Well, give me a call, if anything."

"I'd love to. She's the sweetest thing. But I don't want to mislead you. The list is years long." A spray of silver brightens her temples. "I've already booked myself in, I can tell you."

"You have a pretty trim," I remark. "Very sharp!"

"Thank you." She reaches out and hugs me as if she cannot help it.

"Sweet soul," I say as we pull out. I can't help a backward glance for the green of those baskets is unbelievable. "I knew we should be putting some other fertilizer on ours. You didn't ask them which they use?"

Rachel is quiet. Anxious.

"They were glad to see us!" I insist stoutly.

"I like it," she says. "It's just like a guest house in the country. I'd live there. It's full though."

"Food smells good," I agree. "You want us take a few days off? They won't be full for the rest of our lives."

"It seems they may."

"'No U-turn'."

When we pull up, the house is quiet.

"Dan, your girls are home." I stand in the doorway. No one answers. "Well, if he's out he'll have left a note. Depend on it."

I have hunted till I'm ready to collapse and no note. But then, in my escritoire is an Order of Service, and from the vortex of tattered images the pain sharpens to the old rending, mutilating blade that returns to hack at me as I stumble out of its way. Through my fault? Through my most grievous fault? Door. Grievous. The lock. Please, God, the lock.

Across the road a path leads away among trees that are green, gold and pink. Then browner. Dark water churns out some way from the edge. Birds that were settling to sleep explode from the trees as I approach. Twigs snap under my shoes. The water table is high and the air is laden with too-damp vegetation and rot. Leaves hang low and trail on the water and two small bumps rise gently together and cut the silver-grey sheen, leaving behind an opening V of ripples. A wading bird flaps hastily away. Eyes cruise the surface of the lake, stop, and submerge. Reappear elsewhere. Or are those other eyes? Others appear. Pairs of eyes skimming the surface. What is it like to be submerged and to move in one dimension but see in another?

"Here you are!"

I turn to the glad shout, and they are all about me.

"You're soaking wet!"

"What did you expect?"

But it is good to be back inside. Warm and dry, with a cup of cocoa. The medicines, as usual.

"Can you tell me anything about what happened out there?"

"*Here be dragons,*" I reflect, as the old maps come to mind.

My baby leans towards me curiously, but I shake my head firmly. It's not the sort of thing one would want to keep in one's mind. And what remains I would not burden them with – the darkness, the teeth.

"No." I raise Rabin's hand to my cheek. "It's over." And at last a feeling of well-being, for they cannot trouble us again. Not that lot, at any rate.

"Do you know what?" Rachel regards me anxiously and turns to Rabin. "Those tablets for the side effect are the same as one of Dad's. When he used them first he hallucinated once or twice."

"The doctor said that tablet couldn't have caused that," Rabin reminds her.

"Of course it's the tablets. The doctor doesn't live here, and I do. I'll bring the Melleril back up slightly and watch the Artane. Dad only had one or two episodes before he settled down." She turns back to me. "How do you feel?"

"Good. I don't need any tablets. Dr Maxwell didn't give me any."

"Maxwell was years ago, when I was a child. Dr McDougall sees you now."

"A nice enough young man. But how can I leave the treatment of a man I've known since I was a girl and overturn everything on the advice of . . . of a lad? Who is McDougall? A student? He's graduated?"

"He's very qualified. A specialist."

"Congratulations to him. Let him specialize in someone else. This cake is heavy though. You can't spend cake-money on dumpling. They're robbers."

"Never mind. Don't eat it."

"Well, it's something to put in one's mouth. But how did they get it like this? Must be didn't sift the flour three times. But I'll make the next one. The child shouldn't be subjected to this."

✦

The truth is, I almost forgot but it came to me – I don't know how. I promised to make a cake, and the idea fills me with the solace of the familiar. *This is the hour of banquet and of song.* But must it be chocolate?

"Rachel? Rachel? Sweetie, where's your cocoa?"

Then they can't answer? I'm not making it for myself after all. I'll put out everything till they come.

Run through it quickly: 1 – 2 – 3 – 4: 1 cup milk 2 cups sugar 3 (sifted) cups flour 4 eggs. Half-pound butter, don't forget. Pans? Now look at that. The frying pan full of oil and open in the oven. What an expense, and how unhealthy.

"Rachel? Where you have cocoa?"

Then 375 degrees. I may have to make a plain sponge at this rate. The foot of the stairs leads up into darkness and no one answers.

Perhaps they have stepped over to visit the old lady across the way. Through the window and beyond the bougainvillea her house is ablaze with light. Should I go over? I burrow in my memory. The door is locked in any case. You can't even get to pat the dog. And he looks so frantic. Must be smell his food, for they burning it.

I tell you – it takes patience.

I sit down and lean back in the rocker and call, but no one answers so I gather my strength and bellow, "Then you can't smell you burning the dog food!"

Movement at last, an upheaval upstairs. Voices. Feet thumping down the steps. Shouts and clatter. Let me see what I can do.

But as I turn the handle of the kitchen door Rabin shouts from inside, "Close it! Stay out! Someone watch Mom."

I go into the living room and in the far corner gather the cushion tightly to me. They need not have shouted. Hard as I try, I can't stop the shudders racking me.

Rachel. Rachel's arms.

"It's okay," she sighs. "All under control. Don't worry."

"What is?" I pull myself together quickly as Rabin comes in. "What a way he's sweating!" I gasp. "Too much. He *must* get a check-up."

"I'll put an ad in tomorrow's paper." He slumps into a chair. "We must have someone at night too. Every night."

"Yes." Rachel strokes my face. She looks up at him anxiously. "I had no idea this would . . . . My grandmother lived with us. I thought I knew . . ."

"Mine too."

They stare at me dazedly, but what do any of us know besides what we fabricate in our own heads.

As I get out of bed I begin to construct my circumstances – which, believe me, are not obvious. I feel somehow, perhaps it was so for me once, that I should wake with it all mapped out ready-made, in my head – where I am, whom I can expect to see as the day starts, what is expected of me. I have to do it all from scratch. Well, I've always made cake from scratch, never believed in the boxed rubbish. Yet something went wrong.

Let me see. Something I did that caused trouble. Rabin shocked, sweating.

Jesu. What have I done?

"Dan? Where you are? You can't tell me? Who's there?"

I strain to retrieve connections between flashes of recollection. Nothing except tears, faces in shock. And where is Dan?

Oh God. Oh God, no. "No!"

The door bursts open and Rachel is there, frightened.

"What is it?"

"I don't know. Oh God, what have I done? Who I hurt?"

"No one. You've never hurt anyone."

"Then where they gone? Dan. Mama. Everyone."

"You have been good to them all their lives."

"All their lives. So they're dead?"

"Well, but they were ill. Not your fault."

"But what would make everybody suddenly, fatally ill? What catastrophe? *The Gleaner* said anything?"

"Look. Get dressed and have your tea and I'll tell you everything."

"But after I can't have tea and Dan don't get. Where is he?"

The door to the kitchen reveals ruin, walls black and smeared, the ceiling dark, lowering. The curtain near the stove is ragged. Seared. Now they ought never to do that – hang a curtain near a stove.

"They want me to eat *there*? They think I'm a dawg?"

Suddenly a noise on the steps. Reggae. A word or two that I don't grasp (the argot, you know). Surprised glance around.

"What all you try to do here the one night I spend out? It have bacon, or the fridge burn down too? Aha, yes – fritters, man. No juice?" My boy glances at me again, then at Rachel. "Sick?"

"No, sad for some reason. Trying to get her to dress."

"Nah! Just give her a cup of tea. Why she must dress, to sit in this? Nan, you don't want tea? With plenty condensed milk?"

"Of course. The boy has sense."

By the time the men knock at the door he's gone. I try to open it but it is Viv who finds the key and lets them in.

"Good morning, gentlemen," I say, though I don't know them.

"Yes, yes. Morning, Madda."

Madda me foot. Still, as it is best to keep the peace I polish a glass in my hand.

"But why you wo'king the old lady?" one of the men objects. "How you have she wiping wares? Eh, Madda? Dem shouldn' do you dat."

The man is a moron, but I restrain myself.

"Must do something, you know." Only the very obvious works with some people (the sort Oscar Wilde would have expected to call a spade a spade – I guiltily stifle a guffaw).

"No, no. Is to res'." He puts down the tools he's been holding. And he . . . no . . . actually takes the glass from my hands (and who knows where his hands have been since morning?) and he sets it aside and says, "Res', Madda, res'."

"What have you come about?" I cannot help it if my voice is a bit imperious.

"But, eh-eh!" One of the other men regards me in wonder. "So she always does be? Hmm! How you does manage she? I couldn't take dis wo'k."

"This is my friend." Viv's arm squeezes my shoulders, a brief hug. "Don't mind them. Come."

"Who offered you any job?" I fling after him.

His shriek of laughter strips and reduces me briefly, before I realize what it is. "Poor fellow," I mutter, ashamed of my own callousness. "They can't see he's not . . . right? Why they don't stop tormenting him?"

"He going be fine," Viv answers calmly. "He business is to paint and stop getting on stupid. Look, I doing my work and you working too. Once he start what he come to do everything go quiet down."

"You're a fine woman." I can't explain the break in my voice. "Truly." And I become aware of hushed weeping in the room, of muted mourning, too dignified to be intrusive, to force one's loss on others. Yet inconsolable. As if over some unmotivated attack or betrayal. Poor, poor woman. I rock to the weeping silently, so as not to intrude on her incalculable, irredeemable loss. "Oh, but how will she ever be the same? She can never be."

"Who?"

"The crying woman."

She regards me in surprise. "Where?"

"Can't you hear her? Crying. Inside herself. Poor heart. No one can give it back."

"What, sweetheart? You know what? Come help me make the sour orange thing."

Seville orange! Lovely fat ones to halve and simmer down with sugar. Not chipped up into marmalade, just fat and lush. But it is more difficult than I remember. Perhaps we need the . . . well, the picture is sharp – a concave metal . . . dish with small spikes. But of course a grater will do it eventually. Behind, within, before the wailing wall I carry deep inside, voice after voice raises in mourning for the fragments of lives crumbling through crevices. Yet the Temple of Solomon that it no longer supports materializes at a thought and hovers almost palpably around me.

"*Of whom shall I be afraid?*" Surreptitiously, to avoid upsetting Viv, I wipe away the blood from my grated knuckles before reaching for another orange.

". . . why it should take years? Anyway, I got through to her lawyers today," Rachel announces to Rabin with satisfaction.

"Hammond and Sons?" I interrupt.

"Right."

It seems, they continue more quietly, that a man has paid for some land and has a receipt and a record of paying taxes, but no title.

"... and no record of Dad ever receiving payment for the land."

"And that first lawyer's dead?"

"Long-time."

"The firm?"

"Office burn down."

"Wily Wally," I confirm.

They regard me thoughtfully.

"Mom, just how much land was it that Dad had near Miss Ivy's?"

"Ask him. But I would say twenty-five, thirty acres. I could never distinguish properly between his, Rosemarie's, Ivy's."

"How much in all?"

"Fifty? Don't recall. Is only the piece with the house that Ivy kept. Other small pieces ... I don't know."

"Go and meet the man?" Rachel ponders.

Rabin looks shocked. "Make the lawyer handle it. What we know about this man?"

The talk goes on about land and property. Type of thing I like.

"Stick to Hammond," I advise.

When we are finished, I go and sit at my desk for a little reading, for a file is tied there. The rocker would be more comfortable but a note says that the file is not to be removed from the table. There isn't *one* blank sheet to write on so I have to use tissue from the bathroom – very gently, but I get the number down.

Pansy answers the phone.

"No. She get too hexcited and she talk foolishness."

"But is me paying for it," I argue. "It don't matter what she says. I won't be able to keep it in my head. Let me just hear her voice."

"Who there with you?" Pansy demands. (Damn fast.)

"I'm by myself. What does it matter?"

"Oh, all right."

"Miss Ellie? It's you?" says Rosemarie.

"Yes, yes. How are you, love?"

"Fine." But Rosemarie's voice is strained. "Hold on." I hear her talking to someone else. "You can't give me a chance? A little privacy?" Then "Miss El? You still there?"

"How are you?"

"Oh God!" she whispers. "I now realize it. I didn't know. Ellie, beg the children make me come. I will do anything, scrub floor, clean drain, I will sleep pon floor, sleep in bathroom. I will keep out the way. I can't get out by myself because I don' have a cent of my own money again. But is more than the lock-up, is one evil racket. Some of it I can' even speak. Beg you pay the ticket for me make me come. I won't be no trouble – " She is cut off abruptly.

I am desperate when I tell Rachel, but she hesitates, then says, "But maybe . . . don't you think she sounds . . . really a bit out of touch?"

Why the insinuation goads me so I can't tell. I would normally be the first to acknowledge vulnerability in any of us.

"She's not senile," I say sharply. "Not Rosemarie. And they won't let her talk."

"But she was able to call you."

"I called her."

"Ah." She looks even more doubtful.

And so it comes home to me. Rachel is not sure I know what I'm saying, and who can blame her? I wander to the bathroom, knowing no one will help Rosemarie. Something tells me it was up to me and I have let her down. If she had died, I could have taken it. But to have failed her . . .

And now, try as I may, it begins to rise in me, the flood I suppressed at Mama's deathbed the crises of the business Bonny's stroke leaving my house Rosemarie somewhere nowhere calling out to me Dan my Dan where now – an Order of Service and an empty bed – and I can account for none of them who were all in my care and all the screams I never screamed all the tears I never bled surge together and press up from beneath my diaphragm, one long deep agonizing sob over the face basin racking, racking into another. Viv comes running, Miss Rachel come quickly – no, I don't know what happen.

And I can't tell them. I only know suddenly and finally that I am *no good* and the grief is so overpowering I can register nothing else. Viv is holding out tea Rabin and my own boy all gathered stricken and Rachel locks her arms around me rocking and soothing.

"No good, no good," I gasp. But she holds me against her fiercely.

"You are, you are *so* good," Rabin insists, "incredibly good."

"Poor you." I pat at his face clumsily. "What you know?"

And when he laughs I find a chuckle too somewhere in between the sobs and I sit on the couch with Rachel and after a while it subsides, on the outside.

"I tell you," Rabin murmurs, "Viv won't be able to manage on her own – nor will Doreen if we shift her to weekend. And we can't leave a new person in the house. I think we should postpone the trip."

"I will help Viv," I rally. I mean, I can't leave them in whatever pickle it is. So, sternly, I lock inside this enormous grief and a gathering terror connected, indefinably, with Rosemarie.

"Well, we shall try again," Rachel says, sighing as she negotiates the traffic.

A long exhausting drive. EXIT. No scenery to speak of. Cars flashing by, trucks shuddering above our very heads, *fools* weaving in and out on bicycles as if they are invulnerable – I mean it's stressful – I wouldn't want to drive in this. Even when it slows, among the tall buildings the constant stream of vehicles shoulder one another, squeezing in and out. Shut my eyes, that's it. Draw out a line or two: *and the band played on* – not reassuring enough. Hmm! Reassurance? The Twenty-third.

"*Yea, though I walk.* And it might be *better* to walk sometimes."

"We'll soon be out of it. Look, here's okay."

True word. Clean, orderly rows of buildings. PRIVATE. An electric gate. It slides silently behind us then locks with the faintest cold clang of metal.

"Why would anyone do this to the front of their place?" I wave at the black asphalt paving the whole space between gate and steps. "Grim and forbidding."

"Good morning?" Nurse smiles crisply.

"We shouldn't disturb her work," I whisper to Rachel.

"It's not visiting hours yet." Nurse points politely but severely to the sign.

"We have an appointment." I know Rachel well enough by now to see she isn't pleased. She can grin all she likes.

"You are baring your teeth again." I nudge her, and now she really smiles.

"You have no business reading my mind," she whispers, "but why stop now?"

Nurse ushers us into an office and slips out silently.

After the usual pleasantries the matron asks, "So you say her husband died six years ago? And how has her dementia been manifesting itself?"

And it jars on me, I can tell you. The nurse looked thoroughly efficient – a little distant, perhaps, but I thought she was just a cold fish.

"Wait!" Rachel is flustered, and I don't blame her. "Mom, I'll be a few minutes. You want to have a look at the garden?"

"I'm afraid we don't have one." Matron opens a door to another room. "Mrs Duvall, sit here and watch a little TV with the others." She signals a nurse. "Keep an eye."

The other whats?

"Actually, it's better to be forthright," she advises Rachel as she closes the door behind them.

There's certainly nothing on TV. However, I suppose I can pass the time studying the row of obedient faces in front of it. In fact I can stare to my heart's content – they don't mind me. Dull though. Ah, a window – never mind the bars. I study the paved yard incredulously, then a nurse takes my arm, gently enough, and guides me back to a seat.

"I shouldn't be moving about?" I want to be sensible, after all. "Tell me, Nurse. Remind me why I'm here. I had surgery?"

"Your daughter will soon come. Wait here."

"You're very informative," I respond tartly. "My condition's a secret? From me?"

"Your daughter will come," she repeats, unruffled.

"Listen to her," the elderly gentleman to my left advises. "They know what's best."

"About what?" I think I sound polite, but he does not respond. *Riddle me this and riddle me that.* At least Basil would share the answer.

"*P'raps not*," I sing out the rest of the formula.

But his eyes are turned to the screen though his gaze passes through and beyond the unfolding action. A movement from the woman to my right, the ball of her foot kneading the ground, draws attention to the fact that her feet are far apart, toed in, shanks sloping in to knees tightly squeezed together. Her body is straight and very still, her face slack (mouth disposed in a line of dissatisfied resignation) and propped on her hand. All still but the labouring foot and but for one finger of the other hand rubbing the length of the nose gently, endlessly along a line now raw and wet.

"Where am I?" I whisper to an elderly man to my left.

"St Martin's Home," he responds, and sets something fluttering, fragile as a yellow and black swallowtail butterfly at a window in my brain.

The home, Rosemarie says, is not what it seemed. Evil, she said, *take me out.* And what have I done for her?

"Have you a piece of paper?" I grab his hand. He looks at me blankly. "I have to write it down to remember." Fear grips me, fear of abandoning Rosemarie. *Remember*, Dan prompts. Like leaf-of-life, the little bits of recollection have a vitality of their own, however impossible it is to assemble them. "A sheet of paper, *please.*"

A nurse glances at me sternly and I forget what I meant to write down.

Rachel's hand is under my elbow as we go down the steps and out the grille door, and the padlock snaps behind us. I glance up at the clean grey walls and barred windows but there is no one to wave to.

"Then they don't look out? Or see us off? Cho! Old cuffees."

A nurse turns wordlessly away from the iron gate and I can't resist calling, "Good afternoon to you too, Nurse."

And Rachel giggles almost hysterically as we get into the car and start off. The gate from the premises slides open and we glide through.

"Thank the Lord." I throw up both hands. "Delivered from Alcatraz. Haw!"

In the laughter that follows she literally has to stop the car to catch her breath. But laughter is a good thing, filming, lining, subduing the underlying raw wound, the shattering and the wailing.

Still I can see Rachel is distraught.

"Rabby just has to get this break," she says, "and it's only fair he see his folks, after all he's . . . I'm at my wits' end. What the devil do I do?"

This must be serious business so I rest my hand on her shoulder and say, "You do what is best for him. You know I will help you," and I put my palm up in what, as a child, she used to call the "I swear" position.

"You don't know all I need," she whispers, avoiding my eyes but clutching the wheel with one hand to touch her other palm to mine.

"I will do *anything.* Unconditional."

So we're of one mind.

In Kingston the drive from the airport is familiar but interminable and I cannot help demanding, "Then we not stopping at our house?"

"Which one?"

"Lincoln Road."

You Have a <u>Right</u> to Unleaded Gasoline, instructs a looming notice.

"You know how long since you live at Lincoln Road, Mom?" Rachel keeps hold of my hand like a lifeline.

"Don' mind," the cabbie interrupts. "I going swing past, no extra cost. I wish I had my Mumma wi me still."

I read the sign out loud. "'Car Rims on Sale'."

"People fill them with coal fe use as stove," the driver explains.

"How sensible."

He means well but he has brought us to the wrong place. Dirty walls painted with signs below rolls of barbwire. Slam Go-Go Dancers. But no! A woman's fat thighs open, with a lightning bolt. Good Lord. Don't Piss Here.

"Thank you, brother. You can drive on," I urge.

A church flies by, and goats bustle through the cemetery. On and on.

"Then what about the train?"

"Not again."

But the cashew nut vendors used to run out for a sale when the car stopped at the train crossing. I scrutinize every pedestrian hopefully. One with a black woolly tam has a bundle under his arm but only one leg, and the stump is cocked up on the crossbar of his crutch.

Now a vine draped between two lamp posts is hung with the deepest blue flowers, but we turn off onto a dusty white marl road bordered and overhung with ghostly vegetation. Soon we are back on the main road. Then Detour again. Ferns sprout from the red earth. Over the rocks spray fine saffron flowers. The bauxite film reddens the road, parked trucks, and walls that shade deep red from the base to rims of ochre.

"We can't stop and dig out two plants for Rummy?" I protest. "That is what she would like!"

"We hired this car," Rachel whispers. "The longer we take to get there the more expensive it will be."

"Then not *one* of them could give us a drop?"

"All the people here that I know well enough to ask have stopped driving."

While I try to work that one out we corner back to the wider but shadowed road that is unpredictably dappled by light. Huge spumes of forest bamboo fountain up on the right, and on the left strolls a pedestrian with a large cardboard box balanced on his hand. SPIRITS AND WINES. The road is as I have always known it – wild cocoa leaves and trailing old man's beard. Then SILVERSTONE. LONG VEHICLE. CAUTION AIR BRAKES.

But look how they have love bush killing out the ackee tree. Stupidness!

Paths lead down to the edge of a milky river. A wide bus named *Bompush* groans and rattles past, laden with baskets and hangers-on and marked by deep maroon stripes. In and out between us and the bus weaves a little shrivelled man with his pushcart and, more erratically, butterflies dance around us, black and silver on orange.

Further back, hours or years ago, was what could only be a quarry, vegetation gouged out by a giant claw. Beside it a barefoot man swept heaps of broken bottle from in front of his house. There the roadside was crusted by crushed plastic soft drink containers, exercise book covers and squashed Kentucky Fried Chicken boxes. But all that is broken and painful sweeps away again into oblivion, and here alongside now there is only a young man with a loving face leading a donkey with panniers, each with a small child sleeping, and I touch a kiss from my lips to the window.

NEIGHBOURHOOD WATCH. DELIVERANCE CENTRE. WRAY & NEPHEW SUPPORTS THE DEVELOPMENT OF FOOTBALL. A dull white tent rises awkwardly in preparation for crusade. Elderly devotees sweep and place the chairs. On the bonnet of a car a rug dries, fading. The rusty carcass of a truck lies on its side and dry bush grows through its windows.

"A little time in the hills," Rachel murmurs encouragingly, guiltily, "won't that be lovely? You will know lots of people."

In these small countries, Mama explained wisely, everyone you know knows somebody else who knows you. Sometimes I wished she knew fewer people, especially on Tuesday afternoons when she dropped in on her old people, as she called them. The kissing was the hardest part, the wavering lips that did not connect accurately and strayed damply over my cheek which could not be wiped till later, surreptitiously. One or two of the visits went on till I was grown up and even when I was married I still kept her company on the tram to Miss Minnie.

Past the yams crawling up their stakes to the left is a smooth hill with what used to be a fine old house. Low, coiling walls of grey rock edge the road. A part of the wall declares, GOD A GOD. No arguing with that. Dark limestone with a little moss cover is a seat for an old man in khaki who salutes me. I bow and he is gone.

"But I don't recall a flight, not at all," I assure Rachel. "I know this part of the country though."

"We getting close. You'll soon see Rosemarie."

"Is that so? Great! Does Dan know? Is he with her? Wait. She was in . . . in a . . ."

Rachel stares at me in surprise.

"Rummy is at the home, at Cascade. I didn't know you would remember. You're staying with her for a few weeks. A little holiday while we go to Canada."

"Then I can't come to Canada with you?"

"I'd prefer it." She squeezes my hand. "But the people we staying with wouldn't be able to manage all of us. And then I thought you wanted to see Rummy. She's at Miss Ivy's old place, but they fixed it up. Remember about Cascade?"

The madman looks up from the glass fragments he collects from the roadside and salutes me as I pass.

"Well, Glass Bottle is still with us," I remark. "Mad as a shad."

At the entrance we pause. In the old days we would have gone straight up the steps to the porch that overlooks the garden. But hearing a door click near at hand we bypass the front steps and wander along the downstairs front porch. Down here is not much changed. Pansy – well. After all, marriage to Scotty would age anybody. She envelops Rachel and gushes that it's been fifteen years or more, but what nonsense.

There are the bedrooms on each side of the sitting room and Pansy proudly displays the one she has prepared for me, and I can tell Rachel is pleased.

"I'm glad she doesn't have to bother with the stairs," she says.

"Stairs are good exercise though." Pansy smiles brightly. "And she'll be well supervised."

"Well, they can supervise someone else," I rejoin – pleasantly enough though, I believe.

She is as she always was, slightly stocky in somewhat short tight clothes which she always seems to have only just outgrown. Her hair, if I am not mistaken, is redder than ever, clashing with the bright horizontal stripes – the hair was a sort of ginger to begin with, I think and, yes, the freckles support that. She could have been attractive too, in an impish way, if she dressed less skimpily, gave her hair a chance and jangled less with jewellery. I must have been staring because her small tight eyes shoot suspiciously at me then about the room, over her shoulder. That was how she used to glance at Ivy, I remember, with the slightly narrowed eyes of one trying to peer beyond what is being given out.

The glow of old mahogany lifts me and, almost outside what is to be my door, the old piano is freshly polished, though someone has moved the stool, so how can one play? Besides, across the room is a TV on the piano stool. In the corridor I try a familiar door to my left, but Pansy diverts me.

"Storage. You could fall on the steps. Watch. Remember the herb garden?"

But I glance back at the door to the pantry and in my mind the ficus flicks out a gnarled root and mischievously lassoes the foundations of the house.

"Fool-fool boy," I reflect on Scotty, but I move on. "Ivy's garden had parsley and coriander. Thyme. Scotch bonnet peppers. But locked? No! Then someone would lock a garden? Well! If you want to learn, travel!"

I turn in to the bathroom and the lady with Rachel begins to protest.

"That's for the . . ." But then she waves me on, turns to Rachel and says right out, "We know better than to stop one of them on the way to the toilet."

"Crude!" And I close her out firmly. And then *Them*. Who are *They*?

When I come out we turn back through the house to the front and Rachel is saying, "We have it exactly right now, and I've set out each dose. The white tablet is for the side effects of the green."

"We do everything right here, from laundry service to medicines. We have our own first rate pharmacy. You need not have bothered."

"I've brought a full supply, not knowing what's available."

"Kincaid's for drugs," I confirm. "Good ice cream too." Just a suggestion.

"She has to have *exactly* what I'm leaving for her," Rachel continues. "Sticking to the medication we've arrived at is crucial."

Actually I believe a good thick arrowroot paste would deal with Pansy's pimples but if she must use expensive preparations from the drugstore so be it.

On the porch the guests lounge around, sipping from frosted glasses.

"Writers and business people." Pansy waves to them coyly.

"What did they write?" I enquire, and, when Rachel probes, Pansy tells us about *Society Bride*, a production by some guest named Cerise.

"Quite prestigious. Lots of *aero*dite people."

"No visitors about? Do they have outings? Church? Activities?"

"Well, their children have their own lives. *You* know. We have a minister especially for upstairs where they're mainly Protest*ants*."

"So what sort of *ant* are you?" I nip in, but Rachel digs me with her elbow.

An aging hippie with the most fragile long silver ponytail dangling from the back of his smooth dome ogles Rachel from his chaise longue, but she looks at him as if he has slithered out of some rotten tree. His silver tail reminds me of the puss.

"Marie Antoinette," I say, peering at her empty chair. "Don't tell me they did away with her?"

The beatnik casts his eyes up to heaven then looks steadfastly away.

Rachel turns to Pansy, puzzled. "You mean I really won't see Rummy? I have the taxi waiting and the connection to catch, but I assumed I'd see her. I didn't know she was well enough to go out."

"She insisted on going hairdresser, and Scotty take her. You know how he like to spoil her."

Back outside at the car door Rachel pauses and continues, "You'll let them call? Put it on the bill."

She pins a note on my dress and holds me tight against her. She lets me go so reluctantly that I give her a big grin to make it easier, then she climbs into the car. "I'll be back for you both after Canada," she calls through the window, and I shout after her to eat some of those big black cherries for me. She hangs out of the window waving till the car rounds the bend.

Pansy and I listen to the sound of the engine fading downhill.

"Jarvis!" Pansy snaps.

A man who has been loitering near the gate turns inside as an iron gate grinds across the entrance and he opens a gate in an inner fence, then closes it again. Wordlessly Pansy draws me back in towards the foot of the stairs at the entrance and hands me up the first few steps of the staircase. She swings the wrought iron door at the base of the steps in behind me, and the lock clicks. Rosemarie's voice on the phone comes back to me . . . *beg you get me out this jail,* and Dan's eyes fasten my mind, *Remember* . . . But Pansy shouts above it all.

"You can take her now, Maynard."

A woman leans forward at the top of the stairs, her bosom jutting over me like an oncoming tank.

"Sherman?" I snicker, confident poor Pansy will never be any the wiser, but I mount the steps eager to reclaim that porch, for it had suspended us in evenings of cobalt and flame, of jasmine, coconut drops and liqueur, debate and laughter. "Dan? You're there already?"

But the upstairs porch is all grilled in and there is no sign of him.

"Come." A nurse steers me in from the porch down a dim passage.

An angular man pushing a wheelchair barges out of a door and I flatten myself against the wall.

"All right, Sterling Mess, all right," I mutter, chuckling at Bonny's name for me when I was learning to drive, then I press on.

We stop at a door with a key and they had better not leave any key on the outside of my door lest someone forget themselves and I get locked in, but the door groans inward and an old woman sitting on the edge of the bed raises her head and stares.

"Eleanor?" she whispers.

"Forgive me," I say, "for my head is not so good."

"Oh, Miss Ellie, I never think I would see you again, but I sorry you come to this." Her arms enfold me so tightly I cannot see her face any more. There is only her voice. "Then they send you *here*? Oh Jesus, how they could do you this? How they could do it?"

Her voice.

"Rosemarie?"

TEN

Rosemarie

HOW IS POSSIBLE to feel two opposite way one time? Overjoyed, the laughter bubbling over, yet, same time, horror flooding up like acid in my throat. When I clutch Ellie I so confuse between the joy and disappointment, she tense up and pull away.

"Then you not glad to see me?"

"Of course." I tightened my arms against the hurt in her voice, but when I relaxed and held her away to look at her she started back in shock.

"What happened?" She stared at me.

"Yes. Is not the same Rosemarie."

"Then you stop going hairdresser? Stupidness." She sat me down on the stool, drew a comb out her bag and combed my hair, then a powder puff. "But you must buy powder that match you skin. After you don' want resemble duppy."

Then the door fling open and Jarvis pitch one suitcase through it.

"See de bag ya, Byer."

"Miss Byer to you!" a voice barked out.

"Then they don't knock?" Ellie demanded. "Wait!" For now Byer, thin and sharp like barbwire, dumped the case on the bed and wrenched it open, digging about in it. "What you doing? Atrocious!"

The Byer turn her back unconcern, a fish out one new dressing gown poor Rachel must be pack with her heart full, it so silky and glowing, and this crab-face woman hold it in front her and swing in front the mirror jukking out her boney hip one side after the next.

Well, I dived across and snatched at it. "You strip me of everything but you not starting on her, you dutty tief."

And the response come one time – one stinging clap on my face, make me head ring.

"Jesu!" Ellie's arm was up shielding her own face, even though her body edged across, shaking, in front me. "Oh Jesu!"

But the woman turn away without a word, not a wrinkle of the gown drape on her arm and only the sash aflutter after her before she slam the door on us.

Is then I get afraid for Ellie, fraid bout the shock. For what I living with not something she could imagine, nothing she could grasp without . . . without it crack her mind. I start to think, suppose understanding just overwhelm her, and I bend over her, one hand nursing my face and the other (if it only could) trying to smooth the whole thing from her head.

"Shh, darling. Forget it." She was frozen. "Shh. Forget." So it come to me to try divert her. "Make we unpack. Quick. I have a little place. Watch."

One drawer at the bottom of the wardrobe eased right out onto the floor so I could reach through the space to two loose floorboards and the brown paper lining I had underneath. Knowing how Rachel packed I felt right away for a box deep in the middle of the suitcase and I squealed out when my fingers skidded on the surface. I worked the chocolate box out from between the cloth and stuffed one into my mouth and one in Ellie's. She selected a cookie carefully and pushed it in her pocket, watching me pull out my old biscuit tin from the wardrobe to squeeze everything in tight, chocolate and cookies together, never mind how they crushed.

"But they not fitting," she objected. "Cho! Make them stay in they own boxes."

"No. She might remember see something so in the bag," I explained. "Make the cubbitch old wretch come and find the tin empty. She will say I done eat them out. Watch where I putting our tin." She glanced away hopelessly. "What? You memory not worse, Ellie?"

"I have *no* head."

"Hush." I slid the drawer back in and placed the empty boxes back in the suitcase. "Missis, you are you own sweet self. Not one of them can touch you. Come. Make we walk."

She glanced about, first at Ivy's old TV spitting and snowing in front the chair. Then up. On the ceiling water marks rippled out and overlapped, dark and swollen near the corners. One corner had burst open already and a set of fat cables wormed out, with another tangle of small wires writhing between them.

"Dangerous," she objected. "Rachel would never have that."

So she was well glad to walk out. Only then she turned naturally to Ivy's room, the front bedroom that opened directly on the upstairs veranda.

"Imagine Ivy room come to be matron's office for Pansy, who is just a so-so gaoler," I grumbled, trying to figure out, yet again, how Scotty could have married her, only to feel my stomach dip sickeningly. The continuous disappointment in him echoed through me like a stone down a well, so I hurried on. "Then the facety tourist dem downstairs – they calling the veranda Sundowners' Porch."

"It always did have a magnificent view of the sunset," Ellie agreed, so I let it pass.

All the other bedrooms upstairs opened left of the dining room or right into the passage, but over the years the clutter had built up and I needed space to walk for I could never think sitting still. Now I had to fix my mind not to be greedy to hold onto her and . . . and I had to brace myself to send her back.

"I'll sweep out the office for you if you let me walk with her," I bargained with Pansy. She hesitated, watching me from her eye-corner with her mean calculating self. "How far you think I can get? You think I taking her out to feed you beast dawg?" I waved towards the broad, brown, stump-tailed dog lying against the fence beyond the downstairs entrance, rump pressed up to the heavy chain-link, and it glared back on me and its lip frilled, skinning the long yellow teeth, but it never moved another muscle. Up and down beyond it roamed this mawga black shadow on patrol, constantly stalking, stalking. Like it didn't even sleep. I don't know which seemed worse, the beast lying patiently in wait there or that restless demon self. The last one, the third, lock 'way on the other side, because she in pups.

Eventually Pansy shrugged and unlocked the gate to the downstairs porch. "Just walk her through. Don't sit around and make her chat and thing," she said, adding the usual warning. "The downstairs people can't take it."

At the foot of the stairs Ellie dug me with her elbow as one of Scotty's juiciest finds flounced past.

"They squeeze that one into the white uniform under pressure?" Ellie whispered loud and clear, staring after her, so I hurried into an update on the home.

"You know Scotty promote this place as lifelong holiday. You ever heard anything so wo'tless, Miss El? Watch the size of them TV. Satellite connection, missis, and you cannot imagine the slackness. Then they have Drama Club too, but we make poppyshow of it call it *Last Acts*."

"Nasty." But we tief a little guilty laugh and hug up. "Watch this side now how it change up. Ashmead quarters almost finish makeover. Wall knock out between rooms 8 and 9 so he use the side entrance through the corridor and never have to lay eye on any of us. Good-good hardwood floor tear up to put down tile. Truck come with furniture new bran'. Picture, ornament, stereo, phone, more phone, computer, camera. Then listen – " Is months I dying to tell her the whole scandalous business and at last I whisper, "Mirror on the ceiling over him bed."

"Story! You must tell Dan that one."

"I suppose they must moof arount." The woman with the bleached hair and cigarette holder flicked her eyes away from us and leaned confidentially to another one who should *never* have on shorts. "But I feel it so depressink."

"I c'n, like, tot'lly relate to that. And it's not whad we *paid* for."

I hurry Ellie away because right away she start to mimic exactly: "Not whad we *paid* for," punctuated by a resounding guffaw. "Haw!"

"Shh! Back here they fit in a salon . . ."

"'SILVER LININGS'," she read out.

". . . where Mitzy does their hair – the same lush one." I chuckled. "Is years ago you shoulda see her, when she first come. But she dressing just as scanty now she have more flesh to put out." Then I hugged Ellie fiercely. "I must be don't laugh since I see you last." But it eat into me, how they throw her over. "How they could send you *here*, Ellie? Wait." I grabbed at her when she slipped across the corridor and came to a stop in front of the vault door. "We not allowed here."

"But don't this was the pantry?" She loitered there stubbornly and flashed her brilliant grin, rattling the door handle. "You think it still have pimento dram?" Whatever else she forgot, that long storeroom against the back foundation of the house remained sharp in her mind. "It just comes back to me, Rummy, that earthy smell and the cool bottles tucked between those two roots bulging in. They were good for that at least – wedging the bottles."

But Pansy swoop down flapping like johncrow, and I think, *Eehi! Head red same way.* Her face puff up so her eye squeeze sly and irritable as she hustle us back to the steps.

"What you doing here? The guest complaining upstairs people disturbing them."

"Is loiter we loiter by the storeroom door why she bother with us," I muttered to Ellie. "Never mind. We will see the sunset better up here."

"We can't look in on Ivy?"

"This room is the office now. They deal with the accounts, passports, wills and everything."

Ellie looked troubled. "But government offices close at night."

From my room I pointed out through the bars at the kennels and the rooms for the handler Scotty like to call "Security".

"'K9 CORNER'." I read the faded sign for her. "And the old brute Jarvis is one dawg himself."

Her eyes caught a muddle of scraggy red ginger I had stopped seeing long-time, and roamed over the stained wall and ceiling, the scratched furniture and ancient TV. My room. It was the first I had really seen it for years.

"Ugly." I sighed in agreement. "Hear nuh, take care in that shower and don't look for any no-skid tile. Old man Simpson, who had this room before me, broke his hip."

"I know him?" Her eyes fixed on the mildewed walls and rusty bars at the window.

"No. Nor will you."

But she had stopped hearing me, just stared around. The state of the room paralysed her, and the need to get her out took me by the throat. When I grabbed her arm it shook her out of it.

"But what a desert," she snapped. "Then bedspread, vase, pictures. Lamp-shade. Nothing? I would help Ivy if she's strapped for cash again. What's a couple gallons of paint? I know, let's phone old man Jordan and tell him to touch it up. He'll be glad for the little work."

I stayed quiet and she picked it up.

"Old Jordan didn't die, did he?"

"Oh, years ago. But, but don't you see? You don't realize . . . what this is?"

"What *what* is?"

She patted a stray strand of my hair back in place and her fingers massaged my temples. The delight of being pampered confused with my disappointment in Rachel almost overcame me and I squeezed my eyes tight.

Her voice sank to a whisper. "Where hurts, darling?"

"My mind."

"Well, at least you have one." She put her head to one side to laugh me out of it. "Good for you!"

Then, out through the bars, she caught sight of the sundial and clapped her hands, so I pointed out the rest.

"Watch," I said. "They dig up the small lawn to the side of the house and build a pool for the stream to trickle in. Of course they miscalculate the slope and end up having to pipe in water. Remember they advertise 'Gourmet Fountain Water'? Same pipe. Some of the guests pose off in lounge chairs around the pool – no one goes in. Is cold where they put it, in the shadow of the house. One likkle ole man say he from Michigan an laugh at us when we tell him he wi ketch cold – he take himself in the pool early morning and by weekend, poor fellow, they bury him. Well, nobody swim after that, but they sit round it you know and take pictures to send back. After all, it advertise as 'Landscaped Tropical Gardens with Natural Pool and Falls'."

One set of raucous laughter break out suddenly from beneath the window, and drown me out.

"Dem say Scotty Cunningham neighbour cyan't keep even a female dankey," Byer announced.

"I don't even waalk pas' him cyar." Maynard gestured like she was on stage.

And the blank bewilderment on Ellie's face reminded me again not to accept this . . . this gift, don' mind how I long for it year in year out. I hardened myself to send her back, to find some way. I gathered her against me, her head on my shoulder and rocked her there.

"Listen, Ellie. You listening? I'm going to tell you something to say if Rachel calls. Something you *must* remember as you hear the phone ring. I going put something in your head to say."

"Can't keep anything in my head. You will have to talk to them."

"They won't let me talk. They will let you talk. You must say, *Take me home.*"

"But I am glad to visit you."

"You must say, *Take me home.*" I chant it and beat time.

"You'll come?"

"Say, *Take me home.* Sing."

"See my letter? Tied to my sash?" She held up a card on a ribbon, with Rachel's writing.

Dearest, we have just gone for a little holiday. Coming for you as soon as we get back from Canada.

"That's what they always say." But I was too furious to go on.

As we turned out of our room a slim woman in mauve slacks and a loose floral top stopped and stared at her.

"But don't I know you? Eleanor?"

"Remind me."

"Agnes," I prompted her.

"Bonny's Agnes?"

"Well, hardly," Agnes said sourly. "He never get around to it."

"Only because he was working himself to death to earn you," Ellie rapped back.

"I was a wage?" The justice of it silenced Ellie for a moment and Agnes raged. "I can never forgive him."

"Poor Bonny."

"Him and his stupid pride mash up both our lives. I hope he roast in hell!"

"No! Oh no. Poor Bonny." Even while I tugged Ellie away she wailed back at Agnes, "He idolized you."

But thank God whatever come to Agnes's mouth next drown out in the music blaring from downstairs.

"Mindless," Ellie grumbled. "Then is a party going on or what?"

"Always."

"Then I expect Rachel will soon come for us, for I don't think Dan can take all this buppity-buppity." She gazed around the porch, puzzled, and for the first time in years I thought of it as it had been in the old days, cool with ferns and begonias, flavoured by smells from the kitchen, stewed cashew or sweet potato pudding.

"What they all waiting for?" Her eyes searched the people sitting about. "Lantern slides? Like Valdez," she recalled, and leaned forward to a maid mopping a corner.

"Tell me something. What time is the show to start? Hello? My dear? Hi! My good woman! Ex*cuse* me."

Sybil broke in with her little gasping voice. "The bathroom's that way, Ellie."

And Ellie whirled round on this shrivelled-up woman who called her name. She studied the narrow skirt nobody that age would wear, and the polka-dot top built for one vast bosom, on this woman that look like she don't even have memory of bosom.

"That way," Sybil insisted. "The bathroom."

"Shall I help you get to it?" Ellie offered her hand gingerly.

"Well, sit down, dear." Sybil waved in the direction of a chair. But she went on frankly, "You need to be able to reach the bathroom though, you know."

But by now Ellie was fixed on the nurse. "Hard of hearing, eh? Good of them to give her the little work though." Then she smiled around at the rest. "What is it we're here for?"

Almost every face turned to this new bright voice. Only two stayed sameway, one like stone and the other one, Jocelyn, only straining, "Nnn! Nnnnn!" On and on, at the dress-sash tie down her wrist, her two hand pin to the chair handle.

"For?"

Ellie could never have recognized this dark thin man with the mouth pinched with disappointment in little lines, cut as if by a razor blade.

"What do you mean, 'for'?" His belt gathered the waist of his pants into ample folds and the end dangled before he lowered himself into a nearby chair.

"What are we going to do?"

"You tell us." He looked away, back in time. Sour as barge. "You're the ones who opted out of the original plan. Pity I can't tell the same tale."

"Aah." She pounced on it like a game. "Well, tell a tale then. Whoever is It."

Sybil perked up. "Yes, yes!"

Jocelyn swung her head but, under the blotches that had formed as her freckles spread and merged, her expression never changed. She only babbled loud and furious, and the man with the bitter face considered, then made a snap decision.

"*You're* It," he pronounced.

"Nope. Can't be," said Miss Ellie. "I have no head." When he stared at her she explained, "I forget things. I'll get it mixed up."

"I remember everything." He crashed his fist on the flat handle of the old Morris chair. Then he caught hold of himself and demanded, "You don't know where you are?"

"Yes, man. But, remind me of the occasion."

Fury took him over again.

"You are in hell."

She look around as if things were gloomy enough, but then shook her head. "Cho! Can't be."

"And why not?"

"Because hell is not for me. If I'm here, it can't be hell."

They digested that one for a while, and the old clergyman across the room nodded, satisfied.

Like a miracle, Cecil's face relaxed. "Ma'am, I beg your pardon." He leaned forward. "*Don't* you know me then, Miss Ellie? Really?"

"Remind me."

"Aah. I wondered why you wouldn't speak me. It's Cecil." He stretched his arm towards her.

"Happy to meet you." She kept his hand in hers, patting it gently, and studied his face. "You have a brother I know? A son?"

The lines tightened his face again, but the old days had come back for he pressed her hand speechlessly.

"She doesn't recognize me either now I've lost all the weight. I'm Sybil."

Ellie accepted graciously the brittle hand reached out to her.

"I knew a Sybil once," she said wistfully. "My dear good friend."

"Well. Why we don't really do that?" Sybil accepted the situation briskly. "Tell stories, I mean. It's a good enough plan. I can't talk for long though."

"Copasetic," murmured Archdeacon. "You're It, Cecil."

When I was a young man, I went to America to study medicine. The story had a firm place in her head from the old days, so Ellie gave it only one ear. Here, on the porch, if you sat on the ground, you could press your face against the wrought iron scrollwork and see the garden without the metal bars interrupting the view. *However well I performed, this doctor called me "Boy". Then the orderlies took it up.* "From my anchorage here" – Ellie rocked to and fro – "this green is the greenest green." *. . . was going home but the coloured cleaner said I was letting him down and he asked me why I didn't go into Pharmacy. And that was how I started out . . .*

"Or you can just cash a cheque, or sell a bit of jewellery." A voice rose up from the porch below. "They take care of it for you."

"Jewlree. Take care 'v it for youuu. Haw!"

"Shh!"

Ellie glanced back, but no one looked her way except the woman tied to the chair with the dress-sash, and if Ellie hadn't recognized Sybil she certainly couldn't know Jocelyn.

"Story!" she said in disbelief when I told her. "Jocelyn was no beauty, but she never carried herself like that. And tie up too? Then where's her room?"

That was a tale in itself.

"When the last new retiree, Thelma Chew, come to stay they just pick up Jocelyn throw her in with Eric over on our side of the house," I explained. "Pansy say is two diaper case, so keep them one place – man or woman they don't know the difference again anyway. So they put Thelma in Jocelyn old room, especially since her mind good and they don't have to tie her to prevent her climbing through the window, for that side don't have no bars."

"Bars!"

"What? Don't talk bout iron bar, missis. You don't see grille gate at the top and bottom of the front steps, outside the kitchen door, at the western door where Ivy had the kitchen garden, and at the entrance to the corridor from our porch? And now they rig up one at the top of the inside stair. Mercy, Father! Then, is crime, they say. Stupidness. Whoever hear bout crime inna country? Besides, they not trying to protect us, is jail they jailing us."

"Nnn. Nnnn."

"Nnnn," Ellie responded absently, peering between the wrought iron bars, and I knew what she searched for.

"Where's the lignum vitae tree, Dan? Hey, Dan!" Then she sighed. "Empty all the way to the edge and that is a sheer drop, you know, before it slopes away more gently – but I can't see the rooftops of the houses below from this angle – and there way beyond is the sea. Watch. It's all a huge bowl. Darkness flows into it, and look. Flames licking at the corner of the sky. Wait. Paper rustling? Ah, sensible! Tied right here to my belt. Aah, yes, I can sit and watch the sea for as long as I like till Rachel comes back."

"Get up sit on a chair." Byer swoop down on her. "Next thing they see you from downstairs sitting pon floor, and is unsightly. Get up."

"They can see through wood and tile? Stupidness. How they can see me from downstairs?"

"I say get up." Byer raise her hand, but I shove her aside ferociously.

"Don't rough her." I pulled Ellie up and we went in to the little space that remained of the dining room where we squeezed around table.

The others introduced themselves again, but Sybil and Cecil were like strangers still, and Jocelyn babbled so furiously I wonder if something really lingered somewhere in her head after all. But all these strangely old faces were new to Ellie, and nothing new could lodge in her mind.

"Though Canon Pearce I've known, or known of, for fifty years – looks much the same" – she smiled – "and possibly that baboon, Cockburn, is somewhere here by the sound of him."

"We're all that are left of the upstairs people," Hugh Pearce explained.

And what would have been left of Ellie if she had come here from the first, then lost Dan and lived on through this? I wondered. Then I thought back to our old misunderstanding about the move. After the first shock I had thought it was my mind. That it could have been hers never entered my head. In the end all that mattered was they hadn't just thrown me away.

Mechanically, Byer set down a bowl and spoon in front of Ellie.

"But where the soup?" She tilted the bowl and peered into it.

"No, not soup." I held back her hand as she made to push it away. "Why you don't eat?"

"Don't I waiting for the plate? How I must eat?"

"They mean you to eat from the bowl."

"Eat from bowl? With spoon? They crazy."

Gently I raised a spoon of rice and gravy to her mouth and she ate it in surprise. Then I put down the spoon.

"Pick it up."

She stared at me with wide eyes because my voice was sharp.

"Pick up that spoon," I repeated. Then I went on more gently. "You must be able to take care of yourself. Pick up the spoon. Helpless people don't last here."

"I'll call Old Dr Max."

"No family doctors allowed. You have to use the house doctor."

"Well, I require a knife and fork," she returned, "unless Petrona means to serve soup."

"Make a start, Ellie." Sybil's voice had been quiet when she was young and now it had turned thin like Sybil self, though roughened at times to an asthmatic rasp. "They're so quick to clear the table I can hardly chew the food in time. To avoid the heartburn I start right away and eat what I can slowly till they take it away."

"Well, I'll chew fast enough when I get a knife and fork."

"Pick up the spoon, Eleanor." I hardened my voice to metal. "Stop being troublesome."

She picked it up and flung it back down, but the fear of being a burden made her snatch it back. She swallowed the rice and pronounced coldly, "I shall be returning home. I'll call my daughter."

And I managed to nod approvingly, although it tore me apart.

Later, smiling secretively at her, I folded a napkin and slipped it into my bosom. But she had forgotten the chocolates and frowned, mystified.

After dinner, they agreed to tell another story.

"Thelma, you're It," Archdeacon pronounced.

Ellie studied the small trembling woman and nudged me. "She could be anybody's maiden aunt and she's shaking, but you know, she's much younger than the rest of us."

It turned out to be one long moralizing tale, and Ellie faced the garden again through the grillework, in time to see a peenie wallie drifting by, a point of erratic green light.

"Just so my mind evades attrition," she explained in a whisper. "Ah, Rummy, I remember this smell of angel's trumpet and this . . . symphony of whistling frogs and crickets. Still, one doesn't want to hurt people's feelings."

So then she turned back and dipped her head obediently as if listening, but really she had settled down to observe feet. I followed her eyes to the edge of the group. Despite her stylish trim and tasteful pastels, Agnes offered a mismatched pair, on one foot the second toe twisting over the big toe, and on the other the second toe twisted away.

"As if in alarm," Ellie remarked on the toe and knocked me with her elbow. "For a woman so carefully dressed, I wonder she didn't do anything about that."

No one but I knew what she was talking about, so it passed off as nonsense.

Only later, in my room, when I had propped the back of the chair under the handle of the door, I pulled the drawer entirely out of the wardrobe, prised out the biscuit tin and tumbled out some cookies and chocolates in my napkin then put everything back. We were just finishing when the door crashed open, toppling the chair.

Byer demanded, "Is where you get dat?"

Stuffing the last cookie in Ellie's mouth I held up the bright tin that had been resting on her suitcase and jeered, "Pity you come so late."

"And you couldn't save me one?" The woman slammed out then popped her head back around the door. "I almost forget say Miss Pansy tell me tomorrow consultation day so Duvall fe dress good."

Alarmed, Ellie called after her, "Consult with whom?"

"Lawyer," I said. "Don't tell him your business."

"That's easy." Ellie smirked. "I don't know my business. What? He's a sharper?"

"Crook," I confirmed. "They make you move money, property. Advise you on investment. Next thing you don't know where anything is."

"Call police."

"They not noticing all like us. Once you in a home, that's that."

"Do your hair. Put on your uniform," Ellie urged. "After they must listen to you if you command attention. What about *your* property, though? Is okay?"

"Ask Ivy nephew."

Early early next morning, while I lying there watching Ellie comb her hair with the same old vain tilting of her head to one side, a sweet-face little nurse knock the door to ask whether to sweep now or later.

"How you not in school?" Ellie protested. "What's your name?"

"Cheryl. I did go school at the shelter," the girl said, "but man come a night an rape some of de girls an I did fraid and run 'way. De priest try place me somewhere else but after him dead . . . You hear bout the priest dem shoot down? Me don't know, 'm. Bad dem bad. So I try me bes' an get a work."

"Poor little heart."

"I glad, 'm. Today is me first day. Mr Scotty bring me here las' evening."

No wonder Patsy put her to sweep upstairs.

"The poor pickney safer up here under my eye," I told Ellie.

The morning was bright and hot when Pansy poked her sweetie-sweetie smile around the door.

"Ingratiating." Ellie supplied the word briskly.

"Well. Don't we look pretty and smell sweet today, Miss Eleanor. I see you mean to charm Mr Stockwell?"

"I beg your pardon?" Ellie returned coldly.

"Mr Stockwell always ask me how my old ladies have such pretty legs."

"Well, you can tell your Mr Stockwell he's vulgar and he can go to France."

Pansy patted her arm nevertheless. "You calm down. He's a very brilliant man and we are fortunate he makes his hexpertise available to our clients."

"Remind me," Ellie said at the door, "for I keep forgetting. What's this place called now?"

"Last Resort!" I cackled – infectiously, for I heard her squawk on the other side of the door.

"Don't follow her," Pansy muttered to me. "She should just clear out of here. What she need to fit in is a rehab programme. That is what we need for all like her."

"Rehab," Ellie said. "What is *that* now? In our day when you wanted a clear-out you just took a purge – calomel at night and castor oil in the morning. Later a little salt physic to make sure, then they followed it up with tea to give you a boost. Tea with plenty condensed milk . . ." Her voice faded along the corridor.

In no time at all, though, she was back, hectored by Pansy at her shrillest.

"I done tell you Mr Stockwell is a lawyer."

"Maybe so. But what have I to say to him? Perhaps we'll talk it over when my husband arrives."

"You just vex because he called you Eleanor."

"He *what*? Good thing I never heard. Who the devil is he calling Eleanor – this little rancid boy."

"Stockwell is first class. You going be in good hands."

"I'm going to be in nobody's hands," Ellie retorted, then subsided suddenly with a grin. "More than enough of a handful from I was a child. Well. Let me just potter off with Rummy because I can see you have your hands full and I don't like to keep Dan waiting too long."

As we made our way to the porch, the tall preoccupied man who walked past us with the chair looked older than either of us, and Ellie asked whether he should be lifting such a weight. But he raised it easily enough over his head and smashed it through a window and when the nurses ran shouting to him he looked pleased.

"They might stop economizing on his pills now," I said. "I tell them till I tired. Let me see what them glass panes going cost."

The shower of glass reminded Ellie of the falls, for she said, "And what about Basil? 'You know what de riggle say bout falls, 'm?'"

"What?"

"Broke down Nanny go down hill an cyan come up again!"

"I miss the ole wo'tless myself," I admitted.

"Not dead though?"

"No. Just gone town. Occasionally he come back and look for us."

"Agnes," one of the nurses called, riveting Ellie's attention on the slim woman in the soft floral robe who paused before flicking her lighter to the cigarette.

"No one here by that name. I'm Miss Agnes," she told the nurse.

"Well, *Miss* Pansy want speak to you," Mitzy sneered.

"No interest in speaking to her. I don't get me likkle wine with me dinner almost a week now."

"Well, you know I would want you get it, but Miss Pansy say is you a share it round and when you wine money for the week done, that is that."

Agnes was the only one who had resources left, but these seemed fixed in small allocations for specific purposes. The arrangement was a mystery to the rest of us.

"Some of the money I paying for a decent room could use for the wine then."

"You must be sure an' tell Miss Pansy dat. She say come to the office."

"Tell her to kiss my arse."

Mitzy squealed out in delight and begged Agnes to tell Miss Pansy so in person. So I left them to it and settled Ellie on the porch where her attention fastened on one short stout man struggling to open a tin of salve. When she could bear it no more she snatched it from him and twisted off the top.

"For my joints" – Eric was always grateful for help – "only the joints won't let me get at it." He plastered it on with his awkward fumbling movements. "Used to take some pills but after a while . . ." Her eyes opened up in disbelief when he unfastened the top button of his trousers and tapped the telltale band of white plastic. "Mashed up my kidneys."

"Eric, close up you pants!" Byer's voice rang across the porch making everyone stare at the awkward little man, so he dropped his face, poor fellow, and she cackled, "Then you not so bold again? Big judge – don't you was a judge? I thought you wanted to show us *something*. But you have anything leave, Eric? I did think must be because you don't have nothing leave why you wife drop you here leave you."

Over the years Eric had turned so self-effacing I forgot whatever profession he had had. Now he squeezed together his legs and drew in his shoulders till they almost folded round his head. He just deflated in front of us, tears dripping from his chin. Byer sniggered away, slashing his last rag of dignity.

"You should be ashamed," Thelma managed to say, even this slim, timid-looking woman scandalized into rebellion.

"Nope!" Ellie butted in. "Should be shot!"

The woman in the dirty uniform returned one long vulgar suck-teeth and swaggered off, leaving Eric there shaking in the midst of us while we looked away so he could fade back mercifully from notice, but there was no silencing Ellie.

"Then what? Our mouths are not our own?"

Archdeacon Pearce's habitually gentle voice rose plaintively. "And shouldn't there be such a thing as elder rights?"

"Can't say." It was a raucous response. "Is a grey area." The speaker sprawled back on the threadbare armchair howling as the others eyed him sourly.

"Can only be Cockburn to bray so," Ellie muttered, and I let it pass.

Thelma unfolded one finger and lifted it as if for permission to speak. "You know I was CJ's secretary for thirty-one years. I saw something like that . . ." Her slightly slanted eyes narrowed reflectively.

"CJ was a fine lawyer," Ellie encouraged her. "You retired?"

"Just last year. The younger ones were complaining how Thelma Chew could get to stay on and fill up a senior position. He didn't notice them, but then when . . . he passed away . . ." The agitation set her head rolling, her two hands quivering, and she paused to catch herself. When she met my eye she objected, "Sometimes it's not as bad as this. Last year I could still type most of the time." She closed her eyes to remember. "And there was a folder, Archdeacon: *Intimidation, Molestation and Humiliation of Retired Persons and Institutionalized Elderly.* Another had material on Last Acts. Once, CJ took on a case on failure to fulfil caretaking obligations."

I watched her closely.

"You worked till *last* year? Thelma, you ever used a computer?" I asked.

"Of course!" The question seemed to shock Thelma. "I pride myself on keeping up to date. I spent every leave doing courses. Neither chick nor child and what would I do at home? It's because I was afraid to stay home by myself that I arranged to come straight here when I retired. I was saving for this for . . . oh, years."

"For this." Sybil gestured, her finger a twig shaken at the peeling varnish of the upstairs furniture.

"Well, I read the brochures, Miss Sybil. I went on the Net to compare it to life-shares elsewhere. I visited and as usual they showed me the downstairs rooms. I saved and saved." The tremor was in her voice now as Thelma glanced around defensively. "Well, you all came here of your own choice."

"Not me." Cecil's mouth twisted wryly. "My children treated me to this. Sold me off with my own money. Oh, I intended to come here at first, but when I got suspicious and refused they called me irrational, capricious – soon there was nowhere else to go." Especially as he was by now incurably sour.

"But hurt," Ellie rebuked me softly, reading my face as usual, "wounded beyond healing." How could she know, though? "It's written in his face," she went on, "line by line."

"Miss Pansy?" A voice raised near the back of the dining room. "You don't hear Basil want come back to work?"

Quiet fall one time, for Gladys always worth hearing.

"Basil don' want no work, Gladys, he looking place to live. Beg me if me can put him in the tool room till he can throw up a shack."

"But trough dem bulldoze him house just when him coming back to retire a country. Poor Basil. You not taking him back, Miss Pansy?"

"Make him rot a town."

"Then you did e-mail, Thelma?" I whispered.

"Naturally." The quivering fingers worried the scratched pearl buttons at her breast. "I'm very modern, you know."

"Then you must be understand . . . I can't follow the language."

Around me the others too groped tentatively towards one another, and is only then it hit me that over the years we had been talking less and less.

"And after all," Ellie argued, "if we don't talk to each other, who will?"

"My children don't bother talk to me," Cecil said with finality.

"Phone them till they do," she said.

"I'm not allowed near the phone."

"Insist."

"I used to," he said irritably. "I gave up."

"*No.*" That was Ellie self – loud and unruly at a hint of oppression. "Never give up."

Archdeacon nodded. "She's right, Cecil. And why shouldn't we be open with each other? Everyone else knows our business."

They leaned together and now it was a flood. I lost my footing as strange terms slid past. *Asset management and protection planning. Revocable living wills.* The conversation tumbled around us and the voices overlapped so I could hardly keep up.

"Mine has a clause about termination of life support that I'm worried about now."

"CJ mentioned a senior legal hotline in . . ."

"Well, the one who set it up for my brother in the States was from the National Academy of Elder Law Attorneys . . ."

"There was never a disclaimer, Hugh, but no one would let me phone . . ."

"But does yours actually state directives about end of life medical treat . . . ?"

"Once I was *in*, well the family home . . ."

I broke into the exchange. "Most of our papers store away right here under our feet." Silence fell. "You didn't know?"

"You *know* most of us will only go downstairs when they carry us out," said Cecil.

"Don't let them drive up your pressure, Cecil," Sybil said in her ragged voice and groped for her inhalant.

"The storeroom always had shelves, and the old card table before they refurbished it," I explained. "Now it has cabinets too. Files with documents. Paper and more paper."

"What type?" Thelma leaned forward, her hand demurely to the front of her blouse.

"Pensions, social security information for some of the downstairs people, but mainly insurance contracts, bonds, real estate deeds. I saw a metal pan with . . . I think, safety deposit keys. Safe installed against the wall on the side with the door, then shelves at each end. The other wall is too dusty but they still built a safe into it and the front is metal with a Yale lock, which makes no sense. Anyway, whatever is in the strongroom – that is the heart of everything going on."

Ellie searched her mind for such a room at Ivy's.

"Where?"

"The old pantry," I answered. "They have it like fortress now."

"Cho!" One thought displaced another. "Ignorance top of ignorance. Fool-fool boy."

"What else is down there?" Archdeacon probed. "Are there books?"

"Papers, film, equipment, jewellery. And the cash."

"Have you seen a stamp collection?" asked Cecil.

"Did you notice a painting?" Archdeacon wanted to know. "I wasn't here two months before it disappeared from my wall."

"I don't know. I never stay long."

"What made them let you in the storeroom at all?" Cecil demanded.

"I clean places they fraid to send the servant dem," I fired back. "See here, Cecil, I'm the one they have most control of. I'm *their* old aunt. No child of mine is coming to enquire after me."

"Wait. Stop," Ellie interrupted.

And Archdeacon agreed quietly. "Let's keep this . . . loving. Most of us here have only each other."

"But did you notice stamps?"

"No!" I said, utterly fed up. "No, Cecil, I never see into every drawer and crevice. Is clean I have to clean fast and leave. They hardly send me there." But I paused and dropped my voice. "There were the boxes of cash though. Boxes and boxes." I heard the van and signalled. *"There.* You hear the gate sliding again?"

But then other voices intervened.

"Miss Agnes?"

"Who calling me name?"

"Me Mitzy, 'm."

"What you have nice for me?"

"Nothing, 'm."

"Well, call me when you have something fe me. Wait. Help me here a minute."

"Miss Agnes, Mr Scott say if you need any cheque change, 'm."

"I say help me inside to the toilet."

"But Mr Scott . . ."

"I say help me inside now, mek me squeeze out likkle water!"

Thelma closed her eyes and the others looked far away, but Archdeacon urged in his practical way, "Do lend her a hand, Nurse. It seems terribly urgent."

The sound of an engine distracted us, even as Agnes scurried away uncomfortably.

"That's not the same Agnes who . . . ?"

But I signalled Ellie to be quiet, and darted over to squat at the gate to the steps, leaning to glimpse the porch beneath.

"Is another one," I said.

"With a box?" Cecil leaned forward taut as wire. "Cash?"

"Lord God, Cecil. You can see trough cyardboard? Because me cyan't see trough cyardboard. But, yes, I assume is the same thing."

The phone rang and Ellie sang out, "Rachel."

As she dived in the direction of the ringing, I called, "You can't reach it."

"But it's for me," she insisted, over her shoulder, heading towards the entrance to the corridor.

Then Maynard called, "Duvall!" But she blocked me when I tried to follow.

"Mrs Duvall," Ellie corrected her, and disappeared down the passage.

Afterwards she reported that Rachel asked all sorts of questions she couldn't answer. When was she coming? This was what I wanted to know.

"Soon," Ellie said, and I sighed.

"They all say that."

"I want us to go home," Ellie said decidedly. "I want them."

"But did you tell Rachel that? Did you tell her?" I pressed her, but she couldn't say. Instead she blurted an entirely different question.

"Where the children?"

"Which?"

"Well, for that matter, any children. What about that nice lad, Evan? A little boisterous but decent. Jolly. Long-time I don't see any children. Wait. Don't Pansy has a little girl?"

"She don't come *here*. And she's big – had twenty-first birthday, Lord, over a year now," I recalled. "I don't know when last I saw children up here."

"Dan will be disappointed," she said wistfully. "He's been asking about it."

"Downtown needs so much prayer." Thelma's closed eyes were like two almonds. "War there, Archdeacon. Rema and Tivoli. Gladys says you have to live behind bars." She tucked a strand vaguely into her French roll, trying to skewer it once and for all with a hairpin, but her hand trembled and I slid the pin for her.

"Well then, they have nothing on us," I grumbled. "Stop. You remember Basil?"

"What bout him?" Ellie asked eagerly.

"Where he was living garrison now. Is that why he want come back to country, but now Gladys say his little house bulldoze." Police, gunman – each one want to be badder than the next one."

To my surprise Ellie guffawed. "What the bee say to the light wire?"

"Mercy. You worse than two Basil. Tell us and done."

"Sting me sting but shack you shack!"

"You is Basil 'prentice."

She laughed with her whole body, head thrown back and arms flung wide, arching her spine and rocking from the hip. Even her foot tapped applause and it was this reckless zest that had drawn me in to begin with and I could not hold her there to see it snuffed out. For I was too familiar with this underside of institutions, the separation from the familiar, the dwindling stimulation and the eyes dulling till all the light in them went out. I had seen Ivy disintegrate in her own house when it became the home. Nothing I did could save Ivy, and Ellie too would fold into herself and never laugh again. Of course the condition meant it would happen, in time, wherever she was, but if she stayed at Cascade it would happen in no time at all. And I must watch it happen or give her up to buy back time for her. Time with Rachel.

Then it came to me.

What if I could force a crisis that could close the home? Would that buy time fo her? But then what about the rest of us?

At night I would think aloud to Ellie.

"Is like we get invisible, you know. Scotty and Pansy don't even notice me watching them. Listen." I leaned nearer to her. "Is like Scotty don't have a drop of Jesse blood in him. It wring my heart to say it, but is truth. Scotty like a animal with the whip cracking over his head. It look like he and this man Ashmead lock in some kind of financial agreement that have Scotty adoring him and frighten to death at the same time. Scotty mad fe money, and is that send him to Ashmead in the first place. Now Scotty he sends a monthly statement through the computer, but before he sends he *fixes* them. Every month Scotty changes up the accounts. I mean I see it all on the screen and he even prints it out. They think when you old you harmless, you know, so they don't hide from all like me. But this Ashmead is a *big* man and if he know how they siphon off the money one hell would pop, and all it need is for Massa to see the two set of account – the real one and the fix one."

"Crooks," she said softly. "Stay far from them."

I reassured her. "I not doing nothing stupid, because I don't know where it would end. Is just that I find out bout the double-cross and I hear Ashmead have *one* temper. Must be all that have him pressure so high. But is not me he going mad with." I paused at the thought of a man with blood pressure carrying on so, which led me to think of the rest of it. "You don't remember I tell you bout the mirror on the ceiling and bout the camera and all set up by him bed?"

"Story!"

"Anyway, Thelma say if she can just get in that office . . ."

Ellie settled on the bed, and from the back of my wardrobe I eased out a book that had come with her. I kept it for her use only, within the room, to avoid it going astray or being tossed out.

"*Palgrave's*! From I was a girl." She clapped her hands and snuggled back against the pillow with it, but she glanced up as I slipped to the door with the room key.

"Wait. You not locking me in?"

I didn't know what to say, and I could have kicked myself for letting her see the key.

"If I don't, and you wander into the wrong corner, they will take you from me and keep you lock up all the time. I can't tell you some of what go on – I can hardly think about it myself. Is just that I don't want take my eye off you. Shh! Is just for a little."

"So now, whom do I trust?"

It pierced me and I sat on the stool, having no answer. She laid aside the book and crawled onto the far side of the bed, drew her knees to her chin, and faced the wall.

"Dan will come for me. I don't need one of the rest of you."

"That's why I tell you to get out of here," I said, the words like blades in my own belly. "Tell Rachel pick you up fast."

She closed her eyes to fix her mind on them. "Rachel, Dan, Papa, Mama, Bonny. Bonny grew thinner," she recalled, "harried. He drove himself harder and harder while Agnes married the blasted fortune hunter who insulted and battered her. I never heard how *he* died. People say Agnes lives at Ivy's now, but I wouldn't know."

When she was quiet I came and went, but when I spoke to her she refused to answer me. However, she talked her situation over with herself.

"I can get along on my own. I have my own property, my own account, my own ballot. I have fingers to dial for a cab and I have my cheque book."

After a while, though, when she had ignored me moving in and out for long enough and the empty room had become boring, she must have got up, and the door I had forgotten to lock after all opened easily.

The porch gate always seems closed but in fact it swings out at a touch once they forget to lock it. Through the window of the kitchen, which was upstairs as it had always been, the yard was busy. A burly man with a hoop in his ear clenched his teeth on a spanner and shifted a bedspring swung over his head. An air-conditioning unit and a chest of drawers were moving too. Some of the foreign guests seemed pleasant enough but would pass most of us from upstairs without a look. Who would notice Ellie? Farther out was empty. All the activity concentrated near the house.

As I defrosted the fridge I glimpsed her from the kitchen window upstairs when she had already wandered to the back and unlatched the inner gate that opened a few feet from the house into the fenced area alongside the road. She was in easy earshot, but before I could call I caught a low rumble as the dog raised his head.

"I wonder if you are Rachel's," she sang out. "One stray after the other and she feeds it till it's fat. You can't have been with her for long."

The lean legs strained taut as it advanced slowly, one paw silently before the other, eye fixed on her. My mouth dried, and the danger of startling the animal struck me dumb.

"Good morning," she cried brightly. "What's your name?"

It grumbled a response and she stooped, offering her face right up to the brute's mouth.

"I'm Rachel's mom. Come. Good boy. Sit now." The dog crouched and she shook her head. "You really not such an attractive fellow," she said. "I suppose you don't get much attention." She sank down on a broad root that coiled out some distance from the ficus and settled with the dog at her feet, its head in her lap, thrown back and grinning adoringly in her face. "But, poor fellow, they must feed you better. Watch how you mawga." She ran her fingers along the thin, black legs and gaunt brown chest and terrible mutilated ears. "I'm so sorry," she mourned, stroking him. "Who could have done this to you?"

When he reached forward and licked her chin, though, that was that.

"A bit much, if you know what I mean," she said.

I saw her get up, but thinking her safe after all I was only too glad she had found that much freedom. In truth I was tired too, tired from worrying about what was to happen to her. She must have decided to continue her walk farther afield. She must have closed the pedestrian gate in the outside fence, maybe just to protect the dog from being knocked down.

"You've had your share of trouble in the world," I heard her call, but I didn't look out.

It never enter me head that she take me at my word about leaving the home, and that she pick up her handbag and set off down the road to hail cab.

ELEVEN

Shatter

ONE HARD ROAD fe old woman to walk. What all like her doing alone pon street?

Is what? Is not the same house dem call me to for the job and me can't get in? And watch the beast dawg awalk longside her pon the inside of the fence.

"Aah." Me think she see me but is talk she a talk to herself. "Same road from all the holiday with Miss Ivy. Steep but lush, even among the rocks." She spread out her two hand like she want hug up the road. Then she stoop down and pull out one plant, tell it it belong in Ivy rock garden.

When me ease out in the road de maaga dawg growl and I duck back in the bush. But she look up and wave.

"My friend." An it start to whimper like it see it mumma. "What ho, Gawain!"

Down where rock slide and pile up by the roadside she collect more plant, but then she rest her hand pon her headback and watch the sun, say, "You decide to come out in power, eh? My old jippy-jappa hat is what I need, but that was when I small."

One langula man, a walk up the road, stop. And him stand up watch her good, then start laugh.

"You taking exercise, Miss Ellie. After I hear you did gaan 'way."

"Well, if you know me, you know I can't stand one place."

But me feel say she no recognize him right 'way.

"What make cow walk over hill, m'am?"

She dive forward and grab him hand. "Tell me, Basil."

"'Cause him cyan't waalk under it." Him laugh again and raise him ole hat to her. "Later, 'm."

Almost alongside me she stop again and reach for one orchid plant break off and hanging by vine.

"I sure you going catch." But she hand so full up she look for a shade to ketch herself, and is then she see me.

Well, she study me so good me say she must know me if she see me again, and that mean she have fe dead.

"Cruelly thin." She bend her head and wrap her hand round her body and rock, like it hurt her. Then she watch me again and tell me, "You have the loneliest face I ever saw." She stare at the gold in me eyelid like is too much to understand and she sink down on the tree stump. And she don't fraid me at all. True is a cotton tree on the corner, I say, take care she a duppy.

"I wish you would remind me of your name," she say. Polite, like she a talk to doctor. "And don't vex if I even ask again. My head not with me."

Is then I see how it go and I could relax, for me prefer not fe kill old woman if me can help it. "You nah remember ting good?" I check.

She say no, say she no mean to rude but nothing stay in her head. So me decide fe test it, but me feel better.

"Long-time me nah tell nobady me name." It make me look back over the years and de people I blow away and . . . and some I did care bout.

"But we mus' call you something, man."

"Aright, Mumma. Call me Shatter."

"Shatter?"

"Eehi."

"You live round here, Mr Shatter?"

"Fe now." Me point out me box and the brown bag dem under the hedge.

"Story!"

She hand drop in she pocket and come up with two mint. She give me one rightway. She bite the other one in two, wrap half and drop in she pocket and suck the other one, smiling like pickney.

"Then whe' you family, friend?" She lean forward like she know me. "Don't think me meddlesome, but you should build youself up, man. What about sports? They don't play football in school again? Tell me something, because I think I've been away – they still have Manning Cup?"

And so we talk. True, me no always understand what she say and I don't know how much she follow me but I find meself . . . a talk bout life on me own as a pickney and how I stop school after I steal the toilet from the schoolhouse. Me no know how me end up tell the ole woman me whole life.

"Me madda say talking no good, beating no good – even the murderation she give me with the bust-up bicycle tyre no do nothing. She leave for New York and send back money for a while – "

She stop me. "Then what about you grandmother? Some children . . ."

"True Grannie a good to me what make me soft to old people. Grannie sell soup on the street corner while the boy them play domino in the reggae rhythm and drink Dragon. When me call out to the nice woman them parade past in the batty rider shorts, the Grannie vex; but the men tell her say is good me not no antyman and so me get bold, breed the little twelve-year-old girl who auntie run the beauty parlour, make the Grannie throw me out the house. But she take me back. She did always take me back, and is only that she dead why me end up pon street."

"But you don't mean literally on the street? Not even an aunt?" She look round. "Well, the whole area higgledy-piggledy for true. Watch the rubbish – box juice carton and soak-up brown paper bag scatter all around. But how he could keep the place so sloven? Perhaps nobody teach him." She sigh and look back at me. "Listen, man. People won't want you in their place if you going keep it so. Make them see you are a decent lad so you can get a work. You try get work?"

"The big man did take me in and me begin to make money till ACID pass through the area like fire and mash up the life."

"What name ACID?"

"Is one type of Babylon. Police – "

She cut in again. "Well, even I know Babylon is police."

"Same time me did like a girl but she did cut-eye all the man them till them hold her an battery her. Police threaten to drape them, but the man dem tell Babylon say the girl beg dem fe the agony and the police say it must true because look look how the youth dem call her Mattress. But in truth the girl get the name after the battery.

"Like I sorry for her at first then we get . . . anyway we stay together for a year or more. When she time come and she collapse me couldn't get her to KPH no car wouldn' stop and me put one smooth stone under her head on the sidewalk and run looking help to get her to hospital, but the babymada dead right there pon ground.

"After dat me was like village ram and now me have de sickness."

Me see the old woman lost, and me realize one time all like she nah understand bout no rudeness and she no know bout the sickness. But like she sense something . . . big.

"I can't imagine." She moan and put out her hand, but me no let nobady touch me and me flinch way. "Your eyes," she say. "They swallow up you face. You look . . . hunted. I can't imagine." She close her eyes. Then she go on like she a search for word in the dark. "But whatever it is, you . . . you young. That's what I always tell Rachel. Your whole life ahead of you."

Dat burn me like fire make me tell her say, "After me nah have as much time as you." But then I drop that for I never watch down dat road and me nah go start now, and when I look pon her is remember I remember me grannie, make me talk decent. "Watch." I point back the way she come. "You from the madhouse with the heap of bad dawg dem?"

"No! I . . . I think I'm staying with friends up that way," and she point same place.

"It have one Ashmead live there?"

"I know that name, but whether he's a guest now . . . Is best you ask Miss Ivy, because I don't want mislead you."

"Then you no know who live wid you?"

"Names," she begin like she in pain, so me stop her.

"Is so me grannie did stay. Don' mind." I stretch out the neck of me vest and blow soft on the old sore. De clinic did give one medicine after the nex, and I use all-heal and drink ashes-water, but it always come back and it did big an hot when she catch sight of it. If me wasn't watching her good me coulda never believe me eye.

"Is cry you a cry? Fe *me?*"

"My sister-in-law is a nurse." She stop fe wipe her eye with her dress-collar. "Ask for Matron Cunningham."

"Cunningham?" Is that name I hear along with Ashmead.

"She will clean and dress that. I would try but I have nothing here." She spread her two hand and say how she sorry, but now me mind occupy with the job.

"Is Ashmead I looking. Hear say him might have a work fe me."

She sigh. "I might know him when I see him and I would like to see you in a good job. I don't mind passing on a message for you, but it would have to write down. You know your name just slip out my head again?"

"Shatter, dem call me. Look ya." Me pull the pencil from behind me ear and write it on the sweetie wrapper. "Give Ashmead dat."

"Bless you. Well, I hope you catch up with your people. I going just take my walk."

"Seen. Go in peace, Grannie." Is after she turn away it come to me and I call after her, "Respec'."

"Walk good." She hand raise like is bless she a bless me and she set her foot well strong on the rough road a wind down the hillside like snake.

One more time she stop fe tear out fern from on the roadside and wipe her hand on paper from her bosom.

"Rummy must be put this there, for I never do that. So at least she's near at hand, and I suppose Dan can't be far."

I duck back inna bush when one car round the bend and pull up next to her. And the brown man a drive it stare pon her like him did want fe lick her down.

"Mas' Scotty," she greet him, not too warm.

Him fling open the door and she climb in. But like she not so happy.

"I could wait for Rachel," she tell him. "You sure you have time to give me a lift?"

Him no answer, just a press him foot down on the gas and the car roar up the hill.

But I see how him did watch her face and I think, *Grannie, you woulda more safer with me.*

TWELVE

Archdeacon

AFTER SEARCHING THE premises for Eleanor Duvall we were astounded to see her arrive in Scott Cunningham's car. Jarvis held back the dog, which she addressed warmly as her friend, and Pansy Cunningham hustled her upstairs. There followed an altercation between husband and wife on the usual subject of who was to blame, laced with some of the most profane language I have ever encountered.

"Stop it!" Mrs Duvall shouted. And so they did, staring at her in astonishment. "Are you out of your minds? How can you abuse your mouths with such filth?"

Cunningham lowered his face an inch from hers and hissed, "Old woman, close your arse."

The poor lady's legs simply gave way, whether from shock or exhaustion I cannot say, and she sank onto the chair I was able to slide beneath her. I reached across for her hand although the joints of my own fingers were swollen and painful.

"He's such a hog," I said, comforting her as best I could, "but never mind. At least you were fortunate enough not to have met the dogs." As if on cue the more vicious of the two, a particularly vile Doberman, stalked alongside the lawn, patrolling the fence with his eyes fixed on something moving on the other side.

The other lurched silently over to join the first, sniffing the edge of the fence. "Demons," I whispered. "My dear, you are so, so fortunate. So much to give thanks for."

Rosemarie rushed up from the garden and I waved her over.

"I was searching the yard," she gasped.

"AWOL," I confirmed admiringly. "I had been combing upstairs myself."

"Is that why I tie Jocelyn," Pansy Cunningham muttered. "But all like this one going drop break her hip and bring down trouble on us. And then her *mouth*. I know how she stay from long-time, with all her high-fluting way of talk."

"A wicked set!"

"Who, Miss Agnes?" Mitzy egged her on.

Agnes ignored Mitzy but eyed Pansy narrowly, sidelong, and said, "The whole of them who clear out with the ice cream my money pay for and dem done it out. Jesus? You hearing me? Is Bombay mango ice cream and me never see a spoon of it."

"Miss Agnes, you well get ice cream for dessert."

"Not the Bombay mango dem send Basil for with my own money. All you eat it out. You is a dutty set. Anyhow, stand out of my way make me pass. I say move make me reach the toilet." The corridor from the porch had a bathroom at the far end, just at the top of the inner staircase, and Agnes scurried towards it.

"But she was elegant, in the old days." Mrs Duvall took up for Agnes as best she could. "A bit flighty, but refined enough. Her values were not ours, but, still, they ought not deprive anyone of . . ." As she reflected on what she knew of Agnes, Eleanor Duvall's voice drifted away and she squeezed her eyes closed as if in pain.

In minutes though she opened her eyes and observed me brightly. "You look just like Canon Pearce, but older. Only last night Dan and I were agreeing on what a fine man Pearce is, and what a scholar." She smiled when I thanked her, and continued after a while. "You remind me of my own Canon too, Canon Wortley. You knew him?"

"I wish I had, Mrs Duvall. A saint, they said."

"Mm. Such big ears. Do call me Ellie. Was a sin to think of his ears during the prayers, but I couldn't help it. What a way we loved him though." When she walked towards the altar, she said, the eagle on whose wings the Bible rested glanced sideways at her rather sharply, but she didn't mind because the light streamed in through pointed archways from which doors, flung open, swept upwards too like wings on each side, and in the stained glass above the altar Jesus raised his hands and seemed to dance in a robe of swirling red. "When the bishop walked up the aisle his hat mirrored all the other pointed arches in the church and his staff flashed in the light and the procession was so solemn I felt myself carried forward, towards the altar. But on ordinary days with Canon Wortley, I relaxed with the bright, winged doorways and Jesus dancing."

Even then, she said, Tuesdays were the difficult days and, when she grew up, the hardest Tuesday was still, always, Miss Minnie's. Now even when she and Dan were married, Miss Ellie said, she could hardly abandon Mama to face it on her own. So quiet, so mournful. There was so little said on those visits that she would yearn for her childhood when conscience would not have prevented her from signalling, whispering and at last openly higueing Mama to leave.

One Tuesday Miss Minnie moaned, "Is three years today since Tita die. I never hear from the boy. Her own grandson and he could be alive or dead. I don't know how he turn out. Or what he turn into."

Then, in the midst of these disclosures on the porch, a newscast from the radio just inside the door shattered the evening, startling Miss Ellie from her sleepy recollections.

"... set o' gunman that bomb Denham Town police station?" a woman bawled, cutting across our talk.

"What?" I asked, but no one answered.

Instead Mitzy called out, "Hear them! Is from inside the hospital." And they turned up the volume.

A woman's voice blared over the radio, "... pure gunshat. People just a dead everywhere!"

"Then tell us what it is, nuh?" Miss Ellie shouted.

"Quiet!" Pansy had no interest in the news, just in maintaining an idyllic atmosphere for her downstairs guests.

"Shoot-out, Miss Ellie," Basil responded quietly from just below the wrought iron grillework. "Trouble a town."

Now a radio announcer took over. "Security forces deployed . . . virtual siege . . . bodies decomposing in the road."

"Dem say blood bank out of blood. Den we no can sell?" Mitzy said as she admired her own glamorous hairstyle in a mirror over Ivy's buffet, and writhed complacently in the tightest of tight skirts.

"Sell blood?" Miss Ellie pondered aloud.

Mitzy lowered her voice conspiratorially. "Or what bout we drain the Pansy and sell her owns?" She giggled and drew an answering maniacal shriek from Byer.

Pansy Cunningham issued from the office that had been Ivy's room, casting a quick, suspicious glance at them, but then a quieter, full-bodied woman arrived at the top of the steps to the porch, clicking in the gate behind her, and I greeted her eagerly.

"Gladys!" I said. "How did you get here? What a time you chose for your holiday! Your family in Papine all right? You couldn't have got any rest."

"Res'? What dat? When me last sleep, Archdeacon, I can't tell you. Bullet a rain – blam blam! Me 'queeze under the divan. Yes, sah. Gunshat. 'Queeze me have fe 'queeze. Blam blam round me I smell de gunpowder inna de room. Me sister sewing machine and all the dress heng up to deliver – everyting shoot up, sah.

"Bad boy who take ride up to Papine put on soldier suit and running wi' big gun. Shatter-dem say is send the big man send fe them. Bad bwoy boast how woman and pickney in front them, so security in town couldn't fire back pon the youth but some security don't care so one or two get hit. One bellywoman take a bullet in she neck and the rest of them drag her 'way inna handcart. When the big man see im *have* fe move, him give de order. Everyting fe move. Pickney with paint pan running alongside him a carry bullet an all dem ting.

"True I was to come back to work two day now but I send tell Miss Pansy barricade burning in de road. She no believe me."

She fixed Pansy Cunningham with a smouldering eye and demanded, "Why you no believe me, m'am? Me come to work in rain and flood and when me well sick. And you no believe me?"

"Is my information," her employer said stiffly, "that people calling in sick all over the country and getting money to stay in town and raise barricade. As fast as police clear one part they block up another. So they get two salary."

"And after I work here years, 'm? Quiet, never raise me voice let alone me hand to nobody? And you take me for ole hooligan? But a what dis, Jesus?"

"Viv, calm down, darling," Miss Ellie urged.

"No noise out here!" Pansy Cunningham, her eyes darting to and from Gladys, looked cowed.

"What noise you hear beside you own voice, Miss Pansy? Is what you really expec' from me? Oh Master, to this day people like you think all black people a ragamuffin. You could take out the likkle money from me pay for the two day, m'am, if needs be." She swung towards us. "Archdeacon, all like you I care what you think. See me dress did hang up in me sister house, sah. See de bullet hole ya? A-oh."

I stretched out my hand to steady hers, which was shaking. "Gladys, we thank God you're safe."

"Archdeacon, all like you Jesus will pour down him blessing pon. I cyan't speak fe all." And she swept away without a further glance at Pansy. "Brimstone stack up aplenty too."

The Cunningham woman charged downstairs, clanging in the wrought iron gate behind her and muttering, "I wish I could burn down this whole top floor."

"And that is what it is now? That is town?" Miss Ellie ignored Management as usual, leaning towards Rosemarie, her hand to her heart as if to stop its pounding. "That is what we have to go home to?"

"No," Rosemarie assured her. "Is just right now, and certain areas. Don' mind! Every country have dem bad spot. Most of the places you know in Kingston quiet. We here in the hills peaceful."

"But trouble is all we hearing about," Miss Ellie protested.

"Well, is news. People living civilized – most people – that not news," Rosemarie explained hurriedly, then signalled Miss Ellie to wait and slipped away.

"Some only pretend to be civilized though," Cecil remarked, "and they cash in on the madness."

"Speaking of cash," I mused.

"We don't know anything . . . about *that* cash," rasped Sybil. "Whose is it?"

Our nervousness communicated to Miss Ellie and she whispered, "What's this now, a secret? Why it sound so suspicious?"

"Because it makes no sense," Cecil said, and she nodded.

"But I still think we should cash our cheques," I reflected the next night when, inevitably, the topic came up again. "We have nowhere to spend cheques and no access to a bank. The cash is some security for an emergency."

"Which makes it odd they should allow us cash, doesn't it?" Thelma put in diffidently. "What's wrong with it, why they don't want it? We have nowhere to spend anything anyway."

"That's how the monkey jumps," I agreed. "But let's have what is ours in whatever form we can."

We went round in circles, as we always did eventually when we discussed the flow of cash. Provided you wore it on your body all the time, Cecil said, the cash could keep and be spent anywhere. But while you kept cash you lost interest, Sybil insisted. Though where was the interest going otherwise? Did we know anything about our accounts any more?

"Oh Father!"

We all turned to a strangled cry from Miss Ellie.

"But look at this, in all this anxiety about finances, I've come out without a thing in my hand. Purse, cheque book, nothing."

Rosemarie stepped back from the office to the porch and someone slammed the door behind her.

"Rachel is paying good money," she retorted to the closed door.

"For the mother to *stay*, not for twenty-four-hour nursing. We don't have no money or space fe dat." That was Pansy Cunningham's voice.

Miss Ellie hurried towards Rosemarie. "I'm in *one* fix," she whispered urgently.

"Good thing you realize it," Rosemarie returned tartly.

"I've come out without my purse."

"Oh Saviour!"

"I sorry, Rummy," she wailed. "Is my head. Now I don't have a quattie on me to buy one thing."

Rosemarie calmed her, grooming a stray wisp of hair back from her sister-in-law's face. "Your purse in the room."

"What room?" Miss Ellie gripped her hand in alarm.

"Ours. Remember you're staying with me."

"Aah. So now . . ." Miss Ellie's eyes roamed the bare walls. "What we doing? How do we spend the evening? But stop! Then where the books?"

She must have seen me from the corner of her eye, for she held out her hand and I reached for it gratefully. She searched my face.

"What is this desolation?"

"It's just that they took my books," I confided. "They said they were making my room into a double and they needed the space. I had come here on the understanding I would have my books."

The enormity of it silenced her. No one had grasped it before so completely. She repeated, "They took your books. Who would do that?" And her eyes raked the corners for these philistines.

"They took it all! When they swept everything off . . . The shelf had the Bible my father gave me when I was confirmed. Then they said I could use the Good News in the passageway." I realized suddenly I was crushing her fingers. "I'm sorry." I released them.

"Least I can do."

I leaned back on the mildewed cushion covers. "Without the poetry it is hard to relate . . ." I broke off into confession. "I hardly read now."

"Shh! It's in your head though." Her eyes gazed far into the past. "Look at all the poetry in me and I have *no* head." She found a psalm, drawing me in with her, and soon we were all quoting lustily, rising to a crescendo.

"Hush!" snapped Maynard, a tank-shaped woman in dull white who had come to wheel in Jocelyn.

In the shocked silence we returned to ourselves.

"Then they talk to us like hogs, eh?" Miss Ellie conferred. "No background. . . except . . ." She glanced at Maynard's retreating figure and snickered infectiously.

"Imposing," I confirmed delicately.

"Hush!" She parodied them. "*Hushhh!*"

Pansy flung the office door open again just as Maynard turned back and glowered at us.

"Is what you making so much noise for?" Maynard demanded. "You goin' annoy the people downstairs."

"Blast the people downstairs!" Miss Ellie erupted. "Then there's to be no more free speech? Go to a warm place!"

"You see, Miss Pansy?" said Maynard. "Don't a tell you what a terror this old woman is? Is she stirring them up. She same one start it!"

If Miss Ellie was frightened it did not show, and perhaps she had forgotten what it was about in any case, though she stared daggers back at them.

When the office door closed once more behind Pansy and Maynard had rolled Jocelyn away, Miss Ellie crouched forward to Cecil, whose face, unfortunately, had turned (over the years) sour enough to curdle cream.

"I did something to cause trouble?"

And to my amazement Cecil's face sweetened uncertainly – almost as if he was just remembering how to smile.

"What I did?" she insisted.

"All that you should, Miss Ellie." He got up, took her hand and bent till his lips almost touched the tips of her fingers. Then he straightened up to his old businesslike posture and moved towards the office.

"I'd like to make a phone call, please," he said, rapping on the door. "I shall apprize my children of my continued existence, welcome or unwelcome though the news may be. If you prefer, you can unlock the phone in the corridor."

"Be *pleasant*, Cecil," Rosemarie advised.

"Copasetic!" I settled back amid the upheaval with closed eyes to concentrate on my reading.

It was true that the Cunninghams were at core inept, intrinsically cowardly and, so, ultimately helpless before Miss Ellie's instinctive and uninhibited joyfulness. By teatime Basil struggled upstairs with a burden too heavy for a man his age. He set down a pot of ferns where some fronds could tumble through the rails and off the porch but arranged it so that most would spill forward between our chairs.

"What's the use of putting that up here?" Pansy Cunningham demanded. "After nobody going see it?"

But Basil set his mouth stubbornly and trundled downstairs leaving it in place while his employer stared impotently.

The problem, however, was that the Cunninghams had backing.

It was perhaps appropriate then that, that evening when it was my turn, I had a story to tell about the home's benefactor. I had pieced it together from all the nurses' gossip and what I had overheard from the Cunninghams themselves, for they spoke carelessly in front of us, our connections with the outside world being broken, and especially as we were supposedly falling apart anyway in mind as well as in body. So I had this fragmentary account of Ashmead to pass on.

They say Ashmead began with nothing, as a boy, right in Kingston. The child was battered, and just about when the war ended he ran away. He made his way over to the States by ship, hiding in a crate, and lived on the street. Now here the versions diverge but, whether or not he went to jail, he did meet an old man – Jewish, they say – who turned his life around. I can't work out whether this was in New York or Chicago but he married this man's daughter, who was frail apparently for she ended up in a wheelchair – I don't know, polio perhaps. The father left her well provided for and they must have invested well, from the sound of things.

I confess I've heard nothing about either of them to stir my admiration apart from the persistence and competence it must have taken for him to rise out of his distress. Certainly the Love Nes' suggests room for much improvement in his personal life, especially since his wife is very much alive somewhere to my understanding. He's never brought her here so to my way of thinking she must be confined to Kingston, perhaps by her disability. Whatever his personal morals, mind you, if the Cunninghams are to believed (and that is always a moot point) the Ashmeads are in a position to do substantial good – except that what I've heard tittered over were just elaborate parties, thrown to entertain *the best people.* But Pansy Cunningham loves to drop names, so this is just what is important to her. I really can't say more for *he's* never been upstairs, though he spends a few days downstairs from time to time. He's charming, they say, and of course we know him to be benevolent.

My question to Rosemarie is the same as it has always been: what would a man like that have to do with Scott and Pansy Cunningham? On their side, of course, the reaction is hysterical. As Sybil says, Scott is in jitters over every visit, while Pansy is ecstatic.

"No problem with even a little anky-panky sometimes." It was one of Sybil's good days and she mimicked Pansy Cunningham's giggle. "He deserve to get away from it *h*all now and again." The giggle dissipated in Sybil's wheezing.

"In fact," I confirmed, "Mrs Cunningham proposes that he should 'chrow a little party' right here on one of his visits, *h*as lavish as he like."

Mine is a tale with no end. So far Ashmead has made short visits and closeted himself with Cunningham, although downstairs work is almost complete on a full apartment and a number of guests have been displaced. I've never actually laid eyes on him.

"But what could Scott possibly have to offer him but a room out of sight of his wife?" I demanded once more.

"The Love Nes'," Cecil affirmed. "A 'home' away from home."

"And as far away as possible," Sybil chuckled hoarsely.

"There must be more to it," Thelma muttered. But she would hazard no further guess and as the subject accentuated her trembling we did not press her.

In any case Miss Ellie was up and wandering along the corridor, so in view of her perambulations earlier that day I took the liberty of keeping her in sight. She tapped politely then turned handles. The first door she tried was that of Jocelyn, the quarrelsome woman they kept tied to her chair handles. The same room contained a shy broken man (the Right Honourable Eric Marsh he was once) who had been speechless for the past week and now lay all day on his bed in a diaper, so it was not surprising Miss Ellie closed the door at once.

A voice intervened. "Miss Agnes, where you going?"

So Miss Ellie stepped aside, but Agnes paused, holding her shoes carefully at eye level.

"What business it is of yours?" she retorted.

"Miss Agnes," Gladys coaxed.

"Gladys, just move de rubbige out me way make me walk. I don't want no broken glass in me foot-bottom."

"Come this way, m'am."

"Don't pull me. Leggo! Cruel! Jesus, they trying to trow me down!" She planted her feet with the twisted toes stubbornly apart.

"No, darling," Miss Ellie protested. "Viv was being gentle, I saw her."

But Rosemarie intervened more firmly. "Never mind. I going move the rubbish."

A few sweeping movements on the clear floor around her feet and Rosemarie looked up. "See? No glass left."

"Thank you, Miss Rosemarie. Thank you." The ferocious Agnes leaned forward and kissed her. "Praise the Lord!" She made her way along firmly, still barefoot, with a scornful look at Eleanor Duvall and holding the shoes above her head. "Praise the Lord I can walk in safety now."

I lost sight of Miss Ellie around the corner and followed slowly, my ankles being quite swollen, but it seems that at the next door, the bathroom at last, she knocked scrupulously but without response. When she pushed it ajar, to her confusion there was Scott Cunningham just inside the door trying to push himself up on a girl, almost a child, against the bathroom wall, and I rounded the corner just as he yanked at the door to shut them in, but the girl struggled into the doorway and he snatched back her arm.

"Mr Scott! Please, Mr Scott, to let me go. Miss Pansy will kill me, sah. I will loss de wo'k."

"Is me bring you here and you no like me? Cheryl, you know you like me why you come."

"Me come fe the wo'k, sah." Cheryl apparently pulled free but he closed the door before she could get out, and that was when Ellie flung herself on it and beat on the flimsy wood with her fist.

"Open the door," she screamed. "Open it this instant."

"Get away," he barked from inside.

Ellie raised her voice and yelled with all her lungs, "Pansy. Rosemarie. Dan. Oh Jesu. Come and stop this terrible thing!"

As Rosemarie ran up, the door opened and Cunningham pitched out the terrified little girl, who bolted away, and he came out into the passage, to Ellie's horror, still zipping up his trousers.

Pansy burst into the corridor, panting from the stairs, and before she could speak he bellowed, "This ole woman only molesting people. She try to burst in on me in the toilet now. But who really watching her?"

"You see?" Pansy turned on Rosemarie. "Is exactly what I was telling you. She need something to keep her quiet."

Rosemarie hurried Ellie back to the porch, whispering, "You couldn' do otherwise just now. But as a whole you have to keep quieter. Hear nah: you think everybody who land up here can just stay alive on they own? Is keep they have fe keep them going. All the people in charge have to do is let go. Once or twice it happen that someone turn out to be a nuisance. And . . . was like a purge."

"So in the old days don't everyone took a little clean-out regularly?" Ellie shrugged. "And nowadays medicine not so bitter. I mean, you're a big woman, Rosemarie. Behave yourself."

But Rosemarie turned away in frustration, and since the Cunninghams were by then safely engaged in one of their bitter exchanges of accusation she returned to her discussion with Thelma.

"Thelma, is talk you talking or you *know* about e-mail and computer file and them thing? I can see the two set of figures when he working and I feel Pansy must know about it, but she probably don' do much of it herself because she such a damn-ass."

"Rosemarie." Ellie sounded startled.

"Wait, you awake? Sorry, missis. Me think you did nod off. Archdeacon, sorry, massa."

I diverted Ellie with my quick tour of the night sky. We could just see Scorpio sweeping his tail across his corner of the heavens. Antares winked bloodily and the sting hung poised there, with a twinkle.

Miss Ellie slept later than usual the next morning, after her exertions, and wandered out into the midst of the excitement.

"Gone?" she asked Rosemarie.

"Yes. But how you know?"

"Know what?"

"About Eric."

"I don't even know an Eric. What's happened to him?"

"Dead. In the night."

"Of what?"

Troubled, Rosemarie searched for some phrase.

"Come straight," Miss Ellie insisted.

"Neglect." Her sister-in-law's mouth set in a bitter line. "Is burdensome – the feeding, cleaning . . . Is just what I tell you. If you become inconvenient, is easy to just relax and make things take their course. This place have waiting list and the space full up right away."

In a daze Ellie stared around at the frantic activity. Windows being washed. The porch blocked off and grillework being painted.

"No you can't," snapped Maynard. "You going nasty up the wet paint. It have to ready and dry before the funeral."

"Funeral here?"

But the nurses had no time for any of us.

"His family wanted it here," Rosemarie explained to Miss Ellie. "He don't belong to any church."

"No! Not belong to a church?"

"They bringing a reverend though."

Why now, one wondered.

That night the porch was quiet with its dejected little group avoiding one another's eyes. When Ellie tried to get to the bottom of it, all I could articulate was, "Not a bad fellow. A little tedious at times, but a decent chap."

"Space problems," hissed Cecil, his wronged expression embracing the trials of Eric. "We'll see how far the paint job will go."

Two mornings afterwards a nurse bore down on Miss Ellie with a glass and pills.

"Let me keep it for her till after lunch, Maynard," Rosemarie offered briskly. "It might just upset her stomach now and, besides, it going wear off."

As the nurse disappeared Miss Ellie craned her neck. "What is that I must take?"

"Nothing, sweetheart." Rosemarie poked the pills deep into the moist soil of a potted begonia. "I not letting them dope you up with no sedative." Then she watered the plant gently from the small cup.

"Too much water for begonia," Miss Ellie protested.

Pansy Cunningham bustled out of the office then, giving instructions every-where. "You have to give Jocelyn the shot *early*. Cut the cord if the knot can't loose. We don't have time for . . . yes." As she whisked off she delivered a last instruction over her shoulder. "Lock the door at the step. We no want nobody wander up inna this madhouse."

Gladys's well-built frame slanted forward to lean on her mop as she studied the scene and laughed softly. "A who say slavery done?" she reflected. "When it done, a de Pansy she take it over." She kissed her teeth and stalked away.

"Suck-teeth is offensive," grumbled Miss Ellie. "Stop it." But Gladys had gone inside anyway.

Flowers were borne up the steps.

"Downstairs, downstairs," a nurse ordered.

"*Upstairs*, Mitzy," Pansy Cunningham called irritably from inside. "The downstairs people say they didn't pay to come here to be part of any funeral. Is making them nervous."

"Then make the tourist them come up here, nah? Miss Pansy, if we have funeral up here, how de bax going go up an down dem stair? Likklemost, dem drap it make Eric jus' roll out."

"Keep the flowers in the van ten minutes then. Cho! If the family wasn't thinking to send the brother here I woulda never put up with this crasses."

Soon the porch was crowded with new faces. Bright faces. Makeup, cigarettes, a jangle of bracelets. Newspapers unfolding and the smell of coffee. The downstairs guests whom we rarely encountered appropriated the porch and spread themselves comfortably. Above the noise of furniture being arranged downstairs the chatter of strange voices replaced our own.

"I put something on Renegade, you know."

"Sly dog. How'd ya know?"

"Hot tip, hot tip. Is that beach trip finalized?"

"Some of them don't want to go."

"Why?"

"Disrespect." A chuckle. "As if they knew who he was, or cared." Then the speaker grew serious. "Of course I'm sorry. Someone dies, you know. But it was time. Couldn't even manage himself, poor fellow, or so I understand. But I never laid eyes on him. I can't pretend to cry."

"The minibus come." Byer's voice came from downstairs.

"Aah!" A general chatter and dither, a gathering up of bags and towels and a swooping for bright broad brims – red, blue . . . stripes, black and white.

"Wait! Wait! Is me hat dat fe funeral!" Maynard bellowed, then calmed down quickly. "No, no. That is all right. A little mistake, man. You know Nurse May nah vex fe dat. Enjoy the afternoon."

A sigh of relief as the porch grew quieter. Still we cleared off out of range of funeral arrangements.

"Come make them stay," Gladys agreed. "Leave the old Maynard with im ugly John Canoe hat."

Later, downstairs, the singing rose and fell as the funeral proceeded and at first they kept Rosemarie and Ellie inside, though no one bothered me sitting quietly on the porch. Then in no time I heard the nurses urging them to dress. Quickly, quickly.

"Where my things, Viv? Then you not going?"

"No, Miss Ellie. Gladys not going nowhere. Dey want Miss Rose and Archdeacon where they can see them though, so you can't leave behind either. Then wait. Miss Ellie, you remember one Petrona?"

"Of *course* I know Petrona."

"She sen' 'hello', 'm."

Maynard flung open their door but her powerful figure in black and white screened them from view. "Is wait you waiting for the burying to over? What taking you so long fe put on frock and come out? Who you think looking at *you*?" she demanded.

Mitzy, barely contained in a cocktail dress, piped up from the porch, "Come take a likkle drive out. Dem ready fe go a grave. We all going. After nobady wouldn' want miss it."

Miss Ellie's navy blue was a little tight and she bustled out tugging at it anxiously, while Mitzy sneered at her.

"Is greedy you greedy make you too fat for you clothes."

"No, she is *not* eating too much; she just not getting exercise how you lock us up," Rosemarie snapped.

But Miss Ellie herself was in fine form. "A drive? Me? Great! An outing."

At the cemetery they hustled us out of the car. "Yes, come. Get out fast. They by the hole a'ready."

"Where?"

Pansy Cunningham surveyed the set from her perch on a grave. A woman in deep black touched lace to her eyes. Weaving through the crowd a thin young man, a boy really, seemed out of place in ill-fitting clothes and an eye-stud.

He paused to study the Cunninghams then, halting in front of Miss Ellie, exclaimed, "Eh-eh! Grannie?"

Then he was gone, but Ellie had been transfixed by the stud in his eyelid and dug her elbow at Rosemarie.

"Is nothing," Rosemare whispered. "Some men . . ." She pressed her lips to Ellie's ear.

"Nooo," Ellie blurted out, "then how . . ." But everyone looked at her sternly and the music was so melancholy she put her finger to her lips.

"Like his daughter come to see him fe the last," a spectator behind us whispered, craning his neck. "Poor soul how she eye red."

"She's from abroad?" I whispered.

"Town." Rosemarie grunted. "First time I ever set eye pon *her*."

Scott Cunningham asked to say a few words. Solemn in dark grey double-breasted.

". . . leaving a gap no one will be able to fill" – he paused, reaching for his handkerchief but then stuffing it back bravely – "his cheerful courage a model for us all."

"Oh gawd!" A woman threw back her head, a hand pressed to her mouth and then clutching the hat brim.

Her face was out of sight but it was obviously Maynard. Black and white broad-brim. Black and white dress. Black and white purse? Black and white shoes! Good heavens! Black stockings with sprays of white flowers!

"Oh gawd, papa Eric!"

Others huddled around her, supporting. "Hush, Maynard. Be strong."

". . . bringing continuous light and inspiration to our little evenings on the porch," Scott Cunningham continued. "Deeply sorry he left us before his brother's arrival in our little family."

An elderly auburn-haired man with side whiskers faded to camel-colour shook his head over the casket.

The black and white vision threw both her hands in the air. "Don' take him yet, me Jesus. We not ready. We cyan't go it alone. Not yet, not yet!"

". . . a family of which every member is an intrinsic part . . ." Cunningham rolled out sonorously.

"Big words," reflected Miss Ellie. "Smart clothes with big words." She closed her eyes to play around inside her head. "Sophistication. Sophistry."

A sound system planted on a tomb played "Abide with Me".

"Watch how de daughter a cry," an admiring voice gushed at my ear.

". . . never did enough – " Her voice broke. "I tried. Every comfort money could buy. I deprived my own children at times to ensure Papa's comfort, to keep him in the luxury we felt he deserved. But still, when it comes, one feels it was not enough." Pansy Cunningham squeezed the thick shoulder pad of the elegant black dress on the sobbing woman. ". . . and the debt of thanks I owe to all who make this 'home' a home indeed. I know this is the best possible place for Uncle Den, even though Dad will now be present only in spirit."

A clergyman officiated but our small group at the back could hear nothing. The casket sank from sight while the minister's lips moved inaudibly. For one who no longer got to church regularly, Miss Ellie must have found this the last straw.

"Can't hear you at the back, Reverend," she called.

One thing is certain: they heard her. Rosemarie gripped her hand but she shook her off, refusing to be quieted.

"Stupidness! What? They fraid they wake the corpse?"

"I don't feel so good," Rosemarie whispered in her ear, casting around a desperate look. "Just hold me, Ellie, and keep me very still."

Well, naturally that had the desired effect.

Over their shoulders I could still see Cunningham throw in a clod and take the hand of the elegant woman in black. ". . . personal loss of a spiritual leader," he pronounced. "The nurses were devoted to him too."

Maynard shrieked and threw herself forward on the soft earth and torn grass at the rim of the hole. "Gawd!" As they held her, she struggled. "Let me go wid him. Papa Eric!"

But they drew her back and at last she clung to Patsy Cunningham, smothering her sobs and trailing mud across lavender linen.

"Safe in the arms," Maynard gasped, "safe in the arms."

They supported her drooping figure, which threatened to crumple again at every step, and led her away. Somehow she grasped a flower, holding it aloft.

"I going keep this till I die." She stuffed it in her bosom, a white orchid snatched from the daughter's wreath.

At Pansy Cunningham's car, Maynard paused and glanced regally around, raising the flower. "He will be in all our hearts" – she nodded thoughtfully – "and our hearts will go on."

I glanced back to ensure Rosemarie's door was locked while Maynard seated herself on the other side of Ellie, who sympathetically laid her hand on the nurse's shoulder.

"Watch me dress, ole woman," Maynard hissed.

On our return the steps took me time, my ankles on fire from balancing on the wet uneven ground. By the time I finished the climb, the Cunninghams were in the office whispering about accounts, the door ajar.

"We have the daughter cheque," the wife confirmed, rubbing at the streak of grave mud on her dress.

"How you know her cheque good?"

"Is good. Always late, but good."

"Then is what happen to the June money? Not you tell me the cheque bounce?"

"The son-in-law write that. When I call the daughter she send cash."

"Is that money you turn in only half of."

"Because I did have to pay the fees for Cindy course in modelling. I tired tell you that!"

"Then why you don't bring the children to see us?" Ellie demanded from her perch on a stool near the office door.

"Rosemarie!" Scott Cunningham shouted.

"Facety," muttered Ellie. "Doesn't know how to address his own stepmother. Disrespectful, insipid little ingrate."

Rosemarie hurried over and snatched her away, closing the door a little more, but I could still hear Cunningham's lowered voice.

"You sure them didn' see the sore?"

"After is we dress him! And the doctor certificate in order too, so is not that you must worry about. Is the accounts going cause trouble. Is one hell of a mess you looking to make."

A nurse skittered past, and through half-closed lids I recognized the wiggle without actually seeing the face. She tapped the door and seemed disappointed to find the wife in the office.

"The Jocelyn she tablet wearing off. Mus' give her more, or just tie her?"

"Nothing can tie her just so, Mitzy. Give her more."

"Is one or a half?"

"Me no know. Ask Maynard. Give her the one. What difference it make?"

By supper we caught the rumble of a heavy vehicle labouring up to the gate and manoeuvring the sharp turn between the pillars. A door banged open, pouring out voices, greeting and comparing, and loud self-satisfied yawns. Their voices rose uninhibited.

"Fab'lous day. Beach ws incredible. Y'all shoulda been th'r."

"But I have never done it that way," Ellie was insisting to the nurse pushing the spoon towards her. "I have eaten with a knife and fork all my life."

"Spoon is what you getting here. All like you eat cleaner with spoon. Watch how you hand shaking."

Rosemarie's eyes riveted on Ellie's hand and she set her mouth mutinously. "But see here. Her hand trembling for true. They short her tablets." Rosemarie scraped back her chair and stamped out. "Pansy! What bout the tablet Miss Ellie suppose to take? She have to get Artane with the Melleril. You can't short her so."

But Ellie was otherwise occupied. "All like who? Mus' be you grow up eating with spoon from bowl! Why I must I do everything your bungo way? At least make me have a plate and fork!" She got up, slammed the chair in to the table and marched out to inhale the evening air deeply, still holding the offending bowl.

"Eleanor," Pansy Cunningham shouted.

"Who you calling Eleanor? *You* like to eat from bowl like dawg? Fetch!" She hurled it over the porch rail onto the lawn.

"Aw blimey!" A voice rose from the porch downstairs then dropped a level and continued conversationally. "Thay're just always whining up there nowadays, aren't they?"

"They don't know any better. They can't help themselves."

"They didn't used to though, did they. Kept bloody quiet up to recently, so why don't they shut the 'ell up now and let others help them."

"They don't know they don't know. My mother was like that."

"When?"

"She was my . . . Oh, let's not go into it."

"But was she . . . ?"

"*Don't* go there."

Ellie sniggered. "They don't know it's no point trying not to think." A rhythm cantered back to her and she shouted to them through the bars, *"Yonder's the midden whose odours will madden!"*

Instantly chairs scraped and a table grated as it was pulled back.

Rosemarie bore down on her sister-in-law with a fork in her hand and seated her right there on the porch. If only she would eat quietly, she begged. So I took my own supper out to see whether I could keep her occupied.

But now the voices from below surged hushed but frantic. What were they afraid of? Ellie wanted to know. For once, she said, she was thankful for the wrought iron that spoilt the view but kept out whatever terrors there were.

"For, up here, at least we don't live in hiding. Downstairs they huddle. Is something in the dark they fraid? But most of them – their heads not like mine. They remember their way."

And then it struck me that she could not recall what lay along her most recent paths and every step she took for the rest of her life would be through a minefield.

"But what you going to do?" she demanded. "Just stand and shake?"

As the others joined us on the porch she spread her arms and beat time with her fork. *"I'll labour night and day,"* she warbled, *"to be a pilgrim."*

"Quiet!" A nurse plunged towards her, scandalized.

"But after I not singing anything coarse!" she protested. "Is a lovely old hymn. Then you don't remember it?"

Only then the office door burst open and Scott Cunningham exploded through it roaring incomprehensibly about files. The nurses scattered and his wife, behind him, had obviously been taken entirely by surprise. Rosemarie cast a warning glance around and we made ourselves invisible. Blank stares came naturally to some. I donned my mask of imperturbable civility. Thelma dropped her eyes, the portrait of decorum, and Cecil fell silent, wrapping himself around his own incurable wound. But not Miss Ellie.

"There's *no* need to address people like cattle!" she reproved him, shrugging in my direction when I raised an appeasing hand. "I can be direct with Scotty, Canon. I have known the boy all his life."

Cunningham pointed to her and screamed at his wife, "Confusion from the time she get here."

"She couldn't interfere with no computer. What she *know*? Is you with you smartness get youself into – "

"She stir them up! You can't see the whole mad rass of them out of control? Since she come! The whole dead-an-wake dem come to life. Someone sitting there looking quiet quiet get into the accounts and e-mail all kind a file all over the place."

That was when I saw his fury only filmed the surface. His face was bloodless with terror.

THIRTEEN

Ellie

WHEN SCOTTY AND Pansy hurl obscenities at each other I have no choice but to put my foot down.

"Shh! Stop the nastiness. Offensive!"

Scotty whirls on the nearest nurse. "Get something to shut her up."

She wiggles in the little tight skirt sucked up under her bottom, and pushes out her mouth. "Dem ting don't make no difference to her, Mas' Scotty."

"You see her swallow it?"

"I give Miss Rosemarie it for her."

"Aah, right!" His fingers dig into my jaws, forcing open my mouth, and Pansy locks an arm around, pinning me. Rage builds as he pushes in the tablets and I . . . I must . . . to spit them back at him for his fingers (who knows where last) are all over my tongue. Pansy grips my nose and . . . and air, I cannot help . . . gulp clear my mouth. As I gasp they pour in more water.

"Right!" Scotty loosens his hold.

But the fury swelling in me breaks out, sweeping me along to spew the water directly in his face and he yells and pitches me away, the back of his hand sudden and numbing and my shoulder crunching against the chair.

"No, no." A thin man springs to his feet, his face, etched with years of meditating on his own grievances, transforms as the lines melt into an expression of dismay. "Are you all right, ma'am?"

He helps me up with a courtesy, in fact a courtliness, I would not have expected from a face so taciturn, almost sullen. He sits me on a sofa but soon his words are fuzzy, I can hear them but their meanings are hazy and the clear lines of objects and people seem vague. The nurses curl away like smoke, other faces mourn over me, and through eyes that are neither open nor closed I see Scotty and Pansy gesticulating frantically.

"He might see past it . . ." he says, "behind the . . ."

What is in front and what is behind? Who whispers and why and to hush what? What silent and hidden? Dan murmurs, I tell you, greed cracks its whip over Scotty. But there is something more, a darkening threat.

I try to shift my . . . not exactly thoughts . . . but they wheel far above, seeing my cronies huddled round me and the others gesturing in anger. Or fear? At the back is a door into hell. A front, Dan says. *I know not seems . . .*

I sit the talk tumbling about me but cannot . . . connect with . . . empties my mind or mist creeps overtaking vacant. Words cannot my jaw slackening and even my eyes to blink. Cannot.

"What happened?" Rosemarie. "Cecil! Thelma!"

Pain in her voice pierces me but I only sit, my mind bleeding unstaunched into their cries. Hushed.

"No nothing like that. No stroke. Just forced the tablets . . ."

"No, don't know what . . . some kind of . . ."

"Hit her, the monster . . ."

Phone ringing for me.

"Duvall," someone shouts.

"Well, it's her call," snaps Rosemarie.

"Tell them she's sleeping."

"They won't believe you after this," Rosemarie hisses, "for she never sleeps at this hour. If you don't want a full-scale investigation, you better don't drug her again."

I should move. *Cannot rest from travel.* No map though. *Here be dragons.*

But summon my voice from a remote shore, though cannot assemble. Seize a line.

"Push off. And sitting well in order, smite the sounding furrows."

"Is what? What she doing?" A full-bodied woman bends over me gently, peering in disbelief. "Then she not sleeping, Miss Rose? After what they give her?"

"Quoting the poetry." Rosemarie strokes my face. And the others bend over, exclaiming in admiration, and I may have drifted off to sleep, secure in their closeness, but suddenly I surface again.

"For my purpose holds . . ." But I cannot seem quite keep up.

I open my eyes, at least I think so, in a dim place. A thin wiry woman is bending over me.

"Where's Dan?" It is a struggle to make my mouth move.

She smiles at me a slow expectant smile, opening her eyes wide to catch my full attention.

"He dead," she purrs gladly. "And is you kill him." She draws back and studies me. "Him suffer, you see?"

Even as my mind writhes I assess her and discard her news. When she bends again, I am ready for the old witch.

"Liar!" I lurch up, putting my face full up to her. "I know you for a liar! Meanness written all over you."

She slams me back on the mattress and flounces out clanging the door behind her, and now there is no sleep for me for I am boiling mad.

Still, I draw up my knees and close my eyes and after a while someone, it must be Dan, murmurs *dominus vobiscum*, and the shadows dissipate.

I must have been asleep, but at any rate I've now found myself in a long dim room particularly dark to one end because there is only a single small, high window, barred and partially obscured from outside. Not even the usual hypocritical swirl of today's wrought iron. Just barred. What can it mean?

"Dan? They have you in this jail too?"

Apparently not, thank God. But Rachel will be worried so I must get a move on.

I feel my way along the smooth cold damp wall to a door, but the handle waggles uselessly in my hand, halting at the crucial moment.

"Then why it won't open?" I bend, peeping to see if there is a keyhole, and find it is one of these new types of lock. So I just gather my strength into my arm and slam on the door with my hand, but it has some padding or corky layer and makes no sound. "Who locked this? Open the blasted door!" I listen for running steps, but nothing.

High window.

"They send me to the Tower?" I chuckle. "I better get a move on before they make it the block." So I push a low stool across the room and cautiously climb up on a desk so as to grasp the bars. The floor is below ground level and the small area of window that is not obscured looks out on the base of a breadfruit tree. One is on the ground, full, and close enough for me to catch the miniature quilt pattern on the skin.

"Then they waiting for it to rot? Stop. They need a good pear, and saltfish. Hello?"

Then where is Rachel? I climb down and the floor inside is uneven for two huge roots have worked themselves in through the wall and forked into smaller ones. And now there is no putting off the bathroom any longer. To my horror the door is locked. In truth, a dungeon. No time to argue. Sliding my hand along the wall, I move into the darkness – corner, there are shelves, corner, now a different wall, cold, crumbly in places, slippery. The floor buckles. Here are the knots and gnarls and I lose touch with the wall but now I am returning to the side of the room that is merely dim, hurrying, for now I *must* find a commode, a bottle, a plastic bag – anything – crashing to my knees with the urgency of it, but no bed only a mattress and nothing below the desk or even Ivy's old card table. Jesu, what to do. The door is locked.

"Oh Christ, help me. Hurry."

But it is already too late. The horror of my predicament in this strange place – not my house – with no change of clothes, for I had no idea I would be here any length of time. Of course, I could wash the underwear and put it to dry discreetly. Who could tell what I did or didn't have on by looking at me? I raise the skirt carefully to keep it dry.

But. But what . . . what this is? A plastic binding smooth all around to my touch. A diaper? On *me*? When? Then, in my sleep. Someone came in my sleep and stripped me? I close my eyes. Sweet Jesu, prevent me from going mad. Carefully I run my fingers along the tape till they make out the join. Fingernail. Pick, pick. Aah. Rip it. I roll it up and hurl it at the door as it opens.

Rosemarie jumps back, fielding it with her arm.

"Who?" I gasp. "Who is doing this? This locking of doors. I can't reach a toilet. I find myself in this, this . . ."

"Hush!" She embraces me and holds me hard. "You don't business here. You must get back to Rachel. Come quietly with me, very quietly. By the time they realize you out with me they mightn't bother, once you quiet."

"Who are they to decide I must be quiet? A lousy set. To hell with them!"

"Shh! I taking you out. If you make noise they going lock me up too."

That's different. A thought arrests me.

"You remember somebody had a riddle about a toilet?"

"Mercy, King! Nothing don't stop you?"

"Pickney have a horse. He cyan't ride it facing forwards or to the side. Only backwards."

"Shh!"

We tiptoe along the corridor and go up a stairway. She unbolts the gate at the top and hands me through to Viv.

"Stay with her till I come, Gladys," she says quietly. "I must manage lock back the door." Then she slips back down. Soon enough, however, we are together again in a room that is pretty grim but not absolutely unfamiliar.

"They don't know about paint?" I ask, but I don't wait for the answer because I am shaking all over and have to sit quickly.

"You going find youself with one hell of a case," Rosemarie announces to them just outside the door. "You lucky I get her out here before stroke take her. Look how she shaking all over. Don't is you tell me her daughter call to say she coming for her in the next couple weeks, and look at her. She have to get the exact medication they send, from now on." Suddenly Rosemarie seems to snap and begins to shout at them. "Is why you shorting her? To give someone else? To save money? Is prescription medicine, you cyan't just share Artane around."

"I want to go home," I tell Rachel on the phone.

"And we can't wait to see you." Her voice is bright and eager. "We have pictures of Niagara to show you. But, Mom, you may need to stay a fortnight longer while we do some work on the house, and while Doreen takes her holiday. Can you hold on a little longer? As you have Rummy. But I'm anxious to see you both. I've booked my flight."

"But Rummy's coming back with me, eh, baby?"

"Scotty says she isn't well enough to travel now, but when he comes for his meeting in a couple months he will bring her then."

"Then you not well?" I demand when I can find Rosemarie. "And you couldn't tell me?"

"I too dyamn well for them to let me talk to people outside."

"Come back with me. Cho! Leave them make them stay since they so miserable!"

"No one can take on two old people." She sets her mouth and her jaw clenches. "Anyway. I've worked it out."

In a while Pansy announces that Scotty has business in Trinidad and will take me with him to save Rachel the flight.

"So how you going explain him not taking me?" Rosemarie demands.

"Them could ever expect him to manage two at a time?" Pansy goads her. "One ole higue per trip!"

On the porch, the news is that Ashmead is taking over downstairs. It's not just the apartment he needs; the tourists must go for him to have any privacy. They've had notice and most have moved already. The rest will be out within the week. Ashmead has determined that the place needs fewer old people, so that's that. Now Pansy has served notice, Rosemarie reports that Mr Ashmead will be inspecting upstairs this evening.

"Whatever will make him comfortable. Out in the big world, wheeling and dealing, as they say," Pansy simpers. "Need a likkle hideaway."

For sanity sake I turn my attention from Pansy to a nearby pot of ferns. Mmm. Luxuriant. I wonder if they use the eggshell too or only the tea leaves.

Pansy's gushing interrupts rational thought and I return to them with a sigh. She shows off a tall trim man with a somewhat washed-out complexion, who is looking past us to a door on the other side of the porch. I can't help thinking it must be one of the guests who got the purge Rosemarie was talking about, and a brief snigger escapes me. He glances my way and gazes with sudden but expressionless concentration, his body tense.

"These are some of our upstairs guests, Mr Ashmead," Pansy declares apologetically.

"Do join us." I extend a hand, but he circles us with a lithe ease and enters Ivy's room, and the door clicks shut behind them.

"Old sourpuss," Rosemarie snorts.

"Well, I don't know . . ." I falter, and they stare at me. "I mean, he looks wretched. You think it's the medicine?"

"Rich as Croesus from what I hear," retorts a particularly sour-looking chap, though he's actually very civil to me. "I should be so wretched."

FOURTEEN

Ashmead

AT FIRST I came to the house to get my own body back under control. Hypertension was going to kill me, that asinine doctor at Specialist Associates assured me cheerfully. I required two weeks of absolute rest, and he knew a delightful place – if it was still in operation, he said, for the old lady had been slowing down when he was there many years ago.

That was how I got here, like anybody else – to recuperate.

And I recovered. I kept to myself. I read on the beach under an almond tree, drank coconut water, lived on red snapper and pawpaw. I did a little fishing. When I recovered I went away and left them alone.

Now they twitter outside in a wave of anxiety. And I recognize that aversion. I know it from old. And they know nothing of me – how could they? Who is there to search the crevices, the corners of my mind, to fold back layer after layer of the years in which no one has ever actually seen me.

Only one person ever glimpsed me (glimpsed, in passing, that child in the corner), for what did the other old woman do, for all her soft words. Nothing, and she was nothing to me. Then the girl with the lace collar would visit with her mother, and she would glance at me wondering briefly (what is he doing there, what happened to him, those bruises?) and they would sit down and eat cake sprinkled with sugar and cinnamon. I have seen her since but she has never recognized me, and in those early days she never stopped to ask me anything, to intervene. No one did. They only glanced away as if once I was out of sight I might not be there at all. It has always been like that. From time.

Even in that brief space as I walked past, they stared then flicked their eyes away. Yet I am attractive. I have proven it time and again if the rapturous murmurs of women can be believed, those fortunate to pass swiftly through my hands. Charm. I am an expert in charm. I could give myself a certificate for it – not like Cunningham's, a glossy papering over contempt, charm as a skill for deflecting recognition and deferring rage. Anger management, they call it now. Where were they when I invented it?

I know where I was. I was the child in the corner. For years I studied anger, my area of specialization. I relegated anger to a signal that it was time to talk myself into relaxing. It was a trigger for the story I would begin in my head, the dispassionate account of what had called the anger forth. "Wrath is a deadly sin," the old woman croaked when I answered back. Yes, deadly, for it clouds the mind. So in the corner, in the cupboard, I began to invent my story, searching back for beginnings to unravel my situation, but coiling it forward too, to test alternative developments, probing the way to survive.

Well. I'm out of the corner now. Out of the cupboard, into the packing case, shipping off to freedom; in the hold the bruises on my skin healed, but on the streets of America land of the free my skin was the prison, light as it had seemed at home. When I had the means, I lightened it further as best I could. But, oh yes, there were other beatings, other lessons. Working on the trawler, though, I learned patience and dexterity, and when I could afford leisure for a hobby I took up fishing. Meanwhile, drifting on the street, prison briefly, it was all, all an education, for I had determined sitting in that corner when the boy next door slammed the gate on his way off to school that I too would learn, somehow, at every opportunity. When a passing priest glanced in the direction of my cell, I crossed myself fervently, catching his eye, and when I came out his letter of introduction eased me into an adult literacy programme and so on so on through cleaner, messenger, assistant, manager, my aura of loyalty drawing me closer into the confidence of the old man who eventually employed me.

Whether or not he had completely moved from loan-sharking to processing rum from the Caribbean in the Prohibition years, before I was born, he was well established when we met and he accommodated my move back to Kingston. I worked in Customs and Excise for a time but travelled regularly, for I had met his daughter.

And I thought: *perhaps there will be somebody after all.*

That was the time when nothing mattered but to have her. Not the money, not the business, only the fine curve of her held by her father yet pulling away, drawn taut from his bent form. In his office among the ledgers she blurred into the adding machine, evading the stare of clients until she relaxed into her work and her lips unclenched from their tense tight line.

Whoever married her would have to be of the faith, her father would say, and I at least had the name. So I began to mirror her, self-effacing, respectfully acknowledging her from afar but imperceptibly inching closer. I practised drawing attention to myself through modesty, through maintaining a respectful distance. But the pretence closed on me, grew genuine. Her tense circumlocution of every remark, her mutinous refusal to respond, her turning aside from every approach – it was all to draw me on, a dissembling rejection, seductive as it was meant to be. Carelessly she tightened hold on my mind, my body – I began to move, to think in time to her steps, her shrug could undo me. She exerted a force for which I was utterly unprepared and I stammered at the briefest and most dismissive acknowledgement, alarmed at my legs giving way in a current overpowering and violent.

She was not caught in it, it seemed. She maintained a control that was unwholesome. Infuriating. Even as I became obsessed with winning her I became equally intent on breaking her, on smashing her silence even though I wanted no actual words from her, only to make her moan my name.

Instead she took matters into her own hands.

"This is what we will do," she proposed coolly at dinner.

What was I doing there? Herself, her father, me – it had been an unprecedented invitation. She had dressed with care, it seemed, with every piece of jewellery outside of the bank, presumably to make her point.

"Father will leave everything he has in my name alone until my death when it reverts to charities. My husband will manage the estate accounting to me absolutely, but he will want for nothing. And I suppose Papa will consider some settlement."

I responded to him before he could speak, protesting, "I have no interest in possessing anything but your daughter."

"Which is everything," he concluded dryly, though I shook my head and dropped my eyes in the attitude of one much misunderstood.

But so it was resolved.

I thought of us as allies till I recognized I was a commodity to her. The practicality of the arrangement forestalled any illusions I might have had about her feelings. The poisoning sense of having bought and sold each other dispatched us promptly to our respective corners but kept us watchful of each other. Of course, I wanted her utterly to myself. Not with that brief flutter of hope but with unrelenting fixity – for how could I pretend patience with her father's call on her? I suppose I seemed changeable, adoration swinging to impatience, for it was neglect it amounted to, this preoccupation with her father whom she had never loved nor had cause to love, and because he was ill briefly, trivially, with some prostate complaint. Neglect me? I could feel the heat rising in my blood and the veins in my head contracted. I would show her, without further waste of time. The future tightened to tomorrow occupying me with her compliance in the night ahead, her unfailing presence in the morning whatever her father's medical status in her own country.

Yet when she was disentangled from her father something held me back aloof, turned inward, resentful of her presence always and everywhere. I was alone as I had been all my life, isolated beyond expression or comprehension, but company was nothing I could tolerate – this horrifying persistent intimacy. I would not be left to myself I would not be imposed on I required her presence, immediate but inconspicuous – a shadow to materialize on call. Her face now, its aversion insupportable. Bold or evasive it revealed her flaunting disregard, her availability to whomever she might encounter. I knew if I looked carelessly into this face I would smash it; there could be no coming together face to face, the thought appalled me, and I approached her only from behind. Suddenly, mercilessly, to get it over with.

After yet another faceless encounter, unsatisfying as ever, I shoved her aside. For she could have done better than that. Instead of engaging me she held out on me. I would have been disappointed if I had allowed myself, but between the hurt and my consciousness I managed to position rage.

Powerless to begin with, but I could have shown them had she not been protected by her father's will; this will of this other man, her father, and this powerlessness over her life began to torment me, distract me until I was failing on every approach – or rather she failed to stimulate me as she could have if her mind were on me, *me*, instead of wandering, speculating, fantasizing – I could see it in her pretending eyes. But I could make up for it. Socially. I disconnected from her and focused on my position in the community. From a distance I observed my own response to her neglect and coldness. I was a spectator it meant nothing I was numb when the lamp came into my hand the belt the cigarette stand she provoked me into it to put me in the wrong.

Very well I knew she sought comfort elsewhere, everywhere else. I saw it in the smirk of every accountant in the business, every supermarket clerk. They smiled faking sympathy but it was only their recollection of the night before or their expectation of the night to come. What else was there for them to smile about with her? I masked my need of her, never admitted it. Sleep evaded me, teased me, I sank into it only to be shaken by disruption, the feel and smell of her so near, so cold, and I so alone. The desolation would overcome me and I would plead to begin again.

I raised her worshipped her stripped her crushed her punished her. I begged forgiveness and in contempt for the weakness she had brought on me I made her an example. But to whom? To herself? Myself? Oh, I refuse to have it pinned on me, the consequences of her own disgusting behaviour. It was the times responsible too, all I had gone through, her betrayal.

I remember too well how the night her father died she did not weep; I saw she thought herself free. It was an offence. There is only one way of dealing with these things and I learned it the hard way – one way of reacting to the tightening stress. In the end nothing else works. She did not turn to me when her father died. She drew back from my embrace, thwarting and belittling me in her turning away. She made nothing of me and I put my foot down. Propelling her from pedestal to stretcher. The ambulance wailed out her version of it, and how could I not hate her for what she made me do, the pressure she had put on me. Pressure indeed. She's the one who drove mine up.

I decided to make myself independent of her. A brief experiment with trans-shipment from Colombia had rewarded me with resources for a project of my own, free from foreign control or threat of retaliation. As crime soared out of control in Kingston, I built a thriving security business. Identifying competent managers presented the greatest challenge but eventually I had my team. Money began to come in from those who depended on us for protection. As everything fell into place my blood pressure dipped under control. The country house was increasingly useful, remote and innocuous as it was.

I contributed to improvements that my managers wanted for their various communities, but I kept my connections with them private. My reputation for benevolence, however, my recognition as a philanthropist, reached the *Gleaner*. That was when the young fool running the home contacted me for funding. When he heard my terms he attempted to withdraw and began a series of inept security efforts on his own – the usual fencing, burglar proofing, dogs, what have you. But he came around. He accommodated me with permanent quarters at a particular trying time.

Long before, when my wife was recovering from surgery, trying one foot before the other, holding the chair rolling ahead, she fell again, during that argument, having taunted me at every turn, and the wheelchair became permanent. What was there left to feel for her but hatred for the guilt heaped on me, and nothing but anger can override guilt, even as it overrode fear years ago. I've shown her. She is where she belongs, fixed in her chair, but even there in a sense she controls my life – through her money which beckons, unreachable. Beating me with it *she* abuses *me* while pretending to be some helpless victim. Here, with the mountains between us, I need not set eyes on her, but even apart from that this location itself has turned out to be increasingly useful.

There is good land around Cascade and soon enough I thought of ways in which it might provide me with space for my more delicate negotiations on the North Coast. From a modest base, I reached out with significant successes. Already I had contracts with a number of hotels and two more had included me in their payroll in order to proceed safely with construction. I showed them how to work their budgets around the sums necessary for protection, a quarter million for the smaller operations, a million for the more ambitious projects. A steady flow of cash was passing through pharmaceutical businesses under Cunningham's name but I had growing concerns about Cunningham's accounts, and an e-mail from someone within the home confirmed my suspicions. Gradually it became apparent that other messages were being sent regarding this place and operations in which I was connected with Cunningham. It was on that recent visit to deal with all these matters and to put my own security measures in place that I saw . . . I saw her. There she was. A door opened then closed her out.

And it was like being a child again, in the corner, fixed by that quick glance, a brief flicker of attention, kindly but passing. Eleanor Duvall she had come to be. I knew her because I had glimpsed her occasionally over the years, but she would not have known me. She was upstairs with another woman – always, they told me – a prying old bitch who was Cunningham's stepmother and who may have set on the one who worked the e-mail. There was a small group of them who still had their senses and there were measures to be taken, but it was hard to know where the Duvall woman fit. They said her mind was gone too, and it was borne home to me clearly enough that she wandered about in the night. With that same swift, sure glance.

There was a door to the cupboard in the old house, where I would be locked in after a beating. "Just like your mother," spat the old woman who said she was my grandmother, flailing the tamarind switch in my face. "Too tief to keep a good job and up and down the street like a whore and bring you here for me to mind." I covered my ears while she screamed her usual epithets for my mother (*bitch, slut, whore*) and I sang loudly, loudly even as the switch lashed down, loudly to drown her out, so she pushed me in the cupboard and I sang to block the pain but I may have passed out for I don't know what happened till I woke up. Sometimes when I woke up the cupboard door was open. (Perhaps it was the other old woman, the sister, who opened it, but I put her from my mind when I determined she was no use, for she did nothing for me in the long run.)

Once when I woke up my head was absolutely clear and I knew what was to be done. "I will show her," I said. The future was this and I clung to it. It was what preserved me in the end, one after the other. *"I will show you."*

And one day when I was hardly more than a child I woke up and I was stronger than the old woman, and the young one who visited occasionally had unfastened the back door of the house and left it ajar as a message to me when she went away with her mother, so that instead of striking back (she must have seen it was coming), instead of striking back I might run, only run. Except that I had already awakened to this condition of perpetual rage. Wrath is not an original sin for I took pains to learn it and as I stood in that doorway I had my last moment of uncertainty. I thought, *Before I run I will show you, old woman; or, shall I run now and come back for you later?*

Now only the twisted woman in the wheelchair, my wife, sits between me and complete control of all that should be at my disposal, for as long as I preserve her life – which I must, for at her death her father's property passes to various charities, though I have sought these out with a view to acquiring control of them one by one and then I'll be out of *that* trap. Meanwhile I have patience. I walk hidden in bright daylight invisible in my cloak of benevolence, like charm, donned and doffed at will. What you see is not all there is. Even the rage below is a mantle. Stifled under the charm, under the rage, the child slipped through a crack in the old woman's jailhouse and ran until there was nowhere farther to go but the sea.

FIFTEEN

Ellie

"I EXPECTED SOMEONE younger though, with all this talk about cutting down on the old people." Sybil remarks sadly, "This Ashmead can't be younger than Thelma."

"Cutting down, eh? So, what about us?" demands a thin sour-looking man, but no one responds at once.

"Props, I suppose," Canon reflects after a while. "But how many of us will there be anyway, Cecil? Another funeral so soon."

"A funeral?" I ask.

"They say she wandered away and . . . must have tried to get a lift because she was so unsteady. Whoever picked her up . . ."

"Who?"

"They don't know who picked her up." Barge's response is so low I strain my ears. "The police came and they can't seem to shed any light."

"Who?" I insist.

"Whoever picked up Thelma," Rosemarie explains automatically, gazing out through the wrought iron grillework.

"But, Miss Rose" – Basil stares in from the top step on the other side of the gate – "Miss Telma so 'fraid everything, much less de dawg, and her whole body a shake so, what woulda make her walk trough de dog run and down de hill? Miss Gladys, what you tink?"

From the entrance to the corridor, a woman responds quietly. "Basil right, Miss Rose. And Miss Telma head did good, m'am. It nah make no sense."

"Yes," Rosemarie says. "Her head did well good."

"Miss Pansy say them will have a quiet service here tomorrow. I ask her how dem doing it so quick and she say after Telma Chew don't have nobody for us to wait funeral pon, an best we get it over with."

Only now that I see her I remember her shyness and pearl buttons. The rolling quaver of the hand – what is it called again, Dan? Not enough to kill her. Not yet.

"What did she die of?" I demand, gripping the arm of a big powerfully built nurse.

"Ole age." She shakes me off.

"Stupidness. That's not a sickness. And she mus' be twenty years younger than me. Look."

"That is why you mus' careful," says a voice at my back. I turned to see a wiry, mean-faced woman. "Anyting can happen anytime."

"Oh, Thelma." Rosemarie kisses the pale and forever stilled face.

Characteristically the high-necked blouse is buttoned up to her throat, and there's a nice scarf with a fancy knot, but not matching. I stretch to loosen it.

"Too tight," I argue, but Rosemarie pulls me back to an inconspicuous corner of the room and very quickly it is over.

Afterwards, the nurses talk in front of us as if we are not there and as if nothing important has happened.

"Well, if de big man going spend more time, likkle Loverboy going have fe cool down. Him cyan't compete anyway."

A soft-faced little one asks whether Mr Ashmead fraid Mr Scott or if he can handle him, and whether Ashmead is a church man. They stare at her.

"Then, Cheryl, you no see him *nest*? No see de mirror and ting over him bed? Mas' Ashmead sound holy to you? Look ya. Him have camera recording him wo'k. Him sound fraid to you?"

"But dem say he do a lot of good works, don't it?"

"All like you will make a nice likkle present from Mr Scott. Likkle peace offering gift for Mr Man to goodwo'ks on."

Just as the child runs away crying, Pansy comes up the stairs and I tell her to keep some control over her husband.

"You can't let him run wild terrorizing people little girl pickney," I say. "For God's sake show some guts." But Rosemarie draws me away to her room.

Then, as she helps me out of the tight navy blue dress, she hugs me so desperately I am frightened.

"What is it? Jesu!"

"If Rachel call you, ask them if they can send for us *now*. Beg them. Oh God, beg them."

But when I begin to cry she calms down at once.

"Shh. Is all right."

See, now she brightens up, but it's not a real brightening, I can tell; it's to comfort me.

"Just give my love, if they call, all my love. I feel say I can't be that wrong about them."

Outside, a clergyman whose name escapes me passes along the passage and raises his palm to me, and I cry out, *"Et cum spiritu!"*

And he bows.

Below the window, Scotty tells Pansy to get a grip on herself and ignore whatever it is the old harpy tell her, but a car door slams and his voice falters to a stop.

Obnoxious, calling people names. But I drift away, to avoid him, or it may be some medicine. No, I'm just tired really. Last night (or was it the night before?) I did not sleep as I should. I went walking – Rolling Calf, Rosemarie teases me – and there were two of them. One straight and pale but otherwise strong and active looking, the other dark but emaciated, and they were not together but there was some connection and I was frightened. Not frightened of either of them, just of the connection. Suddenly the song comes to mind now and I belt it out: *"It musa be a duppy or a gunman . . ."* But then I think of Scotty saying, "old harpy."

Tita was a harpy, an old lady said, almost apologetically, one Tuesday. Mama reminded Miss Minnie that she had got on well with the child though.

"Oh yes." Her face softened from its habitual tragic lines. "He was so bright. I felt he would go far, but he could never assert himself to play, to talk even. Tita was so cold to him – imagine, his own grandmother. Cruel. She beat him brutally. She cursed him. She would lock him up without food."

I never told Mama I was the one who unlocked the door, though he was quite capable of doing so himself but perhaps he was conditioned not to, so I did it, I was the one who unleashed him. And one day not long after or perhaps long after, I can't say, I glimpsed him from a tram but I pretended not to have seen, because of what had happened. Blood everywhere, they had said. I was afraid. Suppose it was my fault, suppose . . . I never told a soul.

"I believe she never forgave his mother, why she went on so," Miss Minnie continued. "But she was a hard person to begin with, Tita was. Look how she treated me." Then she turned to Mama, puzzled. "Why I miss her, I don't know. I suppose it was another creature in the house."

Harpy.

I have been sleeping quite soundly and awake to find myself in a dim room, nodding beside a barred window. Outside, people scuttle to and fro, voices I don't know for the most part except for one, but I was never a great admirer of Ivy's nephew, even though he is Rosemarie's stepson too, now I think of it.

By pressing my face close to the bars I dispense with everything but the vista beyond. The ground and its foliage grows indistinct while the sky glows vividly.

The enormity of space. A band of ultramarine at the perimeter of vision thins and bends. Beneath dips grey, slate grey deepening to charcoal, but out at the edges the perimeter glows tyrian, shading up to crimson, heating to scarlet, to flame. I press my face back to the cold bars through which the blazing sky is revealed. *The print of a vermilion hoof.* A grey-white cloud rears from the pit of fire and dark shapes form and vaporize. It's like being on a plane, it occurs to me, flying. The void is a stark consuming enigma but I ride protected by a conviction that there is no journey without a destination. Only, what will it be this time? I have often travelled before, but then I knew the plan.

Clouds like mist drift down, wraithlike. Might they seep in and suck me dissipating out into the atmosphere – a spray of molecules in the already bleeding sky? By now, as it is, to the people running this way and that under the window and past the door, I am invisible. Counted as one of the dead. I suppose it's New Year's Eve because I hear the fireworks even though I can't see them from here, and the party must be somewhere else because I mean there's no lights no little smell of fruitcake no jollification at all.

Jesu. Watch. Scotty running as if the Furies are after him, but it is only the little mawga fellow.

Gone.

So I send my mind out once more. Outside again, I mount the flame-edged clouds and ride over the darkness in which the clappers go off every so often. *"Out of this house," said rider to reader.* For the past is within me, they cannot take it, even the loved ones gone I have can call on in my mind what is death, *where is thy sting?* And this fool who ducked in and slid behind my door is a dead soul and thinks himself alive and in charge but does not know who I have been and will always be. Life as Scotty thinks it to be is a thin surface over the midden. Whose odours will madden. And I laugh suddenly, not loudly but wildly, for I am mistress of the air, chooser of the dead.

The noise startles Scotty and he says to me, "Quiet!" before diving out through the door again. He looks hunted.

Around the black bottom of the pit that is the garden outside the window, a few figures patrol, searching the bushes with a narrow beam of torchlight and the glow of a cigarette and a little way off a phone is ringing.

"What about Rummy? How is she?" Rachel's voice on the phone is tight with anxiety. "Scotty said last time that she is not as she was."

"No one told me," I object. "All this time I thought she was fine."

"I suppose he must know," she says uncertainly.

"Well, I know what I know," I reply "My mind is not a blank slate just because some of it is erased." Even so, the point of the argument is slipping away from me.

"I told him I was coming for you soon but I could tell he didn't believe me, and he said there was no need because he was coming for a meeting and you would travel with him. Then I asked whether Rummy was up to a visit. He said, 'Aunt Rosemarie is quite senile, but if you think you can manage I'll bring her for the follow-up meeting.' He seemed preoccupied. I suppose they really aren't set up to run a hospital."

Images suffuse my mind.

"Because what he's set up to run is a brothel," I say.

"Mom!"

"What? Scotty's so full of *prunes*."

Slick, he is, contriving. *Yon Cassius.* Businesslike, dividing lines upstairs downstairs inside outside.

"You have to draw the line somewhere," he and Pansy agreed. He said it when they were deciding where to send Cindy for ballet, and they dispensed with one teacher who was willing "to let in every likkle chigger-foot pickney". They said it when they were organizing the home, dissolving lines between properties *meum* and *teum*, spinning sidelines, Scotty in black and white funeral suit with ingratiating smile and gravalicious eyes, looking more like Anancy than ever. Only someone else is pulling his threads if what they say is right. But what do they say? Where?

Sometimes at night, I went walking if Rosemarie fell asleep in her clothes before locking up. I knew Ivy's old house so well. Since most people were asleep, the others talked in their rooms as if no one could possibly hear.

"Miss Pansy know you up here tonight, Mas' Scotty?"

"Why we talking bout her. Me no come here fe dat."

"Tell me what you come for, Mr Scott."

When they laughed together in the office I was free to roam. Don't go there, Andy would say if he knew, but I can't not think. Wings beating in my head . . . *as if of hemlock I had drunk.* One of them poured something and made me swallow.

"Atrocious!" I exclaim. Then I comb my hair, anxious to get out into the fresh air. "*Mirror, mirror, on the wall,*" I intone, but something slits my thoughts and I take only a quick glance, which turns out to be less gruelling than I expected. Perhaps it was rereading Sidney Carton, but there is no guillotine in sight. Certain things are best put out of mind resolutely, however, and what I saw on my walk is one of those things, but as I search my brain for a tune that will help me, I recall Rachel's voice on the phone.

"There must be some new treatment," I was insisting, for at last Rachel had called and I was clutching the phone greedily to my ear for the balm of her voice. "Nowadays something is discovered or invented every minute," I urged. "There must be something for my head. Something for the slicing."

So much to tell Rachel, for she might intervene if only I can word it; but, amputated, it throbs there like a ghost pain of the mind, excruciating but intangible.

Remember, Dan urges.

Forget, soothes Rosemarie.

SIXTEEN

Robin

I CAN'T HONESTLY swear I would have undertaken it if I had known all that was involved (perhaps that's why we must not know) but I want to believe I would have done it anyway – because I had loved the old man, because Miss Ellie was and is, even now, a lady of extraordinary grace, but most of all, for Rache. For I could see some of what she thought she held to herself. It was no easy thing, even for me, to see the old man slide into helplessness although his mind remained intact – and I thought that made it harder: he could see where he was headed. But Mom. Brilliant, joyous Miss Ellie, first in denial and fury, then conscious of erosion, clutching at clues, desperate to avoid becoming a burden as the gaps widened between flashes of clarity.

Such a pair, inseparable. I had looked at Rachel with them – they were well and strong then – and I thought, yes. I want *this*. In the end I saw Dan watching Ellie, knowing what lay ahead; I saw her seeing him slip away. Then I watched Rachel, watching them watch each other. Tortured gazes interlocking, the matrix against which to get through the day. And yet, still, the laughter was never far.

Tennis. They used to come and watch a game or two. They snooped and schemed to find what I might need for my game. They bragged to their friends, they read it up. When I began to give it up they protested, but I needed more time, more time with Andy and his schoolwork, more time, the less Rachel had. The tennis was the first to go, and I don't regret it. You take care of your children and your old people, that's what you do.

At work it was a different world. The school ran reasonably, because of its traditions which were so entrenched, the superior teachers we attracted, the best performers in Common Entrance vying for a place. But the chaos outside was leaking in all the time, the unthinkable blotting out all that was taking place in that other life: the fifth former peddling weed and his father, called in, boxing the dean; the watchman smuggling out what he could of the PA system and then, dismissed, sneaking back in to set fire to the lab. It was not a school where shoot-outs occurred between bandits from the district, but it was demanding. Then, when I came home I registered the shock of adjustment, a changing of gears between emergencies.

My own family had moved away over the years, my eldest sister most recently after my mother died, but I saw less of them than we had intended. Only recently we managed that visit to Canada, leaving Mom at Cascade. Now there's a mystery, that place. Rachel tried to solve it through Mom but that was reading more meaning into Miss Ellie's disconnected comments than could possibly be there, though sometimes on a good day she would surprise us. It was best, I felt, to leave Rachel to think what she pleased if it could comfort her, whether she was fooling herself or not, whether there really was substance in some of it. For this Miss Ellie had had a mind so lively . . . Well.

Dan and Ellie. Inseparable, even now he's gone. Once, before she went back to Jamaica, my routine check established that Mom was not in her room but I was not particularly anxious. I went immediately to Dad's study, for Mom was always wandering in search of him. Only afterwards, when I found she was not at his desk, a cold fear took me that she had got outside and lost herself. I found her eventually upstairs in the spare room, curled up in a chair beside the closed window, sitting, rocking, drifting off into her nap with her arms wrapped around herself, shivering without complaint. At the feel of the soft fabric enfolding her she glanced up with the usual grateful smile.

"Aha! You're home, my boy."

"Mm-hmm! I'm the only one here in fact."

"Then you wrapping me up?" She caught my hand and kissed it.

"Just now. Let me pull this dress over your head."

"Why, love?"

"Because you're sitting here with no clothes on."

"How?"

"You must have taken them off."

"I wouldn't."

"No idea then."

"Poor you!"

"Don't worry. Doreen is off today, but Rachel will soon come home. There. Sweet biscuits?"

"Ah. *And not in utter nakedness,*" she confirmed.

Once she had her tea I helped her into bed, because the mystery of getting her teeth brushed was beyond me. If the teeth had lasted this long they would hold for another night, so I stroked her hair and left her rubbing her feet on the softness of her old blanket.

Again and again, we reviewed the strength of her medicine – whether she needed more.

"Or less." Andy wallowed a French fry in a ferocious mess of ketchup and pepper, wagging his head in time to whatever was being piped directly from that noisebox into his brain.

"If you eat that on campus, why you won't have real food when you come home?" his mother wailed.

"Next time," he promised. "Midnight snack while I do the stupid assignment." His head bobbed as if it might drop off.

"What a vision." Mom had regarded the shaggy whiskers incredulously. "Haw!"

And he had shaken with laughter and fallen out of time with his tune.

She kept time with her hands along with the bobbing of his head and after a while she superimposed her own rhythm. She inhaled gratefully as if her personal music that I could not hear filled not only the room but her lungs, and circulated, filming, salving, percolating in through every pore, intercepting each mutation quietly underway in the rhythms of her life. And sometimes she paused in midgesture (for she marked time with her hands) as if pulled away from her melody to brood over something she had been trying to remember. Or, perhaps, to forget. Then, trying to keep in time, she conducted vigorously again.

But the person struggling hardest to keep in time was Rachel, who felt behind in all things – whatever her meticulous attention to scheduling and her paranoia about deadlines – behind so she felt that she could never catch up again in this life.

"What about the letter to the lawyer?" I had urged Rachel. "Or are they supposed to write us? The real process hasn't even begun and it can't start till we find out what went on with Dad's property."

"Will it happen in time for her to get any benefit from the estate?" she asked. "If they're playing the ass let's give it to someone else who will move on it. They're way behind time."

"Behind time, overtime, out of time. Haw!" Mom had slapped her leg in delight.

"Well, at least you're pleased with life."

When Mom laughed, Rachel lit up.

Now, that night there was Rachel on the telephone, talking to her mother at Cascade, and one glance at Rachel's face made me dive over and press the button for speaker. I was more troubled than I cared to show, nagged by something I could not put my finger on. There were random things that seemed to make no sense.

"Mom," I put in, "before you went for this holiday with Rummy – you said you telephoned her?"

"Who went on holiday with Rummy?" Her voice, loving and near, stroked us as surely as her habitual petting of the cheek. ("Little velvet thing," she would purr to Rachel.)

"You did." I sighed, turning to Andy. "Remember Mom told us she called Rummy and we didn't see how . . . but look, it's on the phone bill."

"So?'

"That was the day she cried. So hard. She said Rummy was frantic, begging for help."

"*Rummy* cried?" Andy tried to conjure it. "What the jail is this?"

"Why?" Mom gasped before I could explain, and I could hear her anxiety over the phone. "Rummy's ill?"

"Then you seem to have developed such an *attitude* to Scotty, Mom," Rachel put in. "I wonder if really . . . But I thought this man Ashmead had cleaned things up."

"What he could clean up? Dirty ole brute!"

"Mom!"

But Andy guffawed and she sang out to him, pleased to be in a congenial set, "You agree, big fellow? Dirty ole brute? Haw!"

"If you say so." He doubled up with amusement.

"Mom, I don't think you ever even *met* the man," Rachel said. "Still, if he spends so much on the place, perhaps he's there often and you just forgot to mention it. So doesn't his wife go there too? Especially if it's her money like Rummy said."

"Husband and wife are 'one flesh'," Mom reminded us.

"Listen. Is Rummy there now, with you? When last did you see her?"

She paused so long I wondered if we were disconnected.

"I can't say. But a matter . . . Rosemarie . . . someone . . . something I should . . . relate. Rachel?" Beneath the surface of the past into which she probed, the fragments must have drifted, too elusive to assemble, and as they swirled her voice filled with excruciating pain, as if each edge were a razor.

"What is it you feel?" Rachel keened. "Sweetheart?"

"My head."

"Hurts?"

"No. But something glides . . . something . . . terrible, is it? It slices here, there."

"Pain?" Rachel pressed a hand to her own head.

"Not again. It's faded, leaving only the ferns outside the glass . . . shimmering."

"When I come, I'll walk with you and see these ferns."

"Mm. *Come into the garden, Maud, for the black bat night has flown* . . . But it hasn't, has it?"

"Evan!" Rachel exclaimed. "Rabin, he's the one we could contact. Evan would know how everyone is. Mom, can you say how we'd find Evan?"

"Ivy's boy?" Mom's voice chirped. "Ivy will be able to put you in touch with him. But be discreet how you ask. In our time a girl could never recover from a mistake like that, and her fiancé dropped her too when she contacted him, just as if he had nothing to do with it." She heaved a sigh while Rachel and I stared at each other. "I can never forget Ivy clutching me. Wild. Her eyes were wild. Holding me as if some undertow were ripping her away. Well, well. Evan never had the life he deserved, and it was not his fault. But Ivy was so afraid. And all alone. He seems to have forgiven her – if he even knows."

After a brief space Rachel resumed. "Who else would know Evan, Mom?"

"Scotty. But he's in such a state nowadays. He just ran past with the little fellow behind him. And Bonny knows Evan well."

"Is Ivy's house a nice place for a holiday now that Scotty's fixed it up?"

There was a pause at the other end as if Mom were searching her mind.

"We upstairs people chat, you know. The dog is friendly, poor fellow. They take us for a drive to the graveyard."

"Sounds delightful," I observed wryly. "Who else lives there that we know?"

Silence.

"Pansy is nice?"

"She needs to open her eyes."

"Scotty?"

"The other one is no better."

"How?" I probe.

"Don't know."

Rachel assumed a gossipy tone that I expected to go nowhere with Miss Ellie. "How does upstairs looks now it's fixed up?"

"Like snakes hanging from the ceiling, coiling and writhing, you know."

"What?"

"They could shock you, you know."

"Ah. What about the ceilings downstairs?"

"Mirrors. Equally shocking." Mom snickered, but whatever pun she had uncovered was quite lost on us.

I shook my head at Rachel, and said, "I don't think we'll work it out this way."

And Mom's voice lowered, slowed, then projected itself distinctly as she threw herself into verse:

"Out flew the web and floated wide,
The mirror cracked from side to side,
The curse . . . the curse . . ."

And she broke off suddenly with a strangled cry.

"What is it? Mom, talk to us!"

And Miss Ellie seemed to collect herself for she responded in some surprise, "Tennyson. You know that. Hold on let me see what all that noise is about."

"Mom, don't put down the phone. Miss Ellie, wait!"

But I was too late, for the phone went dead.

"We must go for her," I told Rachel. "We must bring her back. *Now.*"

But to my amazement, she hesitated, her expression horrified.

"But were you *listening*?" she said. "Isn't she's too far gone to bring back, to uproot and separate from Rosemarie again? She sounds completely out of it. Suppose she needs to stay? I'll have to bear it, but . . . Suppose she can't be moved, or just needs Rummy more? But you're right – I have to get there now. Now, and see for myself. But suppose she has to stay there where . . . where they're equipped . . ."

SEVENTEEN

Ellie

I PROBABLY SHOULDN'T have put down that phone because I don't know whether I can recall Rachel's number, but she will call again for, thank God, I remembered myself and replaced the receiver in the cradle. But I had to find out what all the excitement outside was about. Perhaps it's an excursion though it's a bit late for that – unless it's fishing. Dan loves an excursion, especially a fishing excursion. He has all the tackle – well, of course that was how I recognized it for a fishing knife.

Enough of that. I should tidy up before Rachel comes for me, so, quickly, the dressing table. I was a little afraid I might see only a yawning emptiness, that when I look into the glass I might see nothing at all or see what would be better blotted out, but it is not as bad as all that. I peer into the corners behind the woman reflected there, but nothing hovers, nothing I can see. I turn away in relief that there is nothing gory or hideous there, only me – a little bent. Determinedly I straighten my shoulders, and brush my hair.

"But stop! Mama? Don't today is Tuesday?"

No answer.

When I look out everyone is gone (I may or may not be dreaming – though how does one check that?). A key shines on the outside of my door. Bad idea, but thank God no joker turned it. I patrol and call, but no one answers. Now Rachel never does that. She always answers. A note tied to a sash hanging over the dressing table says that she is gone for a little holiday. *Coming for you as soon as . . . Love, Rachel.* A pen lies on the table.

Carefully I hang the sash around my neck and, finding all the inner doors open, walk down the steps at the end of the corridor keeping the paper in hand and gripping the pen firmly as well. Here is a place to sit down to wait, reading it again from time to time. I don't mind keeping watch.

On the television the same scenes are playing over and over. An impact on a towering building, billowing smoke, a plane bursts into a skyscraper, smoke, running, and the whole collapsing into dust and smoke. Every day these films are more far-fetched. They play it over and over and talk to the men in the construction helmets. People are buried alive. They are trying to reach them. It is too much for me and I close it out. I bolt the grille gate to Ivy's kitchen garden for good measure.

I reach back in my thoughts to a house surrounded by a latticed porch, with gables and transoms of the most delicate fretwork. Like lace. Memories like lace.

A tapping stirs me again (*as of some one gently rapping, rapping at my chamber door*) and when I turn the key I find on the inside of the door to the downstairs porch, here is a painfully thin young man. If they let him in through the outside gate they must know he's all right. Out on the other side of the house, Gawain barks furiously so I can hardly hear a word. The lad seems to recognize me and raises his hand.

Turning from him with my message gripped tightly, I pause to push in the chair. He seems tense but you don't just leave a chair higgledy-piggledy for people to come and find the room untidy. Now he puts his head around a door to the big bedroom that used to belong to Ivy's father, the door opposite the pantry, and seems to be looking for someone. There is no sign of anyone around and what would I be staying here for, alone with a young man I don't know? I hurry out to the corridor, to the downstairs phone, and search the numbers listed above it, but I don't recognize the names. Carefully, clutching my pen and paper in my left hand, I press the buttons that are so hard to target unless one is unusually steady. Why they did away with the dials, Lord?

"Hello?"

It is hard to explain that there is a man in the house who is a stranger.

"I don't know him at all," I finish.

The voice crackles at the other end. "I sorry, Mammy. I don't follow you. I feel you get a wrong number. But you in trouble? You can give me an address? Or call out a number you want me ring for you?"

But tell her what?

"Wait. Hold a minute, please." I lay it down, covering the mouthpiece with my other hand to give me time to think, to think what I called about, and to conjure the face of the woman on the other end, but it is no use and I replace the receiver on its cradle carefully in case Rachel or someone else should need to get us.

When I go back to the foot of the inside staircase, a young man who is waiting on someone there demands, "Scott Cunningham upstairs? Or he gone?"

A glance around confirms it, and away in a mirror across the room a woman with nothing to lose (and what could be more unmanageable?) raises her head and straightens her shoulders, and I signal frantically to her, staring as she sweeps her hands back and forth and stirs the air. The lad stands transfixed, for some of these children feel they can bully big people, you know, and they're surprised when it doesn't work.

I close my eyes to gather my thoughts, then I open them suddenly and fix him with a stern look, and say, "What you take me for?" I recall a glint of steel, the sweep of a blade flashing from a recess. "Is hang you want to hang?" I demand, and he stares at me, startled, then I realize – no, it was the other man. "Sorry, son. I think I mix you up with someone else."

Reality melts and reforms continuously around me and I turn away to orient myself, certain that I have no time to spare, and much more than a fool-fool boy to think about. For I have an obligation to fulfil, to Dan, to Rosemarie and . . . others? And although I have always had so much to do, so much to face, it has never been like this. Something hovers – as it has before, but it has never been so big, or had so many teeth. There is a strange young man here, mounting the steps in Ivy's house, so at once, before I forget, pen and paper – in my hand already, and I turn over to the blank side. I write, *Let in the dog*.

Clutching it so that it cannot get away and be forgotten I tiptoe through the ransacked house to the foot of the stairs near the door to the kitchen garden, shaken and more mixed up than ever but grasping my instructions in my hand and here is the grille door lit up by the outside light and beyond, through the glass, the near part of the garden shows up in a riot of colour but peaceful if the dog would only stop that infernal noise, so I pull the bolt . . . Oh Lord. The dog flings himself against the door. Too powerful. Jesu!

The impact is against the wall at my back but the ground slams up, paper floating . . . No. The paper my anchor drifting aside fills me with panic and I roll, snatch and in my teeth so my hands to fend off lest break a hip and finished but the General barges past me straight inside and I shakily, feeling my way along the wall I stumble in and bolt the door so at least the world is safe from Gawain, but he bounds up the stairs.

My limbs quiver and my skin cold and damp all over and, Oh Father, the foot of the step and sink down. Praise Him! Quietly, right here fold my arms my head, aah. Across the way through the open room is a window on the side of the house overlooking the road and the yard is bright but all is quiet. The door of the room right opposite is ajar and a ripple sets off across my mind, the hair on my arms raises as reality dissolves then sets again. A glance confirms it. The mirror reflects a room that is unfamiliar. Its frame encloses a portrait of an unknown person in a life I do not know.

"Help me, do. A glass of ice water."

She says nothing. I reach out but the glass offers no response, and no sign of Dan or Rosemarie or anything to account for the whole yelling and barking and commotion upstairs. In my time, Sunday was a quiet day.

A crash across the way rains glass outside that far window, sparkling as it falls. A thin young man lands on the ground outside and runs awkwardly, one leg crumpling under him.

They will play these wild games. You tell them and tell them.

"Easy does it," I call after him, waving a paper I have taken from between my teeth of all places.

A note on it says, *Let in the dog.* And I make the effort, battered as I feel, to get up look through the nearby door, but the General is nowhere in sight and I close it again gently to avoid making a noise and waking the others. And I sit and catch my breath. I don't know if it is the TV that upsets me so. It perches on the piano stool awkwardly and on the screen they are running and screaming as it crumbles around them. I am afraid of falling and now I feel so utterly exhausted (though God knows why) and this dog sleeping with its head on my instep is so comforting I might just doze off here myself.

Cloudy, cloudy outside and in. Long ago, when the children were away – I think it had something to do with their jobs – we went to visit them in one of these big cities in the States. So alike, some of these cities. But this one, this one dapples my mind with recollection.

There is a lake in New Orleans, like the sea. You stand on the edge and look out and there seems to be no other side. You send out your mind and sense no other edge for the horizon as you know is all a sham. Doesn't mean a thing. A line that seems to be there, a bit like death, if you like, there officially but not there in truth, if you see what I mean.

Rachel said they killed the lawyer. Poor woman. They don't like to upset me, so I pretended I hadn't heard. But now I remember I feel it as if I knew her well. Or someone like her . . .

"He's a great fisherman. Trophies from all about, they say," Rosemarie had reported.

"Dan loved fishing too." That was how I recognized it for a fishing knife.

I cannot assemble or disentangle the pieces, and Rosemarie is nowhere to be found. Yet only I have all the fragments. Somewhere. Only I can fight, and just when I am old.

As I sit here, I can tell you. I close my eyes and I feel it again. Not *again*, for it never really stops, I suppose. Only, when I stop doing everything else I become aware of it. A transformation. Slow, sure, constant.

The concrete becoming insubstantial. Yes, yes. I feel lighter, as though my very body is dematerializing even to the bone. My skin, see? Finer, transparent over a network of veins. And, to my mind, the edges of my life seem porous, so that fragments of experience fall in or out. (*And thin the boundary in between* . . . only I can't catch the tune.) Then, further in, passages grow more spacious, their arched ceilings higher, more imposing. Little things slip by, it is true. But there is room for large issues to roll through in their entirety. Life, death. Hmm. Then there are other areas I had not known about before, darker, echoing. Best not to enquire. Courtyards surprisingly far in, abloom with . . . ah, and the ferns so lush. And such a vista of mountains and mist. Imagine they could get all that in, eh?

So the walls thin to this series of columns broken by windows – webs of light. But what is interesting and I never noticed it before and so perhaps others can't see it is that the light shines out as well as in. Of course I do not know how it looks from outside, for it's a soft light. It would be a pity to miss it.

Perhaps there are people who can't see it even from inside, and that is somehow frightening, for then all it would be would be the dark cellars where I go as little as possible for what business have I there among the fine silencing lines of red wiped invisible with alcohol swabs? No, I like the upstairs with the hanging ferns and, beyond, flamboyants floating in mist that swirls and parts around the mountains.

"She's dead." Rosemarie's anguished whisper.

"Who?"

"Poor timid little soul. Not a relative in the world. No one will even ask for her."

She had done nothing either, according to Rosemarie, but to try to find out . . . find out . . . something or other.

"She just sent the message," Rosemarie said mournfully. "She was the only one young enough to have known what to do, and young enough not to be babbling about it in a year or two. It must be the same way they figure it out too. And they don't think of me at all. Not yet."

We looked at each other reflected in the mirror.

Some days are cloudy, cloudy inside as well as outside. Somewhere is a wound like a fine line, but deep. Between it and me a gap widens, a veritable buffer of emptiness between me and sensation.

Where was I?

Yes. By a lake. And then the bridge. Who could have imagined a bridge over something so vast. Only to conceive the idea was . . . was bold. But people are. Driving across the bridge, you . . . then they drive so fast in these foreign countries. This vehicle – speeding along a road that arches out from the shore into nowhere. Water ripples away in the wind on either side and, behind, the shore rushes away and, before, the road narrows to a pinpoint on the horizon that you know isn't even there. The bridge . . . but how can it be a bridge with only one end . . . road into grey nothing, yet you know it can't be nothing, for why would they drive you along it if it went nowhere? I mean, they have sense. You don't put gas into a car and just run it to use up the gas.

The shore rushes away behind you. After a while, it too is out of sight. Behind you, as in front, the road narrows to a pinpoint at a line that does not exist, and on either side steel-coloured water ripples, foams, wind-whipped sprays turn into mist, or is it a diaphanous rain hazing the surface of water that looks tough but lustrous though even its surface is an imaginary line for where does the water stop and the sky begin in that sort of situation. So I recall. A wet day with a light mist so that even the imaginary lines fade. And there I am again, hurtling through a world without horizons (even such as they are, shams every one) on a bridge that arches from the forgotten to the unknowable. Moving so fast it's no point being afraid and anyway the scenery is like nothing else in this world. Unearthly. I just say my prayers and give myself up to the adventure for within I carry all the people I love and out there, well, just look at the vastness of it. Stunning. I lean back, closing my eyes in contentment. Even when the room around me materializes again my mind clings to these fragments (wouldn't have missed it for the world) so I turn back into my head to see what else is there.

But I am forgetful. *Forgetful, anger, roaming at night.* One night as I walked upstairs, the door to the inside stairs at Ivy's, which people had been bolting from the other side, swung open to my touch. I held the rail tight and set my feet carefully on the steps. In the darkness at the foot of the stairwell where I am sitting now I stopped, because a thin figure blocked the moonlight beyond the iron gate at the end of the corridor. The light over the entrance was too dim to show his face, but gleamed on a stud in his eyelid. He tried the gate but it was locked, and so he tapered away. Thin, almost emaciated, bathed in white light, he may have raised his hand, a spectral greeting, or, perhaps like an apparition he was never really there.

I was afraid to go on and when I went back upstairs that must have been when I saw Thelma coming out of Ivy's room. I glimpsed a screen and the green words "Shutting Down", as she pulled closed the door that said OFFICE.

"At this hour you come out for a snack?" I grinned. "Well. Cockroach must forage."

"Go back to bed!" She led me to another door and woke Rosemarie.

"What a way this house busy at night," I chuckled, and as soon as Rosemarie fell asleep I was off for a walk again.

But now I close my eyes again and there is Rosemarie. We sit together on the side of a bed, for the room has no chair, and as we talk we look at each other in the mirror.

"Trembling all over, but so brave. Poor Thelma."

Thelma. That was another name that escaped me. *Thelma.* For Thelma and I looked at each other in the mirror too. A thin curved blade for gutting fish sweeps a fine red line across her throat. Blood spurts out and hits the wall, trickling down between the bumps in the concrete.

Something must be done. Or it will happen again. *Talk to Rachel*, echoes Dan's voice, then Rosemarie's in my head. *Remember Rosemarie*, Dan urges. *Forget*, soothes Rosemarie. Zкор, a column soars on a mount.

Do not go gentle into that good night. I write this in blood on the walls of my mind.

EIGHTEEN

Rosemarie

I WAS WELL hurt when Dan first shrug off Scotty degree from the college abroad, for I see the certificate myself and Ivy and I say we would cook some rice and peas and make Basil dem kill the young pig. And how Dan respond just throw a damper on the whole thing and it never come off. I suppose I wasn't so sure after that for I not as blind as Dan and Ellie seem to feel, but it was much later that Archdeacon really confirmed no reputable institution was behind Scotty degree. Even then I said, "Is not everybody is a brains can go UWI. Somewhere recognize the boy work and that must worth something."

Only Archdeacon said, kind of offhand, that any work that didn't leave no proper record was not likely to be an achievement. And he try to avoid calling Scotty a fake outright but he say he certain the certificate false.

The first sign of trouble I saw between Scotty and Ashmead was over that same. Ashmead told him something I couldn't work out.

Scotty blustered, "I can go anywhere and work. I have my certificate."

And Ashmead agreed, more polite than I expected, "I know. It was one of your attractions, so obviously manufactured it would put off any self-respecting employer. Besides, false documents lead back to nowhere, so their owners leave no trace." His voice was soft and reasonable.

"Is not that I want another job," Scotty start to whine.

Stupid and treacherous as this boy turn out, I began to fret. After all, he was Jesse's son.

"You know what I think, Miss Rose?" Thelma fluttered after I confided in her. "He must be in some scheme with Ashmead that has got so big and dirty Scott doesn't know where to put his foot."

Next morning Scotty announced triumphantly that he was getting out of pharmaceuticals and starting out in the hotel business. A backhoe come in and start tear down trees on the other side of the private road behind Ivy back fence.

"But that is my land," I screamed at him.

"Is what you want?" he demanded. "You want to keep you piece of wasteland or you want invest in a hotel that going bring in money? Or you prefer sell?" He dive into the office and come out with a paper. "Is a good offer but you would do better to invest in the hotel itself. Listen. Make me give you a couple days to consider. I will work from the other side while you come to you senses."

"The other side is Dan's. Ivy sold it to him. Yours is next to mine and Evan's beyond Dan's."

"Well, the Dan dead long-time. He tenant buy it through the same crooked lawyer and sell it one time and Ashmead have the title. Evan will sell if he know what good fe him. All this ya going tear down."

At the thought of Ivy house knock down my eye grow dark, and when I come to myself I hear him saying how the tourist dem get they notice and done move out. But all that I know long-time. Is true downstairs was empty and only a few of us from upstairs still around.

"But what about us?" I wanted to know. He said arrangements were in train. That was when I came to understand what Ashmead had said at the start of the exchange I heard.

He had said, "You see upstairs? If I have to move those old farts myself you're going with them."

Well, Scotty make up his mind to hold down whatever job he have with Ashmead, and he working flat-out on hotel. But he never trust anyone even to clean the office and he continually looking over his shoulder.

Next thing, Scotty bring in one scrawny boy for protection. A little underfed pickney with a jewellery in him eyelid and look like he can't protect himself, much less . . . When I hear the boy had an injury and I offer to dress it for him that is how I get to see the sore. I see that once in my life before and is nothing I could ever mistake for no injury. Well, I was sorry for his condition but I wanted to know why they lying about *injury* and what this boy was doing going everywhere with Scotty. Is Gladys whisper to me that Mister Scotty think the boy working for him but the boy really a deportee come back and working for Ashmead. I feel she know a lot more than that but she dry up when I ask. All she say after that is, keep 'way from the whole o' dem.

Now just before Thelma die, Ashmead did interrogate Scotty in connection with his accounts and Scotty had to admit that someone get to tamper with the records. Ashmead ask whether it was his wife and Scotty stutter out quick quick that Pansy don't know nothing bout no computer. Then, shortly after, them find Thelma dead and Ashmead leave and gone back a Kingston.

Most of the day pass quiet before we get to hear Ashmead was coming back because trouble start from a set of e-mail that come out from Cascade self, and Scotty start flattering round and round like chicken with it head cut off.

Evening coming on when Pansy and Cindy drive up. They have traveller cheque and ticket and Cindy new luggage fill up the back of the SUV. Scotty only see Pansy when she coming back out the house to the car.

Pansy voice was businesslike businesslike. "I only come for two passport dem from the storeroom."

"Then dry so you going without one word to me?" Scotty shout.

"You think I going stay with you and dead?" Pansy scream. "Or make dem acid Cindy? Next thing they think say all young people know bout computer and is *she* do it."

"Where you think you going? Where you think you can hide?"

"The farther from you and this half-arse country we get, the safer we going be."

"And what bout me? What I suppose to do?"

"Grind Mitzy, nuh! It work for you all this time."

"Cindy." He drop his voice and he whimper. "Cindy, you mean you would leave Daddy? After all I spend pon you?"

"I didn't haux to be born!" she pitch back at him, and flounce inna the car.

Glass Bottle pick up two small stone and fling them at the SUV as it roar out of the gate.

"Not to disrespec de Daddy," he scold them.

One of the stones nick the windscreen, and the fine cracks spin out like spiderweb, and that was the last straw for Pansy. She slam on the brakes and we hear her screech at him, "I going send police to lock up you mad arse." Then she start off again down the road.

Nobody take Pansy serious, because there was no chance to think. Everything begin to happen one time.

Ashmead pull in and pass Scotty on the landing without a word. He signal back to his car and the young boy with the eye-stud come out. When Scotty see him slide out of Ashmead car he yell at Jarvis to leggo the dawg. Two of the dawg dem race out and the boy shoot both of them dead with hardly a glance. How the light fading, we never see the long gun in his hand before – it did just look like part of him hand. Scotty duck and run and the boy take after him round the house. Glass Bottle throw stone and shout not to kill dawg fe nothing and police van draw up and they start to shoot at Glass Bottle.

Ashmead in the office smashing up the computer when Glass Bottle scale the fence, jump over the dead dawg and run take cover in the house. Police swarm after him still shooting, and I scream out, "Oh God, is a old-people home. Him is jus' a madman. Oh Jesus, what you doing? Is a set of old people." But one of them box me down flat and I roll under the dining table while they storm through shooting everything up. And this don't have nothing to do with Ashmead business or Scotty wo'tlessness or Thelma dead. Me don't have no time to tell police what going on, no time to think bout anything but dodge bullet. Cecil stretch out on the floor but I couldn't tell if he was taking cover or he get hit. I know for a fact Sybil dead. And nobody care.

When the police get into the office and start upending everything looking for the madman, I see Archdeacon on the way to the inside stairs and I take off after him, but before I reach the top of the stairs I hear a shout and look back along the corridor and through the door to the porch. Police sight Glass Bottle from the porch and in the dusk he look like he was getting away across the lawn but they shoot him down just near the stump of the old lignum vitae tree. When Archdeacon and I get to the bottom of the stairs we turn straight into the store-room and pull in the vault door.

And is only when we catch ourselves and make to turn on the light that we find the Ashmead in there with us.

NINETEEN

Ashmead

IT IS NEVER as it seems. I see what they think – I see it in their faces, staring, wide-eyed, as if I am some monster, without seeing me. From the first I came to the guest house with no intention of injuring anyone and even now, down here, the gun is for my own protection, what with the madness that fool has brought down on us.

If I had locked the door they would not be here and perhaps I could have slept. But then, here in the dark of the storeroom with my mind slipping back, the tension has gathered my nerves taut and this intrusion at least resets my thoughts.

As they eased the door closed stealthily, I said, "Turn slowly." And they froze at my voice. "Don't touch the light switch."

Now I can see them in the dim light from the high window but their eyes have not yet adjusted and they peer uselessly in my direction. I raise my hand into the faint stream of light so they can see the gun, then call them quietly over to the side hidden deep in shadow and make them sit on the ground. I am on the only chair which is an advantage for I can get to my feet faster.

"But how the door wasn't locked?" I can hear her whisper to the priest.

There must be no talk between them.

"I left it so," I say. I did it purposely, for if the police try it and find it locked it will prompt suspicion, while no cursory glance from the doorway will penetrate the dimness. "If it opens," I go on softly, "don't make a sound." I reinforce this with a brief gesture with the gun in my hand they can now discern.

The priest's eyes search the window, then shift back to the room, pausing to adjust again to shadow. He is confused but only temporarily. His mind is intact – so much the worse for him. His gaze pries into the darker spaces beyond me, but the old Cunningham woman stares at my face, her eyes flickering to my hand then back, burning into mine.

"Don't open your mouth," I tell her. An old woman's voice in my head? And this one – this one probably the bitch who organized the leak regarding my business. I won't be able to stop myself if she starts talking and the cork on these walls won't mute the sound of a shot, for I have faintly heard gunfire upstairs.

As I wait here straining my ears for the muffled noises above to stop, the dull throb of feet running on the wooden floor, the shots, the kicking of the doors, these others flatten themselves away from me against the damp wall, excruciatingly aware of my presence, one unable to look at me, one unable to look away.

The priest stares at the window willing himself beyond its panes and the woman reads my every look and gesture, working forward to my next move. *He will kill us,* her eyes conclude. *He must.* Clear thinking, and every thought written fatally on her face. *But how will he do it without drawing their attention?*

I will show you.

My loathing builds as the minutes drag by towards the time scheduled for my flight. The hours. In this jailhouse. And this is the bitch who did it; she brought me here. The usual tendon tightens in my neck and my hand fondles the hard metal, a finger reaching of its own volition towards the trigger.

"The bathroom is right outside the door," the priest murmurs. "Please."

"Shut up."

"I must relieve myself," he insists, face turned from the woman in embarrassment. "You know I won't run off and leave her here alone with you."

I motion him to a corner between the tree roots. "Do it there."

She won't go though, in front of the two of us. She will hold it in if it kills her.

When he comes back he settles back down wordlessly beside her on the ground. And they stare at me, speculating on what is to come.

I have nothing to say to them and all they have to tell and must not be allowed to utter is throttled even as the concrete wall is muffled with cork. They know how much more they have to fear from me than the guns upstairs. In any case what confusion we could hear outside has passed, leaving behind a great stillness. The silence hangs heavy in the damp air and the smell of loose earth and rusting bolts.

By morning I will be out of here, and as for these . . . Once I secure the room from the outside it will be the silence of a tomb.

TWENTY

Ellie

ALL THE SHOUTING has stopped and I may have slept right here for I am so cramped I can hardly untangle myself. A faint click on the pantry door alerts the dog who has been sleeping on my foot. She raises her head and frills her lip.

"Shh! Behave yourself, General." I let her out through a door to an enclosed part of the garden, flipping off the light switch as the sun is rising anyway, and I nod to the man who emerges from the pantry. To my surprise he squeezes out and slams the door behind himself hurriedly, checking the lock, pocketing the key, then pushing something more bulky into his pocket. His glance skewers me briefly but he offers no greeting, the old cuffee, merely crosses to the room opposite, enters and closes that door too. This sudden appearance from underground in the dim light, his pallor, and some . . . something, a recollection of a wound shivers across my brain but I shrug it off in a line or two from that song. You remember Barnabas Collins, the vampire man on the TV show? Then the song was all the rage: *Out de light, lack you door tight, Barnabas a come a go take one bite* . . . "Haw!"

But in the silence, something. Faint – but listen. Like a pounding on the inside of the pantry door, but it is locked and as I study it a sliver of paper works its way underneath.

Rosemarie's writing. *Help us. Locked in.*

Now I pound the door, and shout for Rachel, but that makes no sense, and while I hold the paper tightly in my left hand, a man appears from a nearby doorway.

"Let me." He guides me away through the passage to the sitting room and I can do with the assistance as I seem to have slept badly and ache all over. He settles me in one of the easy chairs.

"Did you lock that door by accident? Would you like me to call someone?" He watches me closely.

"Yes," I respond desperately. "But whom? My head is not with me."

"And what would you be calling about?"

"I'm not even sure."

He studies my face, and I his. He is faintly familiar. I would think I know his family, yet now I see him there's no placing him after all. A striking face under the full head of glossy hair emits no warmth and his slate eyes are insatiable. He leans forward reassuringly, but who trusts a man with a smile-shaped . . . maw. I shrink back with the odd feeling he might issue flame or contagion, but he sinks easily onto the other chair.

"All this excitement isn't for people our age," he remarks confidentially, as if his pretending to be my age might disarm me. Grey as he is, his face is unlined. Elegant bones, but pallid skin for a coloured man.

"I'm afraid your name escapes . . ." I shiver suddenly, at something more than the cold mountain air in the early morning, but I manage to steady my voice. "Remind me."

"I'm a friend of your family, Mrs Duvall, an associate of Scott Cunningham. Remember Scotty?"

Unfortunately. Grasping. Haphazard principles. Yes. So this is one of Scotty's cronies. Dissolute too, from the slack mouth and greedy eyes.

"We were never close."

I must sound cold, for he purses his mouth and shakes his head a little sadly. The visitor wears a suit of exquisite quality and cut, though slightly dusty, yet something about him disorders what was rather a jolly room in the old days. In fact, oddly enough, some chairs are overturned and a cabinet glass is broken.

"Been a bit of a disappointment to me too," he reflects. "When I think of all that boy could have . . . well, he showed such promise."

"Who?" On the screen they silently replay the rescue work, the digging, the weeping. In the corner runs another picture, smaller and in slow motion, over and over. A plane ploughing into a tower, a dark cloud billowing, and the noiseless crumbling into dust and smoke. The men in the helmets toil on, heaving and uncovering. People are buried alive. They are trying to reach them. "Whom?" I feel for the gist of it, haunted by a sense that I should be digging too.

He regards me with satisfaction. "Scotty. I thought him promising."

I never knew a promise Scotty did not break. Still, not having got the main thrust of the conversation I hold my peace, but he leans forward.

"Heard from any of them lately? Scotty's aunt . . . stepmother, is it? Rosemarie?"

Rosemarie's name hurtles me into chaos. I was there too not so long ago and in my mind the room narrows, lowers, darkens, thuds soundlessly under my fist, bulges with dark knots protruding inward, trips me in the dim light. No one can hear. Rosemarie.

He appraises me suavely. "What's going through your mind?"

The images scatter at his voice, leaving me on the outside of a terrible memory, and his eyes bore into mine, crushing it further and further in.

"Is everything all right?"

Now it is all locked away in the darkness and I attend to the matter at hand. A stranger to be entertained whether I like him or not. Why have they left me with this anarchic grin?

"Do you remember Rosemarie?" he asks. "Rosemarie?" he prompts, a man who should be about my colour, but pale as if he has spent his life underground.

"Rosemarie is my sister."

He looks surprised. "Sister? Or sister-in-law."

"Husband and wife," I respond coldly, "are one flesh." I haven't time to split hairs. "You obviously have no idea how old I am."

"Tell me." He assesses me with interest.

Surely he's not young himself. Not withered, no. I shuffle the words in my head and for a moment Dan and I bend again over the crossword turning over the clue. *Etiolate.*

"How old *are* you?"

"Don't be impudent. You don't ask questions like that!" The gall.

He shifts gear swiftly. "I'm sorry. I never meant to offend you."

I relax slightly. "Well, perhaps you weren't taught. Your mother should have . . ." But it has slipped away, what affronted me.

"I never had one," he remarks, and, in response to my obvious confusion, he adds, "a mother, you know."

And the odd thing is that while normally that would touch me, I find myself at this moment without any sympathy for him whatever.

"Let me tell Dan you're here." Pressing down on the table I raise myself to a standing position, but I pause for my feet to respond. The corridor seems familiar enough but the entrance to the pantry is locked and the way I take leads into the bathroom. And why not? They say the late King George always advised: never miss an opportunity.

When I come out, the passage offers various outlets but I pause at the foot of the stairs where a man of indeterminate age leads me aside to the downstairs sitting room.

"Glad to have you back." He is dressed like an American, but I am not quick enough to place an accent.

"Can I help you to the sofa?" He lays down his leather case to offer me his hand, but I'm not such a fool as to take it, so after a second or two he withdraws his arm and I sink gratefully into the soft cushions opposite the TV. He walks to the door and glances around – for Dan, I suppose. Meanwhile I pick up the small dark case Dan always uses when he travels and I wedge it carefully between me and the arm of the sofa.

On the table are old magazines. *Time. National Geographic.* I turn the pages of one they have left for me, till I see an interesting picture, but an ad warns, *Run, Rhino, run. Extinction is forever.*

The . . . salesman (is it?) turns back to me and takes my hand. Men you don't even know have the temerity to be familiar, as if you were waiting and praying for it. I withdraw my fingers, wipe them on my skirt and clasp them with the other hand. His eyes which pick up everything smoulder, then go cold.

"Tell me, do you have memories of that home Scotty ran? You were on holiday there. Any recent word from them? You may not have had much to do with Scotty, but what about Rosemarie? What can you tell me about Cascade?"

"Let me call my husband. He keeps up to date with the correspondence." At the mere mention of him, all Dan's civility and decorum rise around me, interposed between me and the suave smile of the stranger unaccountably in front of me.

"But I prefer talking with you." He leans closer. "It's always so much more pleasant talking to a beautiful woman." He unravels his long limbs and coils forward with practised elegance, and his eyes flick over me. "You must have been a scorcher in your day."

That's it!

"My husband . . ." My voice trembles, I can't say why. "My husband supplies the compliments I need." And the incredible insult, the assumption that I should appreciate . . . . What makes them think . . . that I need their notice to feel of value, or to be sure I am alive? Ice congeals around my heart. And who the devil *is* this?

"You do forget everything right away, don't you." He relaxes against the cushions, regarding me closely, then goes on in a voice so low that now I have to lean forward to catch it. "So I'll tell you something. You like secrets?" he murmurs. "I've taken care of Rosemarie." My stomach lurches and my eyes squeeze tight, but his voice penetrates and blood spurts on the inside of my mind. "I can kill you too, and any number of old women. They die easily. People are never surprised. And no one misses them." The whisper withdraws like a blade, and his voice turns conversational. "But I'd like to leave a door open for you, so tell me what you remember about Rosemarie and Thelma – what information they sent out and where they sent it." I open my eyes to stare down the nightmare but it is real and stops my breath and my heart plunges into bottomless grief. "You don't remember, eh? Aah. Then you will forget all this as well . . . and soon you will forget Rosemarie too."

"No." I push my face into his. "I will write it down. If I even forget it tonight, I'll read it tomorrow."

"You will forget, you old fool."

"Who are you to call anyone 'old fool'?" I spit back. "Look how you dry up and fade out like something they forget in the dark. Age is on its way for you too." Ha! He had not thought of that, and recoils as if I struck him, but the thread has slipped and I manoeuvre on without a context. "What is it you want with me?"

"Nothing. That's the point. Just to be sure you remember nothing."

"I remember you are vile. And Dan will help me keep track of the rest."

Outside, a man's voice breaks in on us. "The whole place search up, you see. I have to talk to whoever was here."

The man who is with me withdraws quickly and I am alone when Basil shows the policeman into the room.

"Good morning, Officer," I say. "How may I assist you?"

He stares at me without answering, than turns back to Basil. "Oho! Is a insane!" He puts his head to one side and gazes again with his voyeur's eyes. "No, no! I cyan't question all like she. But how you didn' tell me her condition? All right, Madda."

"Madda me foot." But now I think of it – poor fellow, with his head lolling about like that, and a young strong man too. "Officer, would you like a cup of tea?" His laughter recedes as he tramps out through the door. "Can't someone give him a lift? He shouldn't be on his own. Just ask Viv, Petrona, somebody give him a cool drink for me."

I hear the car pull out and soon a tall, sickly looking man emerges from the room near the foot of the steps, and I sigh, "I wish Dan were here." And he leans forward solicitously.

"You must miss him a great deal. Your husband, I mean," he purrs, calculatedly appeasing and about as healing as arsenic.

The space I maintain between us is a relief and in the vacuous numbness I find it in myself to feel surprised.

"Why would I?" I stare, I suppose. "He's never gone for long."

But his attention has wandered. He mutters about his papers, his flight. He glances among the books on the side table. Basil returns and just stands there while the man turns over newspapers, magazines, the phone, exclaiming desperately that he has mislaid his ticket and passport.

"Rosemarie might know where they are," I suggest. "You want to phone her?" I only propose it because if he can clear up whatever it is, he may just go. But from what he says it seems she can't be reached.

"Then send the messenger!" I say, irritated. In all my years in Bonny's business I never let the fool-fool telephone company hold me back. "That little meagre fellow who calls me Grannie. With the stupid thing in his eyelid. Don't he's desperate for any work he can get? Then you can't spare him the little cash?"

The man lurches towards me, staring. "Who?"

"Whom!"

But the thread snaps. He sways inexplicably before me with his hand to his head and his eyes consuming the room.

"Is what papers it is you lose, sah?" Basil probes gently. "Wait. You not well? You want me call anyone? You wife?"

"One flesh," I agree.

He stumbles slightly at the door to the room before us and clutches the knob on his way in as if for support.

"But suppose the ticket and thing tief?" asks Basil. "You don't want call back the officer if he still near, make him help you?"

The other man shakes his head without even thanking Basil, and darts at me a parting glance so piercing I almost flinch, but I reach for a familiar line and hurl it at him,

"They're looking for you, said hearer to horror,
As she left him there, as she left him there."

Basil helps me outside and finds me a seat, and I shut my eyes to lock the other one out from my mind.

All the same that brightness that gleams to all eyes, for it is real – I don't pretend (why would I?) – outshines the shadows that reach below it, twice its depth. I am hardly aware of them myself. Now and then something blunders on them. Still, there is a shield between me and these shadows. (Dark sensations of . . . loss, perhaps?) Shadows of things I need not feel, for now, at least. Pain postponed, it is good to live in the sunshine. Give the rest a wide berth. Anchor myself with this chuckle that is hardly, if at all, a spasm of frustration. I recall the children chatting in the next room. Nice how they get along, like Dan and me.

"The hardest part is working out what's in her head. We don't even know when she's in pain."

But from I was a child we were taught, as girls, never admit to pain. Men are not to know. We learn it to different degrees: when the pain comes, eat it. Clench and swallow. Hold your face composed and focus on what is enjoyable and squeeze the rest to the edge. (Something lies buried, something to be uncovered. In good time.) Even now, when it almost comes to me, I can hold onto the amusing side that almost all things have. And the laughter that I cling to is real. Fun fringed with fury. Scotty running was no joke though and the little meagre boy who jumped down hurt his foot and the thing in his hand was gun and I called out to them but no one heard so I closed my eyes tight. Then under the door into my hand came a message in black and white. Around the edges are metal and stone, but the inside is lined with silence.

I remember my Rachel taking my face so we looked into each other's eyes, and hers were frantic, so when she steadied her elbow on the armrest in the car and put up her palm, I rested mine against it. I would do anything. Then another picture in my mind sharpens, fades, sharpens again. Hands groping along a rough wall. Fists beating the inside of a door. Slivers of light. It fades before I can put words to it.

When I hear the sound of the car starting up I open my eyes again, and from under my arm I pass Basil a small black case I have found in my care.

"The visitor seems to have overlooked this. As you get older," I explain faintly, "you can get a bit forgetful."

"Him must be sick," Basil argues. "Take care is something he eat."

And some men are so greedy. Like Scott. Greedy, that is what Scotty is. And for no reason the song wells up:

"... *an is greedy yes is greedy make dem kill him, uh-huh! ...*"

TWENTY-ONE

Rachel

BEFORE WE WENT to Cascade she took my hand to draw me into the garden.

Here I had a few clay pots but most were cement, not like in the old days. My more fragile plants had long since died of neglect, but lush staghorns flourished and, at the base of a massive tree trunk, healthy anthurium lilies wove their roots through tight fibres of coconut husks. On a branch that reached out to direct light was the orchid Rummy had brought years ago, detached from the notorious ficus behind Aunt Ivy's house and fixed securely to a slab nailed to our tree. Mom traced the delicate lip without actually touching it, only marking the air that bordered it, its pale mauve veined with violet, the bloom mirroring the fragility of her hand.

This hand, sliding into mine, was soft with the softness of muscle loss and uncertainty of direction, yet it was a warm sure hand, ready with solace, and remembering it and feeling it all over again a huge wave of shame swept down on me from a gulf I had not even known was there somewhere inside – a terrain I had had no time to chart for years – a tumult of regret for not having put my hand in hers as Dad slipped from her, while I was overwhelmed by the logistics of nurses and diets and maintenance of household and teenage recalcitrance and looming loss and guilt about crisis as a way of life in the house and terror of being washed away washed away, my fingers loosening their grip and the ground torn away beneath me, and in it all I knew, knew excruciatingly, how much worse it was for her but was so swept away I could never quite reach out fully and now here she was with this slight but infinitely reassuring pressure on my hand, not constraining but simply reconfirming that my comfort was her last remaining priority.

"Do you think they will catch again if we water them regularly?" was all I asked. "The ferns, I mean, for the orchid is flourishing."

There seemed to be some other source, a pipe dripping somewhere perhaps. There were signs of life persisting stubbornly in crevices.

"You believe in the eggshells too?" she cried, peering among a few brittle maidenhair stems miraculously holding on in the shade.

"Blindly," I confirmed, clinging to her hand although I had lied earlier when I said I was never mad at her for being forgetful and consequently unreasonable, for there were times . . . Then that guilt would rise like nausea, for she would never have been angry at someone for a condition they could not help, and shame would overwhelm me.

Between the pots the tree roots reached and grappled. They were in league with time, unstoppable. I noted that the garden had run entirely beyond my control, but it was finding its own way . . .

"Mom." Andy's voice called me back to the present. "Look, I can't stop," he went on, more to himself, dropping a CD on Mom's escritoire. "I need the memory so I dumped this off but it says 'Cascade Accounts' and I know Nan keeps copies of everything. It's two sets of figures, one beside the other. But it don' matter because is only copied to us. What are you doing just sitting here in her room anyway?"

"Trouble at Cascade. Or unless she's raving. I don't know which."

"I wonder if it have anything to do with them figures, Ras," Andy said slowly. (And Mom would have stared at him, for "Why would a decent child use a word like that?" is what she would have said.)

"Figures?" But I was focusing on the phone without my glasses.

When I called, Mom answered at once.

"I was sitting right here." She seemed surprised that I should not know that. "Rosemarie? Wait a bit. There's a note." Then she began to bawl into the phone.

"Locked in. She can't get out. There are people buried alive. Oh Jesu – Rosemarie." She dropped the receiver and I could hear her crying, "Help! Help her!"

"Don't put it down," I shouted. "Mom, take up the phone. Pick up the receiver. Mom, don't leave the phone."

Andy and Rabin rushed in but when Rabin grabbed the receiver there was no one there.

"What is it?" I gasped. "She's crying, that someone has buried Rosemarie alive."

"Who? No, man. That must be the TV – the news," Rabin insisted.

"No! Well, I don't know. How can we be sure? Who can we call?"

"You would think that Dad would have had some record . . . some note that might help us contact someone, wouldn't you?" Rabin muttered. "Something to help work out how to reach Rummy?"

Andy shrugged. "I suppose you done check the file?"

"File?"

He stared at me, surprised. "GranDan and Nan have a file for years. Rummy and thing. The little desk-business here. Full of . . . Look. All this." With a sigh of something between impatience and tolerance beyond the call of duty he pulled out drawer after drawer and dumped it all on the table, found a CD, then turned back to the computer and popped it in. "I saved that last one with the Cascade business because she was always so hyper about records and thing."

Rabin moved to the keyboard and sifted through the file, looking incredulous.

"Is years I surfing from one site to the next," Andy went on. "GranDan was interested and . . . Watch. Accounts I told you about, and something that came earlier. Some sort of report that was only copied to us so."

"Who it went to?"

"Let's see." He took back the mouse from his father. "A whole lot of addresses. Look: Intergovernmental Commission on Anonymous Passbook Savings, Elder Rights International Task Force on Abuse of the Aged, World Bank Commission on money laundering . . ." He stared at us sitting frozen before the screen. "Selassie!"

"Who sent that out? Scotty says . . ." I said faintly. "Scotty said Rosemarie is senile . . ."

"I only have it because we always kept everything. You know how Nan always says nothing makes confusion like lost papers."

His hair clung to his damp forehead. He was so like Dad, copper cheeked, calm eyed.

. . . *on money laundering,* he had read. My limbs went weak and I slumped into a chair.

"Oh Lord! I've let her down." I glanced around wildly. "I didn't believe Rummy was in trouble . . . when I could have done something. I was the only one who could have done anything. I've let them all down." My head crashed to my arms on the table and I whispered, "Dear God, this isn't happening. Tell me I'll wake up."

"What is it?" Andy was horrified, and when I think of it I don't blame him. He would never have seen me like that in all the years. Beaten. "Nan in real trouble then?"

"No, no," Rabin interposed quickly. Too quickly. "But there may be trouble at the . . . at Cascade."

Breaking in on us, the scene in New York played on, over and over.

The TV, of course. It had triggered confusion time and again. And what could possibly go so wrong at Aunt Ivy's old house? Mom's bewilderment was not unique. The whole of them, many in the same condition, must be reinforcing one another. And whichever was there playing with e-mail had to be as batty as the rest, or why would she be there?

"All right," Rabin went on. "I'm booking the flight – flights. I'm coming with you. You crazy? Of course I'm coming with you."

To do what? I wonder. Oh yes, I wanted him to come. I needed the company, the support for what had to be done. But what *was* it that had to be done? All she said about everything to do with the place was so far-fetched, that I could hide from it no longer, it was broken, that last last thread I clung to. She had drifted beyond my reach and there was nothing left to do but to make arrangements.

What was the best I could do for her now?

For her, not for me – this child wanting her mother with a pain like a knife in the belly. For her.

Rosemarie? Establish that Rummy was alive and physically in order, that the home was sound – and leave them together? Hadn't she longed for Rosemarie this sixteen years? How would I separate them now? Hadn't she asked time and again to go home? Ferncot was sold, but Ivy's house was there. Here, it was all strange to her, and perhaps my own home was a place to visit, not the old well-known place deep in her head with Ivy and the whole of them. Wouldn't the mountains alone soothe her? God knows even I, rerooted, yearned for those mountains. She was part of them in a landscape inside her head that nothing else could match.

And she had told me herself (it haunted me, that warning twenty – thirty? – years ago to protect my family even from her if need be). She had insisted on it. And yes, while she was away I had had time to read, to think, to listen, and perhaps I should draw a deep breath and say she is being taken care of. Inhale deep and stifle it, that sob heaving to escape, for if I start I may never stop. Not this, not what I wanted, not what Dad envisaged. But he had not envisaged the alternative either, to watch it overtaking, to have to speed up, always trying to outrun it, to forestall it . . . with it gaining on us all the time. And there are no weapons to fight with. The outcome is inevitable, and I am unreasonable to postpone accepting it, and she had not wanted me ever to go through this.

Less than an hour later I manoeuvred the suitcase down the steps and Rabin looked up from the phone and said, "I got the flight. But what you doing? We only need hand luggage."

"I'm taking stuff for her. If the home is okay, if all this is pure confusion, I may need to let her stay."

Rabin put down the receiver slowly.

"Don't look at me like that," I said. "You know she is making no sense, no sense at all, and this house, this house is . . . our lives are in upheaval. Whatever I *feel,* I have to be rational. There is a point at which the right thing to do is to put your elderly relative in a home." I stood next to the door of her room and rested my forehead on the wall. "And those were my mother's instructions."

"You are doing this for me. Don't do this because of me. You should have enough faith in me to know you don't have to."

"I am doing it for *Mom.* She told me: 'If I get like that, put me in a home.'"

"Dad would not have wanted . . ."

"And you think it's what I want?" I cried. "Dad is dead. Mom is alive." And suddenly I could manage only a whisper. "And I have her instructions."

TWENTY-TWO

Basil

BECAUSE YOU OLD don't mean you turn stupid, for make me tell you say – me same one well old and me not no jackass. Is that why, when me see Miss El a look so full of trouble, me study me head say, Basil, something more a go on.

Of course me want know where Miss Rose and Archdeacon gone to, because dem not like Miss Agnes who head turn inside out. Dem head well good, like Miss Telma; all like them not walking wild wild on road fe lost themself. Dem have to be somewhe'.

Next, me want know where this man, Ashmead, creep out from after all that a go on, and where him was when it did happening. I meet him up with Miss El when the officer gone – but where he was before that, when the same officer did come talk with her? Him say a sleep him sleep. Sleep what? Through police raid and gunshot and house search up? After is not like him head don't righted like one or two of them upstairs. Me say, him lie to rass. Now if him lie bout that, how me fe turn me back pon him with Miss El?

So once me see police gone and take the dead with them and the place look quiet, me drag the dead dog out the way for me know say Jarvis nah come back to show him face anywhere police pass. When me get Miss El outside, me show her a shade to sit, where she can watch the sea. They move the bench longtime but I put two brick and the doormat and she settle comfortable, and me gone back in fe find out what going on with the Ashmead. I move careful because I hear enough to know say me dealing with a smaddy that don and all frighten fe.

"Can help you find what you looking, sah?"

Him no answer, just keep turning over the papers and mopping him face, so me start make up one thing after the other.

"I wonder if police did pick up you paper with everything else dem seize upstairs, sah. You prefer call the station or you prefer wait, because dem say dem a come straight back. Dem did aks after you, you know, sah, but I tell them you gone home a Kingston. They did want talk to somebody who head good and who educate, because me don't know nothing bout Mas' Scotty business. I tell them say you gone long-time, but if you want to wait for them I will say you come back to assist as a friend of the family. I feel say they will just tape off the place leave it empty so, but me no know. One of them say him have a lead."

All the time me watching him in him face and him hand turning over the same papers over again and they scattering by him foot and him don't seem to notice, because the other one of him hand dangle with the finger dem turn down.

And me tell him, "If Mas' Scotty mix ting up I don't know what wi' go on. Next thing is lock up people lock up. Jail fe the rest of dem life."

Him turn look pon me with him mouth slack, and me say, "Make me help you to you car, sah. As you call him early, the taxi waiting. You go straight home, sah. You nah look well."

And me draw him out the room they fix up so nice fe him and get him to the car, make sure it gone down the hill. And after that me never bother bout him because me have more important thing fe think bout.

So then me gone back a Miss El and say, "Miss El, make me aks you some-thing?"

And she say, "Basil you can ask me anything, but my head not good."

And I say, "But nothing no wrong with you heart, m'am. Is a good heart. Me know it from time."

And she smile and squeeze me hand and say, "True Basil?"

"True, is gospel, 'm." Then I ask her what bout Miss Rose and whether she have anything write down can help us, for I done see she have one paper crushup tight in her hand and I know she did always believe in writing ting down. So we spread out the paper and she read it aloud.

She cry out, "Jesu! Rosemarie. Someone said buried?"

"Is all right, 'm. We going get to her." For is only one place in Miss Ivy house that anybody could lock 'way, much less bury. "Miss El, you ever go down in Miss Ivy pantry?"

That surprise her so she forget Miss Rose.

"Yes, man, for the little pimento dram."

"It join onto any other room, 'm, or just the passage there?"

"You can see the fruit trees. Watch them, eh?" Her eye roam all about. "Bread-fruit, pear, mango. And Basil could climb anything. I think they hectored him a bit too much. You knew Basil?"

"Yes, 'm. But me never go inna pantry yet, you know, Miss El. How it stay?"

"Desk, shelves, cupboard, roots and cracks. Remember the old card table? Then one little window with the rubbish accumulating over it."

"Window? So you could dig way the rubbidge and break a window fe get in the pantry?"

"But how a big person could squeeze through that little window, and the bars? Behave youself, man."

"And suppose anybody lock in the pantry, 'm. It have any other way out?"

"Ask Her Majesty." She laugh out and clap her hand, and raise her head look out at the sea, and I tell myself say it not working, for she well los'. Then she smile and say, "When we went on the trip we visited a palace, called Versailles. They showed us the secret passage for the queen to run away, though they caught her anyway. Some of them wore red ribbons around their necks and they danced. Sometimes, in a catastrophe you just put up a good face. Not everyone can."

"Miss El, you know if Miss Ivy pantry really seal up completely?"

"Fool-fool boy, to leave a tree like that to mash up the foundations."

"I trying to help Miss Rose come out the pantry, 'm. Is lock she get lock in. It have any way out, 'm?"

Then she watch me direct and sensible, and that time when she stare out again I wait because I know she looking back into long-time.

"But, Basil. You *must* remember Marie Antoinette."

"The puss, 'm."

"Basil, years ago the puss get lock up in the pantry and it get out."

And I stop breathe.

"Is how the puss get out Miss Ivy pantry, Miss El?"

"Squeeze out through the crack. The roots break up the back wall. Years now."

"Miss El. You head well good."

"Haw!"

Long-time was a crack. Now, the wall crumbling and piece piece a drop out while one heap of small stone and rotten branch and dry leaf full up the space. The hoe and the garden fork throw down at the root of the same big tree, just where me leave dem run 'way when the shooting start, so me pick them up.

The soil well soft and the hoe chop down so deep me say better I hold back – next thing I damage Miss Rose or whoever else down dey, or make the mash-up wall self drop down pon them. But, likkle after, thing a scrape from the other side and Archdeacon voice a call fram inside, and the whole time Miss Ellie asking, "What you going to plant in that big hole, Basil? Is only a tree need a hole that size. But after it don't make sense planting new tree beside ficus. Cho!"

Then she make out Miss Rose voice and get frantic but, praise God, same time the set of dirt and small stone and dry leaf start to slide and the whole thing cave down and we hear them shout, but was from the wall side not no roof falling so it only slide down and them jump back in time and when the dust and rubbish settle we see the two of them well dirty up but safe, huddle gainst the other wall. It take a little time for them to climb over the broke-up wall how some of the stone sharp. But plenty of it crumble up so them come out good, only I have to hold back Miss El because she trying to give a hand and she not up to that. But when them do reach to hug up I see fe once them no have no voice to say nothing, and even Archdeacon had was to wipe eye-water and when he leave them he come put him hand round me and hold onto me like lost pickney when him puppa find him.

Me never experience anything like that in all me days.

After we catch weself we try find out who else leave pon the property and Miss Rose and Archdeacon make me help them get out two rusty box they find down inna pantry when they was looking for way out. Miss Rose say she never think she woulda come through it when she see police that shoulda help them with Ashmead just a shoot down Glass Bottle.

And that make Miss Ellie cry out, "No! Glass Bottle? Why? What he could do for them to shoot him? Then don't tell me he dead? But Glass Bottle wouldn't hurt anybody. You don't mean it?"

We had was to run bring ice water and make her sit down. But good thing she forget as soon as I remind her how Miss Rose and Archdeacon come out safe. Of course she done forget them ever lock up. So me take care no tell her nothing bout Miss Sybil. Likewise, me no mention Mr Scott to Miss Rose except fe say I think he make off inna car – and me lie tell them say Scotty tell me him plan go abroad fe join Pansy. Now what I see the maaga boy drag into Mr Scott car never look like anything coulda go foreign. But me never see good and me no sure, and since me no really care me just let it pass in all of what a go on.

For as the time pass the rest of the old people a shuffle one one out of bathroom and wardrobe or wherever them take shelter – me no know. One one a zigzag out like cockroach. Only one or two of the mix-up ones did huddle up in bed fall asleep, and now dem wake up a look food. Only God coulda send Miss Gladys to see bout them and she land up in the gateway just in time.

As Archdeacon see her from upstairs he sink down inna chair say, "We can manage now. And Cecil can oversee the medication for the rest of them."

And Miss Rose bawl, "Cecil make it? Archdeacon, how you never tell me! Praise God! I did see him stretch out pon floor and no sign of him since then. I search all over. Then where he is?"

"Mr Cecil gone town, 'm. Him was upstairs lying down." I drap me voice. "Him feel bad, especially how we lose Miss Sybil, 'm. But I carry the paper you find and give him, the one you say must get to Mas' Evan – only Mas' Evan flight back to Kingston delay through all what go on a America. But when Mr Cecil see the paper he say he taking it to Mas' Evan daughter right away, don't mind she down a de Kingston branch. Him taking it himself. Him call taxi and gone, and him carry some of the money Archdeacon bring from the storeroom fe pay the cabbie. Gone town, 'm."

"I never see Mr Cecil, 'm," Gladys say, "but as I come up the hill I meet Miss Agnes on the road going down. Me done send her in through the side gate tell her ice cream upstairs fe her."

Gladys say one pickney did run to her yard fe say police shooting up a Cascade. A so Gladys reach find herself on the road up the hill and meet up with the Agnes, for nobody did watching the one who head mix up.

Miss Rose groan. "My fault, you see. I shoulda never let her out my sight. And then, imagine Scotty done run out on us. He must be well tell Ashmead all kind of lie on me anyway, to save him own skin. I can't believe Jesse boy coulda turn out so."

That make me remember, but I hold me tongue.

Only Miss El blurt out, "But don't I heard he died? Scotty was so misguided. I wouldn't be surprised if he brought it on himself." She shake her head like she disappoint, for she woulda never want anybody fe hurt. "They sent the boy to search, and he came back without him, poor mawga little fellow."

Well, that time I had was to put in me mouth.

"No waste time sorry fe dat one, 'm. You no know what old-time people say? 'Sarry fe maaga dawg, maaga dawg turn round and bite you.'" Then I make haste tell Miss Rose it did have a sick in the house but I see him to him taxi, and she might want check if him room in order. Because now I hear car straining up the hill, so perhaps Ashmead well coming back. And who know whether him room have gun and all dem ting, or what him coming back to do? So is that why I make Miss Rose and Miss El gone in by themselves. Then I brace myself and wait to see is what now.

When the car reach and is Miss Rachel get out with her husband, relief almost knock me flat. Me foot get weak.

"Miss Rachel, I glad fe see you. Glad can't done."

Archdeacon hold the door while Mas' Rabin take out the bag dem and pay taximan. One old beat-up taxi, but it make it up the hill.

"Mom?" Miss Rachel cry out, and Archdeacon tell them Miss Ellie well, but explain how she and Miss Rose inside fixing room for a sick.

And it so happen that from outside the house look like nothing no do it. Is ongly the one window break pon the road side, and we done tear down the police tape.

"Then, Basil, you wouldn't get in trouble for moving that?" Miss El did watch me, worried, while I pull it down.

"Nah, m'am. Police just going say we no know what we a do."

Archdeacon did stare at me like he in shock. "Then we not making a full report to the police?"

"Me don't feel good bout that, you know, sah," Gladys tell him. "Me say, not fe mix up police inna you business. If police come lock the place down now everybody might just scatter up, and don't is best you keep together? Why we don't just go on quiet quiet, make them forget us – mind we business till Mas' Evan can get him flight home. Next ting when you call police you find you have them fe deal with now. Police can well ignorant you know, sah."

I see them a consider, so me remind them what old-time people say bout hurrying to do ting you don't think through: " 'Monkey must know where him go put him tail, before him order trousers.' "

"We'll give it a bit more thought," Archdeacon agree with me.

Anyway, is not long after that Miss Rachel reach, and I so tired ready fe drap down me just tell her, "You go in, 'm. Them right downstairs."

Ongly, the two of them did hear the car from where they was inside, and when them run out see Miss Rachel them hug up like them hand dem never going able fe unlock. It do me heart good.

And Miss Rose tell dem, "Thank God fe Basil."

And I did feel well good – true is Miss El really wo'k it out, but still me feel good because I believe say people did used to think me never have no sense.

TWENTY-THREE

Ellie

BUT IN ALL the jollification, they not overlooking something? And I can't work out a thing with the loud laughter distracting me like that.

"Cockburn has come too, I suppose." I can't help the sigh that slips out.

"Cockburn? What Cockburn?" Rosemarie objects. "He dead years ago!"

"But don't I heard his old raucous laugh?"

"Not Cockburn, missis. He gone from before you move away. You don't remember we went funeral? Pansy had on the heap of lace."

"The lace I remember – not that I haven't *tried* to forget."

Rabin calls my boy long distance and presses a button so we can all hear him.

"Rummy too?" That's Andy's voice. My own boy. "This is real bad. No, I mean, *bad.*"

Which is so odd, when he sounds happy. But I am accustomed, as all the images ripple across my mind, to how pain and humour intervene in each other's paths.

"I wonder what Dan has to say?" I enquire. "You haven't spoken to Dan yet?" They shake their heads and really so much was happening all the time that none of us can possibly keep up with all of it. *"I am going O my people on a long and distant journey . . . ."*

Their voices collide and intersect. A trim woman with fiery eyes picks her way barefoot towards Rosemarie, holding her shoes on high.

". . . want me little glass of wine before I go to me bed though!" she says fiercely.

". . . *many moons and many winters . . .*"

". . . not when Thelma sent the message, God rest her soul," says an elderly clergyman, "but afterwards when Scotty started to cry and say they were going to kill him . . ."

"You *weren't* locked in the storeroom then?" Rachel tries to disentangle it.

"Oh yes," Canon confirmed. "He meant us to die down there and we thought we would, for the door you know . . ."

". . . to look like we wander down and lock ourselves in," Rosemarie finishes, for she can be a bit overbearing, I can tell you. She has even tried it with me.

"Then how you got out?" Rachel asks.

I may have been nodding off, but now Versailles occurs to me again with its secret passageway.

"Tell me something," I ask the chap next to me, "Miss Ivy's feisty puss still alive?"

"*What*, Mom?"

Marie Antoinette stalks through my mind, a silvery shadow.

"The cat. You don't know Miss Ivy had one stoshus puss?"

"Scotty and all run 'way," Rosemarie adds.

"But from what?" demands that nice young man hovering around Rachel (and I like the look of him. I only hope he becomes a permanent fixture). "And what about Scotty's wife?"

"Oh, she leave him gone," Rosemarie reports.

"But no!" I throw up both hands. "Still, you see – there is only so much one can put up with – even a dope like Pansy."

Something else though. Something they forgot. Someone besides Scott. Why are *they* forgetting now? That's my job.

The umbrella shelters me but what about my boy (the big one)? Only Rabin pays no attention to the water driving into his face. He bundles me onto the back seat of the car with Rosemarie and Canon, but in no time, Rachel signals him to turn into a long unlit driveway and he helps me out again.

A hospital waiting room at night is tense, frightening – no one stops to tell me why I'm here and they push the wheelchair frantically. What are they racing for, what do I have?

"Tell me!" I cry. "For God's sake!"

"What? What?" Rachel leans an ear towards me as she hurries alongside.

"You driving me through in the wheelchair and you don't even tell me what it is they going do? Surgery?"

They stop.

"No, darling. Not you. You're fine. The hospital called and asked us to come and see someone and we have to move quickly. That's why we giving you this fast drive."

"Praise Him. Just so I know. Carry on."

We speed on, and after a while Rachel tells me, "You're fine, my love, we just need to go quickly to see someone else, why we have you in the wheelchair. You are fine." Which is a relief.

We pause at a doorway, and I really have to remark on it. "But here smells of urine."

"Accurate as usual, Mom."

"Then they must fire the cleaner."

The small waiting area is crowded, the old-fashioned louvred windows crossed by plain metal bars. A few nurses hurry by in white that is a little crumpled but clean. Some younger ones, in pink, seem to be doing what they can, but everywhere people are waiting, hoping, giving up, holding on.

Jolt. Moving again. Swing right.

"There." At the door the nurse points in towards a long white outline on the bed. "When he collapse on the way to airport, the taximan come straight here, but we find little or no identification. Like he lose some papers just when he need to travel. All we can find out is that the driver bring him from some place name Cascade, and is that why we ring. Then we try to get a name from him, someone to call, but all he can say sound like *Ellie*. You know anyone name Ellie?"

I clear my throat. "I'm Mrs Eleanor Duvall."

Rummy's hand is on my shoulder. "It may be one of our people." She slips into her professional voice and extends her hand. "Matron Cunningham. Miss Ellie's sister-in-law."

"I can't let more than three of you in, considering his condition," Nurse says, running her eyes over the group. "Matron, Miss Ellie" – she glances at Canon's worn collar – "and Rev, you come."

Inside, Rosemarie explains, "I'm managing a home for seniors on behalf of the owner who's temporarily away, and this is one of our rather unstable members. He just slipped off."

"Did you report it, Matron?" The nurse sounds almost apologetic. Rosemarie is imposing.

"Not yet. He's often quite competent, though he has his moments. He can tell the wildest stories."

Nurse and orderly exchange smiles.

"He gave us a little of that when he came to – after he collapse and the driver bring him, but he hardly speaking now. He *was* delusional." She grins derisively.

She leans over the bed to take the patient's face in her hands, and she turns it gently to us. His eyes bore into mine.

"He was a businessman, yes, and goes back to the old days sometimes," Rosemarie agrees tolerantly. "Fancies himself wealthy." She drops her voice discreetly. "He's been a charity case, really. I can give you a history." She studies the nurse. "Not speaking, you say?"

An elderly man twists chafed wrists strapped to the metal bedrails. A sturdy, graceful frame, to be struck down so suddenly but – there it is. Sounds blur from one side of his mouth while the other side hangs dead. His eyes are riveted on me and mine are on about the same level as I sit in the wheelchair.

"No head for names," I apologize.

"But remember him from the home?" Rosemarie, thank God, right there to clarify everything. "Ivy's house, on the porch."

But the image that lances in is of a dim corridor and a door opening from it.

"Where?" the lady at the desk probes. "It have any letter about committal? Who put him in the home?"

"You can't always blame them," I reprove her gently. "When your old people get these . . . problems, you mightn't have a choice."

"Hard to manage?" The nurse addresses Rosemarie, ignoring me, but I reply anyway, keeping my eyes on the sagging side of his face.

"Not as he is," I say. "That's a stroke."

"Eey! She sharp, eh?" says the nurse.

"Oh yes," Rosemarie agrees proudly, then says to me, "Remember old man Deering?"

"Shh! A terror. Wife nearly died!"

"This patient must have a next of kin we can contact," says the nurse. She searches his wallet and he glares at it with the expressive side of his face. She pulls a card and reads out a phone number. "I going call this in case he have any close family" – she sighs – "because somebody have to register him."

Faces don't fool me. Eyes speak. Rosemarie is afraid of the phone call.

"Who they calling?" I say in her ear.

"The wife." Matter of fact, mantling the tension.

"One flesh," I protest.

But her eyes say, *Precisely.*

"At least this monster is contained," Canon whispers, only that brings the rest of the story back to me.

I can't help sniggering. "Grendel had a mother."

The supervisor speaks into the phone with her best voice. "Mrs Ashmead, you say? So I got you right away!" She explains that she is calling from a hospital, breaking the news gently. "Really very ill and he can't speak on the phone. Yes, m'am. I can describe him."

Rosemarie is expressionless, but I can see her fingers clenching and unclenching.

As the nurse describes the patient clinically, Canon rests his hand on Rosemarie's shoulder like a benediction, and the man on the bed pierces me with his terrible eyes. I look away but the shining steel side of the hospital trolley returns his gaze and my mind reflects the mirror on the ceiling of a room where a woman beats the air with her hands and slides to the ground at last, clutching her throat. Blood oozes into the pitted surface in my mind.

I lean forward and whisper in his ear, "I know you."

And he stares back, his eyes widening, his jaw working, twisting.

"Mrs Ashmead, Matron Cunningham is right here. Look, I'll put the call on speaker. Go ahead."

"Pansy Cunningham?" From the phone, a small cold voice.

"No. This is her husband's stepmother, Rosemarie Cunningham. Matron."

"Will he recover?"

"Well . . ."

"Speak up! Will he come out of this?"

"His condition is very serious," the supervisor interjects. "He should survive, but he may never be what he was."

"No one should ever be what *he* was." The swift, feral slash in response from the woman at the other end silences the nurse. Then: "Cunningham!"

"Mrs Ashmead?"

"What have you to say?"

"The home will be glad to supply whatever papers you need regarding his condition and . . . and our files will show he's no longer responsible, since . . . there may be transactions of his you may want to distance yourself from. For now, you may want me to register him as a patient here."

Silence yawns like miles between the women on the phone.

"Cunningham!" We jump as the sharp, shrewd tone crackles in again. "Register him. I'll fax the authorization and contact you with further instructions." Then the line goes dead.

Rosemarie raises her shoulders to the supervisor, who rolls up her eyes. The man on the bed stares desperately from one to the other, his mouth works silently and then with a faint wet noise.

The talk flows on around and past me.

Now if I had my head with me I think I might help, but as things stand . . . His eyes. His eyes, now. They . . . reflect nothing, only . . . only searching. A gaze hard to look away from. Compelling, bottomless void. One might have called it a greedy, ruthless face, but now it seems so empty of humanity – hardly a face, the years concealed by absence of lines – nothing etched by pain or laughter. A terrible smoothness.

He stares back. A glance, insanely intense, sucking slyly at my thoughts, leaving gaps. Something his eyes say that I don't catch, and he begins to moan sounds, not words, which slide slippery around me from this . . . beautifully framed but emptied of meaning . . . shell. Fallen from promise. He leans forward and to my horror approximates his face to a smile utterly devoid of humour or warmth – monstrous. I block my face with my arm to shield myself from obscenity as he tugs self-destructively at his restraints. I propel myself out of the chair and cover my ears to shut out the alternative snarl and hiss, and (worse somehow) running through that, a sort of humming. And I close my eyes away from the twisted mask.

"Get her out," Rosemarie orders. "Get her to Rachel."

And Canon helps me stumble through the door as Sister responds, "Calm him down. This could be a second one."

Outside, I open my eyes and there are people about who are ill, injured, patient, resigned, hopeful, weeping, moaning, pleading, grateful. Soon my old friend Canon Pearce is bending over a woman on a stretcher.

"No. No one contacted me to see you," he responds to her, "I'm here on another visit. But I'll be happy to say a few words with you."

There is a braying laugh somewhere off to the left, and where Cockburn could possibly have come from at this hour I can't tell, but with a little luck I may be able to avoid him. And if not, well, he's not that bad. Rachel and Rabin seem tense though.

Two nurses walk out of a door and – for heaven's sake – one could be Rosemarie, looking much older.

"Violent and delusional," the other says. "We can't keep him here once he begins to recover."

"He will recover?" Rachel asks, and looks traumatized by the idea.

But the nurse ignores her, remarking, "The wife look like she in no hurry to take him back."

"She's older, you see, and an invalid herself. Look here – as soon as you are ready to release him I'll take him back to the home and readmit him." It is Rosemarie. And she seems calm though the clergyman behind her stares at her in shock.

As I pass the door, a man strapped on a bed strains till the tendons bulge on his neck, and his mouth, at first compressed to a slit, opens to a snarl and then a gaping hole in the distorted face.

His eyes pierce me with a command – perhaps to recognize him – but it is the glance of a beast at bay, sullen but desperate. A far corner of my mind reflects those eyes that look up and meet mine in the mirror above a limp form sliding sliding down a wall.

"Hmm! He will need real sedation. Restraints too."

"One doesn't like to, but . . ." Rosemarie's voice trails off as the patient stares at me, unblinking. There was a gleam once, sweeping a thin trail of red. "What could have brought it on?"

"Who can say?" Nurse turns tiredly away. "Time catches up with us all."

Pinioned he emits a howl of abandonment at once so threatening and tormented that it draws a hush over the whole building.

I wrap my arms around my head and crouch in the eye of the storm, my own lids tightly shut, while the chaos of images swirls on sickeningly.

As we drive back I rest my head on Rosemarie's shoulder.

"I'm not up to these night jaunts any more," I protest. "And they drive so fast. Leave me home next time. Leave me with Dan or Rachel."

"Slow down, Rabby," Rachel says. "Why you racing so?"

Rabin shakes his head. "You forget we leave Agnes with poor Cecil?"

"Agnes was always a handful," I agree.

Yet, when we get home, a tall thin mournful man tells us he just gave Agnes the glass of sherry she asked for and she settled down and told him the whole story of her life. All *I* want is not to hear it tonight. Still, I'll have a sherry with them. Why not?

Basil is there too, waiting to go home. He's not a young man and I think they drive him a little too hard, but he looks cheerful.

"What man make dat God nah make, Miss El?"

"Tell me, Basil," I urge, and he belts it out, "Mistake!" And the tiredness melts away in laughter.

"How's Petrona," I demand when we settle down. "And Miss Ivy?"

There is a pause before he replies. "Well, M'am. In dem different ways. Well."

He accepts a glass of sherry with a wide grin while I reach for an empty glass on the tray, pour in half my own drink, cover it and set it aside. Then I down the rest thankfully.

"My hair looking terrible," Agnes sighs. "What I going to do?"

"The question is – what will this man's wife be like?" Rachel asks. "You know anything about her, Archdeacon?"

"Husband and wife are one flesh," I remind them. "Probably they're peas in a pod."

"Lord God," mutters Rosemarie. "Beg pardon, Archdeacon." And they look at each other aghast – I don't know why.

Enormous things, sometimes, go on under our noses and we cannot grasp them and perhaps would rather not understand, but I presume it must all make sense in its own outlandish way. For, look at me. How many can understand me, even if some accept? The rest are a joke to me.

One equal temper. As I sit, aah, here – I feel them all about. This cloud of witnesses.

Even if others, some things, are blotted out, it is not a gathering darkness, or an emptying – not that sort of . . . ruin – it is a dappling with light, an iridescence that blinds me to the immediate past – a refilling with lost sensations, a rekindling so that the fragmenting and reassembling radiance can sometimes obscure the shadows of loss.

Mama and Bonny. Dan racing the raindrops. Miss Ivy, Rosemarie and a shower of orchids down a mossy trunk. A creaking gate with verdigris on its hinges.

Each scintilla of recollection hangs there intact before me. I contemplate them separate but gathered at their ends from a single cord, gleaming and colliding like wind chimes. Mama smiles from her picture on my table, a loving, wise face.

"Forget it, Miss Minnie," Mama urged, "and just live your life. Your sister resented the child because she wanted her daughter to be different, and her daughter made the same mistake she had made. Your sister took it out on everyone, but you've survived them all."

Poor child. Never heard a word from the boy. But where did the daughter get this little fair child anyway? (Miss Minnie whispered that old Pastor Cockburn, Agnes's father, was a terror with the young girls, but Mama said the girl would have done anything to get away from that mother. Tita was an old harpy.) Anyway, there was the pickney, pale like a weed in the dark, its eyes watchful, biding time. Bruised – must have been a child always in a fight at school, if he ever attended, but as if bruised inside too.

"You've survived them all, Miss Min," Mama insisted.

I open my eyes to smile back at Mama but she has stepped out, so I push my hand in my pocket hopefully and come up with half a peppermint, carefully rewrapped, and an empty candy wrapper holding one word, *Shatter.* But there is no explanation for any of it. As I try to work it out, their talk intervenes.

"I suppose now they will come back to take it over," Rachel says.

"Well, I come across Ivy will in the pan with the passport dem, and it say the place is for Evan." Rosemarie looks very satisfied. "I give Basil the papers and he pass it on to Cyril to drop at Evan house, so when he manage to get back he will see it. Anyway, Basil say Scotty leave the island gone foreign. And as I see it, best he stay there. All like him would have money over there in any case."

Ivy's will in a pan? Well, why not? I keep my old papers in boxes, and one box of old letters I reread all the time. Sometimes I just close my eyes and . . . and look, look the first one I ever wrote to Rummy:

Dear Rosemarie, You will find it strange to get a letter from me when we have never met (though I hope we do meet and become good friends) but I am taking the liberty of writing you now in confidence to ask a favour. I have a dear friend, Ivy Rousseau, who will be in your part of the world shortly and who stands in desperate need of a friend.

. . .

"Evan's It!" Canon exclaims with such gusto I can only rejoice with him.

"So let it be written," I agree.

And to my satisfaction Canon responds with alacrity, just as Dan would have, "So let it be done."

But I'm not sure what game it is. Harder and harder to keep abreast, a struggle against gathering forces.

"*Cannon to right of them. Cannon to left of them.* Cannons outside them. Teeth inside them."

"What's that?" Rachel calls.

So she's home. Good.

"Oh, nothing. *Volleyed and thundered*, you know."

And I chuckle. I must, all I can, wrap myself in humour. St George fades into legend as I hurtle forward. No point depending on a rescuer from outside. Whatever surfaces through the smoky stillness, I shall flourish what weapons I have, glancing bright – laughter, stronger than steel.

"I must can get a lift to the hairdresser," Agnes moans. "You mean not one of unu will take pity on me?"

He was a coarse materialistic man, they say, that man Agnes married. She grew like him but he never cared for her. I suppose when her life emptied of love there was nothing left to lavish attention on but her own person. Poor Agnes. Of course, one would think that at least Jocelyn had the child, but where is Jocelyn now? They say the child was cold to her in the end. What angry people we leave behind when we are careless. What ripples spread, widening.

Ripples. So they seem from a distance. Far away the sea churns but from here it is restful on the eye which discerns only ripples.

We arrive at the hospital and a nurse finishes her chores with a spattering noise and metallic clank, and vanishes. There is a single patient at the far end of the room.

"Mercy." A shiny black van rolls to a standstill at the door and as best I can I suppress a shudder at the unwelcome reminder. Back doors fold away noiselessly and a slick ramp lowers. Dark suits emerge through the side doors and fade aside. A chair rolls down, polished, plush with crimson leather trimmed with cream and gliding forward as if of its own accord.

"You must be Mrs Ashmead," Rosemarie says, then introduces me and explains that my daughter is in town for a few days or she would have accompanied us, and she adds, "I hadn't thought you could come."

"Really."

The new voice draws a sharp intake of breath from the long still form on the bed.

"I haven't crossed the island for small talk."

Her face is turned away, the hair meticulously coiffed to its smooth platinum sheen, under oversize dark glasses. Cream suit with heavy pearl earrings and one long strand knotted on the chest like a noose. Red manicured nails motionless on the soft cream-coloured leather handle of the wheelchair. Not calm. Lifeless.

Just red spattered on cream. On the footrest, chic high-heels with one shoe tipped showing a sole unused.

"I'd have thought my husband would have made arrangements for both of you."

Rosemarie stares at her, motionless.

"For of course," the woman in the chair continues, without a glance our way, "of course he made arrangements for me too. It was clear my father's will protected me: if I died everything would go to predetermined charities. So my husband set it up that if he predeceased me I would not long survive him. An account was opened for his . . . agent. Only one thing escaped the monster." She pauses and seems to savour the thought. "He put nothing in place for the eventuality of his being declared incompetent." She turns towards the bed, its polished steel gleaming like the sides of the wheelchair. Cold shining panels like mirrors slide in my mind. "Incompetent."

A muscle on the living side of his face twitches.

"I have him now," she says.

His mouth parts crookedly and emits sounds, notes, almost a ragged tune.

"If he recovers?" Rosemarie prompts.

"Organizations who received your message will be glad to find him in circulation again – not that there is anything for him to return to. All accounts in his name have been frozen" – she leans towards the patient, driving in her voice like an ice pick – "including the joint account with the agent who was to take care of me."

The wheels swivel noiselessly as she swings to face us. Skin smooth-stretched, veiled expression nailed in place, and the nose shows only the faintest ridge as if expertly reset. Cheekbones, perhaps elegant once though never beautiful, still are what many would term striking. The mouth, aah.

"Those messages were copied to Eleanor Duvall," she remarks, her lips barely moving. "And what is your condition, I wonder."

"Pretty well, thank you. Head not so . . ."

"You, Matron," she snaps. "What is it you would get out of keeping what's left of my husband, as you propose?" She throws out random figures.

Rosemarie tests each word. "Evan would have to say – the new owner."

A phone flips open and Rosemarie calls a number. Soon, incongruously, Evan's voice fills the dim room.

"Me, Miss Rose? Me tie up myself in they money? Me never feel say me could learn anything but wo'tlessness from Scotty but is one thing he teach me: is true what old-time people say: a greedy make fly follow coffin go a grave. This time round, a we run things. Tell Miss Lady say Evan going take him at our normal rate or not at all." The voice changes, softens. "And give my best respects to Miss El."

"The normal rate?" The voice of the woman in the chair grates in disbelief. "You think what you are getting here is *normal*? What makes you even contemplate taking this off my hands?"

The loathing in her glance at the bed makes me grip Rosemarie's arm. "Then what does *she* want with him? The patient, is it?" I ask.

"He won't recover." The woman pronounces it like a sentence.

"Who is it, Rosemarie? Who it is she wants dead?"

Two fingers barely lift from the chair arm, her very gestures leeched of interest. "What difference would it make if I finished him, unaware as he is. Such anticlimax."

But the thread has slipped away.

"I can't say," I apologize. "Only, I live each day, you know."

"Live." She tries it like a foreign word. "How long since I was alive rather than just undead." Her mouth flinches. Clenches. Probably small to begin with, it pinches at the corners, as if it has never widened, curved, pursed – just tightened not to take up space, not to yield, set in its small straight slit. She bends forward, takes off the big dark glasses and stares back.

"Jesu." I recoil.

Eyes sunken in dark sockets burn into mine, her body tensed as if bracing by force of habit against outrage.

"Years ago, when I recognized murder as my last remaining option and knew there was nothing to wait for but opportunity, I began to wear sunglasses always, everywhere, to keep him from reading me. I suppose I no longer need them."

But the torment and hatred. Bottomless. Lord, shield me from these eyes.

"What brought you here? How did you reach . . . us?" I strain to account for her somehow.

"I flew." She brushes me aside – but it comes back to me, a flight I made, to see Rachel.

In the distance there were buildings of white cloud, solid along the far edge of the sky, and beneath seemed firm but fluffy, like meringue. Then thin layers streaming, widening, flowing above those tighter clusters, around dark, smoky columns – the fluid ones pooled where the sun slanted in and flamed in wide lakes, brilliant, deepening. And I thought in just such a sky they might ride . . . only I am losing track of our exchange.

"And has it been . . . satisfactory? Your visit?" I ask hurriedly.

"I have him where I want him." Her eyes are on Rosemarie. "I believe the matron can be of assistance and the papers are prepared. I can think of no use for you, but . . ." She shrugs dismissively. "What harm can you do? You can't *know* anything."

The patient's face turns, involuntarily it seems, head dropping down to his shoulder, eyes on the metal panel of that side of the chair and trapping my own glance so I can only stare, mesmerized, at the steel surface. He glares as if his eyes neither admit nor blot out images chopping at his damaged brain, and there, see there it is – the reflection that slices back up into memory.

"I know . . . him." I clutch my throat, rocking back and forth; in the distance my own voice moans. "I saw. I saw how it welled out between her fingers and she tried to call out to me but . . . choked . . . sliding, sliding."

"Thelma," Rosemarie whispered. "You were there? Oh God, Ellie."

"Thelma who?" asks the woman.

She startles me out of . . . whatever it was, and my hands drop, for Rosemarie looks faint. Strong Rosemarie, shaking.

"Sweetheart, what?"

But Rosemarie feels for a chair as if her legs cannot support her.

"What is this? I have no time for it," the woman in the chair says, but now my priority is Rosemarie, and I shrug the invalid aside irritably.

"Then, Madam, you are free to go."

And she does, after a moment, glide away to the van as I kneel to put my arms around Rosemarie. Beside the van a man in a dark suit raises his arm, but the woman I do not know – a woman in a wheelchair – motions him aside impatiently and turns away; the man drops his arm and jumps in and the van pulls off; then Rosemarie is sobbing in my arms and I believe I have never seen her cry before.

Rachel is not here and I am alone with it. (*Remember Rosemarie*, Dan said.) Somehow, somehow I must comfort her.

"Not Scotty, then," Rosemarie sobs. "At least not that."

And whatever that means, it seems to bring relief.

Perhaps I have been asleep, for when next I open my eyes we are sitting on the downstairs porch and they are all arguing around me.

"Rachel?" I ask.

"Then you *are* taking him in?" Rabin is demanding incredulously.

"What else do you suggest?" Rosemarie sounds harassed. "*You* want carry Ashmead back to Trinidad with you?"

"I don't know, Rummy. How will you manage?" Rachel holds her forehead, spreading her fingers as if to press back a tightening band. "How can you live with someone so . . . so deadly?"

"Knock him out, man," I propose. They exchange glances, which always makes me anxious. "I'm talking foolishness?"

"Not at all, Missis." Rosemarie hugs me. "You alone talking sense." She turns to them. "You don't see he helpless? And if he even partly recover, what he can do? No one going to ill-treat him, but he going keep under *my* eye. Is the only safe way." Some *coup de grâce* I cannot define.

Basil is a few feet away, in the garden, and he sets his mouth mutinously. "If smaddy no dead, no call them duppy," he mutters.

Best just to let them work it out – yet to keep listening. For we have so much to exchange. A long and distant journey. *Yea, though I walk . . .* Not death though, not death. Not so mundane. Something shimmering, more . . . taboo. Not only unspeakable but unthinkable. Yet I laughed, just now, when I did think of it. And I shall again when it comes back to me.

I close my eyes again, for when foolishness or troubling scenes are on TV it is good to just sit and turn things over in my mind. Somewhere it crumbles, slides, opens another space. Some things fall out and others are covered. Things that would have worried me, dematerialize. *Something there is . . .* and they all join in before we resume the conversation. Or do we talk? Or do we just think, mind to mind? Something has been lifted away and something restored.

Inland far we be, but there's the roar of mighty waters, wings of fire sweeping round me and I am unsinged and steady, frail as I am, in the whirlwind, for I have them all to back me up, all of them from the past, for the future, in my timeless present, and I am full of a kind of strength, built-in armour I hammered out over the years from a metal of my own invention quite quite new and shining out for anyone to see who cares to look at it. They pause to stroke it and wonder at its softness.

"Like silk, ent?"

I open my eyes and Rabin takes my hand. "You want to meet the new puppy?"

"What happened to the General?"

"Oh, Gawain is getting old, but he's okay. He's in Trinidad but we're at Cascade. Miss Ivy's. Watch this little fellow."

"Oh, lovely!" Fat and wriggling and wagging. Little pink tongue curled at the end, and, oh, the ears feel like silk. "What's his name?"

"Rumpus. Archdeacon named him." He passes the puppy back to Basil, who shambles off in his awkward way I've got so fond of, with it under his arm.

We sit on a bench that Basil and Rabin have shifted under a tree in the garden, and the smell of jasmine rises and bats (is it?) flutter far overhead.

"So you're off tomorrow?" Rummy reflects. "And Miss Ellie?"

Rachel regards her in surprise. "Well, we all go together."

"But you brought her big suitcase," Rosemarie says, like an accusation. Then her tone changes. "You could let her stay a little longer, since she has all her things. And the place going to be different now – like what we set out to do with Ivy. After all, nothing wrong with a *good* home."

"Nothing whatever." Rachel laces her arm through mine firmly.

"But you taking her from me?" As Rachel stares deep into herself, like someone reading, Rosemarie relents. "I know the two of you belong together." Rummy's a little sullen still, I must say. "And I only glad you know it too. I woulda like to have her longer though."

"I'm coming home with you?" Incredible. I can't take my eye from Rachel's face in the sheer delight of it. "With you and my boy?"

"Then what you bring the big suitcase for?" Rosemarie demands.

I wish she would let up, for Rachel, the poor child, has seemed so tormented, but the truth is that now the strain has passed from her face.

"Because I was trying to be rational," she confesses. "I thought the state of affairs was . . . different. What has fooled me most was that first fury, years ago, when I thought: *and this is just the beginning*. And I was afraid, Rummy, obsessed with what seemed to be bearing down on me. At the back of my mind, all these years, I've had this . . . this terror. As if something, something unthinkable, would be . . . unleashed. But it's all different to what I thought, and to what she knew herself when she warned me, years and years ago. The fury passes. And in the calm after that storm sometimes, at least in this case, there remains . . . much of the original after all."

When they talk in riddles I know it's about me, and I break in anxiously.

"I did something to cause trouble?"

"No." Rummy smiles ruefully. "Is just that everybody want to keep you and Rachel is It."

Well, of course. But I can't help lamenting, "Then Rummy isn't coming with us?"

"Not yet. But she's free to visit now. Often."

You cannot have it all. And I can feel a rending at the thought of Rosemarie staying behind, even for a while, but Rachel is the life that I have left. And it is so hard to keep track of the plan that I just slide my hand into hers so she will know I'm ready, and when our palms meet some deep wound somewhere else begins to heal.

Yet the car that pulls to a stop beside us is not to collect us after all. Rummy says someone's room is ready but we must wait for Basil to come with the wheelchair.

In the back seat of the car is an invalid whose face is familiar – perhaps a family resemblance – but I don't recall his name. They all seem wary of him as of some drowsy ogre overcome from within by his own venom. But his face is unlined, unmarked as though nothing and no one has ever touched him. Gingerly I put out my hand and stroke his cheek which sags with the dead weight of numb flesh, wet near the strange suction of the useless side of the mouth, feeling if only I can for the tingling, burning edge of the wasted area so that he can know a human touch, but the drooping eye betrays no sensation, and the unwieldy tongue lies still under its sentence of silence. And all response is lost in this vacuum of feeling in which he is imprisoned, perhaps forever.

Monster, his wife said? Harpy, someone muttered? It may have been old Miss Minnie. No. She said Tita was a harpy, that's it. People call each other these things and who knows what makes them what they are.

For now I look at him with the past evaporating all about us and I can't see anything unsettling beyond the damaged face. His eyes are on me and a tear wells over and seeks its way tentatively down the unlined face, so I lean forward and wipe it with the back of my hand to encourage him as best I can.

"Don't worry," I whisper, "Rosemarie will take care of you."

But he cannot have understood, because the eye on the good side widens in horror.

Epilogue

DAYS, MONTHS – what are these. A house reshapes itself according to some original template etched in thought, some delicate structure of latticed porches and intricate fretwork, of wicker chairs outside and cane-seated chairs with delicately carved legs inside around a table spread with cutwork embroidery, and even beyond the window, the philodendrons are fretted with their pattern of holes. Mama's old open-weave burlap bag bulges full of gladioli bulbs again but already the garden is glorious. Through the fine interstices the dirt that clung to them and the little bits of rotting leaves crumble away. Outside the window huge caladium leaves of translucent pink finely speckled with white dip gently. The ferns that network all these roots nod dreamily in the shade, one with the fronds transplanted far and near. The hand that brought the first tangle of them from the Kingston house smuggled offshoots across the sea. Routings and rerootings.

Delicate as the perfume of shrubs, unstoppable as the probing of trees, intoxicating as the tart sweetness of mangoes, is a richness muted by age erupting in the odd guffaw but mostly percolating out through lives touched by this glow and outward still, warming others imperceptibly, an energy transformed but never lost, radiating and transfiguring. It is a composite life among them all, both here and there, this house or that merging, home after home disintegrating the barriers between its innermost rooms and brilliant gardens unravelling geography and time.

Days, months, years. They blur then dissolve. One of the usual crowd might discern them, but there is no need. The immediate is boundless and its radiance sufficient. Yards, miles, equally irrelevant. Somewhere, a gnarled tree chuckles and shuffles its roots through human enterprises, but now there is peace with the roots of the trees that spread invisibly to intertwine with our affairs. What vermin there may have been have lost their venom. Pain, while it grows, is detached now that one is not tightly tethered to the flesh. The world is full of interest but restful. One sleeps until one wakes.

And now look – a young man with a face whose features unite them all peeps around the door and then hurries in, leading a girl slender and brown as a fine branch. Lace sprays about her like fine petals. The sight of them invites applause, a head thrown back in delight.

A bride, a bride! If one can't shout it aloud still it is a matter for celebration, for look at *us,* the times we've had – and not done yet. Reach out a hand, richly veined, and trace the air around a shower of orchids descended from a plant transferred to the ficus bark from the fallen lignum vitae, and now blooming high above the old house. The blooms are edged with fine violet lines.

"Yes, we used your orchid, *and* I brought you a piece of our cake. Do you know me?"

What a question. You're my boy. Feet rubbing together in anticipation mouth opening…there. He pops in a morsel of … aah … mmm . . . fruity, sweet . . .wine tingling the nose. Through the open door music pours in, filling the room.

"Do you think you can get up today?"

Why not? Here is a hand to draw one from the chair and somehow the ground dematerializes beneath the feet. Elbows rise for balance . . . and see? Floating here between the two young people.

"She's brave, isn't she!"

But what does that mean? Just getting up from a chair.

Delicate fabric wafts in and out between the lattice and fretwork that reassemble about us.

The young man extends an encircling arm, then releases the other hand and bows low over it.

"May I have this dance?"

Head inclines graciously, and – stand steady now, swaying to the music while he dips and circles around. A fragment of the tune persists and turns over and returns to mind.

The legs fold one back onto the chair, making it possible to release the supporting hand and place a loud kiss on it. His other hand offers another fragrant morsel. He grins and waves and they are gone, but leaving an explosion of flavour. A raisin, steeped in wine.

The vanishing past and contracting future have taken with them all resentment, mourning and anxiety. These are sensations only barely recalled and of no significance. The dimensions of the world are disentangled to a seamless presence of loved ones, that palm against this palm, a lingering wisdom of counsel and forgiveness, a mainstay of humour. Time, shattered and reconfigured to crowd past and future away before the infinite present, leaves only patience, the joy in an aroma of spice a texture of soft fabric a safety of roots a discernment of guavas and the relief of owning nothing, of power surrendered, of presence in beloved company and of simply and intensely being without having to do yet not a second wasting. A riddle in time, is it – this diffusing, persisting consciousness?

Yes. Aah, all that endures in the long run circles and enfolds me, treasured faces – nameless for no longer distinct from me, and their breath fanning my cheek. *Something there is that does not love a wall,* taken under advisement. *So let it be done.* Their presence warms my skin and I close my eyes and turn over the flavour in my mouth and in my mind I spread my arms and immerse myself in the music – who cares how well I dance or how I seem to strangers when I remember, how I remember. And oh for a rich contralto as a line dawns and shimmers along a corridor like a wisp of silver fur (the mountains are full of silver-ferns, he said), wisps, fronds, lines gleam through. *Then fancies flee away. I care not what men say!*

"How you doing, Mom?" At the door, mirror my face, healed healing, the frantic . . . reconciled. "How, love?" she prompts.

Search for manageable one word one true not sharp only respond to. Aah, triumphant I recall it and life flares back incandescent.

I belt it out. "Present."

And, what here? Look, something quite in my mouth! Mmm, fruitcake. Haw!

Breinigsville, PA USA
26 September 2010
246085BV00002B/2/P